Whispers and Spies

THE SHADOW OF THE BLACK ROSE
BOOK 1

SHERIDAN JEANE

ARE YOU SIGNED UP FOR DRAGONBLADE'S BLOG?

You'll get the latest news and information on exclusive giveaways, exclusive excerpts, coming releases, sales, free books, cover reveals and more.

Check out our complete list of authors, too!

No spam, no junk. That's a promise!

Sign Up Here

www.dragonbladepublishing.com

Dearest Reader;

Thank you for your support of a small press. At Dragonblade Publishing, we strive to bring you the highest quality Historical Romance from some of the best authors in the business. Without your support, there is no 'us', so we sincerely hope you adore these stories and find some new favorite authors along the way.

Happy Reading!

CEO, Dragonblade Publishing

Chapter One

A STUDY IN SILK AND SUBTERFUGE

Half a league, half a league,
Half a league onward,
All in the valley of Death
Rode the six hundred.
—Alfred, Lord Tennyson, "The Charge of the Light Brigade"
(1854)

January 15, 1855
Helena

LADY HELENA ASHFORD entered the Duke of Somerset's ballroom like a chess player surveying the board.

Her jade-hued gown drew eyes—deliberately. Let them admire the silk, the way candlelight caught auburn hair, the picture she made beside smiling Amelia. While society's gaze lingered on surfaces, Helena's attention tracked what mattered: the clusters of men near the windows, the too-bright laughter from the card room, Lord Edward Hawthorne's careful movements through the crowd.

Beauty was the perfect blind. People saw the ornament and missed the observer.

The chandeliers bathed the room in golden light, reflecting

off crystal decanters and casting prismed rainbows from cut-glass sconces. Beneath the music and chatter, however, she listened for murmurs. Names. Codes. Familiar phrasing.

Sir Frederick's note had arrived that morning with his usual brevity: *"Somerset's ball tonight. Hawthorne will be there. Watch him. Note who approaches, who avoids him. Note the patterns more than the people. Use your access and blend in."*

She'd memorized the instructions and burned the note before breakfast. That's how this worked. Facts gathered, sense made of them. That was the work. No written trace.

Which meant that tonight, Helena wasn't merely attending a ball. She was gathering threads.

Her gown flowed like water, the silk chosen not just for elegance but to pass unnoticed. It allowed her to fit in—neither bold nor forgettable.

"Helena, every eye is on you tonight," Amelia said with a grin. "Surely Lord Thomas will finally propose."

Helena smiled, her gaze tracking over Amelia's shoulder toward the card room. "You're relentless."

"I'm observant," Amelia corrected. "You've had his undivided attention for months."

"And yet I remain entirely unengaged." Helena's tone stayed light while she catalogued the room's occupants. Lord Pemberton near the refreshments. Lady Eleanor in mauve silk. Hawthorne still by the windows, now speaking with a military officer she didn't recognize. "Let's hope circumstances don't force me to remain this way forever."

Amelia narrowed her eyes at her. "You're doing it again."

"Doing what?"

"Noting exits and counting suspicious glances." Amelia's voice dropped to match Helena's. "Is this a Sir Frederick assignment or your own initiative?"

"His," she said softly. "Hawthorne's been abroad too often and too covertly. I'm meant to observe and report."

Amelia sighed. "One ball. Just one. I'd like to attend one ball where you're not mentally assembling your report."

"Then you should have chosen a different sister." Helena's tone remained light, but her eyes never stopped moving.

Amelia exhaled slowly. "Fine. But if anyone asks, I'm only here to gossip and drink champagne."

Helena grinned. "As you should be. Though if you overhear anything involving trade, military shipments, or private investments, do let me know."

Her sister executed a theatrical curtsy. "As my lady commands."

As Amelia drifted off toward a knot of laughing debutantes, Helena began her circuit of the room.

She moved like a chess piece—not the queen, but the knight: angled, quiet, unexpected. Each stop calculated. Each smile offered as both invitation and shield. She exchanged pleasantries, noting who responded with too much warmth, who kept their eyes a beat too long on Lord Edward Hawthorne, and who carefully avoided his presence altogether.

Hawthorne himself stood near the far windows, laughing with gentlemen in military coats and diplomatic sashes. His gestures were quick and angular, punctuating words she couldn't hear. His polished grin never reached his eyes.

Twice in the past quarter hour, he'd glanced toward the terrace doors as though expecting someone who hadn't arrived. When the doors opened to admit only a servant bearing champagne, his shoulders tightened with visible disappointment.

Helena filed the observation. *Waiting for someone. Growing impatient.*

She turned just as the Duke of Somerset approached her, cane in hand, his smile gracious despite the strain it clearly cost him.

"Lady Helena. Might I claim a dance before my legs betray me?"

She offered her hand. "The honor is mine, Your Grace."

On the dance floor, she adjusted her grip subtly, steadying him without making it obvious. Despite his frailty, the duke remained a commanding presence—one of the few men whose approval still carried weight in diplomatic circles.

"Your father would be proud of you," he said quietly. "He always spoke highly of your judgment."

The words struck like a blade wrapped in silk. Helena didn't let her step falter. "He taught me to listen before I speak. A rare skill in this crowd."

The duke chuckled. "And a useful one. These days, everyone speaks in riddles. Especially Lord Hawthorne."

"Is that so?"

"A man to be wary of. Far too practiced at hiding the truth."

She met his gaze, her smile warm, and tucked that warning away beside Frederick's. A second voice. A second thread.

From the rotating vantage of the dance, she tracked the room. Lord Hawthorne had moved toward the card room. Lady Eleanor's fan snapped in agitated patterns. And near the terrace doors, a striking woman in emerald silk watched the room with the same careful attention Helena herself employed.

Lady Margaret Fairfax. Widow, society hostess, and avid observer of her environment.

When the music ended, Helena curtsied and guided the duke back to the edge of the floor.

She was making her way toward Amelia when another presence stepped neatly into her path.

"Lady Helena."

She met the gentle eyes of Lord Thomas Chadwick. His expression was warm and hopeful, his tawny hair precisely combed, cravat arranged with mathematical care.

"Would you do me the honor of this dance?"

His timing was inconvenient. Hawthorne's circle had tightened again near the card room, their conversation low and guarded. But refusing Thomas would attract attention—besides which, she didn't *want* to refuse him.

"Of course," she said, folding her fan and taking his arm.

He placed his hand gently over hers. No pressure. No urgency. No spark. Just warmth.

As they joined the waltz, his pleasure was unmistakable. The steadiness of it caught her off guard. It struck her, suddenly, how rare that kind of steadiness was. How rare *he* was.

Steady. Kind. Earnest.

As they spun about the room, she caught snippets of conversations. Unfortunately, no mention of treason caught her ear…not that she'd truly expected it.

"You're very quiet tonight," he said, guiding her into the second rotation of the waltz. "I hope it's not the company."

"Not at all." Her gaze met his. "I was simply listening."

"To the music?"

Her lips curved faintly. "To everything."

Thomas chuckled, clearly not understanding—and not needing to. "I had hoped to speak with you," he said. "I've recently invested in a company that might interest you."

That caught her attention. "A business venture?"

"Indeed. A significant one." His eyes lit with enthusiasm. "A trading company—Sableport Maritime. They've been expanding routes to the Far East, and the returns appear promising. I've taken a position on the board."

Helena's attention sharpened. *Sableport.* The name rang familiar, though she couldn't place why. "That sounds… ambitious. Who recommended it?"

He shrugged, unbothered. "A friend of the family. Lord Hawthorne, actually. He introduced me to one of the partners. Remarkably well-connected fellow."

That sent a chill down her spine.

"And you trust Hawthorne's recommendation of Sableport?" she asked, voice careful.

"Of course. The figures are solid."

Helena smiled politely as her mind raced. *If Hawthorne had introduced Thomas, Sableport wasn't merely commercial. It was part of a broader scheme. Something worth watching. And Thomas, well-meaning as he was, might be walking directly into it.*

"It sounds promising," she said softly.

He brightened. "I've been thinking about what comes next. A quieter life. Something lasting. A home in the country. Travel, on occasion. But mostly peace. With someone I trust. Someone strong, clever… someone like you."

The direction of his thoughts was unmistakable. It should've made her heart race.

It didn't.

Instead, she felt a tug in two directions—toward the safety he offered, and the purpose that drove her. The two were not the same.

"That sounds lovely," she said honestly. "But the world isn't very peaceful right now."

"No," he agreed. "But it could be. Someday. For us."

The music slowed. She curtsied; he bowed.

"You've given me much to think about," she said softly.

"I hope I have," he said, eyes searching hers. "Truly."

She returned to the edge of the ballroom as he stepped away, and allowed herself one deep breath.

She liked him. A great deal. Had hoped something more might grow between them. But now… she wasn't sure she belonged to the life he envisioned.

She turned to retrace her steps toward Hawthorne's group—

—and nearly collided with Lady Margaret Fairfax.

"Lady Helena." Lady Margaret's smile was gracious without warmth. "I was hoping to steal a moment."

Helena inclined her head. "Of course."

Lady Margaret drew her to the piano where she took up her position at the center of a carefully composed tableau. Emerald silk draped her like armor. Her gaze flicked toward the diplomats clustered near the fireplace. "The duke does throw a well-stocked party," she said lightly. "Half the Foreign Office is here, along with all the men hoping to impress them."

"You sound unimpressed."

"Oh, on the contrary. I find all of this"—Lady Margaret

waved a hand at the chandeliers—"immensely useful. People say more when they believe they're only being admired."

"And patterns emerge," Helena said evenly.

Margaret's eyes glinted. "Exactly."

"You were speaking with Ambassador Rowley earlier. Was he going on again about Parliament's reaction to the trade deal? It seems to be his favorite topic."

"Among other things." Lady Margaret admitted. "There's concern in certain quarters about Britain's overreach. Too many treaties signed with too little scrutiny. And now, of course, the Crimea."

"A delicate topic."

Lady Margaret nodded. "One that divides more than it unites. But division has its uses. Especially when it distracts from the real moves being made."

Helena narrowed her eyes slightly. "Moves by whom?"

Lady Margaret's smile didn't falter. "That depends on who's watching. And whether they're clever enough to know what not to say."

The orchestra began another quadrille, and Lord Weymouth arrived. "I believe this is our dance," he said, holding his hand out to Lady Margaret.

As the pair disappeared into the swirl of dancers, Helena watched her go, mind sharp and alert.

Lady Margaret Fairfax was watching the same board.

The question was which piece she believed herself to be.

Helena retreated to a corner of the ballroom, her mind cataloguing the evening's intelligence: Hawthorne's nervous glances, Thomas's Sableport investment, Lady Margaret's unsettling attention.

She would have much to report to Frederick.

The ballroom doors opened. A late arrival.

A man in military dress uniform stood at the threshold, his bearing rigid, his gaze sweeping the room with the focused intensity of someone working, not celebrating. Tall, dark haired, with a slight unevenness to his stance—an old injury, perhaps.

He didn't belong to the celebration. He belonged to something else entirely.

Their eyes met across the crowded room.

And Helena knew, with absolute certainty, that her evening was about to become far more complicated.

Chapter Two

A SOLDIER AMONG SILK

January 15, 1855
James

WHEN MAJOR JAMES Westwood arrived at the Duke of Somerset's ball, the air inside the ballroom felt too warm, too perfumed, and too smug for his taste. Hundreds of candles glittered overhead, reflected in gilded mirrors and polished silver. The laughter was brittle, the music a little too bright.

It was all meant to dazzle. But James wasn't dazzled. He had orders.

If it hadn't been for the mission, he would've gladly kept his distance. Give him a snow-slick trench, a steady rifle, and the silence of an enemy encampment over this theater of satins, silks, and smirks. He adjusted the cuffs of his dress uniform with deliberate precision. The motion was habit, not comfort. His knee ached—a Cossack's saber during a winter raid behind enemy lines, months before the Charge. The blade had caught him across the back of the knee, severing muscle and scraping bone. A field surgeon with fifty other men bleeding out had done what he could, but ligaments torn in the cold never quite knit right.

That night had cost him more than mobility. But he didn't let himself think about that.

The leg ached in cold weather, locked up if he stood too long, and would never carry him through a long march again. But it held his weight. Most days, that was enough. A few heads turned as he passed. Curiosity flickered, then softened into unease. He knew the look well. It clung to him like smoke.

He was the soldier who didn't die. The one who came back scarred and quiet, half ghost. The stories didn't know what to do with survivors. Neither did the people who told them.

He scanned the room the way he'd been trained—points of entry, possible weapons, clusters of conversation where too much stillness hinted at secrets. The ballroom was beautiful, yes. But so were many ambushes.

At his core, James still thought in terms of positioning and advantage. Even here.

Two exits, one heavily trafficked near the refreshments, one barely used leading to the terrace. There were no guards at either. Windows large enough for a man to pass through, if pressed. And near the card room, a cluster of men in diplomatic sashes speaking in voices just low enough to signal intent.

He noted them without effort. Most would never matter. But in his experience, *most* wasn't good enough.

"Major Westwood," drawled a familiar voice behind him, "you are, as always, the very spirit of revelry."

James turned to see Adrian Blackwood approaching with practiced ease. Same stride, same irreverent smirk, though his face had been just enough altered—cheekbones, hairline, posture—that he could pass as an altogether different man to those who didn't know him well. They'd worked together before—missions requiring infiltration more than intimidation. Adrian excelled at becoming whomever the moment required. Tonight, apparently, the moment required a bored aristocrat with too much time and too much wine.

"Adrian," James said, tone neutral. "Enjoying the ball?"

"Immensely. This one's particularly gaudy." Adrian's gaze swept James with affectionate assessment. "You, however, look like someone assigned to guard the wine cellar, not blend into high society. Try smiling, just once. It might confuse the enemy."

James allowed the ghost of a smile. "Noted."

"That's the spirit. Keep that up and you'll almost pass for human." Adrian's attention shifted past James's shoulder, tracking something—or someone—across the ballroom. His posture shifted subtly. Still casual, but focused. "Our mutual friend is near the musicians. Seventh pillar, jade-colored gown."

Lady Helena. So Adrian knew why James was here.

"Seen," James confirmed.

Adrian gave him a light pat on the shoulder, already melting back into the swirl of silk gowns and whispers. James let him go. Adrian belonged to this world of glib phrases and sudden disappearances.

James didn't. His talents ran quieter. Sharper. Built for shadows, not spotlights.

But tonight, he'd need to step into Helena Ashford's light. And hope neither of them burned.

The Crown's reports described her as intelligent, poised, fiercely loyal. But paper didn't capture this—the way her eyes tracked the room like a cipher wheel turning, the way her laugh came late, after a pause too calculated to be careless. She stood beside a younger woman—her sister, clearly—smiling at something she didn't quite find amusing.

She was lovely, yes. But more than that—she was *listening*.

And she didn't belong here. Not entirely. Not any more than he did.

As he watched, a gentleman approached her—Lord Someone-or-Other, he didn't catch the name—and spoke urgently near her ear. Helena's expression never changed. She laughed at precisely the right moment, touched the man's arm in apparent sympathy, and guided him toward the refreshment table where his voice would be swallowed by the crowd.

Whatever he'd been about to say in the middle of the ballroom, she'd just prevented. And made it look like solicitude.

Crown chose well, he thought. *She's not just an observer. She's a player on this board.*

James watched for a moment longer, reading posture and placement like a battlefield map. She wasn't mingling. She was collecting.

She turned.

Their eyes met across ten feet of parquet floor. For a moment, neither moved. James registered details automatically: the intelligence in her gaze, the controlled precision of her posture, the way her hand rested near her sister's arm—protective, but not clinging. And something else. A wariness that matched his own.

"Lady Helena," he said, stepping forward, voice pitched for privacy.

He stepped close enough that the music and chatter would cover his words, but not so close as to alarm her. The scent of something floral—jasmine, perhaps—mixed with the beeswax from the candles. He bowed, careful not to strain his knee.

Her eyes met his with cool curiosity. "Sir, I don't believe we've been introduced."

"Major James Westwood," he said, straightening. "I've come on behalf of Sir Frederick Woolsy."

Recognition flickered in her gaze. Not trust, but awareness. The edge of wariness remained in the tilt of her chin, the slight shift in her stance. She was measuring him. Distance, threat level, purpose. James recognized the assessment because he'd done the same with countless men in countless battles. But her evaluation came wrapped in social pleasantry, delivered with a smile that never wavered.

"I hope Sir Frederick is well. It must be an important message to warrant such… an unexpected intermediary."

He didn't take the bait. "He requests your presence in the garden at your earliest convenience. A matter of some urgency."

Her brows lifted a fraction. Not fear. Calculation.

"This all sounds terribly clandestine," she murmured, tone laced with careful amusement. "Very well, Major. Tell Sir

Frederick I'll join him in ten minutes."

He dipped his head, murmured a quiet thank you, and stepped back into the crowd.

The noise swelled again—music, laughter, the clink of glassware. He moved past it all, barely touching the floor with his steps, feeling the hum of tension settle beneath his ribs like a second pulse.

Near the edge of the ballroom, a uniformed man was holding court, gesturing grandly, surrounded by eager faces. James didn't need to get close to know what he was hearing—a retelling of the *Charge of the Light Brigade*, secondhand at best, spun into gallant poetry and tidy metaphors.

"Theirs not to reason why…"

The line followed him everywhere, clinging like smoke. Quoted by men who'd never stood in bloodied snow. Recited by ladies in drawing rooms with no notion of powder burns or frostbite or the way a man's breath rattled in his throat when he knew he wouldn't make it home.

James kept walking.

He'd learned not to flinch at that line. Just as he'd learned how to disappear in plain sight. Just as he'd learned that wars weren't won only in trenches and charges, but in ballrooms and whispered exchanges.

The war had taught him many things. Chief among them: not every battlefield held men wearing uniforms.

Tonight was proof of that.

And in ten minutes, he'd be in the garden with Lady Helena Ashford and Sir Frederick, preparing to enter a conflict where the weapons were whispers and smiles, and the casualties wore evening dress.

He was ready. The question was: Was she?

Chapter Three

THE GARDEN ACCORD

January 15, 1855
Helena

TEN MINUTES LATER, Helena slipped away from the ballroom, the music dimming behind her as January cold bit through silk and wool alike. Frost silvered every surface—hedges, grass, the iron bench she passed. She pulled her shawl tighter, breath clouding white as she made her way toward the tall hedge where Major James Westwood waited.

He looked as though he belonged to the garden's stark silence—standing so still he might have been carved from the same stone as the statuary. Lamplight caught on the rigid line of his jaw, casting shadows that sharpened already severe features. And his eyes, when they met hers, held the focused quiet of a man more accustomed to holding ground than making conversation.

"Major Westwood," she said evenly.

"Lady Helena." His voice was low, respectful. And far too direct for a garden midnight meeting to be anything but serious.

He unsettled her—not with brashness, but with the quiet weight of his presence. There was nothing decorative about him, nothing polished. He watched the world like a man waiting for it to explode.

Before she could reply, footsteps crunched across the gravel path. Sir Frederick Woolsy and his wife, Lady Josephine, emerged from the garden's edge, dressed in heavy cloaks, their expressions dark with urgency. Whatever had drawn them into the cold tonight, it was no minor matter.

Sir Frederick stepped closer, his breath misting in the cold air. His expression held that quality Helena had often seen—the one that made diplomats forget they'd meant to keep secrets. Even in a frozen garden at midnight, he radiated a calculated charm.

"Lady Helena, Major Westwood," he said, and despite the gravity of their midnight meeting, his voice carried warmth—almost intimacy. "I cannot tell you how grateful I am that you're both here." That smile touched his lips, the one Helena had seen charm information from the most reluctant sources. "I have a proposition for you. One that requires your considerable talents, your discretion, and—if I may be so bold—your trust."

Josephine, standing slightly behind him with her cloak pulled tight, gave her husband a look that was equal parts exasperation and fondness. "Frederick, even in January frost, you manage to make recruitment sound like seduction."

His gray eyes glinted with humor as he glanced back at her. "My dear, recruitment *is* seduction. One presents an opportunity in its most appealing light, emphasizes the exclusive nature of the invitation, and makes refusal seem rather... tedious by comparison." That charming smile touched his lips—the one Helena had heard could disarm foreign ministers. "I find the approach works remarkably well. People so rarely disappoint when you expect the best of them."

Josephine's expression softened slightly, though the exasperation remained. "One of these days, Frederick, you'll recruit someone to be a part of your schemes who sees straight through you."

"Perhaps," he conceded. "But not tonight, I hope." Then, his tone shifting to gravity: "What I'm about to propose requires both your skills and your trust. It won't be simple, and it won't be without risk.

"Let me be brief. The Society has grown bolder. Their tone has grown more extreme. So have their tactics."

Helena's brow furrowed. "You mean the Black Rose Society."

"Yes." He nodded once. "We've identified six separate events in the last month alone—shipments diverted or delayed, communications compromised, officials manipulated. We believe they're planning something larger. Deliberate. And dangerous."

James's eyes narrowed. "Six events in a month. That's not coincidence. That's coordination." His military training showed in how quickly he'd moved from information to implication. "And if they're planning something larger, they'll need resources. Money. Intelligence. Inside access."

"Which they have," Frederick confirmed grimly.

Lady Josephine took over, her voice quieter but no less firm. "They recruit carefully. Members are vetted over time—often through personal ties or shared ideology. They value stability, discretion, and tradition. Most of their senior operatives are married couples or long-established alliances. It's part of how they conceal their hierarchy. Appearances matter. And so does perceived loyalty."

Frederick's expression darkened. "We had an operative attempt to penetrate their circles six weeks ago. William Rawle. Skilled, careful, experienced. He tried to join one of their smaller circles in Lambeth. Went in alone with forged papers and a false persona."

Helena's stomach tightened. "And?"

"He vanished." Frederick's voice was flat. "We found his rooms ransacked, his codebook burned. No body." He paused. "The Society doesn't tolerate deception from outsiders. They investigate backgrounds thoroughly, verify connections. And Rawle had nothing to verify. No attachments. No family ties. He was a ghost trying to infiltrate ghosts, and they saw through him."

James's jaw tightened almost imperceptibly.

"That's why we need you both," Josephine said quietly. "An engaged couple has everything to lose—reputation, family standing, each other. It makes you believable. Human. Real."

Helena's pulse quickened as she understood. "You need us to infiltrate them as a pair."

"We need to get someone inside their inner circle," Frederick said. "And it would take much too long for them to trust a single operative, male or female. Suspicion would follow everywhere."

"But an engaged couple," James said slowly, working through the logic. "Already established in society. Already accepted. No reason to question sudden shared interests."

Lady Josephine nodded. "Precisely. An engagement gives you a pretext to be seen together constantly without raising eyebrows. And if you're careful—"

Helena folded her arms, pulse quickening. "You want me to pose as—what? His fiancée?"

Frederick met her gaze directly. "Yes. The two of you will announce an engagement. You'll attend events together. Move in tandem. Behave, in every way that matters, like a couple deeply aligned in purpose and in trust."

Helena stared at them, breath visible in the frigid air. She hadn't expected *this*. A covert assignment? Yes. Infiltration? Of course. But this?

James spoke before she could. "It's a sound plan. They'll expect intimacy, cooperation, coordination. A real couple has plausible reasons for secrecy. For privacy. It makes intelligence gathering easier."

His tone was clinical. Detached. But Helena felt the shift in her spine—a tightening that had nothing to do with cold.

"You're very quick to volunteer, Major," she said, arching a brow.

He didn't look away. "Because it's necessary."

Lady Josephine's voice softened. "We know what we're asking, Helena. But you weren't an arbitrary choice. You two are uniquely suited. Your reputation as well as your father's—your background, your poise—makes you the kind of woman they'd want to recruit. And James—"

"Has already seen the inside of too many planning rooms," he finished. "They'll assume I'm disillusioned. Disenchanted with command. An easy target for persuasion."

Frederick nodded. "They'll believe in you because they already believe the story they'll tell themselves about you."

Helena's mind spun. The logic was sound. Painfully sound. And yet—

"Lord Thomas Chadwick has been courting me seriously. He spoke tonight of investments, of a future together. He's building toward a proposal."

Lady Josephine's face softened. "I know." Her voice gentled, the edge giving way to something more personal. "He's a good man. And I don't doubt your affection for him." She stepped closer, her expression touched with something more maternal than official. "This life asks too much of the heart sometimes. It isn't fair. But neither is what's coming if we fail to act."

Helena lowered her gaze, throat tight.

Josephine's gloved hand brushed Helena's arm. "If there were any other way, I would insist on it. But the Society trusts no one who seems unmoored. They'll be watching for any cracks, any inconsistencies. I wouldn't send you into that unless I believed you were strong enough to carry it. You'll need to end it. Quickly."

"I understand," she said. It came out smaller than she meant it to.

James said nothing.

Frederick stepped forward. "You don't have to answer now. But we'll need your decision by morning. If you accept, we'll begin arrangements immediately."

He and Josephine turned, their footsteps retreating down the frozen path.

James remained behind.

The silence thickened, broken only by the distant echo of

music from the ballroom. Helena turned to him, her voice barely audible. "This will ruin things with him."

James was quiet for a moment. When he spoke, his voice remained steady, but something in his eyes shifted—acknowledgment, perhaps, or regret. "Then don't say yes because Sir Frederick asked it of you. Say yes because the mission matters."

Her throat tightened. "It always matters."

He gave a small nod. "We can do this. We'll make it convincing. But not complicated."

His words were practical. Measured. And they told her nothing about the man behind them.

But something in his eyes—quiet and unflinching—made her wonder just how well he played the roles assigned to him. And whether he ever came out of them whole.

Helena's lips pressed into a thin line. She exhaled slowly, frost crystallizing between them like the unspoken words neither had said.

"Give me the night to consider it," she said at last.

She turned toward the ballroom, shawl pulled tight. But before she disappeared into the light and warmth, she glanced back.

James stood where she'd left him, solid and still, his eyes never leaving her. Not watching her leave. Watching to make sure she made it safely back.

Something in her chest twisted.

Then she was gone.

Chapter Four

COLD TRUTHS

January 15, 1855
James

J AMES STOOD ALONE in the frozen stillness, watching Helena's silhouette retreat through the garden's far archway until it vanished into warmth and candlelight. The door clicked shut behind her, muting the music and laughter spilling from the ballroom. Only the hush of wind remained.

The cold crept in with purpose. Frost bit along his jawline, and the wool of his uniform couldn't quite hold it at bay. But James didn't move. His knee throbbed—the cold always made it worse—but he stayed planted. Pain was preferable to the uncertain ground he was about to walk.

He let the silence settle over him like a second skin.

It wasn't the assignment that unsettled him.

It was the woman.

Not because she was reckless or emotional—quite the opposite. Helena Ashford was composed, intelligent, unnervingly observant. In the short time he'd known her, she'd spoken with precision, acted with control, and withheld more than she gave. And yet... he'd seen it in her eyes. The quick pivot from hesitation to resolve. The careful weighing of duty against personal cost.

She was a soldier, whether she knew it or not.

But she was also a woman courting thoughts of a quieter future with a respectable man. A woman who had just agreed—almost—to give up security and simplicity for a mission defined by deception. With him.

And that was what twisted inside his chest.

Not the danger. Not even the pretense.

It was the risk of being the reason she lost something real.

A faint shift of gravel behind him pulled him from his thoughts.

Sir Frederick stood under the arch of bare branches, his great-coat draped like armor, his gloves clasped behind his back. The firelight from the ballroom flickered faintly on the snow-dusted path between them.

"She's everything you said she was," James said quietly.

Frederick stepped closer, boots crunching frost. "That worries you."

"Yes." James kept his gaze fixed on the garden beyond—silvered branches reaching into a pale sky, the moon sharp edged and cold. "She's considering it. That should reassure me. Instead…"

"You're afraid you'll fail her."

James didn't deny it.

"Still unsure?"

James exhaled, breath turning to mist. "She's not the problem. I am."

Frederick stepped closer. "That's not like you."

James turned, his eyes darker than the night. "You asked me to protect her. To partner with her. And yet I've seen what happens when I lead men into dangerous territory with false confidence. I've buried too many."

The faces rose unbidden. Lieutenant Morrison, dead in the snow because James had pushed the reconnaissance one mile too far. Corporal Davies, cut down by Russian fire when James's intelligence about enemy positions proved wrong. His entire company…

Too many men. Too many coffins. Too many letters James had written to families who would never understand why their sons, husbands, brothers weren't coming home.

"I won't add her to that list."

"You won't," Frederick said, calm but certain.

"You can't know that."

"I know you," Frederick said. "And I've seen you carry the weight of guilt longer than most men carry a rifle. It's time to put it down."

James held his breath for a beat, then exhaled slowly, fog curling past his lips.

"I'll see it through," he said. "If she agrees.

Frederick gave no smile, no praise. Just a hand on James's shoulder, firm and brief. "Then we may just stand a chance."

He stepped back into the night, following the path Josephine had taken. His coat disappeared into the darkness like a final thought left unspoken.

James stood alone.

He inhaled the cold and let it settle into his bones.

This was war.

But not the kind fought with rifles and regiments. Not the kind where enemy lines were drawn in blood and territory.

This was the war of whispers and wagers. Of secrets that killed and lies that saved lives.

And Helena Ashford would be his counterpart in it.

If he could keep her alive long enough.

Chapter Five

THE SHAPE OF HER FUTURE

January 15, 1855
Helena

ONCE THEY RETURNED home to the Ashford townhouse, all was still—save for the faint crackle of the fire and the occasional sigh of wind pressing against the windows.

Helena sat before her dressing table, her reflection framed in warm lamplight and shadow. The faint clink of pins against porcelain marked each careful movement as she unfastened her hair. Auburn waves slipped free, catching gold from the flames behind her.

The terrace doors remained locked, as they had been for three years. Mother used to take her morning tea there, reading letters and watching the dawn. After her death, Father had bolted them shut. Helena had never opened them.

Until now.

She rose, crossed the room, and tested the bolt. It slid free easily. The door opened to cold night air that tasted of coal smoke and coming rain. She stood on the threshold, bare feet on warm rug, terrace stones just beyond.

Not tonight. But the door was unlocked now. That felt like something.

As her maid built up the fire, Helena barely felt the chill in the air. The uncertainty lived deeper now—lodged behind her ribs, curled quiet and watchful beneath her heart.

The door clicked shut behind her maid, dispatched for chamomile tea. Helena leaned forward, studying the woman in the mirror with clinical distance.

"I can't become him," she whispered to the reflection. Her breath clouded faintly on the glass. "I can't love so deeply that losing it destroys me."

But the words sounded thin in the hush. As if her heart already knew she was lying.

She turned away and crossed to the hearth. A steady warmth glowed within, but it could not banish the memory of Thomas's voice—measured, eager, full of the kind of promise people mistook for security. *A trading company. A future. The country. Simplicity.*

There had been a time when that dream had soothed her. A quiet life beyond London's noise and bloodstains. But now, it felt like a corset drawn too tight—a life designed for someone gentler, someone less entangled.

She could pinpoint the shift: three months ago, after her first task undertaken for Sir Frederick—observing a French diplomat's wife who was passing naval intelligence to Moscow. Helena had followed her to a milliner's shop, decoded her purchase order (which was actually a list of dead drop times and locations), and reported back. That night, she'd returned to her room vibrating with purpose. Alive in a way she hadn't felt since before Mother's death.

Thomas's pastoral dreams had lost their luster that same night. Though she hadn't admitted it until now.

She picked up a hairpin from the mantel and turned it between her fingers. She tightened it in her fist. It bit into her palm. Not painful, just… grounding.

She crossed to her writing desk. There, beside her blotter, rested her father's silver letter opener—its hilt engraved with the

Ashford crest. Solid. Heavy. Unyielding. Like him. Or at least, like the man he'd once been.

Her father had wielded diplomacy like a weapon, elegant and effective. Ambassadors sought his counsel. The Crown valued his insight. But after Mother's death three years ago, he'd turned that razor-sharp analytical mind inward—dissecting every moment with her, cataloguing failures, punishing himself for not recognizing the fever's danger sooner.

Within six months, he'd resigned his post. Within a year, he'd retreated to the country estate where he still lived, technically, though the man Helena had known was long gone. What remained was a shell that read but didn't retain, walked but didn't travel, breathed but didn't truly live.

That's what loving too deeply cost. Everything.

Helena had learned the lesson. Compartmentalize. Focus on work. Keep emotional entanglements manageable, controllable, safe.

But then James's face surfaced in her mind, unbidden. The way he'd stood in the garden—solid, scarred, steady. The way his blue eyes had held hers without flinching. He carried his own wounds, his own dead. He understood the weight of responsibility in ways Thomas never could.

And that made him far more dangerous than a pleasant suitor with pastoral dreams.

Father's pocket watch sat on her nightstand—the one he'd given her before retreating to the country estate. She'd had it converted to a small clock. As she wound it carefully, the familiar rhythm soothed. Three turns, no more. The precision mattered. *Some things you could control, even when everything else slipped through your fingers.* Its quiet ticking filled the room, a steady counterpoint to her indecision.

She pressed her forehead briefly against the cool window-pane. Outside, the rooftops stretched in dark silhouettes, sharp and indifferent beneath a moon that cast more silver than warmth. From here, the city looked almost peaceful. But Helena knew better.

Her hand drifted to the letter opener again.

"I can't become what he did," she said softly. "I won't."

But even as she said it, James's face surfaced—his voice, low and grave, echoing through the garden. The stillness in him. The scars he carried like armor. He unnerved her. Not because he felt dangerous, but because he didn't.

He felt… real. Too real.

She turned sharply away and left her chambers, shawl wrapped tightly around her shoulders, footsteps muffled by the thick rug runner. A glow slipped out from beneath Amelia's door.

Of course she was still awake.

Helena knocked once.

"Come in," came her sister's familiar voice.

Amelia sat cross-legged on the bed, a novel in her lap, the fire throwing amber shadows on the wallpaper. The scent of lavender tea lingered faintly in the air.

"Helena?" Her expression shifted to surprise. "It's late. Did something happen?"

Helena sat at the edge of the bed, her posture too straight, fingers gripping her shawl like a lifeline.

"It's about Lord Chadwick."

Amelia blinked, then smiled cautiously. "Did he finally propose?"

"No." The answer came too quickly. Too tightly. "But he intends to. I think. He spoke of… a future."

Amelia studied her face. "And you're unsure."

Helena hesitated. "He wants a life in the country. Far from all this."

Amelia's voice was gentle. "Isn't that what you used to want?"

"It was." Helena folded her hands in her lap. "But I've changed."

"Because of your work?"

"Because of who I've become doing it." Her voice dropped to

a whisper. "He doesn't know. And even if he did, he wouldn't understand."

Amelia reached for her hand. "You shouldn't have to explain the most important parts of yourself. The right man will already see them."

Helena's throat tightened. "Thomas is good. Kind. Safe."

"Safe," Amelia repeated softly. "Is that really what you want? Or just what feels manageable?"

The question landed with unexpected weight.

Helena didn't answer. Couldn't. Because Amelia was right. Thomas was manageable. Predictable. He offered comfort, not challenge. Security, not understanding.

And somewhere in a frozen garden, a scarred major who understood duty and sacrifice and the weight of impossible choices had looked at her like he *saw* her.

"Perhaps," Helena said carefully, "I need someone who understands that some wars must be fought in ballrooms instead of on battlefields."

Amelia studied her face. "You've made your choice, haven't you?"

Helena stood. "I'm making it now."

Back in her chamber, Helena returned to the writing desk. The fire had burned low—embers glowing like watchful eyes. She set pen to paper with steady hands, but her pulse betrayed her.

Sir Frederick,

I have made my decision. I consent to the course proposed. Please provide further instructions at your earliest convenience.

Yours faithfully,
Helena Ashford

She stared at the words. Final. Irrevocable. Once this letter was sent, she became Major James Westwood's fiancée in the eyes of the Crown and, soon, society.

Her hand didn't shake as she reached for the sealing wax.

Thomas offered safety. James offered purpose.

Father taught her that safety was an illusion. Mother showed her that purpose survived everything.

She sealed the letter with the Ashford crest, the wax cooling quickly in the January air, and rang for her maid, issuing quiet instructions for immediate delivery.

But even after the door clicked shut behind the woman, Helena sat still, hands clasped tightly in her lap.

This is the right choice, she told herself.

And she believed it. But right did not mean easy.

She found herself at the terrace doors again. They stood open to the night—an invitation she'd given herself earlier. Cool air drifted in, carrying the scent of the city. She stepped forward, just to the threshold. Bare feet on the rug, terrace beyond.

Not tonight, she thought. *But one day.*

She would sit there as Mother had. With tea and letters and morning light. She would prove that loving and losing didn't have to mean destruction.

Just not tonight.

She closed the door gently and returned to the desk. Her thoughts turned to the necessary arrangements—public appearances, rehearsed affection, a chaperone.

Amelia, unmarried and bright-eyed, would draw more scrutiny than she could deflect.

Helena needed someone steel-tipped and scandal-proof.

The answer arrived unbidden—and brought a faint smile.

Aunt Prudence.

Helena reached for another sheet.

My Dearest Lady Prudence,

Recent circumstances have led me to require the assistance of someone with your particular skills and experience.

I find myself suddenly engaged to a gentleman of excellent character but brief acquaintance. London society, as ever, demands finesse.

Your presence would be both a comfort and a shield.

As always, your discretion is essential.

I shall explain more fully upon your arrival, which I hope will be swift.

Yours affectionately,
Helena

The wax seal hissed beneath the press. After ringing for a footman, she handed it off with a soft, "Send it at once."

Alone again, Helena remained at her desk, two sealed letters before her.

The fire whispered behind her. The clock ticked its steady rhythm. And through the open terrace doors, London breathed its restless midnight breath.

The choice had been made.

Tomorrow, she would become Major James Westwood's fiancée. She would step into the world of secrets and lies that Frederick inhabited. She would put herself in danger for Crown and country.

And perhaps—though she barely dared acknowledge it—she would discover whether a heart that had learned to guard itself could ever learn to open again.

The cost would be high. She knew that.

But she'd already paid the price of safety. Paid it in boredom and distance and a future that felt like a prison dressed in pastoral silk.

This path might destroy her.

But at least she would be *alive* when it happened.

Chapter Six

A MOST CONVENIENT ENGAGEMENT

January 16, 1855
James

FOLLOWING A RESTLESS night and a knee that ached with sullen stubbornness, James sat at his desk in his modest lodgings, gray morning light seeping through threadbare curtains. A single candle guttered beside him, casting a pale circle across the note from Sir Frederick Woolsy.

He read the line again, though he'd memorized it an hour ago: *Lady Helena has agreed to proceed. Await instructions.*

Helena had accepted the engagement.

He hadn't expected her agreement—not so quickly, not after her hesitation last night. She'd looked at him in that frozen garden like he was a variable in an equation she was still solving. Now she'd provided her answer.

Something had changed. Or perhaps she had made the decision he feared most: to treat this as duty, and nothing more.

It shouldn't matter. It was better this way—cleaner, simpler. And yet…

He stood and moved to the window. Below, a costermonger called his wares, his voice competing with carriage wheels on cobblestones. No gunfire. No smoke. No enemy positions to map. Yet anticipation settled into James's chest like a coiled wire.

The mission had begun. And this field of engagement would test him more severely than any ground he'd crossed in Crimea.

THE ASHFORD RESIDENCE was exactly what he'd imagined—elegant, restrained, steeped in generations of carefully curated decorum. Portraits of stern-faced ancestors lined the entrance hall. The carpet runner muffled his footsteps. Even the air smelled expensive: beeswax, rosewater, and old money.

The maid who greeted him showed no surprise at his arrival, only brisk efficiency as she led him down the carpeted hall to the drawing room.

Helena stood near the window, her profile touched with light. Her hair, burnished auburn, caught the sun like firelight through amber. She turned at his entrance, expression unreadable.

"Major Westwood," she greeted, voice cool and measured.

"Lady Helena."

"Allow me to introduce my sister, Lady Amelia Ashford."

A younger woman rose from the settee—clearly Helena's sister, with the same auburn coloring but a warmer, more open expression. Where Helena observed, Amelia radiated.

"Major Westwood." Amelia curtsied with barely contained energy. "Helena has told me almost nothing about you, which means you must be fascinating."

James bowed. "I hope not to disappoint."

"Oh, you won't. Helena never chooses boring people for her schemes."

"Amelia," Helena said warningly.

Before more could be said, someone rang the bell at the front door. Moments later, the butler appeared in the doorway, his usual composure slightly ruffled.

"Lady Prudence Ashford has arrived, my lady." He announced it as one might announce an approaching storm.

Helena's lips curved. "Aunt Prudence."

Amelia's eyes widened. "Aunt Prudence? Here? Saints preserve us."

Moments later, Lady Prudence swept into the room like a ship under full sail—black silk gown, fur-trimmed hat, eyes like a hawk beneath a veil of feigned distraction.

"My dearest Helena," she declared, arms outstretched. "You summoned, I came. And who," she added, turning a hawkish gaze toward James, "is this young man skulking by the fireplace as though he's dropped something important behind the mantel?"

James straightened instinctively. "Major James Westwood, my lady."

"Ah. The fiancé," Prudence said, as if pronouncing a diagnosis. Her sharp gaze flicked over him. "Sturdy enough. Not the fainting type. He'll do."

Amelia stifled a laugh behind her hand. Helena said nothing, though the corner of her mouth twitched.

Prudence settled into the nearest chair, crossing her ankles with regal elegance. "Now then. What on earth have you dragged me into, Helena?"

Helena remained poised. "We need a chaperone. And more importantly, someone whose presence will discourage curiosity. Your reputation speaks for itself."

"I should hope so," Prudence replied with a sniff. "I haven't played that role since your father stopped letting me choose his waistcoats. But for you, my dear, I'll make the sacrifice."

Helena glanced at James. "It's a fabricated engagement—for infiltration purposes. We'll need to move through society without raising suspicion."

Prudence arched a brow. "You and your clandestine affairs. You take after your father, I'll give you that. Fabricated or not, society adores a love story. And nothing inspires more scrutiny than a sudden engagement between strangers." Her gaze pinned

James. "Tell me, Major. Can you pretend to be absolutely besotted with my niece without looking like a fish left out in the sun?"

"I believe I can manage," James replied smoothly, a faint smile on his lips. "Though I welcome any coaching you care to offer."

Prudence gave a satisfied nod. "He has wit. I'm already inclined to keep him."

Prudence settled more fully into her chair, her theatrical air fading slightly. "Now then. Fabricated engagement aside, I assume there's actual danger involved? You wouldn't have summoned me for mere social theater."

Helena's expression sobered. "There is."

James leaned forward. "May we speak freely in front of Lady Amelia?"

"Amelia already knows more than she should," Helena said. "And she'll be attending events with us initially. She needs to understand the stakes."

Amelia straightened, her playful demeanor shifting to something more focused. "I can keep secrets, Major."

He nodded. That settled, they could begin.

James turned the conversation toward practicalities. "Frederick's sources are incomplete. The Society operates in shadows—whispers of discontent among veterans, rumors of something called 'Eclipse.' Some speak of 'purifying the Crown.' But none of it's solid yet."

Helena picked up the thread. "I've heard similar talk. Discontent about mismanaged supply lines in Crimea. Officers promoted by birth rather than merit. The kind of grumblings that take root when leadership fails."

"After Balaclava, trust in command fractured," James said, his voice tight. "Men died for lack of boots and tents while supplies rotted in London storehouses. It breeds the justified kind of resentment—which makes it dangerous."

Prudence's fan stilled. "Justified rage can be weaponized."

Amelia leaned forward. "But surely the Crown is addressing the supply problems? The reports in the papers—"

"Are carefully curated," James said. "The Society—if these voices are connected to it—doesn't want reform. They want revolution."

"Surely that's going too far, especially during wartime," Prudence protested.

Helena's gaze didn't waver. "Which means we must make order of this chaos. Convince the Black Rose Society they should recruit us."

Amelia clapped softly. "This is going to be fun. Aunt Prudence loose in London with a scandal to manage? They'll be writing songs about it."

Helena sighed. "Let's hope it doesn't come to that."

James allowed himself the briefest smile. The dynamic among the women was unexpected, but undeniably effective. He had a feeling Lady Prudence could win a war with a well-placed eyebrow.

Prudence tilted her head. "One question remains—do you dance, Major?"

"I do."

"Good. A fiancé with two left feet would hardly suit a woman like Helena. We'll need to plan appearances. Dinners. Balls. The opera."

Helena raised an eyebrow, her amusement evident. "Don't let her intimidate you, Major. Aunt Prudence thrives on theatrics."

"Thrives on theatrics?" Prudence exclaimed, her hand fluttering to her chest in mock offense. "Helena, I'll have you know my theatrics have secured more diplomatic agreements than any treaty ever signed."

James bit back a smile as he took a seat opposite Helena. "Our goal is to be seen. To convince others of our bond without giving them reason to doubt."

Helena nodded. "Which means learning each other's habits.

How to move as a pair, appearing familiar and natural."

Amelia leaned forward, mischief glinting in her eyes. "Not like two strangers attempting civility at the altar?"

James gave her a dry look. "Precisely."

They began to chart a course: upcoming invitations, likely encounters, excuses for their presence.

Amelia, resting her chin in her hand, said dryly, "You'll need to practice those glances. You currently look like a man sitting across from his commanding officer, not his intended."

James's lips twitched. "I wasn't aware my resemblance to a commanding officer was so pronounced."

"Oh, it's quite pronounced," Amelia assured him. "All you're missing is a saber and a few shouted orders."

"You simply need to practice," Prudence said cheerfully. "You must learn to look at her like she's the sun and you haven't seen daylight in weeks."

James's voice lowered. "I'm more comfortable in shadows, I'm afraid."

"Well," Prudence said, rising and brushing imaginary lint from her sleeve, "then perhaps Helena will be the one to teach you the value of warmth."

The comment lingered longer than anyone intended.

Helena turned toward James, her expression carefully neutral. "Shall we begin planning the next event?"

"Of course," he said, standing.

The practical details came quickly after that—which invitations to accept, how to coordinate arrivals, the importance of being seen together in public before any formal announcement. But James's attention kept snagging on Prudence's words. Warmth. As though it were something he could simply decide to show.

When he finally took his leave—polite goodbyes to all three women—and stepped into the cold London air, his thoughts remained behind. Especially on the woman with fire in her eyes and walls around her heart.

He wasn't sure yet how much of this engagement would be fiction. But as of today, they were committed to the lie.

And if he wasn't careful, it might start to feel far too real.

Chapter Seven

THE FOREIGN OFFICE ANNEX

January 17, 1855
Helena

T HE ADDRESS SIR Frederick had provided led to a narrow-fronted Georgian building just off Bloomsbury Street near Russell Square. Its faded red brick façade and painted white cornices spoke of modest governmental purpose—unremarkable enough that Helena's cab driver hadn't given it a second glance as he'd driven away.

A discreet brass plaque beside the black-painted door read: *Foreign Office—Annex.*

Helena adjusted her gloves, studying the building. The windows were curtained but not shuttered. No obvious guards. Nothing to suggest this was anything but an outpost for clerks.

But she'd learned that the most dangerous places often looked the most innocuous.

James reached for the door handle. It opened before he could turn it.

A thin, sharp-eyed man in his late sixties stood in the entry hall, dressed like a civilian clerk but with the bearing of someone who'd spent decades taking orders and giving them. His gaze swept over them with practiced efficiency.

"Major Westwood. Lady Helena Ashford." It wasn't a question. "Sir Frederick is expecting you. First floor, end of the hall."

Helena blinked, surprised that he knew their names. "Thank you, Mr...?" Helena prompted.

"Leech, my lady." The faintest hint of amusement touched his weathered face. "Tea will be sent in shortly."

The entry hall was narrow and dimly lit by a single oil lamp, dark wainscoting absorbing what little light filtered through the frosted-glass fanlight above the door. A long runner muffled their footsteps as they moved deeper into the building.

Through an open door to the left, Helena glimpsed what appeared to be a clerk's office—two desks stacked with ledgers, shelves of outdated gazettes, and a harried-looking clerk pushing papers with methodical precision. The perfect picture of bureaucratic tedium.

Except the secretary's eyes had tracked their passage with the same sharp assessment Mr. Leech had employed.

Everyone here was watching. Always.

They climbed a narrow staircase to the first floor, James's slight limp more pronounced after the morning's exertions. At the end of the hall, he knocked twice on a heavy oak door.

"Enter."

Sir Frederick Woolsy's office was everything the clerk's room below was not: lined with locked cabinets, a wall of maps pinned with wax-sealed tags, and a long desk positioned near a window that was shuttered from the inside despite the afternoon hour. A fire crackled in the hearth, and the scent of tea and tobacco hung in the air.

Lady Josephine occupied a chair near the fire, her expression warm but watchful. And arranged around a long table that had been brought in from what must be an adjoining room were four other individuals Helena didn't immediately recognize.

"Lady Helena. Major Westwood." Frederick gestured them forward. "Thank you for coming. I believe it's time you met the others working this matter."

Helena's pulse quickened. *Others*. Not just her and James, then.

"The Black Rose Society is larger and better organized than we initially believed," Frederick continued. "Which means our response must be coordinated. You'll be operating in the field—publicly, visibly. But you'll have assistance."

He turned to a young woman seated at the table—petite and graceful, with chestnut hair swept into a simple chignon and warm brown eyes that assessed everything with quiet intensity.

"Miss Charlotte Sinclair. Our foremost cryptographer. If the Society communicates in cipher, Charlotte will crack it."

Charlotte rose, offering a small curtsy. "Lady Helena. Major Westwood." Her voice was soft but precise, each word carefully measured. "I've heard a great deal about you both."

"All good, I hope," Helena said.

The faintest smile touched Charlotte's lips. "Accurate, at least."

Helena studied her. There was something almost... withdrawn about Charlotte. As though she'd built walls not just around her heart but around her entire self. She wore a simple blue dress, no jewelry save a small locket, and her hands bore faint ink stains—the mark of someone who spent long hours with pen and paper.

"Charlotte works behind the scenes," Frederick explained. "She won't be attending social events. But any coded messages you intercept come directly to her."

"My father, Sir Anthony Sinclair, occasionally accompanies me to social events," Charlotte added quietly. "However, he's unaware of my work for Sir Frederick, so please use discretion when he's nearby."

James nodded. "Easily done. We'll pass along whatever coded information we come across."

"I don't need much," Charlotte said. "Just the ciphers."

Frederick moved on to a tall man lounging against the far wall with studied casualness—the same man James had spoken with at the Duke of Somerset's ball.

"You've already met Adrian Blackwood. Former Lieutenant, 11th Hussars. Master of disguise and infiltration."

Adrian straightened with a grin, sketching a lazy bow. "Lady Helena. A pleasure to be formally introduced. You may not have seen me, but I've often been nearby when Sir Frederick found occasion to make use of your talents."

Helena looked at him in bemusement. How did he know her when she'd never seen him before?

"Adrian can become whomever the mission requires," Sir Frederick said. "He's been tracking Society members in contexts where a uniformed major or a lady of quality would draw immediate suspicion. Taverns, dockside meetings, workers' meetings."

"All the places respectable people avoid," Adrian supplied cheerfully. "It's rather liberating, actually."

"It's dangerous," James said flatly.

"That too." Adrian's smile didn't dim. "But someone has to do it. And I'm rather good at not getting caught."

Sir Frederick indicated a woman standing near the window—elegant despite her subdued clothing, with dark hair and the bearing of someone accustomed to command. She wore a simple gown of lavender silk that spoke of half-mourning.

"Lady Arabella Langley. Widow of Lord Richard Langley, who fell in service to the Crown."

Arabella inclined her head, her expression composed but her eyes sharp. "Lady Helena. Major."

"I'm sorry for your loss," Helena said quietly.

"Thank you." Arabella's voice was steady, giving nothing away. "It was over two years ago. I've learned to carry it."

"Arabella has proven invaluable in social infiltration," Frederick said. "As a widow in half-mourning, she can move through certain circles without attracting undue attention. She's also skilled at disguise when situations require alternative approaches. She's decisive and sees more than most. I suggest you trust her insights."

Finally, Frederick turned to a man standing slightly apart from the others—tall, dark haired, with the posture of someone trained to long hours on his feet and the quiet competence of a man who'd seen too much suffering.

"Dr. Sebastian Ramsey. Formerly a surgeon with the British forces in Crimea. Now providing medical cover for our operations here in London."

The doctor nodded, his expression somber. "Lady Helena. Major Westwood."

James studied him with interest. "Recently returned from Crimea?"

"Three months ago." Something flickered in Ramsey's expression—frustration, perhaps, or old anger. "I saw enough men die from failures of supply and mismanagement to last several lifetimes. The conditions were indefensible."

"And now?" Helena asked.

"Now I try to prevent more unnecessary deaths," Ramsey said. "When Sir Frederick's people are injured and cannot safely seek ordinary medical care, they are brought to me. I also consult on certain matters. Poison identification. Cause of death analysis. Whatever is needed."

Frederick stepped to the center of the room, his gaze sweeping across all six operatives.

"The Society has been operating in shadows for years," he said. "Building on the foundation the Chartists laid—their networks, their rhetoric, the discontent of the working classes. But where the Chartists were open about their demands, the Black Rose Society is covert. They're building something, recruiting carefully, planning operations we still don't fully understand. And whatever they're doing, they're keeping it to themselves."

He paused, letting that sink in.

"But they've grown confident. Bolder. They believe themselves untouchable. That's their weakness."

"I've been hearing more chatter in the past month," Adrian

added. "Workers' meetings, dockyards, veterans' taverns. Someone's stirring up organized discontent."

"And I've intercepted two coded messages in the past week alone," Charlotte said quietly. "Both referenced 'the spring reckoning.' I haven't fully decrypted them yet, but the implication is clear—they're planning something for March or April."

Helena's pulse quickened. Spring. Only a few months away.

"Which brings us to assignments," Frederick said. He turned to Arabella. "What have you learned?"

"I've been tracking Lady Eleanor Bennet," Arabella said. "She has considerable influence and a particular interest in military reform. She hosts small gatherings—very selective, very careful. I've attended twice under different pretexts, but I haven't yet confirmed whether she's recruiting for the Society or simply hosting legitimate political discussions."

Helena leaned forward. "What about Lady Margaret Fairfax? She hosts a Thursday salon—philosophical discussions, reform talk. Very intellectual. Very… selective."

Arabella's eyes sharpened with interest. "I know of her salon but haven't attended. You've observed her yourself?"

"Briefly. At the Duke of Somerset's ball. She spoke passionately about obligation to the poor, about those of us with position using it for more than social advantage. It could be innocent reform sentiment. Or it could be recruitment rhetoric carefully calibrated to sound plausibly noble."

"That matches the Society's methods," Frederick said. "They recruit through shared ideology first, revealing their true nature only once trust is established."

Arabella nodded slowly. "I'll shift my attention to Lady Margaret as well. Between Eleanor and Margaret, we should be able to map their social recruitment network."

"Very good." Sir Frederick reached for a leather portfolio upon his desk. "Within these are accounts of those known—or believed—to be in league with the Society. I expect you all to acquaint yourselves with them thoroughly. Miss Sinclair, I shall require discreet methods for the exchange of ciphered correspondence. Major Blackwood, you will continue your rounds among the taverns. Lady Arabella, keep a close watch upon Lady Eleanor and Lady Margaret. Dr. Ramsey, extend your circle among the medical men; we may yet have need of places where one might recover unseen."

He turned to Helena and James. "And you two practice being enamored of one another. Because if the Society suspects for even a moment that this engagement is a sham, everything we've built collapses."

The meeting drew to a close amid a discussion of practical arrangements—signals to be employed, places where messages might be discreetly left, and measures to be taken should matters go awry. As they prepared to leave, Charlotte approached Helena.

"Lady Helena, if you should happen upon any written communications—notes, letters, or writings set in cipher—I beg that you leave them precisely as you find them. In such work, context may prove everything."

"Of course," Helena said. Then, on impulse: "Would you teach me? The basics?"

Charlotte's eyes widened slightly. "You want to learn?"

"I want to understand. Even if I'm not the expert, I should recognize what's important."

For the first time, Charlotte's smile reached her eyes. "I'd be happy to. Though I should warn you—it's rather tedious work."

"I excel at tedious work," Helena assured her.

Mr. Leech appeared in the doorway as if summoned by thought alone. "Your carriage is ready, Lady Helena. Major Westwood."

Outside, twilight had settled over Bloomsbury, the gas lamps beginning to glow along the street. Their cab waited at the corner, the driver hunched against the cold.

"What did you think of them?" Helena asked as they climbed inside.

James considered. "Charlotte's brilliant but fragile. Adrian's competent but reckless. Arabella's driven by grief—that makes her dangerous to herself. And Ramsey's seen enough preventable death that I suspect he's stopped fearing his own."

"And together?"

"Together, we might actually survive this."

The cab rumbled through darkening streets. Helena stared out the window, her reflection ghostly in the glass.

Somewhere in this city, the Black Rose Society was planning something. *The spring reckoning.*

They had three months, perhaps less, to infiltrate an organization that eliminated anyone who threatened it.

Three months to become people they weren't.

Helena wasn't sure which would prove more difficult—deceiving the Society, or deceiving herself about what this partnership with James was becoming.

Chapter Eight

THE RUSE AT THE OPERA

January 20, 1855
Helena

THE GRAND FAÇADE of Her Majesty's Theatre gleamed under the glow of gaslights, its gilded columns casting long shadows over the bustling street. Carriages lined the curb, liveried servants called out names, and the air hummed with anticipation—perfume, horses, velvet, and ambition all mingling beneath the winter stars.

Helena adjusted her gloves, careful not to wrinkle the silk, and glanced at James beside her. He wore his dress uniform with that same impossible composure—as though military regalia were as natural to him as breathing. Yet his gaze swept the crowd with calculation, not admiration. Even here, he was working.

Behind them, Amelia all but bounced on the balls of her feet.

"Is this your first time at Her Majesty's Theatre?" Helena asked James, voice pitched just above the bustle.

Before he could answer, Amelia chirped, "It's only my second time. The first, I was far too young to care about anything but the gowns." She gazed up at the gilded façade. "Isn't it glorious, Major?"

He offered a faint smile. "It is. The theater back home had

three pews and a curtain held up by wishful thinking."

Lady Prudence, already halfway up the steps, turned with a sniff. "Do try not to gawk, Major. You're quite dazzled by chandeliers."

James's brow lifted. "I thought I was meant to appear enamored, not indifferent."

"With Helena," Prudence shot back. "Not the plasterwork."

Helena glanced sidelong at him. "You'll manage, I'm sure."

Amelia took Helena's arm with a grin. "And if not, I'll lend you my opera glasses. They magnify flirtation beautifully."

Inside, the theater opened like a jeweled music box—mirror-polished walls, gold filigree, and chandeliers blazing with gaslight. The red carpet muffled footsteps and gossip alike.

Helena's gaze swept the tiers of boxes rising around the horseshoe-shaped auditorium. Each one held its own small drama—jewels glittering, fans fluttering, whispered conversations behind gloved hands. Somewhere in this sea of silk and society, members of the Black Rose Society were watching. Listening. Recruiting.

She just had to find them.

Their box was well-positioned, if slightly to the left. Prudence pounced on the flaw immediately.

"Whoever placed us in this box should be thrashed," she declared, eyeing the usher. "Verdi demands proper acoustics."

Amelia leaned in. "Perhaps if you tilt your lorgnette at just the right angle, the sound will follow."

"Impertinent child," Prudence muttered, but her lips twitched as she settled into her seat.

As the usher departed, Helena's attention caught on a box across the way—less prominent than theirs, positioned in the second tier where the view was adequate but the prestige diminished. A young woman sat beside an older gentleman, her chestnut hair styled simply, her dress a modest blue that suggested neither fashion nor poverty but something carefully in between.

Charlotte Sinclair. And beside her, the silver-haired man must be her father, Sir Anthony.

Charlotte's gaze swept the theater with the same quiet intensity Helena had observed at the Foreign Office Annex. Even here, surrounded by music and spectacle, she was working—cataloguing faces, noting associations, building the mental map that would later help her decode the Society's communications.

Their eyes met for the briefest moment. Charlotte's expression didn't change, but her hand moved to adjust her shawl—a simple gesture that meant *I see you. I'm watching.*

Helena turned back to her own box, satisfied. They weren't alone in this theater. The Crown had eyes everywhere.

James had claimed the chair beside Helena. Even seated, his attention never fully settled—scanning the boxes across from them, tracking movement in the aisles below.

Helena leaned toward him, her voice low. "If you keep looking everywhere but at me, someone might think you've never been to the opera before."

James's lips curved into a slow smile. "But I haven't."

"Then pretend," she replied, eyes on the stage. "We're engaged, remember?"

"I do," he said, turning to face her fully. "How's this?"

His gaze held hers—steady, intense, and far too intimate. Helena's breath caught.

"Convincing enough," she said, managing to look away first.

The overture began, and the audience's attention shifted to the stage. Yet Helena found her gaze wandering to the theater's perimeter.

In the standing area at the back of the orchestra level—where tickets were cheapest and those without boxes could watch—a young man in working-class clothes leaned against the rear wall. His cap sat at an angle, his coat worn but clean, his attention ostensibly on the stage.

But Helena recognized the set of his shoulders, the way he held himself despite the humble clothing.

Adrian Blackwood, dressed as a tradesman or clerk. Blending perfectly with the theater's less affluent patrons, watching the boxes above with the same careful attention he'd employ in a dockside tavern.

He didn't look toward their box. Didn't acknowledge Helena's recognition. But she knew he was there, watching for Society members who might attend the opera, tracking who spoke to whom during intermission.

The Crown's reach extended from the finest boxes to the cheapest seats. And no one would suspect the shabby young man at the back was the same Lieutenant Blackwood who'd served with the 11th Hussars in Crimea.

Helena's thoughts strayed to the man beside her. That overt stare…a false act of affection… had felt disarmingly natural, and she struggled to remind herself that it was just that—an act. That was the story. That was the game.

She needed to remain above it—to remember that affection, however convincing, was still part of the deception.

At intermission, they emerged into the gilded crush of the foyer. Laughter and perfume filled the air; whispers curled beneath the rustle of silk skirts. This was where the real performances took place—where alliances were forged and secrets traded beneath the guise of social pleasantry.

Helena touched James's arm lightly. "I see Lady Prescott. I should pay my respects."

He understood immediately. "Of course. I'll wait here."

Amelia, bless her, swept in with practiced timing. "Major Westwood, you simply must tell me more about your service. I've heard such varied accounts of Crimea…" She drew him slightly away, providing cover for Helena's departure.

Helena slipped into the crowd, her movements unhurried but purposeful.

Near a marble column, Helena lingered at the edge of a conversation. Sir Talon Bridewell, unmistakable in his height and silver-touched temples, stood among a cluster of men.

"The shipment's arrival is confirmed," Bridewell murmured. "Our benefactor was quite clear—timing is everything."

"Tied to the speech?" another asked. "Still pressing that reform angle?"

"Prescott's stubborn," said a third. "Thinks one public address can turn the tide."

A fourth voice, lower still: "Let the winter do our work. Starvation persuades more than rhetoric."

Helena's blood chilled. They were content to let people starve as a political tool.

"And the target?" someone asked. "Still the—"

A burst of laughter from a nearby group drowned out the rest. Helena shifted position, trying to catch the response, but Bridewell and his companions didn't elaborate.

Across the foyer, Lady Margaret Fairfax's laugh rang out, drawing attention just as Prudence swooped in.

"Lady Margaret," she cooed, eyes dancing, "is that a Worth original? You must tell me how you managed it before the rest of Paris caught wind."

Margaret turned, her expression shifting from sharp awareness to social pleasure so smoothly that Helena almost believed it genuine. "Lady Prudence. How kind of you to notice…"

The diversion worked. Helena leaned slightly closer.

"The ambassador's been unusually quiet," one man said.

"Quiet?" another scoffed. "He's meeting privately with that group—the black—"

A burst of laughter nearby drowned out the rest.

Helena's pulse quickened. *The Black Rose?* Had he been about to say it? Or something else entirely?

She strained to hear more, but the speaker had moved on to safer topics—horses, or perhaps hounds. The moment had passed.

Before she could manage to overhear another exchange, Amelia's voice rang out—too loud, too bright, perfectly timed. "Helena! There you are! I've been looking everywhere."

Helena turned, schooling her features into a pleasant smile. "Forgive me. I was caught in conversation."

Amelia linked arms with her, her voice dropping to a murmur as they walked. "Prudence's signal. Time to extract you before you're too obvious."

So Prudence had noticed Helena lingering too long near Bridewell's group. Her aunt's social instincts were impeccable.

James appeared at Helena's other side, his expression mild. "Shall we return to our box? The second act begins shortly."

THE APPLAUSE FROM the opera's final act still echoed through the grand hall as guests began filtering toward the exits. Most would linger to see and be seen, but Helena's attention caught on two men moving against the current—away from the crowd, toward the shadowed corridor that led to the theater's private rooms.

Sir Talon Bridewell, and with him a man Helena didn't recognize. Foreign, by the cut of his coat—subtle braided trim along the lapels in a style she'd seen on Eastern European diplomats. His bearing suggested military training, though he wore no uniform.

They disappeared into the corridor. Helena glanced back at James—still engaged with Prudence and Amelia, providing perfect cover. She had perhaps three minutes before her absence would be noted.

"Amelia, stay with James," Helena murmured as she passed. "I'll only be a moment."

She slipped away before either could object.

The corridor was dim, hushed, lit only by widely spaced gas sconces that created pools of shadow between islands of weak light. The carpet runner muffled her footsteps, but every rustle of her skirts sounded deafening in the close space.

She kept fifteen feet back, using a marble pillar for cover

when they paused.

"…securing future influence," Bridewell was saying, his voice low but clear in the empty corridor. "The arrangements are nearly complete."

"And the payment?" the other man asked, his accent unmistakably Eastern European.

"Handled. The Raven has seen to it."

Her heart skipped. *The Raven.* The name hovered like smoke in the shadows.

She leaned closer, straining to hear—and her elbow clipped the plaster wall. A dull thud that seemed to echo forever.

Silence. Complete, suffocating silence.

Then footsteps. Turning toward her. Deliberate. Closing.

Helena's heart hammered against her ribs. She pressed herself flat against the wall, mind racing. If they found her here, alone, clearly eavesdropping—

"Dearest!" Prudence's voice rang out from the corridor's entrance, sharp and imperious. "You've wandered again! Come along before we lose our carriage."

Helena exhaled shakily and stepped into the light, arranging her features into apologetic embarrassment. "Aunt Prudence, I thought I saw Sir Reginald and Lady Prescott come this way—"

Sir Reginald. Father's old friend. Did he still smell of cigars and bay rum?

Then Helena blinked, quickly adapting to the ruse. Prudence's figure emerged at the corridor's entrance, the epitome of effortless composure, her fan snapping shut with a sharp click.

Bridewell stepped into the light, his smile thin and utterly unconvincing. His eyes moved from Prudence to Helena, assessing, calculating. "Lady Prudence. Always a pleasure."

"Ah, Lord Bridewell," Prudence returned, her tone honey sweet. "It's been much too long since we've spoken. You always did have a knack for vanishing at the most unusual moments." Her fan tapped against her palm. "You'll forgive me for retrieving my niece, won't you? She has a dreadful habit of wandering off in search of old friends."

James appeared at Prudence's side, positioning himself slightly in front of Helena—casual but unmistakably protective. His tone remained light. "Lady Helena, there you are. I thought you'd gone to find Lady Prescott."

Helena smoothed her expression into polite chagrin. "I was certain I saw her slip down this corridor, but I must have been mistaken."

Bridewell's companion said nothing. His eyes—cold, evaluating—lingered on Helena a beat too long before he turned away. She'd been noted. Assessed. Perhaps even recognized as a potential threat.

That was decidedly not ideal.

Helena seized the moment, keeping her voice steady. "Lord Bridewell, may I introduce my fiancé, Major James Westwood?"

Bridewell's gaze shifted to James—taking in the uniform, the medals, the bearing of a career soldier. Something flickered in his expression. Interest? Calculation? "Major. Crimea?"

"The 17th Lancers," James said evenly.

"Ah." A pause, weighted with meaning Helena couldn't decipher. Then: "Enjoy the rest of your evening."

Without another word, Bridewell and his companion turned and disappeared into the shadows.

Outside, the cold wrapped around them like consequence. Their breath misted in the January air.

James pulled Helena aside, his voice low and tight with suppressed anger. "What were you thinking?"

"I was thinking I might learn something," she said, matching his volume. "And I did. The Raven. A foreign contact, possibly Eastern European. Payment arrangements. Future influence—"

"You could've been exposed. Do you understand what that would mean? Not just for you, but for all of us?"

Helena's jaw tightened. "I do. And I wasn't caught."

"Only because Prudence rescued you."

"Which is precisely why we work as a team," Prudence interjected, stepping between them with the authority of someone accustomed to managing volatile situations. "Children. The point is not to be brave. The point is to be effective. Dead spies gather no secrets."

She fixed Helena with a stern look. "You took a risk. It paid off this time. But don't mistake luck for skill."

Helena lowered her gaze. The words weren't unkind. But they landed with the weight of truth she couldn't dismiss.

She'd been reckless. Prudence was right. She'd gotten close enough to learn valuable intelligence—but also close enough that Bridewell and his foreign associate had seen her face. Noted her interest.

That couldn't be undone.

As the carriage rumbled away from the opera house, Amelia yawned and tucked her gloved hands into her muff.

"What took you so long?" she asked, peering at Helena. "Did Aunt Prudence stop to lecture someone about propriety again?"

"My dear Amelia," Prudence said with exaggerated dignity, "I never lecture. I simply enlighten those less informed."

Amelia grinned, clearly skeptical.

James's attention remained fixed on Helena, his voice quiet but firm. "You must be more cautious."

Helena turned to the window. Her reflection met her gaze in the glass—pale, composed, unreadable.

She didn't answer.

Her silence wasn't agreement, but determination. She'd do whatever she believed the mission required, promises or no promises.

Chapter Nine

REFLECTIONS AND PLANNING

January 21, 1855
James

PALE MORNING LIGHT filtered through the threadbare curtains of James's quarters, casting soft, crooked bands across the wooden floor. He sat at his desk, his journal open, pen hovering over a blank page. His hand remained still. Too many thoughts jostled for space, and none of them belonged in an official report.

The opera had been a spectacle—soaring chandeliers, velvet-draped tiers, and voices that pierced the air like blades. Far removed from the quiet parlor recitals of his childhood, where music had meant worn sheet music, off-key pianists, and tea served in cracked china. Her Majesty's Theatre was a different world entirely. Sharper. More dangerous.

And not just because of the Society members circulating through the crowd.

But it wasn't the grandeur that lingered in his mind this morning, nor the intelligence Helena had gathered in that damned corridor.

It was Helena herself.

She'd moved through the night like she belonged to it— poised, intelligent, effortlessly in control. Until she wasn't. Until he'd heard Prudence's voice echo down that corridor and known, instantly, that Helena had gone too far. Had pushed too close. And when he'd reached her—standing there with Bridewell and that cold-eyed foreign operative assessing her like a threat to be eliminated—he'd seen it. Just for a breath. Fear flickering behind her composed expression before she buried it beneath practiced social grace.

She'd been afraid. And she'd hidden it so well that anyone else would have missed it.

But James had spent years reading men's faces in the moment before battle. He knew fear when he saw it, no matter how skillfully concealed.

And something in him had shifted at the sight of it.

He couldn't afford to dwell on her. Personal connections made a man weak—he'd learned that lesson watching Lieutenant Morrison bleed out in the snow, crying for a wife who'd never see him again.

To trust someone, to let them in, was to hand them a weapon they could use against you. Or worse—to give yourself something to lose.

And men with something to lose made mistakes.

James tapped the pen once against the desk before setting it aside. He should be writing a report for Frederick—names observed, conversations overheard, associations noted. Measured. Objective. As befitted an officer's duty.

But Helena's voice kept drifting through the analysis, turning facts into something closer to memory. The way she'd said "I wasn't caught" with that defiant tilt to her chin. The tension in her shoulders during the carriage ride home. Her silence when he'd asked for a promise she had no intention of keeping.

He pushed back from the desk.

Enough. Time to act.

LATER THAT MORNING, the butler at Ashford House led him to the drawing room. Sunlight slanted through tall windows, catching dust motes in the air. Helena sat near the window, a notebook in her lap, head bent in apparent concentration. Her hair caught the light, burnished copper against the pale morning sun.

She didn't look up at his entrance. Not immediately. The slight delay felt deliberate—a small assertion of control after last night's confrontation.

Lady Prudence lounged nearby with a teacup, watching them over its rim. Amelia fussed with a stubborn arrangement of winter roses, humming under her breath.

Finally, Helena glanced up. Her expression was composed, polite, and notably distant. "Major Westwood. Punctual, as expected."

Prudence peered over her teacup. "And here I was hoping you'd arrive late enough to give me time for a second cup. But no. Military men. Always on time, always upright, rarely interesting."

James inclined his head. "I'll endeavor to be less disappointing today, Lady Ashford."

"See that you do," she replied, waving her hand as if swatting a fly.

Helena gestured to the chair across from hers. He took the seat, noting the tension in her posture—the way her hand pressed just a little too firmly against her notebook, the controlled set of her shoulders.

"We need to discuss tonight's ball," she said, her tone perhaps a shade too brisk. "I'll be speaking with Lord Chadwick. Private-ly."

James stilled. "To end things."

"Yes." She met his gaze directly, but something in her eyes suggested the decision cost more than she'd admit. "If our engagement is to be believed, there can't be lingering attachments. Thomas deserves clarity. And I need to… close that door."

Prudence made a faint, unimpressed sound. "You say that as

though men accept rejection gracefully. Even reasonable men can surprise you when their pride is wounded."

"Thomas *is* reasonable," Helena said, though her voice carried less conviction than her words suggested.

James kept his expression neutral, but his jaw tightened. He didn't like this plan. Not because Thomas posed any real threat—the man was a gentleman by all accounts—and certainly not because of jealousy.

That would be absurd.

But the thought of Helena alone with a man whose hopes she was about to crush, in a secluded corner of a ballroom where anything could happen… No, he didn't like it at all.

"If he's as fond of you as he seems," James said carefully, "it may not be simple."

"Which is why I'll be careful." Her smile held a trace of defiance. "I've managed far worse. Thomas is a gentleman. He won't make a scene."

"You hope," Prudence interjected. "Reasonable men remain reasonable until they don't. Confidence is commendable, Helena. Overconfidence, less so."

Helena's expression tightened slightly. "Noted. But it needs to be done, and delaying won't make it easier."

James shifted forward. "And after you've spoken with Thomas?"

"I'll focus on Lady Eleanor Bennet." Helena's expression sharpened, the personal matter already compartmentalized. "Sir Frederick wants her watched closely. Arabella says she has considerable influence in military reform circles and has been hosting private gatherings. If she's recruiting for the Society, I need to confirm it."

"How?" James asked.

"Carefully." Her lips curved slightly. "I'll express interest in her reform work. Ask intelligent questions. Show sympathy for veterans' complaints about supply failures and incompetent leadership—complaints you can substantiate from personal experience."

James's eyes narrowed. "You want to use my service record as bait."

"I want to use the truth as an entry point," Helena corrected. "Your frustrations are legitimate. Lady Eleanor will recognize that authenticity. And if she's recruiting disaffected military men, a decorated Crimean veteran engaged to a well-connected lady would be exactly the sort of couple she'd want to cultivate."

"You'll need more than charm," Prudence said, setting her teacup down with a decisive clink. "Lady Eleanor has hosted some of the sharpest political minds in London. She doesn't suffer fools, and she has an unerring ear for insincerity. You'd do well to bring reinforcements."

Helena raised an eyebrow. "You mean the major?"

"I mean someone who can keep his wits about him," Prudence said with a pointed look at James. "Though if you must bring the major, make sure he doesn't glower like a man at a funeral."

"I'll do my best to look enamored," James said, his tone carefully neutral.

Helena's eyes sparked with amusement. "You'll need to improve substantially. Currently, you fluctuate between bored and vaguely dyspeptic."

James's eyebrow lifted. "Dyspeptic?"

"Suffering from indigestion," Helena clarified helpfully. "I thought it more polite than my initial assessment."

Amelia laughed from her position by the roses. "Oh, this is delightful. Please tell us your initial assessment."

"I'd rather not," Helena said primly, though her lips twitched. "The major might take offense."

James fought back a smile. "I appreciate your restraint."

"Try practicing affection instead of sparring," Prudence suggested, her tone shifting to something more instructive. "Start small. Shared glances that linger just a moment too long. Gentle touches—his hand at the small of your back, your fingers brushing his sleeve. The appearance of unconscious intimacy."

James met Helena's gaze across the space between their chairs. "It's not that difficult to pretend."

Something flickered in her eyes—surprise, perhaps, or uncertainty. Her breath caught almost imperceptibly before she collected herself. "Good. Then we're making progress."

But her voice had lost some of its professional edge.

They turned their attention to the evening's logistics. James appreciated Helena's methodical approach—the way she cataloged details, anticipated reactions, identified potential complications. It reminded him of planning sessions before a campaign. Except this time, the terrain was drawing rooms and dance cards, not enemy lines.

"What about Amelia?" he asked as they wrapped up. "Will she continue attending events with us?"

"For now," Helena said. "Once our engagement is formally announced, Aunt Prudence alone will provide sufficient chaperonage. Amelia can resume her normal social calendar."

"She's been useful," James observed carefully. "Good instincts for when to create distractions."

"She's my sister," Helena said quietly. "Not part of this work. The longer she's involved, the greater the risk that she'll be identified as part of our cover. I won't expose her to that danger."

James studied her for a moment. "You're protecting her."

"Of course I am." Helena met his gaze directly. "Wouldn't you?"

He thought of the men he'd led into battle. The ones who hadn't come back. "Yes."

As the conversation wound down, Prudence rose with a dramatic flourish. "Remember, my dear niece, and you too, Major—London society loves a good performance. Let's make sure ours is the talk of the season."

Helena smirked. "Subtlety, Aunt."

Prudence snorted. "Subtlety is overrated."

As James rose to take his leave, Prudence gave him one last

lingering look. "Just remember, Major. You're not playing soldier here. You're playing suitor. Different tools. Different rules."

He inclined his head. "I'll learn quickly."

"You'd better," she said, her gaze sharp despite the lightness in her tone. "Because Helena plays to win."

That, James thought as he made his polite goodbyes, was precisely what concerned him. Helena would see this through—he had no doubt of that. She was too intelligent, too determined, too skilled.

But at what cost to herself? And what would she sacrifice in the name of victory?

Outside, the cold air cut sharper than it had the day before. James adjusted his collar as he stepped into the quiet street, Prudence's words still echoing.

He had his orders. He had his role. Play the enamored fiancé, gain the Society's trust, gather intelligence.

Simple. Clear. Calculated.

And yet, as his boots echoed on the cobblestones, it wasn't Sir Frederick's voice echoing in his mind, or Prudence's warnings, or even his own strategic calculations.

It was Helena's. The way she'd said "I've managed far worse" with that defiant lift to her chin. The moment her expression had faltered when he'd said pretending wasn't difficult.

And that, more than anything, made this mission dangerous.

Because he was beginning to suspect the greatest danger wasn't the Society at all—it was the woman he was meant to deceive.

Chapter Ten

A WALTZ OF SECRETS

January 22, 1855
Helena

FROM THE TOP of the staircase overlooking the intimate ballroom, Helena surveyed her chessboard.

Smaller than the Duke of Somerset's grand affair, Lord Woodhaven's ball held perhaps eighty guests—intimate enough that every conversation could be overheard, every alliance noted, every suspicious glance catalogued. Candlelight shimmered across polished floors, reflected in silk gowns and gleaming shoes. The string quartet near the hearth played softly enough that whispers carried.

Unlike the grandeur of the opera, tonight's ball was warmer, quieter—and far less forgiving of a poorly played move. Here, there was nowhere to hide.

She descended the stairs on James's arm, aware of the eyes following them—some curious, some assessing, a few openly speculative. Their sudden engagement had been the subject of considerable gossip, and tonight would be their first appearance at a smaller, more intimate gathering where scrutiny would be unavoidable.

His posture was impeccable, but there was always something

about the way he moved—alert, calculating—that made it clear he was still more soldier than suitor.

Behind them, Lady Prudence swept in with theatrical flair, her garnet gown rustling like a stage curtain. All eyes shifted to her.

"Dearest Lord Woodhaven," she exclaimed, her voice carrying across the room, "your ballroom positively glows tonight! I only hope my poor gown doesn't dim the effect."

Her arrival pulled everyone's attention, as intended. Laughter rippled nearby. Knowing smiles appeared on faces that had been openly staring at Helena moments before.

Amelia, in a dusty-rose gown, paused halfway down the stairs and flicked her fan open with practiced grace. "Oh, Helena, this is far more inviting than the opera, don't you think? So much warmer. Major Westwood, you must be relieved not to navigate those balconies."

James's mouth curved faintly. "It certainly feels less… theatrical."

Amelia laughed, the sound bright and unforced. "You're developing a sense of humor, Major. Helena must be a good influence." She spotted someone across the room. "Oh! I see Lady Caroline. Excuse me—I simply must greet her."

She drifted away, quickly absorbed into a cluster of young women. Helena noted the ease with which Amelia navigated the room. Her sister's energy served as the perfect cover—friendly, social, utterly unthreatening.

James's gaze swept the room like a silent reconnaissance. She nudged his elbow lightly.

"Try not to look as though you're evaluating a battlefield," she murmured.

"I thought I was blending in."

"You look about as comfortable as a cat in a bath."

Prudence appeared at Helena's shoulder, sipping from a tiny glass of cordial. "Give the man some credit. He's performing admirably for someone raised in a barracks. Don't let her rattle you, Major. A touch of stiffness adds to your charm."

James inclined his head. "Your encouragement is always appreciated, Lady Prudence."

Prudence waved a hand. "Of course it is."

They moved deeper into the ballroom, where rosewater and beeswax mingled in the air. Helena's gown whispered with each step. She spotted Lady Beatrice Cavendish weaving through the crowd, blue skirts swishing and eyes bright with mischief.

"Helena!" Beatrice beamed. "And who is this dashing man by your side?"

Helena kept her smile serene. "May I introduce Major James Westwood. Newly returned to London and already my indispensable companion."

"A daunting task, I'm sure," James said with a respectful bow. "May I bring you both refreshments?"

Helena nodded. "That would be lovely."

As he walked away, Beatrice leaned in, eyes alight. "Is it true? Have you accepted his offer?"

Helena let her gaze linger a moment on James's retreating figure. "Yes. Though it's not public yet."

Beatrice clasped her hands. "Then announce it at my musicale tomorrow night! It'll be positively romantic."

Helena hesitated, appearing to consider. In truth, the musicale would be perfect—smaller than a ball, more intimate than the opera, with an audience of carefully selected guests. Exactly the sort of event where Society members might be present and observing.

"I wouldn't want to impose on your program," Helena said carefully.

"Nonsense! I'll make space. It's settled." Beatrice beamed, clearly delighted with herself.

James returned with two cups of punch. Beatrice took hers with a grin and excused herself, leaving Helena and James alone just as the opening notes of a waltz began.

James extended his hand. "Shall we?"

Helena hesitated for the briefest moment before setting her cup aside, and placing her hand in his. "Of course."

As they moved together across the dance floor, Helena found herself too aware of every point of contact. Her skirts brushed against his uniform with each turn. His hand rested at her waist—light but it claimed its place there. His movements were sure, practiced, restrained. He'd learned to dance properly somewhere, despite his modest upbringing. Another unexpected layer to Major James Westwood.

But it was the steadiness in his eyes that unsettled her most. That focused intensity he usually reserved for field assessments, now directed entirely at her.

"We have an audience," she said softly, though her voice wasn't quite as controlled as she'd intended. "You'll need to look more besotted."

"I thought I was doing well."

"You'll need to convince me otherwise."

Their gazes locked, and for a fleeting moment, Helena forgot the room around them. James leaned in slightly, his playful expression giving way to something deeper. Staring into those eyes left her feeling decidedly off balance.

His breath came warm against her ear as he murmured, "And here I thought I was the one being charmed. But that smile, Helena… that wasn't for the audience."

Her breath caught. He'd seen it—that unguarded moment when her carefully constructed façade had slipped, revealing the genuine attraction she'd been working so hard to deny.

Her smile faltered before she caught herself, but the damage was done. He knew.

Around them, candlelight flickered and guests murmured and music swelled, but Helena felt suspended in this moment—exposed in a way that had nothing to do with espionage and everything to do with the dangerous territory her heart was entering.

She'd asked him to play a part—but had she forgotten her

own?

The waltz ended, and scattered applause broke the spell. As they stepped from the dance floor, Helena drew a steadying breath, grateful for the excuse to put some distance between herself and James's unsettling perceptiveness.

She needed to focus. They were here to work, not to… whatever that had been.

James guided her toward the refreshment table, his hand still at her waist—maintaining the appearance of an enamored couple. But his voice, when he spoke, was all business.

"Hawthorne's in the card room," he murmured. "With three men I don't recognize. Military bearing, all of them. Too old for active service but young enough to have opinions about how the war's being run."

Helena accepted the glass of punch he handed her, using the motion to glance toward the card room's doorway. "Disaffected officers?"

"Possibly. The Society recruits from that sort. Men who feel the Crown has failed them."

"Can you get close enough to hear what they're discussing?"

James's jaw tightened. "Not without drawing attention. A major approaching a group of senior officers uninvited would be noted."

Helena thought quickly. "What if you weren't uninvited? What if I sent you to ask Hawthorne about Thomas's investment in Sableport? An innocent question. Let him believe you're curious about a profitable trading company…"

James's eyes sharpened. "That could work. Gives me a legitimate reason to approach, and Sableport's connection to the Society means they might reveal something in how they respond."

"Or even in how they avoid responding," Helena added. "Either way, we learn something."

James set down his punch glass. "I'll approach now, while they're between hands. Watch Lady Eleanor—she's near the window with Lady Margaret. If they react to my conversation with Hawthorne, that confirms they're watching him closely."

Helena's pulse quickened. He was right. If Eleanor and Margaret were part of Hawthorne's network, they'd be attuned to any potential threat to his cover.

"Be careful," she said softly.

His eyes met hers briefly. "Always."

She watched him cross the ballroom with that distinctive gait—the slight unevenness that marked his injury but never slowed him. He paused at the card room entrance, catching Hawthorne's attention with a deferential nod.

Helena couldn't hear the exchange from this distance, but she could observe. Hawthorne's initial expression—mild pleasure at the interruption. Then James spoke, and something shifted. Hawthorne's smile tightened. One of the other men leaned back in his chair, arms crossed.

Defensive postures. They didn't like the question.

Helena's attention shifted to Lady Eleanor and Lady Margaret, still conversing by the window. Had they noticed?

Yes. Eleanor's fan had stilled mid-flutter. Margaret's gaze had cut toward the card room, just for a moment, before resuming her conversation.

They were watching. Which meant they knew Hawthorne. Knew to watch for threats to him.

The connection was real.

James returned a few minutes later, his expression carefully neutral. "Hawthorne was… evasive. Said Sableport was a sound investment, that Thomas had made a wise choice, but he deflected when I asked about specific trade routes or shipping schedules. Called it 'a private concern.'"

"And the others?"

"One asked if I'd served in Crimea. When I confirmed, he made a comment about 'supply line failures that could have been avoided if someone in Whitehall had been paying attention.' Testing me. Seeing if I'd express discontent with command."

Helena's eyes narrowed. "A test."

"That was my assessment. But I agreed—the provisioning was a disaster. Gave them a little. Enough to interest them."

"Good." She touched his arm lightly. "Did you notice Eleanor and Margaret?"

"Watching us?"

"The moment you approached Hawthorne. They're in league with him, I'm certain of it."

Later, as the dancing continued, Helena positioned herself near the column where Lady Eleanor and Lord Hawthorne were conversing. Close enough to observe, far enough to seem coincidental.

Lady Eleanor Bennet was formidable—fifty if she was a day, but with the bearing of someone accustomed to power. Her sapphire silk gown was expensively tailored, her raven hair pinned in an elaborate chignon that must have taken her maid an hour to construct. She spoke in measured tones, her voice pitched just loud enough to be overheard by those she wished to overhear.

And Helena suspected that was deliberate. Eleanor wasn't careless. If her voice carried, she meant it to.

Helena's breath caught. Spoken aloud, the words were merely political observation—the sort of thing anyone might say at a private gathering. But the way Eleanor said it, with that edge of satisfaction rather than concern…

Not treason. Not exactly. But certainly not loyalty.

And Hawthorne's response was telling: a slight nod, as though confirming something already agreed upon.

Hawthorne's eyes flicked toward Helena. The movement was subtle, but Eleanor caught it immediately. Mid-sentence, she adjusted her shawl and turned, melting into the crowd with practiced ease.

They'd seen her. Knew she was listening.

James appeared at Helena's side, his voice pitched for her ears alone. "Subtle."

"Too subtle to be innocent," Helena agreed, her mind racing. "They knew I was there. Eleanor left deliberately, to prevent me from hearing more."

"Which means they're aware you're watching them."

"We need to be more careful."

Prudence appeared at Helena's elbow with impeccable timing. "The punch is scandalously weak tonight," she announced, loud enough to carry. "Helena, you must try the ratafia instead. It's far superior."

Helena understood the coded warning—Prudence wanted her to move immediately and stop hovering near the column. "Of course, Aunt."

As they walked toward the refreshment table, Prudence murmured, "You were staring. Eleanor noticed. She's sharp as a blade, that one."

"I was careless," Helena said quietly. "But we confirmed the alignment between her and Hawthorne. And they confirmed that they're aware of being watched."

Prudence's expression didn't change, but her voice dropped. "Then you'll need to be cleverer when you eavesdrop. Or more reckless. I'm not certain which is worse."

"I'll follow Hawthorne," James murmured.

"Don't take unnecessary risks," Helena warned.

His look was pointed. "That's *my* line."

As he moved away, Helena's attention caught on a figure standing alone near the terrace doors, his profile silhouetted against the glass. Lord Thomas Chadwick, holding a glass he wasn't drinking from, watching the dancers with an expression of studied detachment.

But she knew that look. She'd seen it on soldiers' faces after bad news. The careful blankness that covered hurt.

It was time. And delaying wouldn't make it easier.

Helena crossed the ballroom, her steps measured, her heart surprisingly heavy. She'd known this moment was coming since she'd accepted Frederick's mission. Had known it when she'd stood in that frozen garden and agreed to pose as James's fiancée.

But knowing and doing were different things.

"Thomas."

He turned, and something in his expression shifted—hope flickering before being carefully extinguished. "Helena." His voice was warm, but guarded. "You look lovely tonight."

"Thank you. May we speak? Privately?"

His jaw tightened almost imperceptibly. "Of course."

He guided her to a small alcove off the main ballroom—not entirely private, but removed enough for quiet conversation. The sounds of music and laughter felt distant here, muffled.

For a long moment, neither spoke.

Then Thomas said, very quietly, "You're going to tell me about Major Westwood."

It wasn't a question.

Helena met his gaze directly. She owed him that much. "Yes."

He exhaled slowly, setting his glass on a nearby table with exaggerated care. "I had wondered. When I heard the rumors. Hoped they weren't true." His smile was painfully self-deprecating. "But here we are."

"Thomas, I'm sorry—"

"Are you?" The question came sharp, surprising her. "Forgive me, but you don't look particularly sorry. You look... resolved. As though this is simply another task to be completed."

The observation stung because it was partly true. She *was* resolved. This was necessary. But that didn't mean it cost nothing.

"I never meant to hurt you," she said quietly.

"No. I don't suppose you did." He studied her face, and she saw him searching for something—regret, perhaps, or the remains of whatever affection they'd shared in recent months. "May I ask when it began? With the major?"

Helena chose her words carefully. "We were introduced very recently."

"Recently." He repeated the word as though testing it. "And yet you're already engaged to him. That's remarkably swift, even by society's standards."

She said nothing. What could she say? That it was a lie? That she was using a fake engagement to infiltrate a treasonous organization? That her real life had diverged so far from anything he could understand that honesty was impossible?

The silence stretched.

"I had plans," Thomas said finally, his voice thick. "For us. The house in Surrey—I'd already begun negotiations to purchase it. Thought I'd surprise you with the details once the Sableport investment matured. I imagined…" He stopped, shaking his head. "It doesn't matter now."

"It matters," Helena said softly. "It matters that you cared. That you thought about our future. I'm honored by that, Thomas. Truly."

"Just not interested."

The bluntness landed like a blow. But he wasn't wrong.

"I'm not the woman you think I am," she said carefully. "The life you're offering—the quiet country house, the distance from London, the simplicity—it's a beautiful vision. For someone else. But I… I've changed. I need something different now."

"Something *he* can give you?" There was an edge to the question.

Helena thought of James. The missions. The danger. The way her heart raced when he looked at her with that focused intensity. The feeling of partnership, of being matched with someone who understood the weight of duty.

"Something I didn't know I needed," she said honestly. "Until recently."

Thomas was quiet for a long moment. When he spoke again, his voice was steadier. "I can't pretend this doesn't hurt. That I'm not… disappointed. Angry, even. But I'm not going to beg you to reconsider. If the major is what you want, then I hope he deserves you."

"Thomas—"

"No." He held up a hand. "Let me finish. You deserve someone who sees you more clearly than I did. Who wants the woman you are, not the woman I imagined you to be. If Westwood is that man…" He exhaled. "Then I wish you well."

The grace in his words made it worse somehow. Made her feel the loss more keenly.

"You're a good man, Thomas Chadwick."

"Not good enough, apparently." The bitterness was brief, quickly suppressed. "Forgive me. That was unkind."

"It was honest. And deserved."

He picked up his glass, looked at it, set it back down. "I should go. Remaining here would only make this more difficult."

"Will you be all right?"

His smile was sad but genuine. "Eventually. Though I'll likely need to drown my sorrows in Sableport returns and rural property purchases. A wounded man needs his consolations."

The attempt at humor made her throat tight.

"Goodbye, Helena."

"Goodbye, Thomas."

He bowed—formal, correct, final—and walked away. She watched him retrieve his coat and hat from a footman, watched him disappear through the main doors without looking back.

And she felt it. The door closing. The path not taken.

She'd hurt a good man for the sake of duty. And though it was necessary, though she'd do it again, it still cost something.

Helena stood alone in the alcove for a moment, collecting herself. Her hands were shaking slightly. She pressed them together, willing them to steady.

This is the price, she thought. *This is what it costs to serve. Personal happiness. Normal futures. Good men who offer comfortable lives.*

She could still have chosen Thomas. Could have told Frederick no, maintained her quiet existence as Lady Helena Ashford, society ornament with a modest secret life gathering occasional intelligence.

But she'd chosen this instead. The missions. The danger. James.

She'd chosen herself. The woman she was becoming. Not the woman Thomas had wanted her to be.

And that had to be enough.

When James returned a few minutes later, he must have read something in her expression. His hand moved as though to touch her arm, then stopped—they were in public, after all.

"It's done," she said quietly.

His eyes searched her face. "Are you all right?"

"I will be." She straightened her shoulders, compartmentalizing the emotion as she'd been trained. "Did you learn anything from Hawthorne's group?"

"Helena—"

"Please, James. I need to focus on the work."

He hesitated, then nodded slowly. "They were discussing military matters. Supply routes, specifically. One mentioned that 'certain inefficiencies' in the procurement process were 'not accidental.' Another said the spring would bring 'necessary corrections.'"

Helena's mind sharpened, latching onto the intelligence like a lifeline. "The spring reckoning Charlotte mentioned."

"Possibly. They noticed me, ended the conversation. But Hawthorne invited me to his club—White's—next week. Said we should discuss mutual interests."

Despite everything, Helena felt a spark of satisfaction. "He's recruiting you."

"So it seems."

"That's good. That's exactly what we need."

James's voice softened. "It can be good *and* you can still feel what you're feeling. Both things can be true."

She looked up at him, this man who read her too clearly, who saw past her professional façade to the woman underneath.

"I know," she said quietly. "But not here. Not now."

He nodded. "When you're ready."

And somehow, the fact that he didn't push, didn't demand she process her emotions on his timeline, made him more dangerous to her heart than any amount of pressing would have done.

Chapter Eleven

THE MUSICAL SOIRÉE

January 24, 1855
James

C ANDLELIGHT SPILLED FROM the windows of Lady Beatrice Cavendish's townhouse, casting soft halos over the freshly fallen snow. James stepped from the carriage, adjusting his cuffs as Helena joined him, her gloved hand sliding through the crook of his arm with practiced ease. Her gown—deep-green silk, understated but striking—caught the light with subtle brilliance. Perfectly chosen. Just enough to draw attention without seeming to seek it.

This was a small gathering. Perhaps forty guests—carefully selected, each one influential in their own sphere. The sort of intimate evening where alliances were tested and secrets traded beneath the veneer of musical appreciation.

Behind them, Prudence emerged with theatrical flair, inhaling the icy air like a connoisseur sampling vintage port. "Ah, Beatrice's soirées never disappoint," she declared, her voice carrying across the snow-hushed street. "Such charming intimacy."

"Charming," Amelia murmured, fan in hand, "but intimate enough that every word we say will be overheard, analyzed, and repeated by breakfast tomorrow."

As they climbed the steps, James leaned toward Helena, his voice pitched for her ears alone. "Am I to endure an evening of questionable musical talent and finely sharpened social curiosity?"

Helena smiled, eyes gleaming with amusement. "Consider it training for far greater horrors, Major."

Inside, the warmth enveloped them—beeswax, perfume, and the particular tension that always preceded a Beatrice Cavendish event. The drawing room hummed with anticipation. Less grand than the opera house, but far more dangerous in its intimacy. Every conversation could be overheard. Every glance noted. Every alliance tested.

Beatrice's musicales had always been more about social maneuvering than musical talent. This was a gathering built for whispers and strategic positioning.

Among the gathered guests, James noted several familiar faces: aristocrats, minor parliamentarians, and a wealthy merchant attempting to purchase respectability through cultural patronage. But his attention caught on a couple standing near the hearth—slightly apart from the main cluster, but positioned with the watchfulness of those accustomed to observing without being observed.

The man was perhaps thirty, tall and broad shouldered, with dark hair and the bearing of someone keenly aware of newfound authority. The cut of his coat suggested wealth recently come into its own—or old wealth returned with altered priorities.

The woman beside him was striking in a way that had nothing to do with conventional beauty and everything to do with presence. Auburn curls arranged in an elegant but practical style. A gown of deep sapphire that suggested mourning without proclaiming it—half-mourning, then. A widow. She held herself with the contained stillness of someone trained to observe without drawing observation.

And her eyes—sharp, assessing, constantly moving—marked her as someone accustomed to observation. Not merely society.

Not entirely.

Helena had noticed them too. Her hand tightened almost imperceptibly on James's arm.

"The Duke of Westbridge," she murmured. "And Mrs. Violet Heatherington."

James's interest sharpened. Sir Frederick had mentioned the duke. He'd inherited the title unexpectedly when his uncle and cousin died at sea. The circumstances had been suspicious, though officially ruled accidental. Sir Frederick hinted otherwise.

And Mrs. Heatherington… He didn't know that name, but the way she stood beside the duke suggested more than social acquaintance.

"They're part of Frederick's network," Helena murmured, "though I've never been formally introduced." Her gaze remained on the couple. "She's observing the same way we are."

Before James could respond, Lady Beatrice approached, glowing with delight. "The newly engaged couple! How radiant you both look." She dropped her voice conspiratorially. "And how fortunate we are. I've forbidden any talk of Crimea tonight. No mismanagement or military blunders. I refuse to let it ruin my festive mood. I want music and merriment, not talk of wounded soldiers and failing ministers."

Helena answered smoothly, "Your soirées are always the perfect escape, Beatrice."

Beatrice beamed, turning to James. "You must be quite taken with her to endure my musicale, Major."

James offered a wry smile. "I've faced many trials, Lady Beatrice. This may be the most harrowing yet."

She laughed, clearly charmed, then gestured toward the musicians beginning to assemble. "Do find comfortable seats. And prepare yourselves—I've secured a rather enthusiastic soprano for this evening."

Helena caught James's eye, amusement dancing in her expression. "You've been warned."

Prudence worked the room like a diplomat at court. "Have

you met my darling niece and her dashing fiancé?" she called to a cluster of matrons, ensuring every guest took notice. "They've been inseparable since the moment they met. Practically fused at the hip."

Knowing smiles appeared. A few fans fluttered with barely suppressed amusement. One elderly lady leaned to her companion and whispered something that made them both chuckle.

The story was taking hold. The whirlwind romance. The sudden engagement. Society loved nothing more than young love triumphant.

Helena looped her hand through James's arm, the gesture automatic now after days of practice. "You owe me for this," she muttered, though her smile never wavered.

"I'll add it to your account," James replied. "Which is growing concerningly long."

Movement at the edge of the room drew James's attention—a maid in simple black, balancing a silver tray with practiced ease as she moved among the guests. Her posture was impeccable, her movements efficient but unobtrusive. Exactly how good household staff should appear.

But something about those movements caught his eye. Too precise. Too deliberate. Too controlled.

The woman was playing the part of a maid too perfectly—and perfection, in such roles, was its own kind of flaw. Real servants had tells: nervousness around aristocrats, hesitation about where to stand, small adjustments to find comfortable positioning. This woman had none of that uncertainty.

She approached their cluster near the fire, offering glasses of sherry and cordial with a deferential nod. As she stepped between Helena and Amelia, her hand brushed Helena's lightly—too quick, too light for accident. A note passed. No pause, no flicker of recognition on her face. Just the serene, anonymous grace of household staff.

But James had been trained to see through disguises. And beneath the starched cap, the lowered gaze, and the plain black dress stood Lady Arabella Langley—widow, aristocrat, and one of Sir Frederick's most trusted agents.

The recognition process took perhaps three seconds. He neither acknowledged her nor looked away too quickly. Just allowed his gaze to pass over her as it would any servant.

He said nothing. Neither did Helena. The only sign she'd registered the interaction was the way her fingers curled slightly around the folded scrap of paper now palmed against her fan.

As the "maid" moved on, blending effortlessly with the other staff along the periphery, James exhaled softly. Arabella had always excelled at becoming invisible. He'd seen her do it before—at the Foreign Office Annex, she'd disappeared into shadows while standing in plain sight.

"Trouble?" he asked under his breath, his lips barely moving.

Helena's response was equally quiet. "Information, more likely. Or a warning."

"Can you read it here?"

"Not without being obvious. I'll find a moment."

When the violins finally fell silent—to James's profound relief—Beatrice stood, beaming with delight. "My friends, what a wonderful evening. And how fortunate we are to celebrate the engagement of Major Westwood and Lady Helena." She turned to James with expectant pleasure. "Major, we'd be thrilled if you would say a few words about your lovely fiancée."

James stilled. He cast Helena a sharp look.

She leaned in, her voice low and apologetic. "I may have encouraged her. Reinforcement of the narrative, you understand."

James rose, drew a measured breath, and accepted a glass of champagne from a hovering footman. The room's attention settled on him like a weight.

"A toast," he began. His voice came out stiffer than intended. He glanced at Helena—who looked equal parts mortified and amused—and inspiration struck.

"It all began the first time I laid eyes on Lady Helena. She was rescuing a kitten from a rather tall tree."

Laughter rippled, polite and surprised. Helena's lips parted in surprise, then curved into a well-trained smile.

"Yes, a kitten," James continued. "A perilous endeavor—but she handled it with grace, climbing that tree in a delightfully rumpled frock."

More laughter.

"I, of course, contributed very little. I have no head for heights. But I did save her bonnet from a rogue branch. Heroic, truly."

The guests chuckled again. James's voice softened as he lifted his glass.

"In truth, Lady Helena possesses a daring spirit and a mind sharper than any saber. I can only hope to match her courage—though with fewer kittens involved."

As he sat, Prudence announced with perfect timing, "The girl's always been reckless! Once jumped from a tree to escape hornets! Nearly gave her poor mother a fit of apoplexy."

Laughter rippled through the room. Several guests raised their glasses. One elderly gentleman called out, "To reckless ladies and the sensible men who save their bonnets!"

More laughter. The mood in the room had shifted—warmer, more convivial. James had won them over.

Helena leaned closer, her voice dry but laced with reluctant amusement. "A kitten?"

James smirked. "It worked."

"You put me in a tree."

"At least I admitted my fear of heights."

"I'll remember this, Major."

As the applause faded and conversations resumed, James noticed the duke and Mrs. Heatherington making their way toward them.

"Major Westwood," the duke said, extending his hand. "Evan Harrington. Please, call me Evan."

After completing the introductions, Violet curtsied, her sharp eyes assessing. "Lady Helena. Major. What a lovely toast. Though I must confess, I'm now desperately curious about the actual story of your meeting."

Helena's smile was warm but carefully controlled. "I'm afraid the truth is far less romantic. We were introduced at a ball by a mutual acquaintance."

"Ah, yes. Our mutual acquaintance," Violet repeated thoughtfully. "How fortunate that your paths crossed." The phrasing was innocuous, but her tone suggested she knew exactly which mutual acquaintance had orchestrated that meeting.

Sir Frederick. She was confirming they were all part of the same circle.

"Very fortunate," Helena agreed. Then, with perfect social grace, she shifted the conversation. "Mrs. Heatherington, your gown is exquisite. The color is remarkably sophisticated."

"Thank you." Violet's hand moved to the sapphire silk—half-mourning, James noted again. "I've been wearing darker shades for some time now, but I'm beginning to reintroduce color. It's a delicate balance, navigating propriety while not wanting to appear frozen in grief."

"You were recently widowed?" Helena asked.

"Nearly three years ago." Something flickered in Violet's eyes—pain, perhaps, or anger carefully banked. "My husband passed unexpectedly. It took time to find my footing afterward."

Helena's hand moved almost unconsciously to touch Violet's arm—a brief gesture of solidarity. "I'm very sorry for your loss."

"Thank you. However moving forward, rather than dwelling, serves me better." Violet's gaze shifted to Evan with something that looked like warmth beneath the professional exterior. "And the duke has been… instrumental in helping me reconnect with society."

Evan's expression softened almost imperceptibly. "Mrs. Heatherington has been invaluable to me as well. Navigating the unexpected responsibilities of the dukedom after my uncle's and cousin's deaths has been… complex. Violet's insights into London society and business matters have proven essential."

"I understood there was some question about the circumstances of their deaths," James said carefully. "At sea, wasn't it?"

Evan's jaw tightened slightly—barely noticeable, but James had been trained to read such tells. "Yes. Their ship went down off the coast. Officially ruled an accident, though the investigation raised… questions. Questions that were ultimately deemed unanswerable."

But not laid to rest, James thought. The way Evan said it suggested he had his own theories about what had happened.

"How terrible," Helena said. "To lose family members and gain a title under such mysterious circumstances."

"It was." Evan's voice was level, but something in his eyes suggested the difficulty went beyond grief. "I'd been abroad for years, serving with the 93rd Highlanders. Hadn't expected to inherit. Hadn't wanted to, truth be told. But here we are."

James felt a spark of recognition—the particular weariness of a man who'd served, returned, and found the civilian world no less complicated than war. "The 93rd. You were at Balaclava?"

"No—I'd returned to England before that disaster." Evan's expression turned grim. "The Thin Red Line, they're calling it now. Though from what I've heard, it was more desperate stand than heroic line."

"The 17th Lancers. I wasn't there for the Charge either—had already returned to England before that particular debacle. But I lost many friends that day. Men I'd served with."

A moment of shared understanding passed between them— men who'd seen the same hell.

"I'm fortunate to have found a reliable partner to ease my way back into civilian life." Evan glanced at Violet.

Violet had been conversing with Helena about fashion, but James suspected she'd been listening to every word of the men's exchange. Now she smoothly redirected the conversation.

"Lady Helena, you have an excellent eye for detail—I noticed you observing the room earlier. Do you find society events exhausting or illuminating?"

Helena smiled slightly. "Both. Though I suspect you understand that better than most."

"I've learned to watch carefully," Violet admitted. "Widowhood teaches you to be observant. You see patterns in behavior that others miss."

"Patterns," Helena repeated. "That sounds like a valuable skill."

"It can be. I've been applying it to financial records lately—shipping manifests, trade routes, company ledgers. My late husband left me with some business interests that required... careful review." Violet's tone was casual, but her eyes were sharp. "I've developed quite an unexpected talent for finding discrepancies."

"What sort of discrepancies?" Helena asked.

"The kind that suggest not everything is as it appears," Violet said carefully, lowering her voice. "Shipments that don't match declarations. Routes that make no commercial sense. Money moving in interesting patterns."

James understood. Violet was investigating financial irregularities—likely connected to the Black Rose Society. Following the money.

"And you've found such irregularities?" Helena pressed.

"Enough to keep me occupied," Violet said. "Our mutual friend finds my work useful."

Evan stepped in. "Violet's facility with numbers combined with the access my position provides—we've been coordinating our efforts. She identifies what matters in all the information."

A partnership, James realized. Something beyond the personal.

"It sounds like important work," Helena said. "If companies are operating improperly during wartime, they should be exposed."

"Agreed," Violet said. "Though exposure requires evidence. Concrete, irrefutable evidence. Which is why the work continues."

Evan's expression lightened deliberately. "But enough business at a musicale. We should meet again soon. Somewhere we can speak more freely."

"I'd welcome that," James said.

"As would I," Helena added.

They exchanged nods, and Evan and Violet moved away.

Helena leaned close to James. "She's following the money. Looking for financial connections to the Society."

"And Evan's using his position to access records she couldn't get otherwise," James added quietly. "They're building the financial trail while we work on infiltration."

"Different approaches, all to the same end," Helena murmured.

James nodded. The circle was larger than he'd realized. And they were all closing in on the Black Rose Society from different angles.

Later, James watched from near the hearth as Helena approached Lady Margaret Fairfax, who stood by the pianoforte, wine in hand. Fairfax moved with careful confidence, the kind that concealed as much as it revealed.

"You must find these times quite turbulent," Margaret said. "With so many shifting alliances, one must remain… adaptable."

Helena's reply came with her usual composure. "Adaptability is essential."

"Yet stability is so often underestimated." Margaret's gaze lingered. "I hope you and Major Westwood find your own kind of stability. A solid match can be a… useful thing."

James couldn't read her tone—approval or warning. Perhaps both.

Helena offered a courteous nod. "We understand each other well."

"Mm," Margaret replied. "A bit of discord can be enlightening. It forces one to pay attention."

From nearby, Amelia muttered to Prudence, "Surely that man's violin can't be intentional?"

"If it is," Prudence replied, "it's revolutionary—and not in a good way."

Lady Margaret chuckled, then turned back to Helena. "You have delightful company. I envy you."

Once the final performance concluded—a pianist who, mercifully, had actual talent—they gathered Amelia and Prudence and made their farewells.

As they made their farewells to Beatrice, James noted Evan and Violet near the door, also preparing to depart. Evan caught his eye and nodded slightly—a wordless acknowledgment of shared purpose.

Outside, the cold air was sharp after the drawing room's warmth. Their breath misted as they walked toward the waiting carriage.

"Well," Prudence declared, "that was productive. The engagement announcement landed beautifully, and James managed not to embarrass himself during his speech. I call that a successful evening."

As the carriage rumbled away from Beatrice's townhouse, Helena finally unfolded the note Arabella had passed her. In the dim interior light, James could just make out the cramped handwriting:

L. Eleanor hosting private gathering next week. Wednesday evening, 10pm. Her residence. Small group, carefully vetted. Confirmation received that military veterans specifically invited. Watch for your invitation. –A

Helena passed the note to James, who read it, then turned the paper over. On the reverse side, rows of seemingly random letters filled the page—a second message, this one encoded.

"Two messages," James observed, handing it back.

Helena turned it over and examined the code. "The second… I'll need to decode, but the first is immediate intelligence—Lady Eleanor is hosting a gathering," Helena said. "Veterans specifically invited."

"Another attempt to enlist sympathizers," James said. "They're moving quickly."

"And whatever's in the encoded message may tell us why," Helena murmured. "The spring reckoning. Whatever they're planning, they're building the structure to support it now."

Prudence's voice was uncharacteristically serious. "Then we must move quickly as well."

Chapter Twelve

THE TIP OFF

January 24, 1855
Helena

THE CARRIAGE RATTLED over cobblestones, wheels clattering as city lights blurred past frosted windows. Helena leaned back against the plush seat beside Amelia, but her thoughts didn't rest. Across from her, James sat next to Aunt Prudence—posture relaxed, face unreadable.

The musicale had been a success—unexpectedly so. James's kitten toast had done more to solidify their false engagement than any number of carefully planned outings. They were inching closer to their goal.

And yet, her thoughts kept drifting… not to the Society. To him.

To the way he'd looked at her when he said "daring spirit." To his hand at her waist during the waltz. To the question she kept pushing aside: What happens when this ends and the pretense becomes unnecessary?

Prudence, wrapped in a lavish winter cloak, cast a keen glance between Helena and James.

"Anyone who doubted your engagement," said in a low, conspiratorial tone, "will be singing a different tune after tonight's little performance. You, dear Major," Prudence said with mock gravity, "are quite the master of improvisation. Who knew kittens could be so effective?"

James inclined his head. "I hope I didn't overdo it with the bonnet."

She patted his arm, her eyes gleaming with amusement. "Nonsense. You did splendidly. We want them all just intrigued enough to see you both as a genuine couple, not a contrived act."

Amelia tucked her cloak snugly around her shoulders. "Thank you, Aunt Prudence. At least now I can sleep knowing no one is whispering about my sister's scandalous romance." She glanced at Helena, brow furrowing. "Though I suppose it must be exhausting, always pretending…"

Her voice trailed off in a yawn. She nestled a cushion beneath her head, resting against the carriage door, eyes fluttering shut within moments.

Helena found herself watching him again—how he sat so still, so attuned to his surroundings even in this mundane setting. She wondered what it would feel like to have that calm confidence beside her… off the battlefield. In ordinary moments. Morning tea. Evening walks. A life that wasn't measured in missions.

The thought startled her.

"It's refreshing," she said, breaking the silence.

James's brow arched slightly, his sharp gaze shifting to hers. "What is?"

"Being with someone who knows." She gestured absently. "Someone who understands this… life. Most men would shy away from the danger—or worse, try to shield me from it as though I were made of glass."

His lips twitched. "From what I've seen, anyone who mistakes you for fragile deserves whatever comes to them."

Helena laughed softly, the sound easing the tension in the air. "You're surprisingly adept at this bantering business, Major."

His gaze lingered, and for a moment, the faint humor in his expression shifted to something more sincere. "We make a good team," he said quietly.

The simple words carried unexpected weight. Not just about the mission. About them.

Helena looked away, out toward the frosted window, though she wasn't seeing the city rush past. It was strategy, yes. But it was also trust—and something else, something unnamed that tugged at the edges of her thoughts.

James understood her world. Not just the danger, but the discipline. The masks. The solitude required to live two lives at once. How rare that was.

How dangerous it could become if she let herself need it too much.

The carriage hit a rut, jolting them. Amelia murmured in her sleep, adjusting without waking, and Helena shifted her focus to the note burning in her reticule.

After confirming Amelia was still soundly asleep, Helena retrieved the folded parchment. It was slightly crumpled from being tucked away, but its significance was undiminished. She unfolded it, her eyes scanning the cryptic markings.

"What is it?" James's voice, low and even, cut through the quiet.

"I still need to read the other message from Arabella," Helena replied in a whisper. "The cipher part."

James's posture straightened, his focus sharpening. "I'd nearly forgotten."

She pulled a small pencil from her reticule. Balancing the parchment on her knee, she began decoding the message, her pencil darting across the page as years of practice guided her hand.

The cipher was a simple substitution—amateur work, really, which meant Arabella had set it down in haste, more obscured than concealed.

James watched in silence, his presence steady and grounding.

Across from them, Prudence shifted slightly, craning her neck to observe Helena's scribbles.

"A cryptogram," Aunt Prudence murmured, keeping her voice low. "Your father was always so fond of them. I never did master those puzzles. They do make for intriguing bedtime reading."

Helena gave her aunt a faint smile and continued working. As the final pieces of the puzzle fell into place, Helena's lips pressed into a thin line. She read aloud:

"The gathering tomorrow night. It's at the Black Cat Tavern in the East End. The pass phrase is 'The moonlight reveals the truth.'"

The words hung in the air between them. The Black Cat Tavern. Helena knew the name by reputation—a rough establishment frequented by dockworkers, smugglers, and those who preferred their business conducted in shadows. Not the sort of place aristocrats typically patronized.

Which made it perfect for a clandestine meeting.

James frowned. "The East End is dangerous. That's not a place where strangers go unnoticed, even cloaked and masked."

Helena's tone remained firm. "Which is precisely why we must act. We might not get another chance to insert ourselves without suspicion. If we delay, we look hesitant."

His jaw tightened, but he nodded. "We'll need a solid plan. No missteps."

A faint smile curved her lips. "That's why I have you—to temper my recklessness with caution. Between us, I think we'll manage."

Prudence cast Helena a knowing look. "I shall be there, of course. In case you need a splendid diversion. I excel at them, as you've seen. I once derailed an entire ambassador's ball with a wind-up automaton that played 'God Save the Queen' off-key. You'd be amazed how fast a room clears." She turned toward James with a conspiratorial wink. "But I'll leave the 'reckless heroics' to you young people."

James's voice softened, breaking the stillness. "Helena, you understand the risks. If we're discovered—"

"I know," she said, meeting his gaze. Her tone was steady, though her heartbeat quickened. "But you've faced risks before. So have I. This one…" She hesitated, then continued. "This one matters. If we can gain entry to the Society directly, we might finally understand what they're planning."

James studied her for a long moment before exhaling. "Then we'll prepare. Every precaution."

"Agreed."

Their silent agreement carried them the rest of the way to the Ashford residence. As the carriage slowed, Helena gently shook Amelia awake. James stepped out first, the cold night air steaming faintly as he opened the door and turned to offer his hand. Prudence gathered her skirts, stepping down with effortless poise, adding with a low chuckle, "I'll expect you both first thing tomorrow to discuss the details. I do hope you won't keep me waiting."

By late afternoon the next day, sunlight slanted through the drawing room windows, gilding furniture edges in warm gold.

Helena paced the room, her thoughts spinning as she rehearsed the details of their plan. Aunt Prudence sat by the window, flipping through a thin stack of correspondence and occasionally issuing suggestions about disguises or escape routes.

She paused when the maid entered, her cautious expression betraying unease.

"My lady," the maid began quietly, "there's a man at the back entrance. He says his name is Nathaniel Clarke and that you would wish to see him."

Helena stilled, her mind sharpening. Nathaniel Clarke was one of Sir Frederick's most resourceful informants, though his motives were often more self-serving than noble. "Send him to the side garden," she instructed. "I'll meet him there."

Prudence looked up from the letters, arching a brow. "Be mindful, dear. If this man's nerves are anything like his reputation, he'll be glancing over his shoulder at every step. Need I accompany you?"

Helena shook her head. "I'll be careful. But thank you, Aunt."

Prudence rose, crossing the room in a rustle of skirts. "Do let me know if you need a dramatic distraction. One can never be too prepared."

Moments later, Helena stepped into the sheltered corner of the garden, shawl drawn tightly around her shoulders against the chill.

Nathaniel Clarke stood near the ivy-covered wall, lean and narrow shouldered, his threadbare coat pulled tight against the cold. His boots were scuffed, his gloves fraying at the seams, but his stance was coiled—casual, yet alert. The gleam of a knife at his belt was the only thing about him that looked freshly polished.

His eyes swept the garden, sharp and quick, never resting long on one spot.

"Nathaniel," Helena greeted, her voice composed.

"Lady Ashford," he said, bobbing his head in greeting. "'eard you're thinkin' of stickin' yer neck in at the Black Cat tonight."

She arched a brow. "Word travels fast."

He gave a lopsided smirk. "Always does when folk don't watch their bleedin' tongues. This bit came from 'is lordship direct. Thought you might want a word."

"Go on."

"Meetin's in the storeroom out back. Rear entrance. Every bloke in there'll be wearin' a black cloak and a mask—standard trick, keeps identities fuzzy-like. Passphrase at the door's wot gets you in. 'The moonlight reveals the truth.' And mind the smell. Place reeks of old ale and desperation. You'll want to breathe shallow-like till yer nose adjusts."

His eyes flicked up to hers. "Don't muck it up. They're sharp in there. Smell a lie faster'n a rat smells bread."

"Anything else?"

"Yeah," he said, with a faint scoff. "I'm your driver tonight. Pick-up and drop-off. I'll be waitin' with the cab—same alley you go in through, and I don't want to be kept hangin'. If you don't show, I'm leavin' with or without a body."

She gave a slow nod, absorbing each detail. "And after?"

Nathaniel's smirk faded into something tighter. "After, you report. Sir Frederick wants your briefing straightaway. No detours. No delays. He'll be waitin' three streets over, near Redbridge Lane, in front o' that little bakery wot smells like burnt walnuts."

James would know the spot. Reliable cover. Sparse foot traffic. Helena filed it away.

"Understood," she said.

Nathaniel's smirk returned, lopsided as ever. "Knew you would. You always pay on time and don't ask fool questions. That's good business. The rest's just noise."

She slipped a few coins into his gloved hand. He pocketed them without a glance.

"Just don't go gettin' yerself stabbed," he added, already backing toward the shadows. "Wouldn't fancy explainin' to 'is lordship how I lost the both of you in one go."

And then he was gone—vanishing into the darkness without so much as a crunch of gravel behind him, leaving Helena alone in the garden.

The weight of his words pressed against her chest as she made her way back into the house, where James and Prudence were waiting in the drawing room.

Prudence's voice carried from the threshold: "There you are, child. You've been gone longer than I like in this chilly air. Come—tell us what your mysterious visitor said, and then let's plan how best I can make a spectacle if you need one."

Helena stepped inside, drawing the shawl tighter as she met their eyes. "He had details about the tavern gathering tonight. The meeting is real. We'll need to move quickly."

James straightened, alert. "Confirmed then. Tonight?"

She nodded. "Yes. Black cloaks, masks, code phrases—it's all in place. We'll need to slip in, blend, and extract whatever we can."

Prudence pursed her lips. "As much as I adore a good masquerade, you cannot take me with you. The East End is no place for someone of my somewhat ungainly abilities—not unless we want to cause a scene before we've even crossed the threshold."

Helena gave her aunt a small, grateful smile. "Thank you, Aunt. I wouldn't ask it of you. But I will need you nearby. Perhaps you could remain at a location a few streets away. If we don't return within a set time, raise the alarm. Discreetly."

"Oh, I do discreet very well," Prudence said, her tone arch. "But I'll also have a flask of brandy and a warm shawl. If you take too long, I'm sending in the cavalry disguised as a choir of wayward nuns."

James glanced between them. "Let's hope it doesn't come to that."

"But if it does," Prudence said, wagging a finger, "you'll wish you'd let me in from the start."

Helena's lips twitched. "Duly noted."

She turned toward James, her expression sharpening into focus. "We have only a few hours. Let's finalize the plan, double-check the exits, and get our disguises ready. Tonight, we take the first step inside."

He nodded once, crisp and certain. "No mistakes."

Helena felt the weight of what they were about to do settle over her. This wasn't observation from the periphery anymore. This was walking into the Society's inner circle, surrounded by enemies, with nothing but their wits and a password to protect them.

If they were discovered, there would be no rescue. No second chances.

Their eyes met—two soldiers on the edge of enemy territory, bound by purpose, trust, and something unspoken. Prudence settled back into her chair with a dramatic sigh and a murmured, "Well, then. On with our little deception."

Chapter Thirteen

THE BLACK CAT TAVERN

January 25, 1855
James

THE CAB CLATTERED to a stop at the mouth of the alley, swallowed by the fog curling through the city's underbelly. Nathaniel Clarke held the reins loosely, his hat pulled low, jaw tight.

"This is close as I get without drawin' eyes," he muttered, eyes flicking down the dim, slick alley. Every muscle in his frame was coiled, like a man ready to vanish at the first hint of trouble.

Helena donned her mask and tightened her cloak, her gloved hands steady. "Thank you, Nathaniel. Wait here. We'll signal if we need a fast exit."

His gaze didn't leave the shadows. "Be quick, and watch your backs. I ain't fond o' cleanin' up corpses."

James stiffened at that, then stepped down, his boots hitting wet stone with a dull splash. He adjusted the brim of his hat and exaggerated the limp as they'd rehearsed, playing the desperate man—a soldier wrecked by war, clinging to hope.

He offered Helena his arm. "Shall we?"

The alley stank of stale beer and rot, just as Nathaniel had warned, the reek of old ale and desperation thick enough to taste.

Rats darted across the cobbles. Voices drifted from unseen corners, low and dangerous. James's training surged to the surface, every step deliberate, every sound catalogued.

Helena walked beside him with unnerving calm. "Remember," she said quietly, "you're not a soldier tonight. Just a man desperate to change his lot."

"A desperate man with a limp," James replied, his voice dry.

Ahead, the tavern's rear door loomed—heavy wood, rusted hinges. A hooded guard emerged from the shadows.

James didn't hesitate. "The moonlight reveals the truth."

The figure stepped aside. The door creaked open, releasing a wave of smoke, sweat, and something older—like soaked wood and old secrets.

Inside, a low-ceilinged storage room glowed dimly under guttering lanterns. Barrels and crates lined the walls—potential cover, but also traps if fighting broke out. The air was thick with damp tobacco and tension. Masked figures moved like shadows draped in black cloaks, whispering.

Helena entered with feline grace. James followed, letting the limp slow him just enough to be noticeable.

Three exits: the door they'd entered, a second door in the far corner (locked?), and a narrow gap between crates that might lead to the main tavern. Twenty-three people, most armed—he spotted knife hilts, a few pistols poorly concealed. Lighting: two lanterns, both near exits. Easy to extinguish for cover.

He filed it all away. If this went wrong, he'd need every advantage.

A slim, masked man climbed onto a crate, commanding immediate silence with a raised hand.

The whisper of his name rippled through the room—"*The Raven*," before the room fell silent.

Even behind the beaked mask, his voice carried—raspy, but assured. Charisma layered over menace.

James had commanded men. He recognized another leader when he saw one—someone who didn't need volume to compel obedience. The most dangerous kind.

"We're here because it's time to act," he said, sweeping an arm toward the oak table beside him, where a floor plan was laid out. "Our target—we'll call him *Bramble*—has been a thorn in our side too long. A voice that carries weight in Parliament. A man whose words could turn the tide of public opinion. Removing him will create the gap in authority we need."

A faint hum of approval rippled through the crowd. He let his gaze drift across the group, cataloging the masked faces and mannerisms of those around him, mentally labeling each one for easier tracking.

"The Bramble upholds a monarchy that sends boys to Crimea with broken rifles and empty bellies," the Raven went on. "They call it strategy. We call it slaughter."

James's jaw tightened. He'd *seen* the slaughter. Watched good men die because Whitehall couldn't manage a supply line. The Raven wasn't wrong about that—the system *had* failed them. But assassination wasn't justice. It was just more death.

Helena moved closer to the table. James kept watch as the room's mood shifted—grievance, bloodlust, conviction.

A tall man stepped forward, his stance parade-ground perfect even here in this dim tavern. Silver touched his temples, hands moving as if tracing maps on an invisible table. Military. Officer class. James pegged him immediately.

British Army—but not Crimea—he carried himself different-ly. Not parade-ground pride so much as discipline held on a short rein.

"Half my company died at Gwalior. Not from enemy fire. From cholera. Because supply officers couldn't be bothered to secure clean water." His voice was clipped, controlled. A man who'd learned to channel rage into precision. "The system that killed them is still in place."

The Raven's voice dropped. "Unforgivable."

The man pointed at the floor plan. "We enter here. Side entrance. Lightly guarded. Silent work. In and out before anyone knows we've been there."

A woman across the room scoffed. Tall—taller than most men James knew—with dark hair visible at the edge of her mask. Green silk flashed beneath her black cloak, and when she stepped forward, a sharp, medicinal scent cut through the tobacco smoke. James had seen her whispering to others before the meeting began, leaning in with urgent intensity, only to be politely but firmly dismissed. When she straightened, her hands had curled briefly—fingers hooking like claws—before she forced them flat again.

Overlooked. Angry about it. James filed that away.

"Silent?" Her voice held scorn, not grief—the cold fury of someone who'd been ignored too many times. "That's cowardice. The Crown only understands spectacle. They feast while our boys die. Quiet work accomplishes nothing. We need a statement that cannot be ignored."

The Raven raised a hand, silencing the rising murmurs of disagreement. "The Bramble's death will send a message," he said, his tone colder. "Chaos. Uncertainty. Fear. The Crown will scramble, and we'll step in to exploit their weaknesses. But it will be *my* message. No deviation."

More voices chimed in—suggestions, threats, quiet schemes. James listened, memorized, assigned nicknames as if this were a battlefield. The *Slim Man,* all slick calculation. The *Failed Merchant,* clinging to faded prestige. And in the corner, two men exchanging a folded slip of paper. That slip passed hands twice. It must be important.

James committed the pair to memory: First man, shorter, nervous hands. Second man, broad shoulders, confident. If he saw either again without masks, he'd recognize them by movement alone.

Near the edge of the group, the *Failed Merchant* in a well-tailored but slightly outdated coat shifted forward. His gloved hands fidgeted with something in his pocket—coins, from the soft clink. When he spoke, his voice had the oily precision of someone accustomed to negotiating. "Bribes might be simpler. I've calculated the cost—three guards, fifty pounds each. Cheaper than bloodshed, and far less likely to trigger investigations." The voice—something about it struck him as familiar. Could that be Hawthorne?

The Raven let the arguments play out before stepping down from the crate, his boots hitting the floor with a deliberate thud. The room fell silent once again.

"This is not a debate," he said coldly. "I welcome your insights, but this undertaking will proceed as I dictate. Once I've made my decision, any deviation from my plan or breach in security will be met with the full wrath of the Black Rose Society."

Then—

"Who are you?" The tall woman in green silk—James had mentally dubbed her *Querulous Woman*—stepped forward, her pale eyes fixed on Helena with open hostility. Not suspicion. Something more personal. Resentment.

James kept his stance easy, deferential. "Just a believer. Like the rest of you."

Her stare could slice skin. "Then why are you watching people instead of focusing on the task at hand? A spy, are you?"

The room seemed to hold its breath.

Twenty-three against two. If this turned violent, they'd never make it to the door. James's weight shifted imperceptibly, calculating: *Querulous Woman first*—she was the threat. *Then the guard at the door.* Three seconds to cross the distance. His leg would slow him—damn the injury. And Helena… he had no idea if she could fight, or if she'd freeze. An unknown variable in an already impossible equation.

He could feel her beside him, tense and alert. Whatever happened next, he'd have to trust she could handle herself. Or protect her trying.

Before the tension snapped, Helena stepped forward—smooth as ever.

"A spy?" Her laugh was light. "My husband can't cross a room without tripping over his own feet. He's lame, not treacherous. Surely you don't think he's a threat?" Her hand settled on James's arm, fingers warm and steady.

Querulous Woman's eyes flicked to James's legs, her suspicion undimmed. "Lame or not, he doesn't belong." Then her gaze flicked to Helena. "Funny," the woman sneered. "You've barely stepped into the room and already you're shielding this man like you run the place. Who, exactly, are you supposed to be?"

James let the moment stretch—then feigned a wince, staggering sideways. "I don't want trouble," he muttered, injecting just enough fear to make his act convincing. His hand brushed the pocket of the *Jaded Aristocrat*. Paper slid into his palm as he stumbled. Pickpocket technique, learned in the rookeries during his first posting. He'd never thought he'd use it for the Crown, but here they were.

The man shoved him hard. "Watch it, you idiot!"

James went down, his bad leg buckling beneath him. He hit the floor with a grunt, the impact jarring through his knee. Pain flared hot and immediate—not feigned this time.

Damn it.

The fresh aggravation sent fire shooting through his thigh.

The *Querulous Woman* in green silk seized the moment, her voice rising with vindication. "They don't belong here! *I've been warning you*—strangers walking in, gaining trust too quickly. Worming their way in. They're spies! I'm certain of it!"

Her emphasis on "I've been warning you," told James everything. She'd raised concerns before. Been ignored. Now she was desperate to be proven right.

His pulse hammered, but he kept his movements measured, climbing to his feet and brushing dirt from his coat as though thoroughly chastened. He caught Helena's sharp glance, her expression tight but composed.

And then the Raven's voice cracked like a whip. *"Enough."*

Silence fell. But the damage was done.

"No one leaves," the Raven said, his rasping voice thick with warning. "If there are spies among us, they'll be dealt with—*after* we've finished. There are priorities."

The crowd shifted, edginess crackling like static in the air. James straightened, his hand brushing his pocket where the stolen paper now rested. He could feel the edges pressing against his thigh—a small prize he could only hope had been worth the risk.

Next to him, Helena's eyes met his—steady, composed, but edged with urgency. She'd seen him take it. Good.

The meeting devolved into smaller clusters of conversation. Questions muttered under breath, plans spun in whispers. The Raven disappeared into one knot of conspirators, his presence like a slowly retreating storm.

James angled himself toward the wall, dragging his bad leg with more weight than usual. The pain was real now, blooming hot behind his knee. Helena moved with him, graceful and unflinching, adjusting her pace to his without making it look like she was.

"Keep moving," she murmured, voice barely audible.

"I'm trying," he said through gritted teeth. "But the fall did some damage. The limp's not an act anymore."

Her hand brushed his arm in response—a grounding touch. Wordless reassurance.

They neared the rear door. The same guard stood watch, arms crossed, face unreadable beneath the mask. His eyes tracked them with feline intensity.

James flicked his gaze to the alley behind the door, then to the barrel wedged beside the wall. Options. Not many.

Helena shifted beside him—subtle, poised to move. He caught her signal, gave one in return. A flick of his fingers: *Go right. I'll draw him.*

She nodded once.

James feinted left. The guard moved.

Helena darted right—fast and sure—and James struck low, sweeping the man's legs out with a twist of his own. The pain screamed through his knee, but he didn't stop, even when something tore. Muscle or tendon, he couldn't tell. Didn't matter. They had seconds.

As the guard stumbled back, Helena struck him once—sharp and clean—sending him to the ground in a heap.

"Go!" James growled.

Helena flung the door open. Cold air hit like a slap. The alley stretched dark and slick before them.

They ran.

Shouts exploded from behind. Boots pounded floorboards.

"The spies are escaping!"

Helena slammed the door shut with her full weight, bracing it with her shoulder. "We need to block it!"

A heavy thud from the other side jolted the door outward. Helena gasped, bracing harder.

James's gaze darted around, landing on a barrel leaning against the wall. Ale, from the smell. Full—maybe two hundred pounds. Ignoring the searing pain in his leg, he staggered over and shoved it against the door with his shoulder. It scraped across stone, heavy and final.

The wood shuddered and groaned as fists slammed the other side. The ale-filled barrel shifted slightly, scraping against the ground.

"They're breaking through!" Helena warned, her voice tight.

"Move!" James barked, his tone sharp, sweat beading his brow.

Helena slipped under his arm, wrapping it around her shoulders as they stumbled down the alley. The sound of splintering wood behind them drove them forward, each step a race against time. James leaned heavily on her, his breaths ragged but controlled.

A shout behind them.

A sharp whistle cut through the chaos, piercing the dense fog.

A cab rounded the corner at full speed.

Nathaniel at the reins.

He pulled hard, bringing the horse up short in front of them.

"Get in!" he shouted, his voice tight.

Helena hauled James into the cab, pushed him inside, then climbed in after. The moment the door slammed shut, the wheels jolted forward. The cab lurched into motion, rattling over uneven stones.

"They're not stoppin'," Nathaniel growled, eyes flicking from side street to side street. "Better pray I lose 'em."

"They can't catch us," Helena said, breathless but certain. She looked over at James. "Not tonight."

He sat back, chest heaving, leg stretched awkwardly before him. "We've got what we came for," he said. "Whatever that paper is, it mattered to someone. I saw it pass hands three times. And we've got faces. Movements. Voices." James shifted, easing weight off his injured leg. "Four main players, I think. The Raven—obvious leader. The tall man with the military bearing—India veteran, from his story. Organized. Methodical. And that woman who challenged us. She wasn't just angry. She was grieving. And the man focused on finances? I think that might have been Hawthorne."

"Hawthorne… are you sure?"

"No, but the man's voice—there was something about it."

Helena nodded, her expression already sharpening into analysis. "We'll keep investigating him. The woman. Did you notice the way the others seemed to dismiss her?"

"Querulous," James agreed. "Makes her more dangerous, but also shows a vulnerability. She'll want to feel vindicated. Seen. She believes."

"At least no one saw past our masks. We're still ghosts."

Outside, the streets blurred past, the fog swallowing the cab whole.

Then quieter: "That woman. She didn't just suspect us. She was looking for a reason to strike."

"No," James said. "She *wanted* us to be guilty. To point the blame at someone."

Helena's jaw tightened. "Because she saw us as a threat. Not to the mission. To *her*."

From the front, Nathaniel kept his eyes fixed ahead, but his voice drifted back. "Let's just hope 'er memory's fuzzy under that mask. Otherwise, you two better vanish when this job's done."

James didn't reply.

Helena looked over at him, her voice soft. "Tonight we were lucky."

She reached across the space between them, her hand finding his in the darkness. His fingers closed around hers—warm, solid, alive.

They rode the rest of the way like that, hands clasped, every clatter of the wheels beneath them a reminder: They'd survived—but only just.

Chapter Fourteen

BOLTHOLE ORDERS

January 25 – late night
Helena

THE CAB RATTLED to a stop on a frost-laced street, wheels crunching over gritty cobblestones. The tavern infiltration still clung to Helena's skin—smoke, fear, adrenaline. Beside her, James was silent, his jaw rigid with pain. The weight of his injury sat between them like a second passenger.

Atop the driver's perch, Nathaniel cast a sharp glance down the road, then back toward them. "This is it," he muttered. "His Lordship'll meet you here. Say your piece, then you're switchin' carriages. Orders."

Helena gave a small nod. She reached for the door.

"You'll want to be quick about it," Nathaniel added, his voice lower. "Streets like this don't stay quiet long."

A tall figure stepped out of the shadows. Sir Frederick, coat buttoned high, eyes harder than the night air. He didn't waste time. "Report. Now."

Helena climbed out, boots skidding slightly on the icy street. James followed more slowly, the pain obvious in the set of his mouth even though he said nothing. Helena wanted to tell him to stop being so proud. She didn't.

She turned to Frederick. "The meeting was larger than expected. The Raven laid out plans for an assassination—more than that. Of throwing the government into disorder. Supply lines in Crimea, assassinating a Crown diplomat. They had maps. Codes. Floor plans. This isn't an idle rebellion—it's organized. Methodical."

"And they have a target," James added, his voice tight with pain and urgency. "Codename 'The Bramble.' They spoke of him like he's significant—someone in Parliament whose voice carries weight. They're planning his assassination."

Frederick's expression darkened, but Helena caught something else beneath the tactical assessment—genuine concern. "Did they say when?"

"No specifics," Helena said. "But soon. The planning is advanced."

Frederick turned to James. "Were you recognized?"

"Not exactly. But someone grew suspicious. We drew attention. They chased us. We got out… barely."

Frederick was quiet for a moment, and Helena recognized the look: He was already three moves ahead, calculating contingencies they hadn't yet considered. She'd seen that expression before—in briefings, when he'd anticipated outcomes no one else had yet considered. The spymaster's mind at work.

His gaze fell to James's leg. "And the limp?"

"It's nothing," James said flatly.

A hot flush of frustration ran through Helena. "It's *not* nothing," she cut in sharply, sharper than she intended. "He wrenched the same leg he injured in Crimea."

"I'll have Dr. Ramsey see to that leg," Frederick said, his tone gentler now. He met James's eyes with something that looked almost like understanding. "I've learned not to trust soldiers when they say they're 'fine.' You're too valuable to this operation to let pride cripple you."

Frederick's expression hardened again. "If there's any chance they identified you, returning home is out of the question." His tone left no room for argument. "You'll lie low at one of my safe houses. It's above a shuttered stationer's just off Lovell's Court, behind Paternoster Row. Clean. Unmarked. You'll stay there until I say otherwise."

Helena's stomach sank. "What of my family? Will they be safe?"

"I'll have them watched and warned—quietly. Your aunt and sister will be told you've gone to the country with the major. A romantic retreat to avoid scandal. Prudence will manage the story."

He turned to Nathaniel. "Take them there and make sure they're settled."

Nathaniel rolled his eyes. "Aye, fine. But I'm no nursemaid, Woolsy. I'm not tuckin' them in."

Frederick ignored him. "Stay alert," he told them both. "We can't afford mistakes."

He turned, melting back into the darkness.

Helena helped James into a second cab, Nathaniel flicking the reins without a word. The ride was silent save for James's occasional sharp intake of breath and the jangle of the harness. She wanted to say something—to acknowledge the tension, the pain in his face. But nothing felt safe enough to offer.

They stopped on a nondescript shop on a deserted street. The sign overhead was chipped and faded. The windows were dark, the alley damp.

Nathaniel pulled the cab to a halt, scanning the road behind. "Top floor. Door's unlocked. Bolt it behind you."

Helena climbed down, the night air bitter against her cheeks. She reached up to steady James as he stepped out. The flash of pain in his face was unmistakable. She swallowed, wishing she could snap at him to stop being so stubborn—but that would do neither of them any good.

Nathaniel flicked the reins and disappeared without a parting word, leaving them huddled on the frozen doorstep. So much for seeing them settled.

The stairs inside were steep and unforgiving. Each time James shifted, he hissed through gritted teeth, leaning on her for support. She bore his weight in silence, her body aching but her mind louder. *Don't feel sorry for him. Just get to the top.*

But even as she thought it, she knew it was a lie. She already cared. Far more than was wise. *Caring too much leads to ruin.* She'd seen that happen before, after Mother died.

Yet here she was, caring anyway.

The flat was small—two rooms, one battered stove, no luxuries. But it was clean. And it was safe. For now.

James locked the door behind them, his shoulders sagging. Helena lit the nearest lamp, golden light flickering over peeling wallpaper and cracked plaster.

James sank into a chair, stretching his leg out with a muted groan. "This is going to be a long night."

Helena didn't answer. She set her reticule on the table and moved to the stove. Someone had left coal. She worked in silence, laying the fire, striking the match.

When the first heat began to spread, she wiped her hands on a towel and finally turned to face him. He looked exhausted, the sharpness dulled by fatigue and stress. "Long, indeed," she murmured.

The silence that followed was heavy—not just exhaustion, but everything unspoken between them.

Helena fiddled with the lamp's wick, adjusting the flame. Once it was glowing, she perched on the edge of the table, hands clenched in her lap.

"The Bramble," she said finally, breaking the silence. "We need to determine who he is."

James shifted in his chair, stretching his injured leg with visible effort. "A voice that carries weight in Parliament. Someone whose words could turn public opinion." He frowned, thinking. "That describes dozens of men."

"But not dozens who would threaten the Black Rose Society enough to warrant assassination." Helena's mind was already cataloguing possibilities. "Someone currently vocal about the war. Someone defending the Crown's decisions in Crimea, perhaps."

"Or someone advocating for continued engagement despite the casualties," James added. "The Society sees the war as government incompetence. Anyone justifying it would be their enemy."

Helena nodded slowly. "Lord Palmerston is too obvious. Too well-protected. They'd never get close."

"And if they killed the Prime Minister, it would unite the country against them," James agreed. "They want chaos, not martyrdom. The Bramble is someone important enough to matter, but not so prominent his death would backfire."

"A diplomat?" Helena suggested. "Someone with Continental connections who could influence foreign support for the war effort?"

"Possibly." James's expression darkened. "Though the way they spoke… it felt personal. As if this isn't just strategic. Someone they particularly despise."

"Sir Frederick, perhaps?" The thought made Helena's stomach clench. "He has influence in certain circles. His voice carries weight with the military command."

James considered this. "Frederick keeps a low profile. I'm not sure the general public knows his name well enough for his death to 'turn the tide of opinion' as the Raven said."

"True." Helena exhaled. "Then who? A general? A Member of Parliament known for war speeches?"

"Or a diplomat who's about to broker something crucial," James said. "A treaty. An alliance. Something that would strengthen Britain's position."

They sat in silence, turning over possibilities. The fire crackled. The lamp hissed.

"We'll need to ask Frederick," Helena said finally. "See who's scheduled to speak publicly in the coming weeks. Who's making waves in Parliament or diplomatic circles."

"And we'll need to warn whoever it is," James added. "Though if we're wrong…" He trailed off.

"If we're wrong, we reveal we have insider knowledge of Society plans," Helena finished. "Which could compromise our infiltration."

"Exactly."

Another silence, heavier this time. The weight of what they'd undertaken—the danger, the complexity, the lives at stake—settled over them both.

Then James spoke, his voice quieter. "You were extraordinary tonight. The way you deflected that woman's suspicion. The way you got us out."

Helena looked up, startled by the shift in tone. "We got each other out."

"Still." His eyes held hers. "I wanted you to know."

James exhaled slowly, then again, as if steadying himself. His gaze dropped to his leg, stretched awkwardly before him, and calculation flickered across his expression. When he spoke again, the warmth from moments before had vanished.

"You shouldn't have told Frederick about my injury," he said abruptly, the vulnerability of the moment closing off as quickly as it had appeared. His voice was edged with frustration. "It could compromise everything."

Her head jerked up. "You think I should've lied?"

"It could compromise the mission."

"You can barely walk," she snapped. "You were limping before tonight, and now you're barely upright. You think that goes unnoticed?"

"It's my business."

"No," she said, standing now, fury rising. "It concerns us both. If we're partners—if what we're doing matters—then your injuries matter too. We work together or not at all."

He rose unsteadily, bracing himself against the chair. His face was pale, drawn tight with pain and anger.

"It's not Frederick's concern."

"Yes, it is!" She stepped closer. "And mine."

His voice dropped, bitter. "I don't need your pity."

"This has nothing to do with pity," she said. "This is me watching someone I trust push himself past the point of reason. That fall could've made things worse. You should rest—heal."

"Don't call it a war wound," he muttered. "Sounds too honorable. It wasn't taken in battle."

She blinked, caught off guard. "Then where?"

"Behind enemy lines. It's complicated."

She softened. "Then explain it."

But he shook his head, the shutters closing again. "It doesn't matter."

"It does to me." Her voice dropped. She moved closer, brushing her fingers against his arm—a gesture that felt startling in its intimacy, crossing a boundary they'd both been carefully maintaining. "*You* matter."

His gaze locked on hers. Something cracked between them—some dam, some boundary—fractured. Her chest tightened with a rush of longing.

"Helena…"

It wasn't wise. It wasn't planned. But when he reached for her, she didn't pull away.

The air seemed to thrum with unspoken emotions. Helena stared up into his eyes, seeing the depth of his weariness and worry, and something in her refused to turn away. James's hand slid to her waist, tugging her closer.

"This is a mistake," he murmured.

"Maybe," she whispered. "But I don't care."

Their lips met, fierce and breathless. A collision of everything they'd tried to bury—fear, pain, longing, defiance. His arms wrapped around her, and she melted into it, heart thudding wildly against his chest.

The fire crackled. The lamp hissed. The world shrank to just this: warmth, breath, touch.

Then—*a knock on the door.*

Helena broke away, breath ragged. James's arms tightened instinctively, his eyes sharp again, protective. The moment shattered, instincts flaring.

Another knock—louder this time.

Helena pulled back fully, pulse hammering, lips tingling. James moved toward the door, positioning himself between it and her—protective instinct automatic.

Whatever had just begun between them would have to wait.

But it *had* begun. And there was no taking it back.

Chapter Fifteen

BETWEEN PAIN AND PROMISE

January 25 – Just past midnight
James

JAMES'S HEARTBEAT THUNDERED in his ears, the knocking at the door landing like a rifle crack. For a moment longer, he held Helena close, her breath warm against his cheek, her lips parted in surprise.

Then—reality.

He released her with a sharp intake of air, the distance between them opening like a chasm. The cold rushed in at once—into the room, into his chest. If the knock had come even seconds later…

He couldn't afford to dwell on that.

But he *was* dwelling on it. On the softness of her lips. On the way she'd yielded, then pulled him closer. On the fact that for those few seconds, nothing else had existed—not the mission, not the danger, not the impossible complications.

Reality reasserted itself with brutal force.

"I—" Helena began, breathless, but her gaze flicked to the door, just as it rattled again with impatience.

James straightened, ignoring the ache flaring in his calf. That kiss had been a mistake. A beautiful, all-consuming, treacherous mistake. He couldn't risk that kind of closeness. Couldn't risk needing her the way he already knew he did. Not now. Not ever.

He crossed to the door, schooling his face into something close to indifference. He opened it to find Lady Josephine Woolsy, bundled in a heavy cloak, and a tall, lean man beside her whose boots were already dripping from the frost.

"We nearly froze to death out here," Josephine said, arching a brow. Her gaze swept past him to Helena and didn't miss a thing.

James stood frozen for half a breath, gaze flicking to the man at her side—Dr. Sebastian Ramsey. Tall, lean, sandy-blond hair, green eyes that missed nothing. He had the composure of someone who'd stared death in the face and found it unremarkable. His coat was immaculate despite the cold, his doctor's satchel carried like a soldier's weapon—naturally, with intent.

Calm. Controlled. Too observant.

Adrian had passed along stories about him. Field surgeon in Crimea, worked behind enemy lines, saved men others had written off. His name passed between wounded soldiers like a rumor of survival.

"Apologies," James said, stepping aside. "We were… occupied."

Josephine's smile tilted in a knowing way. "So I gathered."

The doctor gave a low, polite grunt. "Fascinating," he murmured. "Shall we come in before we become icicles?"

Josephine swept inside, drawing off her gloves finger by finger. "Major, I believe you already know Dr. Ramsey—renowned miracle worker, although too modest to admit it. Frederick thought it best to send someone who knows how to patch up a soldier too stubborn to admit when he's broken."

Her eyes flicked to Helena with something that might have been sympathy. "And someone to ensure Lady Helena doesn't spend the night alone with her fiancé in a situation that might invite speculation. Appearances, my dear."

"Doctor," James said, forcing civility through gritted teeth.

Ramsey's gaze flicked to James's leg, then returned to his

face. "Let's take a look," he said with unhurried certainty, already setting down his bag.

"I'd only just returned from Lady Heatherington's ball," Josephine added breezily, "and barely kicked off my slippers before Frederick sent us out again. You do know how to attract attention."

Helena hovered nearby as James lowered himself into the chair with a grimace. He could feel her watching him, but he couldn't bring himself to meet her eyes.

Ramsey knelt and began loosening James's boot with practiced efficiency.

"Steady," Ramsey murmured, as he loosened the boot with practiced ease. "You're fortunate. Another inch and you might have cracked the fibula."

James hissed in pain but said nothing. He bit down on the sound, even as the fire in his leg flared brighter. He didn't need sympathy. What he needed was to forget the way Helena had tasted when she kissed him back.

"You injured this same leg in Crimea, then?" Ramsey asked.

"Behind enemy lines," James said shortly.

Ramsey's hands stilled for just a moment. "I treated a lot of men behind enemy lines. Early in '54?"

"Middle of '54."

A flicker of recognition crossed Ramsey's face. "The raids. Before Balaclava."

James shrugged, jaw tight. He didn't want to talk about it.

Ramsey, mercifully, took the hint and returned to his task without further questions. The examination was brisk but thorough. James endured it in silence, but his mind wasn't quiet. Behind his eyes, the past unspooled: snow falling on dead men, smoke thick enough to choke on, blood dark against white ground. The weight of a dying man in his arms—"Tell Sarah I tried"—gasping his last while James dragged him toward cover they'd never reach.

The weight of failure.

That same weight pressed against his chest now, stealing his breath.

"Major?"

He blinked hard. Ramsey was watching him, brow furrowed.

"You've done yourself no favors," the doctor said. "But you'll recover—if you stay off it for the next day or two. After that, I'll teach you a strengthening course of exercises. For now, you'll take this." He produced a small tin from his bag. "Analgesic powder. Mix it with hot water. Willow bark and laudanum. Enough to dull the pain without clouding your mind. You'll need your wits about you if Frederick's sending you back into the field."

"I'll do it," Helena said quietly, already reaching for the kettle on the stove.

She moved around the small space with practiced efficiency—no wasted motion, no fuss. The same maddening grace James had always admired. One more thing he didn't deserve.

One more reason to keep his distance.

Ramsey took in James's pained expression and smirked. "Better me than a field surgeon with a saw."

Josephine, meanwhile, was busy brushing snow from her cloak. "Frederick's watchers haven't seen anything unusual near your homes," she said. "He's sent word to your family, Helena—nothing alarming, just enough to keep up appearances. If everything stays quiet through tomorrow evening, you'll be cleared to return. Until then, stay put."

"And Amelia?" Helena asked quietly. "Prudence?"

"Safe at home, none the wiser," Josephine assured her. "Prudence is telling everyone you've gone to the major's country estate for a romantic interlude. Very scandalous, very *them*."

Despite everything, Helena's lips twitched. "Of course she is."

Helena turned back to the kettle, but James caught the subtle shift in her stance. Relief, tightly contained. Not weakness—she wouldn't allow herself that. Just breathing room.

Ramsey rose, brushing off his knees. "No heroics," Ramsey

added mildly as he repacked his bag. "You've only one leg to stand on when it comes to pride."

"I'll restrain myself," James muttered.

Josephine handed Helena a small basket. "Frederick sent provisions. Not out of concern for your hunger—he just doesn't trust you to stay put without supervision."

Helena accepted it with a composed "Thank you," already moving with that infuriating, unshakable grace. Problems like sarcasm, frost, and broken plans barely registered with her. James didn't know what he'd done to earn that kind of dignity from her. Probably nothing.

Josephine, satisfied, tugged her hood back into place. "We'll check in tomorrow. Try not to re-injure yourself in the meantime." Her eyes flicked between them with unmistakable implication.

The door closed behind them. The quiet that followed was colder than anything outside.

Helena moved to the stove and poured hot water into a cup, then stirred in the powder. The scent was bitter and earthy, clinging to the air like steam from a battlefield. She handed the mug to James without ceremony.

Their eyes met briefly—then both looked away. The kiss hung between them like smoke, invisible but impossible to ignore.

He accepted it, his fingers brushing hers. "Thank you."

She nodded once and turned away, starting to unpack the food. No tension in her movements. No accusation. Just that same infuriating composure. He drank the mixture in silence, wincing at the aftertaste.

After a long stretch of quiet, she turned toward him. "Tomorrow. Josephine said we might go home then. Are you... all right?"

"I'll manage."

It wasn't a lie. But it wasn't the truth either.

She searched his face, and he wondered what she saw. Pain? Exhaustion? Or the truth he was trying to bury: that he wanted to pull her back into his arms and consequences be damned.

And then the moment was gone. She gave a small nod and disappeared into the other room, closing the door softly behind her.

James sat alone in the circle of lamplight, the warmth of the drink spreading through his limbs. His calf still pulsed with dull, angry pain, but that wasn't what kept him awake.

Helena was here. Just a room away. Her presence seeped through the walls, through the silence. He could feel it. The shape of her. The weight of her absence.

He pictured her mouth, her breathless intake of air, the way she'd leaned into him as though—for that moment—she'd wanted him just as much.

And maybe she had. That made it worse.

He dragged himself to the small cot and lay back, arm across his eyes, breath tight.

He shouldn't have kissed her.

He couldn't stop thinking about it.

But he had to.

He'd lost too many people already. Every man he'd led into ambush. His closest friend at Sebastopol. The ones who trusted him and died for it.

He couldn't lose Helena.

Which meant he couldn't have her. Couldn't let himself need her the way he already did. Because needing someone meant giving them the power to destroy you when they left.

And everyone left. Through death or distance or disappointment. Everyone.

He turned over, wincing, leg aching. The cot creaked beneath him.

He couldn't sleep.

The pain didn't help, but even more unbearable was the thought of her lying in the next room, just beyond reach. Just beyond reason.

He stayed awake long after he turned down the lamp. Listening to every quiet movement, every sigh of the wind beyond the shutters. Wondering if she, too, was staring at the ceiling. Wondering if her lips still tingled the way his did.

Letting her close meant risking everything. It meant letting her see the parts of himself he'd buried: the guilt, the failures, the nightmares that woke him gasping. It meant giving her the power to destroy him when—not if, *when*—she realized what he really was.

A man who led good soldiers to die in an ambush.

A man who couldn't save the people who trusted him.

A man who would inevitably fail her too.

And if he lost her after that—after letting himself love her, after letting her matter more than breathing—he wouldn't survive it.

So he lay in the dark and told himself what he always did.

Stay away.

Even if it kills you.

But it was already too late.

He was already lost.

Chapter Sixteen

THE UNVEILING OF A THREAT

January 25 – Morning
Helena

HELENA WOKE TO a stale chill pressing against her cheeks. The stove had gone lukewarm in the night, and the air in the small room was cold and filled with her own quiet regret. She pulled the blanket tighter, wishing it could shield her from the knowledge of James's presence just one thin wall away.

She had heard everything—his restless shifting, the soft creak of the cot, the occasional sharp breath when pain flared. Each sound had underscored how closely their lives were now entangled.

She'd lain awake for hours after closing that door between them, replaying the kiss. The way his hands had cupped her face. The desperate hunger in it, as though he'd been starving and she was sustenance. The way she'd responded—no hesitation, no shame, just want.

And then the terrible hollow feeling when she'd walked away.

He's a distraction, she reminded herself. *You saw what happened to Father—losing Mother tore him apart. You can't let that happen to you.*

But even as she thought it, she knew the comparison was flawed.

Father had been destroyed by grief, yes. But he'd also been destroyed by having *nothing else* once he'd abandoned the world of diplomacy. No sense of himself beyond that of devoted husband. When Mother died, he'd simply… stopped. Stopped living. Stopped trying. Let despair make every decision for him.

Helena had the mission. The team. Her own skills that belonged to her alone—observation, deduction, courage earned through action rather than inheritance.

She had *herself*, in ways Father never had.

And last night, kissing James hadn't felt like weakness. It had felt like choosing. Like asserting her own will. Father had surrendered when grief consumed him.

Father had stopped choosing. Had become passive in his own life.

Helena refused to do the same.

The realization settled in her chest, strange and uncomfortable. She'd spent years assuming love inevitably led to devastation. But what if the devastation came not from loving, but from having nothing else? From building an entire existence around *one person* and then losing them?

What if she could love James without losing herself?

The thought was terrifying in an entirely new way.

She pushed the blanket aside and slipped into the main room. Morning light filtered through the thin curtains, catching the dust in gold shafts. She set about preparing breakfast—bread and cheese from the hamper, a pot of tea on the stove. The motions were simple. Familiar. Oddly grounding. She hummed softly while arranging the food, determined to keep her mind steady on their mission.

A soft rustle signaled movement behind her.

"Breakfast," she called, keeping her tone neutral. "You should eat before we discuss anything else."

James emerged from the shadows, his steps steadier than

yesterday. Still cautious. Still wounded. She could see it in the way he favored one side, though he didn't mention it.

"Dr. Ramsey's powder seems to be helping?"

"It is," he said, lowering himself carefully into the chair, testing his knee. "The swelling's gone down, but I still need to be careful."

She passed him a mug of tea. Their fingers brushed—a fleeting touch, but it lingered. Warmth bloomed across her neck before she could suppress it.

She saw his jaw tighten. He'd felt it too—that spark, that connection. And like her, he was choosing to ignore it.

For now.

He cleared his throat. "Leg aside, we have a lot to go over."

She nodded. "Yes. We do."

But the tension in the air—soft, magnetic—challenged her every resolve. She pulled the second chair from the back room, sat beside him at the rickety table to sift through the coded notes and half remembered details from the infiltration.

Morning light filtered through the threadbare curtains, illuminating the rough edges of the safe house.

They leaned in, shoulders nearly touching, the air between them charged with memory and words best left unspoken. She could smell the soap he'd used—same as last night, cedar and something else she couldn't name. Could see the shadow of stubble along his jaw. Could remember exactly how that jaw had felt under her fingertips.

Focus. Duty first.

But focusing was becoming increasingly difficult when every cell in her body was aware of his proximity.

Helena bent over the page. "The Bramble is no obscure target," she said. "They spoke of him with intent—like someone well-placed. Important enough to cause real damage if he falls."

James rubbed his knee absently. "If they're planning an assassination, it'll be carefully orchestrated. We need to identify him before they act."

"Frederick might have ideas," Helena said. "Someone in Parliament, well-connected, vocal about the war. There can't be that many who fit the description."

"Unless it's not about Parliament at all," James mused. "Could be diplomatic. Someone brokering alliances or treaties."

"Or military," Helena added. "A general whose voice carries weight with the troops."

They were speculating in circles. They needed more information.

She blew out a breath. "I never realized the Black Rose Society had such scope. The scale of it—it's daunting. They were so bold last night. It was chilling. They *invited* spectacle."

"They're confident," James said. "That's dangerous. But we'll manage. We do work… well together."

That small truth slipped between them like a thread pulled taut. Her mouth twitched upward before she could stop it.

We do.

And there it was again—that recognition she'd had this morning. Father and Mother had never worked together like this. Mother had supported, smiled, charmed, coddled. But she'd never been Father's *partner* in his work. Never strategized with him. Never shared the burden of decisions. And he'd preferred it that way.

But when Mother died, everything came tumbling down. Father lost his whole world because she *was* his whole world.

But Helena and James were building something different. Equal. Balanced. Last night, she created the cover story; he executed the theft. She deflected suspicion; he planned the escape. Together, they were stronger than either alone.

That's the difference, she realized. *Father never had this.*

Then she remembered the kiss—the heat, the longing, the way her body had betrayed her vow to keep distant—and uncertainty flooded back. Understanding the difference between her situation and Father's was one thing. Having the courage to act on it was another entirely.

She rose abruptly to clear the dishes, needing distance to think.

She didn't look at him. She didn't have to. She could feel the disappointment in the silence.

She gathered the last plate, set it aside, and gestured toward their scattered pages. "We might be missing something obvious."

This time, when their hands brushed, she didn't flinch.

Progress, she thought wryly. *Glacial, terrifying progress.*

James's brow furrowed. "At the meeting—there was a woman. Half mask. I recognized her face, but couldn't place it last night. Just now... it came to me."

He looked up, sharp. "Lady Clarissa Montague."

She blinked. "Clarissa? But she's—"

"Everywhere," he said grimly. "Respected. Connected. Always hosting something."

Her frown deepened. "If she's involved with the Black Rose Society..."

"Then we've underestimated them," he finished.

She reached out, placing a hand on his forearm—without thinking, without caution. "We'll tell Sir Frederick. But we need more than suspicion. Clarissa is untouchable without proof."

"I know." His voice was tight.

She offered a dry smile. "I always found her parties dreadfully dull. Treason is a new low."

He huffed a quiet laugh. "No argument there."

The tension between them eased, just slightly. This was safer ground—mission analysis, strategic planning. She could handle working with James.

It was everything else that terrified her.

Then came the knock.

She stiffened. James straightened. They exchanged a glance. Helena crossed to the door.

Sir Frederick Woolsy stood on the step, snow dusting the shoulders of his coat. Beside him, Lady Josephine offered a bright smile.

Helena exhaled. "Thank goodness."

"No suspicious activity at your homes," Frederick said briskly. "You'll leave with us and return home. But stay cautious."

The moment they stepped inside, Helena launched into her report—Clarissa Montague, the half mask, the confirmation. Frederick's expression tightened with each word.

Josephine's lips pursed. "Clarissa's soirées were bad enough. Who knew sedition would be her next attempt at livening them up?"

Frederick looked to James. "Make discreet inquiries among your military contacts. See what whispers they've heard. Helena, remain attentive to what is said in society. If Lady Clarissa's entangled with foreign interests, we need to know fast."

"And the Bramble?" Helena asked. "We still don't know who the target is. Have you had thoughts on likely candidates?"

Frederick's expression darkened. "Several. I'll provide you with a list of names—men currently vocal about the war, scheduled to speak publicly in coming weeks. If any of them mention upcoming appearances, we need to know immediately."

"Understood."

Josephine drifted to James's side and peered at him like a hawk. "And you? Dr. Ramsey said you were to take that powder. Still following orders?"

James stiffened. "Mostly."

"He's been taking it," Helena said, trying not to sound too pleased with herself.

Josephine's smile curved with mischief. "I knew you'd be fussing over him."

Helena flushed. James looked vaguely horrified.

Before the teasing could deepen, they began to pack. Notes were tucked away. Frederick and Josephine stepped outside to wait for them in the carriage.

Helena paused in the center of the room. Once a sanctuary— now something else entirely. A place where things had shifted. She hesitated, torn between wanting to speak about the kiss and knowing duty must come first.

James lingered near the table, steady on one leg. Silent.

"I suppose we'll be returning to our normal lives," she said softly. "Though with Lady Clarissa in the picture, I'm not sure *normal* applies."

"We'll figure it out," he said. "As long as we keep investigating."

Something in his voice—something low and unguarded—wrapped around her like a promise. She wanted to reach for him. She didn't.

She forced a small smile. "We'll see each other soon. Stay safe, James."

"You too."

For a moment, she thought he might step closer. Touch her hand. Say something about last night—acknowledge it, dismiss it, *something.*

He didn't. He just watched her, expression unreadable.

And she realized: He was waiting. Waiting for her to decide. To choose whether to step forward or step back.

The longing she felt warred with the weight of their mission, with her fear of becoming Father, with the terrifying realization that she might already be past the point of no return.

She stepped back.

Not because she didn't want him. But because she wasn't ready.

Not yet.

The moment passed.

Outside, the carriage waited. Josephine fussed briefly about ensuring James had a seat with sufficient space for his injured leg. Helena sat beside her, placing a careful distance between herself and James.

The safe house disappeared behind them.

She stared out the window, jaw set, hands folded in her lap.

She'd told herself it was a relief to leave. A relief to return to normal life, to the clarity of their roles: betrothed in pretense, partners in purpose, nothing more.

But the hollow space beside her—the careful distance she'd placed between herself and James—made a liar of her.

Whatever had passed between her and James, whatever it was becoming—it hadn't stayed behind.

And it wasn't finished.

Chapter Seventeen

WHISPERS AND LEDGERS

February 1–8, 1855
James

T HE COLD WIND off the Thames stung James's cheeks as he stood outside a nondescript tavern on the first evening of February. His leg still ached from the mishap days ago, but the pain had eased. He rolled his ankle gently—just as Dr. Ramsey had shown him. Still stiff, but improving.

Nearly two weeks since the Black Cat. Two weeks since the kiss he couldn't stop thinking about. Two weeks of making inquiries while trying not to think about Helena's lips or the way she'd looked at him in that safe house.

He was failing spectacularly at the latter.

He lengthened his stride, refusing to let discomfort dictate his pace. Too much was at stake.

Tucking his collar high against the chill, he stepped inside. Pipe smoke, lamplight, and the low murmur of conversation welcomed him like an old acquaintance.

He'd spent the past two days moving back and forth across London—quiet inquiries, subtle meetings, back-room confidences. Old military contacts greeted him with hearty slaps on the back and curious looks at his limp. One or two even teased him about rumors of an engagement, which he brushed off with curt amusement. Each jibe made him bristle, not from dislike of the notion but from how much he didn't mind it. How easily he could picture it being real.

My fiancée. Even thinking the words made something in his chest tighten. The lie was becoming dangerously comfortable.

It felt perilously close to something he couldn't afford.

This assignment was about the Black Rose Society, not Helena.

Even so, he couldn't stop the flicker of memory: her hand brushing his, the quiet intensity in her gaze.

The biting cold outside contrasted with the hushed taverns and back rooms where he found leads: fragmentary rumors of an influential trading company quietly funneling money toward anti-government agitators, coded talk of nobles with questionable loyalties, and—most intriguing—whispers about a "closely guarded diplomat" whose upcoming speech had certain parties nervous.

The Bramble? James wondered. But no one would confirm the target's name. Just vague warnings about "someone who shouldn't be speaking publicly" and "a voice that needs silencing."

And there was the repeated mention of Lord Edward Hawthorne hosting a grand birthday celebration soon.

One afternoon, while passing the east side of St. James's, James paused outside Brooks's Club under pretense of lighting a cigar. He wasn't alone for long.

A tall man emerged from the building's side entrance and paused just beside him, his familiar profile shadowed beneath the brim of a low-crowned hat.

"Terrible odds for the fourth race," said the new Duke of Westbridge, his voice carrying the dispassionate weariness of a man discussing horses. Then, lower: "I wouldn't wager anything... unless you had inside knowledge."

He didn't look at James. Just passed a small, folded ledger page into his palm and added, *"Meridian."*

Without waiting for a reply, he vanished back into the crowd.

James didn't unfold the paper until he was half a block away. Just a fragment of financial entries—Sableport shipping manifests. But the name was unmistakable.

So Violet and the duke were still digging at Sableport... Good.

They were investigating any financial wrongdoings while he and Helena worked the social angle. Different approaches, same target. Just as Frederick had planned.

Beside him in most of these meetings was Major Adrian Blackwood—simply Adrian Blackwood now, preferring not to draw attention to his former rank. Resourceful, irreverent, and this week dressed plainly to blend into tavern crowds: worn jacket, scuffed boots, the look of a man who'd seen better days and wasn't particularly bothered by it.

It was a performance, of course. Adrian was always performing. But unlike most actors, he was good enough that people forgot they were watching a show.

His unassuming manner often opened more doors than James's rank ever had. Men talked more freely around someone who seemed harmless, unremarkable. And Adrian had perfected the art of being both.

Adrian unwrapped a scarf as they entered yet another tavern, the third that week, revealing a new persona beneath—this time, a weary clerk. "You might want to hurry things along, Westwood," he said with a sly grin. "London's alive with rumor, and if you delay too long, people might decide your 'fiancée' needs protecting. I hear gentlemen queue up for that sort of thing."

He paused, then added with mock solemnity, "Though I suppose being heroically lame does add to the appeal. Very romantic."

James shot him a dry look, pulse spiking despite himself. "Attend to the matter at hand."

But the thought of Helena—unguarded, alone—dug under his skin. So much for distance. He'd promised himself he wouldn't make that mistake again.

Late on the evening of February third, they moved through shadowed rooms cluttered with half-emptied bottles in a canteen near the edge of Whitehall. An informant—a wiry man with a twitchy gaze and a persistent cough—sat hunched over their table, scanning the door every few seconds. The flickering lantern light made his nervous features starker.

"There's a company," the man murmured, fingers white-knuckled around his cup. "Respectable on paper. Shipping, mostly. Far East routes."

James leaned in, pen poised. "Name?"

The man swallowed hard, shifting. "Sableport Maritime. They've got investors—respectable ones. But…" He glanced toward the door again. "Word is, some of their money's moving in… unusual directions."

"What kind of directions?"

"The kind that don't show up in ledgers." The man's voice dropped to barely a whisper. "Private donations. Political causes. That's all I know. And I'd like to keep breathing, so that's all I'm saying."

He didn't linger—just pushed away from the table and vanished into the crowd.

James exhaled and closed his notebook.

Adrian watched the man vanish, then murmured, "He's terrified. Which means Sableport's influence runs further than we supposed."

"Or someone's making examples," James said grimly.

"Either way"—Adrian lazily swirled the dregs of his ale—"the deeper we dig, the more questions we find."

He arched an eyebrow. "Though I suspect you'd rather be confirming all this with Lady Helena than brooding with me over a pint of ale."

James almost smiled. "Her insight would be useful," he said. Then, after a beat, "And yes."

Adrian's grin widened. "Good. At least you've stopped deceiving yourself. That's something."

James shot him a look. "Don't you have somewhere to be? Someone to spy on?"

"Always." Adrian stood, stretching. "But watching you pine is far more entertaining than most of Frederick's assignments."

OVER THE NEXT few days, he relayed intelligence to Sir Frederick in coded letters and hurried rendezvous. Some messages were passed off by hand in unmarked envelopes. Others, he delivered to the spymaster himself, either at his home or at the Foreign Office Annex off Bloomsbury Street.

Occasionally, he met Helena at a museum or café. It was important for them to be seen together since they were engaged. Too many times she was already there waiting for him, cloak draped over a café chair, tea cooling beside her. She never scolded his lateness—only offered a soft remark about soldiers losing track of time. The teasing helped. More than it should.

Prudence, of course, made her entrance in her usual fashion—flamboyant, exasperating, and oddly efficient. One afternoon, just as James approached to hand Helena a message in the British Museum, Prudence intercepted it mid-motion.

"Really, Major Westwood," she declared, plucking the note from his fingers. "You do like handing things off like a smuggler in a market square. Have some flair next time—I live for spectacle."

James bowed slightly. "Duly noted."

He didn't laugh, but Helena's eyes sparkled. Prudence's flamboyant style was the exact opposite of his own carefully measured approach. It was no wonder Helena had such sharp wit—she clearly came by it honestly.

Bit by bit, the evidence came together: Lord Edward Hawthorne's name surfaced repeatedly in connection to the Black

Rose Society. His upcoming birthday event, whispered to be grand and well attended, was the next likely setting for a critical move. And Lady Clarissa Montague's presence on the guest list only deepened their suspicions.

By February eighth, James had compiled enough intelligence to fill half a journal. That afternoon, he visited Helena at her home to discuss his findings.

She greeted him with calm efficiency and ushered him into a warm parlor, where a small fire burned low in the grate. Prudence lounged on a settee like a woman auditioning for a painting, while Amelia flitted in and out, curious but unaware of the stakes.

James laid the latest documents on the table. "Lord Hawthorne's masquerade party is confirmed—in two days' time. And Clarissa Montague will attend."

Prudence arched a brow. "She's everywhere there's gossip. And if this Black Rose crowd wants a well-dressed audience for their little coup, a birthday party is the place to be."

"A dramatic setting for sedition," James said.

"Is there any other kind?" Prudence replied sweetly.

Helena returned from the hall, the last traces of cold clinging to her cloak. As she reached for the papers, James continued.

"There's also a company that keeps appearing in our inquiries. Sableport Maritime."

Her brow creased. "Sableport..." She paused, thinking. "Lord Thomas mentioned them. At the Duke of Somerset's ball last month."

James's posture shifted. "What did he say?"

"He'd invested. Taken a position on the board, even." Helena's expression darkened slightly. "Lord Hawthorne introduced him to one of the partners. He called it 'an opportunity for men of vision.'"

James exchanged a glance with Prudence. "Hawthorne's recommendation."

"Exactly." Helena folded her arms. "Thomas spoke of expansion to the Far East, impressive projections. It all sounded… legitimate."

"It may well be," James said carefully. "We're only hearing rumors at this stage. Money moving in unusual directions. Nothing concrete."

"But enough to investigate," Helena finished.

"Yes."

A shadow crossed her face. "I should warn him."

James hesitated. The breakup between Helena and Thomas had been painful for both of them—he'd witnessed the aftermath. Reopening that wound would be difficult.

"Can you reach him without raising suspicion?" he asked gently.

"Perhaps. Through mutual acquaintances." She frowned. "Though after our last conversation, he may not welcome advice from me."

"If there's a way to do it quietly," James said, "it might save him from unwitting entanglement. We don't know enough yet to say Sableport is criminal—but if they're funding seditious activity, anyone publicly associated with them could be caught in the net when things unravel."

Helena nodded slowly. "I'll find a way."

Before more could be said, Sir Frederick and Lady Josephine arrived, carrying fresh intelligence and a final guest list.

Helena scanned it quickly. "Lady Beatrice Cavendish will be there. She's loyal to the Crown."

Josephine gave a dry smile. "Let's hope her loyalty can balance out Clarissa's influence. One flutter of her eyelash and half the room's under her spell."

"If only infiltration were that simple," James muttered. "Still, we'll need to make use of every ally."

Prudence leaned forward with a gleam in her eye. "You'll allow me to create a bit of harmless chaos? I've already decided which gown will scandalize half the room and distract the other half."

James gave her a rare smile. "You're a boon, Lady Prudence."

"Don't sound so surprised."

As the final plans were laid, Josephine and Frederick took their leave. Amelia remained behind, pretending not to eavesdrop. James lingered near the table, Helena at his side, their shoulders nearly touching.

"I'll confirm a few last pieces with my contacts," he said. "Before the party, we need to know who's likely to act—and who's already been bought."

Helena looked up, the firelight catching her eyes. "We'll be ready."

Their gaze held—just a moment too long.

Prudence cut in, wagging a finger. "No more gallivanting off alone, you two. You'll allow me to weave my particular brand of distraction, if you know what's good for you." She tapped her chin, bright-eyed, as though envisioning which outrageous gown she might wear to cause a stir.

James half smiled at her theatrics. "We welcome any advantage." He was surprised by how genuine the words felt—he had begun to trust not just Helena, but her entire eccentric family.

When it was time to leave, James stood at the threshold with a sense of something far bigger than infiltration swirling between them. He knew the mission was only growing more perilous, but so was his awareness of her—the way she moved, the way she thought, the way she made everything else fade into background noise.

She offered a small, poised smile, glancing once at his leg with veiled concern. "Until next time, Major."

"Soon," he returned, keeping his voice measured.

The cold night pressed in as he stepped outside, but her quiet presence stayed with him. He told himself he'd leave it there—at the door, in the warmth of her parlor.

But as he limped toward the street, Adrian's words echoed: *At least you've stopped deceiving yourself.*

He'd already taken the first step toward her. And there might be no turning back.

The question was whether she'd take that step too. Or whether he'd be standing alone when this was over, having risked everything for someone who'd chosen safety.

Chapter Eighteen

SHADOWS BENEATH THE MASQUERADE

February 10, 1855 – Hawthorne Estate
Helena

THE CARRIAGE ROCKED to a stop, lanterns casting halos through the winter fog. Helena took James's offered hand, grateful for the steadiness. Outside, Lord Hawthorne's estate rose in sweeping lines, its windows ablaze with candlelight. Music trickled into the courtyard where liveried footmen helped masked guests alight onto the frosty gravel.

Close behind, Aunt Prudence emerged in a flurry of silk and feathers, carrying a trio of black dominos, her sharp eyes glittering behind her half mask. The brim of her flamboyant headdress brushed the carriage's roof. "I do hope there's decent punch," she declared, her voice echoing above the hush of the night. "All this pomp is wasted if I can't wet my throat between witty remarks."

Helena smiled faintly. Prudence never missed a chance to command attention. At her side, James exuded calm authority, though tension showed in his posture. His limp had faded over the past two weeks—barely noticeable now unless she watched for it. Dr. Ramsey's regimen seemed to be working. Still, she caught the way James shifted his weight after standing too long, the careful way he tested the knee before committing his full weight. A long evening of standing and dancing would test him, but he'd never admit it.

She took a steadying breath. This was what they'd been sent to do. Hawthorne was no mere social host—if he truly provided financial backing to the Black Rose Society, tonight might offer the proof they needed.

They were dressed in Italian Renaissance attire. Her burgundy gown shimmered with gold-thread embroidery, its wide panniers hiding cleverly designed compartments. Her half mask glinted with garnets under the lantern light. She moved carefully, wary of being recognized by scent, silhouette, or step despite the disguise.

James wore a knight-inspired costume—a dark tunic cut in fourteenth-century lines, a short mantle trimmed with discreet silver thread, and a soft black satin mask shaped like a visor. The effect was medieval, martial. Fitting.

"Helena," he murmured, leaning in. "Are you ready?"

She nodded, her spine straightening. "Yes. Let's keep our eyes open."

They entered a marble foyer awash with music and movement. Guests in domino cloaks and elaborate masks swept past, trailing perfume and laughter. A masked woman brushed past her, lingering a moment too long. Another figure in white whispered something indistinct before vanishing into the crowd. Her instincts prickled. This was no mere fête—it was a ballroom of masks, and not everyone here was simply a reveler.

At the threshold stood Lord Edward Hawthorne, dressed in a dark cloak with gold trim. His half mask was ornate but didn't hide the precision in his features or the practiced warmth of his smile.

As guests passed, some gave names, others small bows, all maintaining the elaborate fiction that no one truly recognized anyone. Still, Helena and James stepped forward together—deliberately.

"Lady Helena Ashford," she said with a poised smile, her voice clear beneath the mask. "And Major James Westwood. Thank you for including us, my lord."

He inclined his head, his gaze flicking to her gloved hand and then to James. "Ah—Lady Helena. Major. I'm delighted you could attend. In uncertain times, stability is an undervalued treasure. Allow me to offer my congratulations on your engagement."

She curtsied. "Your estate is as magnificent as ever."

Prudence swept forward before he could speak, her fan snapping open with flair.

"My lord," she declared, eyeing the nearest arrangement, "I must protest—these flowers are quite reckless."

He blinked. "Reckless, madam?"

"Entirely," she said, gesturing grandly. "Winter roses beside hothouse orchids? Half the room will suspect a political message. The other half will wonder at the cost."

A flicker of amusement crossed his face. "No statement intended. Only abundance."

"Abundance always speaks," she replied, her voice dropping with conspiratorial warmth. "Especially when one has the means to indulge it. Still, I commend you—nothing unsettles one's rivals like effortless extravagance."

His smile deepened. "Then I'm glad my arrangements meet with your approval."

"Oh, they do," Prudence said breezily, turning to beckon Helena and James forward. "Now, come—this centerpiece is even more provocative. One must be precise about these things."

As she glided on, Hawthorne turned to greet the next arrivals, and Helena and James slipped into the crowd.

Couples glided across the polished floor to the rise and fall of the waltz. Chandeliers sparkled overhead. Crimson-draped pillars framed the dancers like a stage set. Her skirts swished, the weight of hidden ledgers a constant reminder.

A stir rippled near the main staircase as a new arrival descended into the ballroom like a reigning empress entering her court.

Lady Clarissa Montague.

Even masked, she was unmistakable. Crimson silk and black lace, jet beads catching the light with every gesture. The feathered mask echoed the dramatic sweep of her upswept hair, and each step commanded attention without seeming to seek it.

"She does love an entrance," James murmured beside her, his tone dry.

Clarissa paused at the bottom of the stairs, accepting murmured greetings and subtle bows from nearby gentlemen like a woman entirely accustomed to deference. Then she turned with a stage actress's elegance, laughing at something whispered by the Marquis of Elcombe, and took his arm as if she hadn't a care in the world.

Nothing about her demeanor suggested intrigue. If anything, she appeared perfectly at ease—as though scandal and revolution were inconveniences reserved for lesser women.

Helena's gaze lingered. "She's making no effort to conceal herself," she said softly. "If she's involved, she's thinking several moves ahead."

James gave a thoughtful grunt. "Or she's just as she appears— uninvolved."

Helena wasn't so sure. But Clarissa's attention never flicked their way, and within moments she disappeared into the glittering tide of dancers, leaving behind only the scent of rose attar and a wake of admiration.

A flicker of motion caught Helena's eye: Lady Beatrice Cavendish, radiant in a pale-blue gown, her mask perched elegantly atop her hair, swept through the crowd. Helena and James stepped forward to greet her, exchanging the usual pleasantries.

Beatrice looked them up and down. "You two make a striking pair," she teased.

Helena flushed. Beside her, James stiffened ever so slightly, always unsettled when their engagement was treated as more than subterfuge.

"Your engagement has all London whispering," Beatrice continued. "I suspect you'll be the talk of many a ball this season."

Helena smiled politely and rested a hand lightly on his arm—a cue they'd rehearsed, though it felt increasingly natural. He gave a subtle nod, playing his role.

They drifted away just as two powdered gentlemen passed behind them.

"…If Hawthorne pours any more Sableport coin into Parliament," one quipped, "they'll have to rename the Commons the Company's counting house."

"At least then we'd get better tea," the other replied dryly.

The pair vanished, leaving only cologne and implication in their wake.

Helena met James's gaze. He arched a brow. She gave the slightest shake of her head, as if to say, "Did you hear that?" but neither spoke. The jest rang with a note too pointed, too well-informed to be idle gossip. If Hawthorne was buying influence in Parliament…

Nearby, Sir Talon Bridewell appeared in quiet conversation. Helena recognized him from the opera fiasco: He'd nearly caught her eavesdropping on him in the corridor. Under the pretense of examining a tray of refreshments, she and James inched closer. Bridewell's low voice carried hints of fervor.

"…financial guarantees from the East," Bridewell murmured. "Parliament's collapse means profit—if one's positioned correctly."

She only caught fragments: "Profit born of instability," "Foreign investors." "Replace the Crown with capable men."

These weren't reformers. They were orchestrating a coup in polite language.

"If Bridewell is courting Russian money," James whispered beside her, his lips close to her ear, "the Society's influence runs deeper than we feared."

"Helena."

She turned—and startled.

Lord Thomas Chadwick stood just a pace away, her former suitor rendered almost unrecognizable by the simple black mask that failed to hide the strain in his expression. She hadn't expected to see him, let alone have him approach her. Not after the way things had ended. He looked nervous—more than nervous. His eyes flicked to James, then quickly back to her.

"I—beg your pardon. Might I... speak with you? Just for a moment. Privately."

She hesitated. The request caught her off guard—unexpected, though not unwelcome. She felt no lingering affection, no unresolved feeling. That chapter had closed. But she did feel a flicker of concern. Something was wrong.

James's jaw tensed beside her. She could feel the shift in his stance without even looking.

"It's all right," she said gently, placing a gloved hand on James's forearm to steady both him and herself. "Just a moment."

James nodded once, curtly. "I'll be nearby."

He stepped back, close enough to intervene if needed, but far enough to offer them the illusion of privacy.

Helena led Thomas a short distance to the shadowed edge of the ballroom, next to a marble column. The music swelled, giving them cover.

Thomas exhaled, clearly uneasy. "Thank you. I wouldn't have approached, but... I overheard something. Two men speaking near the terrace. They appeared not to notice me at first."

"What did they say?"

"They were talking about investors. Said some should 'mind their business.' The one man looked straight at me as he said it." He ran a hand through his hair. "It felt like a warning."

Helena's stomach turned cold. "Thomas, have you been questioning your Sableport accounts?"

He jerked his chin back, then gave a short, humorless laugh. "That's it exactly. How did you know? I noted some discrepancies. Small ones, at first. I made inquiries. Too many, apparently. I should have paid attention when you questioned Hawthorne's recommendation at the duke's ball. You asked if I trusted him, and I brushed it off. Said the figures were solid." He laughed bitterly. "The figures are solid. It's what's beneath them that's rotten."

Her gaze sharpened. "And now you think you're being watched?"

"I don't think," he said quietly. "I know." His eyes darted toward the crowd. "I've seen too much. I don't understand half of what I've uncovered, but I can feel danger closing in. I've had the feeling I was being followed recently, and then overhearing that conversation…well, I admit they've made me nervous."

Helena's voice softened. "Then you must stop your inquiries. Withdraw entirely. Sever yourself from it, if you can."

He stood a bit straighter. "I'll do exactly that. But Helena—" His voice caught slightly. "Thank you. For listening. For not dismissing me outright. And for giving such excellent advice. I feel like a reckless fool."

Helena swallowed hard. She knew his pride, his need to prove himself. "You've always been careful, Thomas. Diligent. That's not the same as reckless."

His smile was grim. "Maybe I should have seen the signs."

"No," she said softly. "Sableport presents itself as legitimate. Anyone would've seen the company as an opportunity. But they've hidden something beneath it. You can't blame yourself."

He looked relieved to hear it, though tension still lined his frame.

Before she could reply, James reappeared at the edge of the dance floor, his expression unreadable. Helena touched Thomas's arm.

"Be careful," she said. "And don't speak of this again—not until you're certain no one else is listening."

Thomas nodded and stepped back into the crowd, his figure quickly swallowed by masks and candlelight.

Helena was left with a gnawing sense of foreboding. Did Thomas realize just how close he teetered to a lethal game?

She turned toward James, her pulse thrumming. The noose was tightening—for all of them.

As the night deepened, Aunt Prudence launched into a dramatic anecdote at the center of the ballroom, capturing a ring of amused onlookers. Her flamboyant voice soared above the music—exactly the sort of spectacle Helena had hoped she would create. The subtle wave of Prudence's fan signaled Helena that the diversion was in place.

Under that cover, Helena guided James toward a less-trafficked corridor branching off the main hall where Aunt Prudence had hidden their black domino cloaks. They draped them over their costumes and switched their masks for plain black ones, further obscuring their silhouettes. She'd memorized the map showing the layout and knew exactly where to go to find Lord Hawthorne's office.

Helena's heart pounded as they crept along carved paneling, the muffled waltz receding behind them.

They found the study easily. The door itself was unremarkable—carved oak, polished to a discreet sheen—but once inside, the room was dark, with a velvet-draped window and thick rugs muffling their steps. Helena lit an ornate porcelain oil lamp and scanned the room.

Helena noted how the luxurious trappings clashed with an undeniable sense of secrecy. A massive mahogany desk stood near the single tall window draped in dark velvet. Her lamp flickered low, casting the corners in dusky shadows.

"There's something concealed here," she said. "Secret rooms always leave a clue."

James gestured to the eastern bookcase. "That wall's deep enough."

They split up. He searched near a tapestry. "I've found something. A seam of sorts." He pressed against it.

A muffled click.

The panel gave slightly, revealing a narrow recess—barely more than a cupboard. Empty shelves. Dust. A forgotten walking stick.

"A decoy," he muttered.

"Or misdirection," Helena said. "We keep looking."

"Or there's no secret room and there's nothing to find," James said.

Helena turned toward the desk. "No. There's more. There has to be."

He watched her. "You're sure?"

"Yes."

She noticed the worn patch in the rug—faint but clear. She crouched, fingers brushing the spot where the pile had been rubbed thin.

"Here," she whispered. "This is wear from a hidden door. Repeated use."

She rose and ran her hand along the adjacent panel, searching. James moved in beside her, more careful now. "Let's try together."

With careful pressure, she pressed the inconspicuous edge. A softer click echoed this time, and the panel shifted. The hidden door creaked open, revealing the narrow chamber beyond.

This was it.

Helena exhaled, the rush of exhilaration threading through her limbs. That moment of doubt hadn't broken her focus—but it had reminded her just how high the stakes were.

Inside, the narrow chamber was packed: ledgers, bound envelopes, crates with obscure shipping stamps.

Helena set the lantern down and opened the nearest ledger. Russian funding. Sableport Maritime. Cryptic references to "The Raven." Bridewell's name appeared multiple times.

This was it. Proof.

She gestured to James. He scanned the page, expression darkening. "This is it. Hawthorne's in deep. This will damn him."

As James packed ledgers into her panniers, a marginal note

caught her eye: "investor divergences" and "contingency plans for overly curious parties."

Thomas's name wasn't mentioned explicitly. But the implication was.

They'd warned him tonight for a reason.

She tucked the entire ledger into the large basket hidden under her skirt's right-side pannier. James did the same with another on her left side. They were heavy, but her costume had been designed for just this task. They stepped back out into the main room.

Footsteps outside. The rattle of a doorknob.

"I locked it," James whispered.

They closed the secret door behind them. Helena set the lamp on Hawthorne's desk and lowered the flame. James pulled her close, lifted his mask just enough to grin—and kissed her.

The lock turned.

Lord Hawthorne stood in the doorway, mask in hand, eyes narrowed.

He took in their embrace in the dim light, the black dominos hiding their costumes.

"Who are you?" His voice cut through the stale air. "This is my private study."

She stayed in character, leaning into James, but her pulse thundered in her ears.

"We were looking for a private spot," James said, voice gruff. "This suited our needs perfectly."

Hawthorne stepped closer. "Strange place to tryst. Especially with a forced lock and a scent of lamp oil." His gaze flicked toward the wall.

James shifted to block his view.

Helena stepped forward with a soft laugh. "Perhaps your staff was careless. The door was open and we came in. We've done nothing but steal a moment."

Hawthorne studied her. "Someone broke into this room a few months ago. I keep it locked now. Don't lie to me."

Her hand moved toward the lamp.

"My lord," she said, voice low and intimate, "does this strike you as the conduct of thieves?"

James added, "If we meant to steal from you, we'd have taken greater care to leave no trace."

Hawthorne's eyes narrowed. "Or you're arrogant enough to think theatrics can mask your true intentions."

Her breath caught. Her fingers tightened on the wick regulator.

"Not until I understand precisely what you're doing here," Hawthorne said, stepping closer.

She twisted it.

The flame went out.

Darkness swallowed the room.

Chapter Nineteen

ESCAPING THE ESTATE

February 10, 1855 – Hawthorne Estate
James

D ARKNESS SMOTHERED THE room in an instant.

James heard Hawthorne's sharp intake of breath, followed by a snapped, "Stay where you are."

A single heartbeat throbbed, urging him to protect Helena—then instinct took over.

James dropped into a defensive stance. His leg held for the moment. No time to worry about it now.

Hawthorne lunged. They collided—hard. James seized his wrist and twisted sharply, driving him backward. Hawthorne staggered, came back swinging.

Pain flared in James's knee as he pivoted. He ignored it. The leg held. Good enough.

Helena hovered just behind, sharp and poised. Whenever Hawthorne tried to gain the upper hand, she darted in—grabbing at his coat, shoving his arm, never hesitating.

Hawthorne fought like a man with everything to lose. James shoved him hard. He crashed into a chair, its legs scraping loudly.

"Out," he told Helena. "Now."

The door stood wide open—an escape route. She slipped

through first. James pivoted, slammed his shoulder into Hawthorne's side, then darted after her.

He slammed the door shut then seized the key still lodged in the lock and twisted it hard. The bolt slid home with a satisfying clunk just as Hawthorne's boots pounded the floor beyond the door.

"Help!"

Answering cries. Rapid footsteps. Reinforcements coming.

James grabbed Helena's hand. They ran, footfalls sharp against polished stone.

"Keep up," he said.

"I am," she shot back, breathless.

They veered into a wider hallway leading back to the ballroom. In one fluid motion, James yanked off his black domino and tossed it behind a curtain. Helena followed suit, her hands clutching at her panniers with their hidden contents.

"Can anyone tell?" she asked.

James scanned her. "Not at all," he assured, glancing down at the wide curve of her skirts.

For a fraction of a moment, they were still—breathing hard, hearts pounding. Then the distant strains of violins and lively conversation swept them back to their purpose.

From beneath his mantle, James retrieved their original masks and handed hers over. They slipped them on, not missing a beat as they stepped past the velvet drapes onto the swirling dance floor.

The ballroom burst around them—light, sound, color. Music swelled. Dancers turned. No one noticed the two figures rejoining the crowd.

But James noticed everything as footmen in Hawthorne's livery rushed to one entrance, eyes sweeping the room.

Helena saw them too, eyes widening behind her mask. They'd barely made it back in time, but they still needed cover, fast.

Prudence emerged from the throng, smiling as if nothing

were amiss. "Trouble?" she murmured.

James dipped his head. "Footmen. Searching for us."

Prudence's gaze cut to the doorway. "Leave that to me."

She drifted away with practiced ease, veering toward the refreshment table. A massive crystal punch bowl, flanked by decorative candlesticks, sat poised like an accident waiting to happen.

Prudence paused, then gave the enormous bowl a calculated nudge with her elbow.

It toppled.

Crystal shattered. Brandy ignited in a burst of flame across the floor—not a towering blaze, but enough to send shrieks rippling through the crowd. Guests trampled each other's hems as they scrambled back, hair feathers bobbing in panic.

Prudence stepped back with a look of saintly surprise. "How unfortunate," she said with the faintest smirk.

James couldn't quite smother a wry grin. Chaos now reigned. Hawthorne's men were swallowed by the mass of terrified guests rushing for the exits.

He touched Helena's arm. "Now. While we can." They skirted a toppling candelabra and ducked out a pair of doors that led to a moonlit garden path behind Hawthorne's estate.

A figure emerged from the hedge-lined archway ahead. James tensed, hand moving instinctively toward his concealed knife—then he recognized the silhouette.

"Mrs. Heatherington," Helena said, relief clear in her voice.

Violet stepped from the shadows, still masked but unmistakable. Another figure moved behind her—taller, broader. The Duke of Westbridge.

"Our mutual friend sent us. Thought you might need an alternate exit," Evan said, his voice low and measured. "Violet predicted things would go badly when you didn't return to the ballroom after twenty minutes."

"Thirty," Violet corrected. She pulled a folded document from inside her cloak. "And I was right."

She pressed it into Helena's hands. Heavier than expected—multiple pages, not just one.

"Shipping manifests," Violet said quietly. "Evan traced them through three intermediary firms before finding the connection. Hawthorne's been moving cargo through Sableport that doesn't appear in any official ledgers."

James glanced at Evan. "How did you get these?"

Evan's expression was unreadable behind his mask. "I bought a minor stake in one of the shell companies. Gave me access to their books." He paused. "Legally, of course. I'm a proprietor reviewing his investments."

"Brilliant," James said.

"Thorough," Evan corrected. "There's a difference."

Violet's gaze flicked between Helena and James. "The manifests show weapons. Small arms, mostly. Shipped to addresses in London that don't exist." She paused. "Someone is stockpiling arms."

Helena's fingers tightened on the papers. "For the Society."

"Most likely," Violet confirmed. "But we need more proof before the Crown can act. These manifests are a start, but they're not enough for arrests."

"Combined with what we took from Hawthorne's study—" James began.

"—it might be," Violet finished. She studied Helena for a moment. "You found something, then. In his office."

It wasn't a question.

Helena nodded. "Ledgers. Financial records connecting Hawthorne to the Society. Russian funding. Bridewell's name appears multiple times."

Something passed between the two women—a moment of recognition. They were both doing the same work, different methods. Violet through financial investigation, Helena through social infiltration.

"Frederick will want both," Violet said. "The ledgers prove conspiracy. The manifests prove they plan to act."

Evan touched Violet's elbow. "We should go. If Hawthorne's men are searching the grounds—"

"They won't look for us," Violet said calmly. "We're respectable guests leaving a party that's gone chaotic. But you two"—she looked at James and Helena—"make yourselves scarce. Now."

"Our carriage is waiting," James said.

Violet's eyes crinkled behind her mask. "Good. Then go." She stepped back into the shadows, Evan following. "We'll send word to Frederick about what we found. You do the same."

And then they were gone, melting into the hedge maze like ghosts.

Helena tucked the manifests into her panniers alongside the ledgers. The combined weight of the evidence pressed against her hip.

"Come on," James said.

As they left the garden and burst out into the estate's front courtyard, they found themselves caught up in a flood of frantic guests.

A line of carriages sat along the drive, wheels crunching in the gravel as horses shifted anxiously in reaction to the panicked people streaming through the doors.

One driver stood out. Nathaniel Clarke, half risen from his perch, reins clenched tight. He spotted them and nearly fell from the box.

"Major—hell's teeth, you're lucky I came back to the carriage when I did—"

James skidded to a stop, his knee barking in complaint. "We need to leave. Now."

Nathaniel didn't argue. "Right. Up, quickly."

Helena climbed in first, her face pale but determined. James followed. Footmen spilled out onto the steps behind them, scanning for fleeing intruders.

Prudence bustled out the main entrance, cloaks clutched in her arms, cheeks flushed with glee. She clambered in, thrusting a wrap at Helena. "Put this on before you catch your death."

Nathaniel snapped the reins. The carriage jolted forward, wheels grinding across cobblestone.

Prudence jolted back in her seat, then settled herself. "That punch bowl never stood a chance," she murmured with satisfaction.

Inside, the carriage lanterns cast a warm glow. James noticed a bruise forming on Helena's arm.

"Are you hurt?"

She shook her head. "No. You?"

"Fine." His leg ached, but it had held. That was enough.

Opposite them, Prudence fanned herself, eyes gleaming. "Glorious evening," she declared. "Really, I've always suspected brandy had dramatic potential. Now it's confirmed."

James's mouth curved. "Your distraction exceeded expectations."

"One should always aim for excellence," Prudence replied primly.

From the driver's box, Nathaniel shouted back, "Next time try not to set the 'ouse on fire, all roight? I'd like to keep me job."

James huffed a quiet laugh as he shifted in the carriage seat, easing the pressure from his knee. The fight with Hawthorne had aggravated it—he'd feel that tomorrow. But they'd escaped. Worth it.

Helena shifted as well, settling against his side as the carriage bumped along. She was warm. Alive. Safe.

They'd done it.

James looked out at the moonlit road ahead. The ledgers pressed against Helena's hip—Violet's manifests hidden alongside them—enough evidence to bring Hawthorne down. But exposure came with a price. He would know they'd been stolen. Retaliation would be swift. The mission had succeeded. Now came the dangerous part.

Chapter Twenty

PRESENTING THE EVIDENCE

February 10, 1855 – London-Foreign Office Annex
Helena

T HE CARRIAGE SLOWED before a modest Georgian townhouse on a quiet stretch just off Bloomsbury Street. To anyone else, unremarkable—just another brick façade with curtained windows and a brass plaque: *Foreign Office—Annex.*

But Helena knew better after her visit here last month.

She stepped down into the crisp night air, the weight of her stolen documents still tucked in the baskets hidden beneath her panniers. James followed, steady as ever, and Prudence descended behind them with a rustle of silk and a satisfied sigh.

The door opened before they reached it. Mr. Leech, the Annex's ever-watchful gatekeeper, peered at them through the frosted fanlight and swung it wide with his usual brisk efficiency. Thin as a quill and twice as sharp, he gave Helena and James a once-over that suggested he already knew everything that had transpired.

"If you're here to requisition more paper," he said dryly, "I regret to inform you the Ministry's squandered its budget on nonsense for the month."

Helena offered a weary smile. "We've brought our own this

time."

James gave a brief nod. "We're expected."

Leech stepped aside without further commentary. "Then do try not to linger in the draft."

They stepped into a narrow hall lit by a single oil lamp. Dark wainscoting lined the walls, and a long runner softened their footfalls. Even in the hush of midnight, the place hummed with quiet intent—a space that knew secrets and held them tightly.

Prudence's voice broke the stillness. "Such understated charm. It's like slipping into a secret drawer."

Leech offered no response, merely gestured them forward and led the way toward the rear of the ground floor. The waiting room was modest, gentlemanly—an armchair here, a faintly smoldering hearth there, and a tray of untouched tea already laid out on the sideboard, as if anticipation had preceded them.

He paused at the base of the stairs, head tilting slightly as though listening to some internal confirmation. Then, without ceremony, he said, "They're ready for you upstairs."

James gave a nod of thanks, and they followed him to the tight stairwell. Helena took each step with measured care, the hidden weight beneath her skirts growing heavier with every tread.

They emerged into the council room—a long chamber dominated by a wide oak table, maps pinned with tags along the wall. A fireplace glowed behind Sir Frederick Woolsy, who stood with Lady Josephine at his side. Her posture was stiff, knuckles white around a dispatch she clearly didn't like.

Sir Frederick's gaze swept the trio. "You wasted no time," he said evenly.

Helena curtsied. "We didn't dare."

She stepped forward and slipped her hands through the slits above her panniers. The gown's hidden framework—reinforced stays and lightweight baskets—had supported the documents all evening. The carriage ride had given her shoulders relief, but climbing the stairs to Frederick's office had reminded her just how heavy the ledgers were.

Now, one by one, she withdrew them: coded ledgers, creased letters, foreign dispatches with brittle seals, and a map inked with names they barely dared speak aloud. Each piece landed on the polished table with a soft thump.

When the last document was laid down, she straightened. The weight was gone. She could breathe easier.

James stood beside her. Steady. Present.

Behind them, Prudence let out a pleased hum, clearly delighted by the theatrical reveal. Helena's gaze remained fixed on the table.

Helena exhaled. "We found account books, coded messages, correspondence suggesting foreign backing—including Russian. One ledger shows money passing through successive parties. The names are… notable."

She opened the topmost ledger and skimmed quickly. Her heart stumbled.

"Montague," she said aloud. "Lord Edwin Montague."

Lady Josephine's head snapped around. "Lady Clarissa's late husband?"

"Yes," Helena confirmed. "And not just a token amount. Look at the figure listed."

James leaned in. "That's a substantial sum."

Sir Frederick frowned. "He's been dead three years."

Lady Josephine's tone was crisp. "Clarissa controls the estate now. If that money remained active—if she benefited from it— she's implicated. Intentionally or not."

"James thought he saw her at the Black Cat Tavern," Helena added quietly.

Josephine pursed her lips. "If Clarissa's turning a blind eye to Sableport's questionable activities…"

Sir Frederick tapped the table. "This doesn't prove guilt, but it gives us a financial thread to pull. Follow the flow of money from her late husband's accounts. See if Clarissa ever redirected it. If we find clean hands, we can clear her name. If not…"

James's voice dropped. "Then she stands revealed as a traitor."

Helena nodded, scanning the list. Then she froze.

Thomas Chadwick.

His name, the sum beside it staggering. Far more than Lord Montague's.

Her hand moved before she could think. Slid a sheet over the ledger.

The others kept talking. No one had seen it.

She'd warned him at the masquerade. Told him to divest. But if he'd invested this much—if Frederick saw this—Thomas would be arrested alongside the conspirators.

Later, she told herself. *Once I understand what it means. Once I know if he's a fool or a traitor.*

Her chest tightened. She'd just hidden evidence from her own spymaster.

James added, "We overheard Sir Talon Bridewell discussing large foreign investments, likely Russian. He mentioned Parliament's collapse as an occasion for profit. If he wasn't referring to Sableport, I'll eat Prudence's hat."

Josephine's eyes darkened. "So they're not just whispering—they're preparing to seize the reins."

Sir Frederick let out a slow breath, his features hardening. "And preparing for profit. Classic sedition cloaked in gentlemanly investments."

James's voice dropped a shade. "They're not just planning upheaval. They've laid their plans beyond the upheaval—who gains, who falls. That kind of confidence means they've already purchased influence."

Helena laid down another packet of notes, thoughts racing. Thomas's confession at the masquerade. His fear. His investment.

Why had he invested so much? Did he know what he was involved in?

James, close enough to notice her distraction, caught her eye. A silent question.

She gave a small shake of her head. *Later.*

He nodded once and turned back to Frederick.

Prudence, examining a scribbled letter, chimed in. "Here—foreign names. Cyrillic, if I'm not mistaken." She tapped the paper with a gloved finger. "We'll need to know if these are diplomats or just hired hands."

Her calm tone and razor-sharp comment startled Sir Frederick, who paused and studied her as though seeing her for the first time. "Lady Prudence, you've a keen eye."

Prudence smiled, serene. "People underestimate me. I find it useful."

Sir Frederick turned back to the documents spread before him. "The scale is immense. We'll need to move quickly." He looked up at Helena and James. "The gala is in two weeks. By then, we need to know exactly who we're dealing with and what they're planning."

Helena felt a flicker of pride. They were no longer shadows. They were guiding what would come next.

The meeting wrapped up quickly. Frederick gathered the documents with care.

Helena turned for the door. James followed.

In the foyer, Prudence murmured, "I'll sleep soundly knowing I caused a spectacle and unearthed Russian spies. Splendid work, if I do say so."

Helena allowed herself a faint laugh, though her thoughts kept circling back to Thomas's name in that ledger.

James leaned close. "We make a good team."

Helena glanced at him. "I didn't expect that."

"But you don't mind?"

She thought of Hawthorne's study. James stepping between her and danger without hesitation. The way he'd kept his head when hers nearly spun.

"You locked the door with Hawthorne's own key," she said. "That was quick thinking."

"I had motivation."

She turned toward him, shoulders nearly touching. "We're more than a good team. We're a capable one."

James met her gaze. "And you're far more formidable than anyone gives you credit for."

She looked away, faintly embarrassed. But she didn't move.

A throat cleared.

Prudence stood ready at the door. "Shall we? I'm eager for a pillow and less eager to watch you two make moon eyes."

Outside, Nathaniel Clarke sat slumped on the coach box, reins in hand, scowl on his face.

"Took you long enough," he muttered. "Backside's half frozen."

Prudence swept toward him. "Next time, bring a blanket. Or better, a better attitude."

Nathaniel groaned. "Just get in the carriage."

James helped Helena up. Inside, they settled onto worn cushions, the glow of streetlamps slipping past.

The documents were delivered. Frederick would act. The Society would be exposed.

But Thomas's name was still hidden in her memory, a secret she'd kept from her own spymaster.

Helena closed her eyes, exhaustion settling in. She'd deal with that tomorrow. Tonight, they'd won.

James sat across from her, steady and present.

For now, that was enough.

Chapter Twenty-One

SHADOWS AND STRATEGIES

February 12, 1855
James

T HE HUSH FELL the moment they crossed the threshold.

James felt it like a shift in atmospheric pressure—the swirl of silks and perfume slowed, a collective intake of breath barely concealed behind fans and raised brows. Not for him. For Helena.

"A fire at Lord Hawthorne's estate, wasn't it?" someone whispered near a marble column. "During the masquerade. How terribly dramatic."

"I heard Lady Helena was present," came another voice, too delighted by scandal, "with Major Westwood."

James clenched his jaw, his fingers tightening around his gloves. A full day had passed, and still, the embers of last night's chaos glowed—transformed now into whispers and sidelong glances. The ball had ended in flames. The rumors had not.

The murmurs stirred a memory: Sir Frederick's office, that morning. Pipe smoke hanging thick. The folder sliding across the desk.

"Lord Hawthorne is in custody," Frederick had said. "We moved quickly—arrested him at dawn before he could flee or destroy more evidence. The documents you retrieved gave us enough leverage to act."

James had exhaled. "So it's done?"

Josephine had corrected him. "Hardly. Hawthorne is a thread, not the tapestry. Pull one, the rest tightens. He destroyed his remaining documents before we arrived—burned them in his study's fireplace. But what you brought was damning enough."

Now, with those words echoing in his mind, James offered Helena a small tilt of his head, a silent cue to press forward.

But before they could make it more than a few steps into the glittering crush, a dowager in voluminous lavender silk intercepted them, her ostrich-plumed fan already mid-flutter.

"My dear Lady Helena," she trilled, "you *must* tell me—*were* you at Lord Hawthorne's masquerade last night? I heard there was a fire!" She leaned in, eyes gleaming with theatrical horror. "They say it nearly engulfed the ballroom. And someone threw a punch bowl?"

Helena opened her mouth, only to find no suitable reply available.

Prudence, of course, swept in without hesitation. "Not thrown, dear Lady Crowthorne—*toppled*. Though in fairness, it didn't survive the experience. One might say it shattered under the weight of the evening's excitement."

The dowager blinked. "So you *were* there?"

"Oh, certainly. But I assure you, the fire was really quite democratic—no one important was harmed. Except the brandy. *Tragic loss.*"

Helena gave a delicate cough to mask a laugh. "Aunt, perhaps we should let Lady Crowthorne retrieve her shawl before she faints from the scandal."

"Of course," Prudence said sweetly, taking Helena's arm. "But truly, it was a perfectly respectable blaze. Very tasteful. No singed wigs or scorched costumes at all."

They moved off, leaving the dowager frozen in place, fan fluttering like a trapped bird.

The drawing room glittered, each guest arranged like a museum piece: poised, polished, and ready to feign shock or outrage depending on where the gossip fell. Lady Marlborough's townhouse had never looked more theatrical.

Prudence plunged into the crowd ahead of them, fan fluttering like a war banner. Helena walked beside James, spine straight, expression serene despite the scrutiny. She knew the stakes. Tonight wasn't about comfort—it was about keeping up appearances, preserving the illusion of normalcy before suspicion spread too far.

James guided her toward the dining room. Near the hearth, lounging with false ease and a glass of port, was Sir Talon Bridewell—traitor, opportunist, reformist in name only. James's pulse ticked upward. Lord Hawthorne had been dealt with. Bridewell was next on his list.

A footman directed James to a seat at the glittering table— conveniently close to Bridewell. Helena, with Prudence, was led to the opposite side.

The chair's rigid edge bit into the back of James's knee the moment he sat. He suppressed a grimace. Of course the fashionable furniture would be designed by someone who'd never spent an evening standing on an injured leg. He kept still, knowing that shifting would only draw eyes.

Dinner blurred. James kept his expression neutral as conversation rose and fell like a tide. Bridewell, ever bold, was holding court.

"…a monarchy built on birthright alone is bound to falter," Bridewell said, swirling his wine. "Britain needs men of merit. Visionaries. Men chosen for capability, not titles."

James raised his glass. "An interesting notion." Deliberately vague. Just intrigued enough.

Bridewell's smile sharpened.

Let him think he's recruiting me, James thought. *The bolder he gets, the easier he'll be to trap.*

But even as James played his part, Josephine's voice haunted him: *Cut one thread, and another pulls tight.*

They'd exposed Hawthorne. But they hadn't stopped the Society.

Not yet.

Later, when the ladies withdrew to the salon and the men lingered over cigars and port, Bridewell tried to manipulate Lord Marlborough into complaining about Queen Victoria's husband, Prince Albert, but he refused, immediately retiring to the salon.

When the men rejoined the ladies in the salon, James scanned the crowd for Helena. He found her in quiet conversation with Lord Thomas Chadwick near the far window.

Thomas's normally genial expression looked strained. Helena's posture was too careful—that particular stillness she adopted when worried.

James's chest tightened. Not from suspicion. From jealousy. Unreasonable, but real.

Thomas gave a strained smile. Helena touched his arm briefly, then glanced across the room. Her eyes met James's.

He started toward her, but she gave a small shake of her head. *Later.*

It stung more than it should have. He had no claim. But the pretense was becoming harder to maintain—especially when she turned back to Chadwick, leaving James—her pretend fiancé—standing alone.

AN HOUR LATER, they left the townhouse in near silence. Prudence climbed into the carriage with exaggerated weariness, fanning herself and closing her eyes like an overworked actress. James wasn't fooled.

As the carriage jostled into motion, he spoke. "You seem shaken after speaking with Chadwick. What happened?"

Helena's fingers smoothed the folds of her gown. "He's heavily invested in Sableport, and tonight he received an anonymous note. It said: *'You're asking the wrong questions. Best to stop before you lose more than money.'"*

James sat forward. "That's not a warning. That's a threat."

"I know." Her voice stayed calm, but her fingers worried the edge of her glove. "If the Society sees him as a liability, they'll silence him."

"You're certain he's unaware?"

She nodded. "He's idealistic. Ambitious. But blind to risk. He didn't recognize the signs until too late."

James hesitated. "You still care for him."

"Not like that." Immediate. Certain. "We don't suit. I know that now. But that doesn't mean I'll let him be used—or killed."

The honesty eased something in him. Though it still stung that Chadwick had been her first choice once. He pushed that thought aside.

"What do you want to do?"

"Encourage him to step away. Withdraw his funds. Convince him to leave London if I can manage it."

James studied her. "You'll need help."

Her mouth twitched. "Yes. Yours."

He gave a slow nod. "Then you have it."

The gratitude in her eyes cut through him, sharper than any blade.

THE NEXT MORNING, they stood in Sir Frederick's office at the Foreign Office Annex, the chill of the February air still clinging to their coats. The hearth burned low, casting amber light against the locked cabinets and shadowed maps that lined the walls. The weight of what came next pressed down with the same gravity as the ledgers they'd delivered only days before.

Sir Frederick didn't look up immediately. He stood at the

long table, hands braced on either side of a sheaf of intelligence reports, the candlelight catching the silver at his temples.

"Pretend you have a faltering loyalty to the crown," he said at last, eyes sharp. "That's the only way forward. Bridewell is growing bolder, and the Society is expanding its net. You must step into its path before others are caught unawares. You'll be positioned as sympathizers—quietly discontent, seeking change."

James straightened. "Understood."

Helena gave a single nod. Steady. Resolute.

Lady Josephine, seated near the shuttered window, added, "Build your roles on truth. James, the Crown left you disillusioned after Crimea. And Helena—your father's fall from grace has already shaped public perception. You need only let the Society believe it's soured you completely."

Sir Frederick turned to them, his voice low but resolute. "We cannot afford hesitation. The Black Rose Society must believe you are theirs before we can learn what they intend next."

James nodded slowly. The strategy was sound—thorough, calculated—but the vulnerability of it made his skin itch. He hated the idea of stepping into enemy sympathies, of pretending to align with the very men he'd vowed to unmask.

Sir Frederick studied them both. "You're uniquely positioned for this. Lady Helena, your father trained you well—observation, deduction, the maintenance of composure under pressure. His lessons will serve you now more than ever."

Helena's jaw tightened at the mention of her father, but she inclined her head. "Yes, sir."

"And you, James…" Frederick's gaze turned solemn. "Your incursions behind enemy lines during the war prepared you more than you realize. You've operated with limited support, gathered intelligence under fire, and navigated hostile territory."

The memory hit: smoke, gunfire, stillness. Twelve men. Every one of them gone. He'd trusted the wrong informant, led them into an ambush. Only he came back.

He forced his voice steady. "I understand the stakes."

Sir Frederick didn't press, but his expression acknowledged the weight behind James's words.

"Adrian Blackwood arrives tomorrow," Frederick said. "He'll work with you on fieldcraft—disguises, false identities, code phrases, sleight of hand. He'll test you until you can lie convincingly to men who might kill you for hesitating."

Helena shifted slightly. "We'll work from my home?"

Sir Frederick nodded. "Your residence offers both discretion and familiarity. We need a controlled environment—somewhere trusted, with minimal comings and goings. Inform your staff that you're retiring to the country for a few days. Give them leave to visit their own families in the meantime."

Helena gave a small nod. "That should raise no questions. Most of them haven't had time away since Epiphany."

Frederick's expression remained serious. "Exactly. Let it seem like an act of seasonal generosity. Meanwhile, we'll use that quiet to prepare you both for what's ahead."

Prudence, ever buoyant, clasped her hands together. "Marvelous. I do adore a rehearsal."

As they stepped into the corridor, the hush of the Annex settling around them once more, James glanced at Helena. "Are you certain you're ready for this? It's no small thing—feigning disloyalty to the Crown. Turning your father's disgrace into strategy. That's not easy."

She paused beside a tall, arched window, where the morning sky hung dull and silver. Her gaze swept the street below, but her voice was steady. "It isn't easy. But it's necessary." She turned to face him fully, chin lifting. "If we're to stop the Society, we can't flinch from difficult choices. I'd rather use my family's fall from grace for something meaningful than let it remain a shadow over my name."

James studied her, the strength in her bearing unmistakable. He touched her elbow. "I understand the cost. You're not walking into this blindly."

Her expression softened, but her eyes stayed sharp. "We risk exposure on both sides. If we succeed, no one will know how close we came to ruin. If we fail, we may be remembered as traitors."

"But not to each other," James said.

Silence. Then Helena nodded. "Then let's make it count."

His hand lingered a moment longer. *I won't let you fall alone.*

In the carriage ride home, Prudence was already deep in strategizing mode—though not, it seemed, with any concern for realism.

"We could say you're both fleeing scandal," she mused, fanning herself briskly. "A torrid love affair exposed by a misplaced letter and a parrot that won't stop repeating your secrets. Quite tragic."

James raised an eyebrow. "A parrot?"

"Or"—she leaned forward, eyes sparkling—"we claim you're working on an ambitious book. A *Naturalist's Guide to Courting*, written from the perspective of a disgraced noblewoman and a disillusioned major. Research, of course. Deeply immersive."

Helena bit back a smile. "Would the publisher be sympathetic to treason charges?"

"Only if it made the third edition more salacious," Prudence replied without missing a beat.

James caught Helena's gaze across the carriage. Despite the looming danger, something in her expression—steady, wry, quietly daring—matched his own resolve.

They were already in enemy territory. Soon, they'd be walking straight into the lion's den.

But for the first time in years, he didn't feel alone.

Chapter Twenty-Two

SECRETS AND SYNERGY

February 12, 1855
Helena

T**HE HOUSE WAS** unusually quiet with the staff on leave. Prudence's footsteps echoed as she swept to the door.

"Come in, come in," she declared, ushering James and Adrian inside. "I promise to provide tea and minimal interruptions— unless I decide your new traitorous backstory needs... embellishment." She winked. Adrian offered a surprised smile.

Helena led them to the library, sunlight filtering through tall windows. She met James's steady gaze, drawing reassurance from it. After days of tension and upheaval, she welcomed the calm of focused planning—even if the stakes were perilously high.

Adrian spread a stack of blank pages across the desk. "We'll start with your false pretenses—why you'd join the Black Rose Society. Keep close to the truth. Too much invention, you'll be caught in inconsistency."

James nodded. "We'll cite personal grievances. My experiences in the Crimea. Helena's father's fall from favor."

Helena sat straighter. "The Society must believe we've turned because the Crown failed us. That we're useful—and angry."

Prudence hummed. "And my part? Disillusioned dowager?

Perhaps the monarchy refused to sponsor my charitable efforts to build a home for displaced squirrels."

"Stick to the truth," Helena said quietly. "Your anger after losing your husband. The Crown's investigation never gave you answers."

Prudence's smile faltered. "No," she said. "They never did." A pause, then she cleared her throat. "I was never quite the same after that."

Adrian moved on without pressing. "Let's focus on Helena and James for now."

They worked in companionable silence, shaping motivations. Helena spoke of her father—a respected diplomat who unraveled after her mother's death. His grief made him unreliable. Missed meetings. Confused names. The Foreign Office quietly pushed him aside. No scandal. No fanfare. Just silence.

James, seated beside her, spoke of the war.

"The Crimea was chaos," he said. "We lost men to frostbite because someone forgot to requisition boots. We were given food for two days on a ten-day march. Officers ignored maps. Orders made no sense. And when I brought home the dead— men I'd trained, fought beside—no one in Whitehall wanted to know why."

He looked down at the page, voice taut. "One of my own captains leaked our position to the Russians. I all but proved it. Whitehall had no interest. No inquiry. No consequences. Just silence."

When he looked up, his eyes held something she'd never seen before—something raw and unguarded.

"I spent a year rebuilding myself. Not just my leg—my faith. I wanted to believe in the cause. I still do. But I can't forget how quickly they turned their backs."

Adrian stilled, pen forgotten. "That kind of pain convinces. The Society will believe it."

James gave a bitter huff. "They'd be right to. By every outward measure, I'm perfect for them. Disgraced. Bitter. Skilled.

Principled enough to feel betrayed and dangerous enough to matter."

Helena touched his hand.

"They'll see all that," she said. "What they won't see is the choice you made. You had every reason to turn your back on the Crown—but you didn't. That's what makes you dangerous to them."

The sharp edge in his eyes eased. "Let's hope they never realize the difference."

The heaviness lingered until Prudence broke in brightly. "Let's say your turning point was a dog tax. A loyal hound named Parliament, silenced by bureaucracy."

James cracked a reluctant smile. Helena rolled her eyes. "An Irish wolfhound? And Parliament howled through every cabinet meeting, I assume?"

"Endlessly," Prudence said, deadpan. "A true voice for the people."

Even Adrian chuckled. The tension eased, though not entirely.

Still, it was hard work. Blurring truth with fiction required more than clever phrasing. Every resentment they created was rooted in something real. No matter how many absurdities Prudence threw in—"What if the final straw was an over-boiled egg?"—the weight remained.

Just as their rhythm returned, a sharp knock broke the moment like a dropped teacup.

Prudence peeked through the lace curtain and groaned. "Oh, *good*. Beatrice Cavendish. Likely bearing gossip. Or a plot. Possibly both."

"She didn't write ahead to say she'd be calling," Helena said, surprised.

"Of course not. That would give us time to hide."

Moments later, Beatrice breezed in, clutching a paper-wrapped box like a diplomatic dispatch.

"Did you hear?" she said. "The Duke of Wexford's daughter

fainted in Madame Giroux's shop—between the feathers and French netting. Your engagement was the final blow, apparently. It's her third season, poor thing. She's been paraded like a prize calf, and now you've gone and secured yourself a war hero. It's all very dramatic."

She set the box down. "I've come to recruit you for my next salon. I need clever company, and you're currently the talk of London. The usual lot is unbearably tedious."

Then, pausing, she glanced around. "Where is your staff? I had to knock. Twice."

"On leave," Helena said smoothly. "We're enjoying a few days of quiet."

Beatrice sniffed. "A brilliant idea, if unusual. I never trust anyone who insists on being observed while eating breakfast."

Before she could delve more deeply, Prudence swept in. "Come, Beatrice. I must show you Lady Willoughby's fichu disaster. It looks like she stole it off a distressed curtain rod."

With practiced ease, she propelled Beatrice into another room.

Helena exhaled in the quiet, returning to the library with James. The scent of leather and ink was grounding. As they cleared code phrases and half-written notes from the table, their hands brushed again—once, then again.

"This room always reminds me of Father," Helena said, tracing a book's spine. "He taught me to look beyond the surface and go deeper. Cultures, languages, unspoken agendas. He said diplomacy wasn't about who shouted loudest—it was about understanding what wasn't being said."

She paused, glancing toward a low cabinet. "He also taught me clockwork. Gears, mainsprings, balance. I used to fix watches and mantel clocks for fun. Still do, when I'm anxious. I trace imaginary gears with my fingers or design new ones to work in concert. It helps."

Reaching for a bit of twine left from Adrian's drills, she drew a small folding knife from the pocket of her gown. The blade flashed as she sliced the twine in one clean motion.

"Sometimes you need something sharp enough to cut through nonsense."

She tucked the blade away and offered a faint smile. "He always used to say—never go unprepared."

James studied her. "He sounds remarkable. And a little ahead of his time."

A pang bloomed behind her ribs—bittersweet and sharp. "He was. Brilliant. But after Mother died… Whitehall had no use for a grieving diplomat. They thanked him for his service and forgot him before the ink dried. No ceremony. No outrage. Just the quiet closing of a door."

She ran her fingers along the edge of the table, steadying herself. "He spent his life shaping peace from shadows, and in the end, the shadows swallowed him. I remember thinking, *if I ever found myself in that darkness, I'd learn how to fight from inside it.*"

She met James's eyes. "He taught me to speak five languages and read people before they opened their mouths. He trained me to be a diplomat's wife. Or a spy. I chose the one with sharper teeth."

James reached for her wrist. "No one should have to watch that. I'm sorry."

"So am I. But I'm not sorry I stayed in the fight."

"You're a lot like him," James said. "Strong. Sharp. Fiercely loyal."

She smiled. "He'd have liked you."

"Let's hope Amelia does," James said, though his voice had lost its earlier ease. "We should include her—at least partially. If she stumbles into the truth without warning…"

Helena nodded. "I'll speak to her. She'll be delighted, honestly. She's been desperate for a bit of intrigue. And she's been a steady help this past year. I trust her."

James didn't answer right away. He leaned back slightly, gaze drifting toward the hearth. His fingers laced together, then tightened—tension telegraphing through the small motion.

Helena stilled, watching him. "That's not what's bothering you."

His eyes flicked to hers. "No. It's not."

She waited, quiet but present.

"I should tell you more about that betrayal I mentioned earlier. It was one of my captains—Ethan Turner—he chose our guide, planned the route. Then claimed illness at the last minute and disappeared. The Russians were waiting. I believe he sold us out."

"You trusted him."

"He was my friend," James said flatly. "And he left me with a limp and a graveyard." He stared past her. "I tried to prove it. He vanished. No answers. No justice."

She reached for his hand. "That's unforgivable."

He nodded. "If I ever see him again, I won't be calm."

Her thumb brushed his knuckle. "Then I hope, if that day comes, you'll have someone beside you who understands why."

His eyes searched hers. Their hands remained clasped. Something unspoken settled between them.

THEY SPENT THE rest of the day drilling with Adrian—lockpicking, code writing, disguises and impersonation tricks. Helena bested James at one of the tougher locks.

"Told you clockwork was useful," she said.

Adrian raised a brow. "You've done this before."

"Watches. Music boxes. I even built a mechanical mouse once."

James chuckled. "If we find a bomb, you're handling it."

She grinned. "Let's hope it doesn't come to that."

Eventually, they moved on to developing potential code phrases they might need if pressed to communicate in secrecy while among members of the Black Rose Society.

"How would we insert code phrases without everyone guessing we're speaking in code?" Helena asked.

Adrian straightened from the desk. "Here's a notion: You could use tea varieties as a code," he suggested, glancing between Helena and James. "Tea is ubiquitous enough that no one bats an eye when you speak of it. For example, you might say, 'Have you tried the winter Darjeeling?' where Darjeeling signals a need for caution, or 'I've just acquired a remarkable Assam' means the task is complete."

James raised an eyebrow. "You truly believe we can pass information by just mentioning tea?"

Adrian offered a wry smile. "People share all sorts of polite small talk over tea. In a hushed drawing room, no one would think twice."

Once Adrian judged they were sufficiently prepared, he made Helena and James practice disgruntled rhetoric about the monarchy in front of Lady Prudence and a delighted Lady Amelia, both of whom offered comedic critiques:

"How does one eat one's soup in a traitorous manner?" Amelia teased, nearly choking with laughter as James tried to muster a fierce scowl at the contents of his bowl.

"One slurps with seditious intent, dear. Preferably while cursing Parliament between bites," Prudence advised.

Adrian watched them with faint approval. "This is good. But remember—convincing lies often require action. The Society may demand a show of loyalty. No doubt it will test your conscience as well."

Helena's smile faltered.

James caught her eye. "With luck, it won't come to that. And if it does, we'll find a way to do as little harm as possible."

She nodded. The banter continued, but her thoughts stayed with his words. They would find a way.

THAT NIGHT, HELENA found herself in the garden. The cold air helped her think.

James appeared in the doorway. "I wanted to make sure you weren't freezing out here alone," he said with a half smile.

"I needed air."

He joined her, breath misting in the darkness.

"All of it—your captain's betrayal in Crimea, Thomas's foolish investment, what the Black Rose Society might demand of us in a test of loyalty—it's a lot."

"And it's only beginning." He glanced at her. "That's why we're preparing."

"Having you here helps. As my partner, I mean."

"You help me too. I've learned trust isn't weakness." He paused. "We make each other stronger."

In a surge of boldness, she lifted her hand to his lapel. "You mean more to me than I expected."

The words hung between them.

"You as well," he said quietly. "If there's a chance we can keep each other safe and find happiness in the process…"

They stood, the night pressing close.

He brushed a curl from her cheek. She leaned into his touch and smiled.

No matter what these next weeks bring, I'll cherish this moment.

Then, before she could think better of it, she rose on her toes and kissed the corner of his mouth.

He stiffened briefly, then leaned toward her—

An owl hooted, sharp and sudden—sounding too much like a scandalized chaperone.

They both startled, then laughed.

Helena took his arm. They walked back together, the winter air crisp around the sense of something new.

Chapter Twenty-Three

THE SUMMONS

February 13, 1855
James

THE ASHFORD LIBRARY felt colder without the fire lit. Morning sun spilled across the table where Helena's notes regarding the role she'd play lay in careful rows, her handwriting neat, deliberate. His own was sharper, pressed into the page like he'd carved it.

Disillusioned.
Resentful.
Useful.

Adrian had called his cover story credible. James just thought it was true.

At least his knee had finally stopped protesting. Three weeks of Dr. Ramsey's exercises, and the joint moved smoothly again. The scar tissue from the Cossack's blade would always be there—a permanent weakness. But the strain from the Black Cat had finally healed.

He leaned back, rubbing his neck. The confession he'd made to Helena the night before still echoed—Ethan Turner's betrayal, the men lost in the forest near Sebastopol, the silence afterward. She hadn't tried to fix it. Hadn't offered bright-eyed reassurance that it would all make sense one day.

She'd simply understood. That mattered more than anything.

The door creaked. Adrian entered, shaking the chill from his coat. "Didn't think you'd be up this early."

James grunted. "Didn't sleep well. Came here early to get a start on things. Amelia was up early. She let me in." He reached into his coat and withdrew a folded sheet of ivory paper, laying it beside Adrian's notes.

"This arrived at my flat an hour ago. No signature. Black wax seal."

Adrian scanned the contents, reading aloud:

"Major Westwood—

We would be pleased if you and Lady Helena would join us this evening at Lord Marlborough's townhouse for a philanthropic committee meeting. Several members are eager to make your acquaintance. Your perspective on recent matters would be most welcome.

Eight o'clock. The address is enclosed.

Discretion appreciated."

His mouth tightened.

"A summons disguised as courtesy."

James nodded. "They're inviting both of us. Me and Helena."

He met Adrian's gaze. "Judging our suitability. Observation, not interrogation. But it won't be casual. What do you think?"

Adrian tapped a knuckle against the tabletop. "This is beginning sooner than we hoped. They're moving fast. Adjusting their methods." He leaned against the sideboard. "Hawthorne burned everything before we reached him. Ledgers, letters, records—all gone. All that remains is what you managed to smuggle out. With him in custody, the Society's scrambling. Changing patterns. Shifting their meeting places. Cutting off old ties. They're watching each other now. And watching us."

James frowned. "So this rendezvous—is it a trap or a test?"

"A test," Adrian said. "They'll see how you and Helena conduct yourselves. With your war record, it's easier for them to believe you. The focus will be on Helena. What she says. What she doesn't say."

James let out a slow breath. "Who do you think will be there?"

Adrian's expression didn't shift, but his voice did. "Lord Bridewell, certainly. And a few others whose names we haven't confirmed. Some you've met in passing. Some you haven't. They'll be watching you both closely."

James nodded slowly. "So it's not just about Helena's performance."

"No. You'll both need to be convincing."

James's eyes drifted to the notes again. Helena's script was precise, almost elegant. With her father's training, she had a diplomat's mind, and with Frederick's, a spy's instincts. She was a woman with the spine to face down men who'd unmake the country if it suited them.

He admired her, but there was also something more in what he felt.

Adrian shifted toward the door, pausing before he left. "Don't underestimate these people, James. They don't care about war records. They care about who can be compelled. If they sense what she means to you—"

"They'll use it," James finished.

Adrian nodded once. "Make sure you're ready for that."

HELENA ARRIVED MID-MORNING, Prudence trailing behind with her usual dramatic energy. She swept into the library like a small storm, already critiquing the weather, the state of the tea service, and James's choice of cravat—all before she'd settled into her chair.

"Black wax?" Helena said, examining the envelope James

handed her. Her voice stayed calm, but James saw the slight tightening around her eyes as she scanned the contents. "A committee meeting tonight?"

James gave a nod. "Adrian thinks it's a test. The first of several. Bridewell will be there, so we know it's more than a simple meeting."

Helena nodded slowly, adjusting her cuff button with studied calm. "Subtle questioning. Familiar setting. Just enough to see how we carry ourselves under scrutiny."

"Exactly that," James said. "They won't try to trap us outright—not yet. They'll watch. Judge."

Prudence peered over Helena's shoulder at the summons. "A philanthropic committee meeting. How tediously respectable. Though I suppose sedition does require order, after all. Can't overthrow a government without proper record-keeping."

Despite the tension, James found himself suppressing a smile. Prudence's ability to find absurdity in everything was oddly steadying.

Helena set the summons down carefully. "What's the strategy?"

"Be exactly who they expect," James said. "Disenchanted. Useful. Believably bitter about the Crown's failures."

"But not eager," Helena added. "Too much enthusiasm reads as false. We need to be subtle."

"Precisely. You're wavering because you've lost faith, not because you're looking for a cause to champion."

Helena met his eyes. "And if they ask questions we haven't prepared for?"

"Stay close to the truth. Adrian's advice was sound—too much invention and you'll trip yourself up under questioning. Use your father's story. Use my Crimea experience. The pain is real. The anger is real. We're letting it point where they expect."

She nodded. "I can do that."

"I know you can." The words came out warmer than he'd intended. Their eyes held for a moment longer than necessary.

Prudence cleared her throat with theatrical emphasis. "Well, this is all very touching, but shouldn't you two be discussing what you're going to wear? First impressions matter terribly at treasonous gatherings. I imagine there's a dress code."

Helena turned to her aunt. "You're not coming."

"Obviously not. Chaperones rather dampen the treasonous atmosphere. But I'll expect a full report. Preferably with details about the refreshments. One can tell a great deal about an organization by the quality of their wine selection."

BY THE TIME James stepped into the drawing room of an elegant townhouse in Mayfair that evening, he had buried his nerves under something colder. Purposeful. Steady.

Helena walked beside him, the image of the devoted fiancée. But her posture was tighter than usual, shoulders too straight.

The scent of varnish and oil paint clung to the high-ceilinged gallery. Gaslights glowed low, casting long, amber-lit shadows. Paintings lined the walls—seascapes, portraits, still lifes arranged with calculated precision. He noted the exits. No one appeared to be carrying a weapon, but looks could be deceiving.

Eyes followed them across the parquet floors—some curious, some calculating. No one smiled too widely. No one asked idle questions. The air itself seemed tuned to a sharper frequency.

They weren't exposing them.

They were measuring them.

James made sure they found nothing.

A familiar voice cut through the hush.

"Lady Helena. Major Westwood."

Lord Talon Bridewell emerged from behind a column, smile polished, eyes sharp. "So good of you to come to our committee meeting. Not all our supporters show such... enthusiasm for public appearances."

"We're pleased to be of service," James said. "I understand you do good work."

Bridewell offered James a nod, then lowered his voice. "Several are eager to hear more of your convictions. Particularly Lady Agatha Vexley."

James followed his gaze. A poisonous-green gown caught his eye. The Querulous Woman from the Black Cat. He recognized her in an instant—that rigid spine, those piercing eyes watching them with the same intensity. She stood beside a floral still life, spine rigid, gaze cool. The same sharp medicinal scent he remembered from the Black Cat.

Bridewell continued smoothly, "She sits on our philanthropic committee—has for years. A sharp mind. Sharper opinions."

"Lady Vexley," James murmured, testing the name aloud.

Bridewell's smile thinned. "You'll find her support… illuminating. Or blinding, depending on the direction of the wind."

He drifted off, leaving them in the soft echo of his warning.

"I recognize her," Helena said quietly. "From that night at the Black Cat Tavern."

James nodded. "The one who accused us of spying."

"She was right, of course."

"Which means she's dangerous."

Vexley stood stiffly beside a portly earl, discussing an upcoming War Widows and Orphans committee meeting. But her gaze flicked toward them with just enough venom to curdle the air.

Helena leaned in, voice low. "Everyone's watching how I navigate this room. What I say. Whom I flatter. Whom I ignore."

"Then let's give them a performance worth watching," James replied.

At the far end of the room, a painting of a Crimean battlefield hung crooked above a lacquered sideboard. It wasn't there for beauty. It was a statement. Provocation—death framed in gold leaf.

A voice spoke at his shoulder. "Do you find it beautiful, or appalling?"

James managed not to flinch as he turned. Lord Percival Grey—James recognized him now as the one he'd dubbed Slim Man—sipped claret, his pale gaze curious but guarded.

"That depends," James said. "Is it meant to inspire outrage, or justify the carnage?"

His mouth curved, though his eyes stayed flat. "An answer worthy of our circle. You've adapted quickly, Major Westwood."

"I lost too many good men."

Helena inclined her head. "When the Crown abandons its people, it's natural to admire those who act instead."

Across the room, Lady Vexley turned sharply at that. Lips pressed tight. Not surprised. Not scandalized.

Challenged.

Moments later, the murmur of conversation shifted. Quieted.

A door at the far end opened.

The Raven entered—cloaked, masked, silent.

Postures straightened. Power had entered the space.

He didn't speak to the crowd. He turned to Helena and approached.

James tensed, watching as Vexley's stare pinned her like a needle.

This wasn't just a test.

It was a stage. And this was the performance everyone had come to witness.

"You spoke of institutional decay," the Raven said to Helena, voice low and deliberate. "I'd like to hear your solution."

This was the moment they'd been training for. She stepped forward, her voice steady.

"Systemic rot begins at the root," she said. "If the corruption has reached its core, pruning branches won't save the tree. And if the soil is poisoned—if privilege is prized above merit, wealth above wisdom—then the rot must be torn out by hand."

A few murmurs stirred the air.

She held the Raven's gaze. "Reform isn't born of mercy. It's born of clarity. And resolve."

The Raven tilted his head. "Spoken like someone with true convictions."

"I believe I am just that."

The Raven nodded. And with that, Helena passed whatever test the Society had set for her. The Raven nodded once before moving on, leaving the silence ringing in her ears.

A SHORT TIME later, they were quietly excused from the remainder of the meeting. Lord Bridewell approached as they gathered their things.

"Impressive performance, Lady Helena," he said quietly. "The Raven was… intrigued." He glanced at James. "We'd like to continue the conversation. Tomorrow evening. Just a small gathering at my townhouse. A few others you should meet."

The wording was careful. More instruction than invitation.

James nodded. "We'd be honored."

Bridewell's expression grew serious. "A word of caution. Lady Vexley will be there. She was impressed by what she saw tonight, but impressed doesn't mean convinced." He lowered his voice. "Agatha has been with the Society since the beginning. Longer than most. She's seen people come and go. Seen enthusiasm fade. Seen betrayals."

"Which makes her cautious," James said.

"Which makes her *thorough*," Bridewell corrected. "She'll ask questions. Hard ones. If she senses hesitation or fabrication, the evening will end badly."

Helena met his eyes. "We have nothing to hide. Our grievances are real."

Bridewell studied her for a long moment. "Good. Then tomorrow should go smoothly."

AS THEY STEPPED into the entryway, a footman pulled open the tall glass doors with quiet precision. The warm glow of the gallery spilled out behind them, gilding the threshold for a fleeting moment before the doors whispered shut. Outside, the gaslit street was hushed and heavy with fog, their footsteps the only sound against the damp stone.

James offered his arm. "You didn't just speak their language tonight. You became one of them."

Helena let out a slow breath. "That was the goal."

"They'll remember every word." He glanced sideways. "So will Vexley."

Helena followed his gaze. Behind a tall window just above street level, Lady Vexley was still watching. No conversation. No mask. Just quiet observation.

Her empty wine glass drooped in her hand, forgotten.

When Helena met her gaze, Vexley smiled. Not with warmth. Not with welcome.

With intent.

James murmured, "We may have convinced the Raven. But not Vexley. She's competing. With you."

"No," Helena said. "She's measuring me."

Their carriage waited at the curb. As they climbed inside, James felt the weight of the evening settle over him. They'd passed the first test, but Bridewell's warning about tomorrow echoed in his mind. Vexley wouldn't be swayed by one speech. She'd probe. Test. Look for cracks.

"That wasn't just a test," he said as the carriage rolled through the foggy streets.

"No," Helena agreed. "That was a proving ground—and we passed."

She looked out at the streetlamps sliding by, their glow diffused by the fog. "Vexley has just decided she wants to see me fall."

James's hand found hers in the darkness. "Then we'll make sure she's watching when you don't."

Chapter Twenty-Four

BRIDEWELL'S GAME

February 14, 1855
Helena

HELENA HELPED JAMES from the carriage outside a modest townhouse in a discreet quarter of London. The windows were dim, the lanterns muted. No outward sign of sedition—just quiet, controlled discretion.

James knocked once.

A footman led them into a fire-warmed drawing room where Bridewell waited, along with Lady Agatha Vexley and Lord Percival Grey, their expressions opaque as ever.

"Ah," Bridewell said. "Our guests of honor."

Introductions followed—perfunctory, cautious. Vexley gave Helena a nod that might have been approval—or assessment. Hard to tell.

Bridewell's earlier warning echoed in Helena's mind: *Agatha has been with the Society since the beginning. She's seen betrayals.* The woman's cool gaze suggested she was already looking for cracks in their façade.

The drawing room was elegant but understated. No ostentation. Just quiet wealth and careful taste. A fire burned in the hearth. Wine waited on a sideboard.

They settled into chairs in the dining room. Helena chose a seat that gave her a clear view of both the door and the windows. "New habits becoming ingrained."

James sat next to her, close enough that their shoulders nearly touched. A show of unity. A reminder that they were in this together.

Dinner was simple but precise. Roast pheasant, winter vegetables, claret that tasted expensive. Conversation flowed carefully—politics, Parliament, the war. Nothing treasonous. Not yet.

Midway through, Vexley set down her glass and leveled a cool stare at James.

"You speak with conviction, Major. Why such bitterness?"

Helena felt the room shift. This was it. The scrutiny Bridewell had warned them about.

James let silence stretch, then leaned forward slightly. "I led men in Crimea who froze because no one had requisitioned boots or coats. I buried friends while Whitehall covered its ears. No court-martial. No inquiry. Just a thank-you letter for my service and a permanent limp." His voice dropped. "I'd see someone answer for that."

Vexley didn't blink. Didn't soften. But Helena saw something flicker in her eyes. Recognition, perhaps. Or respect.

Then Vexley turned to Helena. "And you, Lady Helena—your father's disgrace must've stung. But was it the loss of your family's influence or his loss of purpose that wounded you most?"

The question was a blade. Precise. Cutting.

Helena didn't flinch. "It was watching a man with competence discarded when what he really needed was their understanding. I learned early how disposable service becomes once it's no longer useful. Loyalty only flows in one direction."

Bridewell's smile flickered. "You speak with clarity, Lady Helena. The kind we need."

Vexley's wineglass paused midair. She didn't speak, but her stillness spoke volumes. Then:

"Some of us earned our place with blood and years of risk," she said. Her voice stayed level, but the edge was unmistakable. "Not sentiment. Tell me, Lady Helena—did your father's disgrace hurt more than his irrelevance?"

The words landed like a slap, all the more biting for the smile she wore.

Helena stiffened but didn't blink. "What hurt," she said evenly, "was watching a capable man dismissed while fools were promoted. Woman to woman, I imagine you understand how that feels." She raised her glass. "To Britain. And the patriots she forgets."

Vexley simply stared at her.

For a heartbeat, the room held its breath.

Then Bridewell lifted his own glass. "To Britain."

Vexley followed a beat later. Her eyes never left Helena's.

They drank.

The tension eased—not gone, but loosened. Like a rope slackening after a tug-of-war.

Grey, who had been silent through most of the exchange, finally spoke. "You both carry your wounds well. That's rare. Most people wear their pain like armor. You two... You've sharpened yours into weapons."

"Is that approval?" James asked.

Grey's mouth curved. "It's acknowledgment. Approval comes later."

Bridewell set down his glass. "Speaking of which—there's a matter we'd like to discuss. A larger gathering will take place soon, and I think you both should attend. It's more... significant than this evening's conversation."

Helena's pulse quickened, but she kept her expression neutral. "How significant?"

"Significant enough that you'll need to wear masks," Bridewell said. "Where identities are protected and commitments are made." He leaned forward. "The kind where there's no turning back."

Vexley's eyes glittered. "Be prepared to swear loyalty. Once you stand among the Society—truly stand among us—withdrawal becomes nearly impossible."

James met Helena's gaze briefly. A silent question. She gave the smallest nod.

"When?" James asked.

"Two nights from now. We'll send details." Bridewell stood, signaling the evening's end. "Enjoy the rest of your claret. And prepare yourselves. What comes next will test more than your words."

THE CARRIAGE RIDE to the Foreign Office Annex was quiet. Helena stared out at the passing streetlamps, her mind replaying Vexley's interrogation, Bridewell's warnings, Grey's cold acknowledgment.

"You handled her well," James said finally.

"She wasn't testing my answers. She was testing whether I'd break under pressure."

"And you didn't."

"No. But she's not convinced. Just… willing to watch me prove myself."

James's hand found hers in the darkness. "Then we'll give her a performance worth watching."

At the Annex, Sir Frederick was waiting in his office. As they told him what had transpired that evening, the fire burned low, casting long shadows across the maps and documents that covered every surface.

Lady Josephine stood beside him, her expression grave.

"You passed," Frederick said once they'd finished speaking.

"For now," Helena corrected.

"For now," Frederick agreed. "But you're about to see the Society's real face. Once you take that oath, you're committed to this path. You understand that?"

James nodded. "We understand the stakes."

Josephine's voice was quiet but firm. "The moment you swear loyalty to them, you become complicit in whatever they plan next. If they demand action—if they ask you to prove yourselves—"

"We'll find a way to minimize real harm," Helena said. "We discussed this with Adrian. We know there may be… choices that will test our principles."

Frederick's expression darkened. "Then prepare yourselves. Because whatever they ask of you, refusing will destroy your cover. And accepting may compromise everything you believe in."

The room fell silent.

Finally, Helena spoke. "We're committed. Whatever comes next, we'll handle it."

Frederick studied them both for a long moment. Then he nodded. "Then God help you both. Because in two nights, you'll be beyond my reach."

Chapter Twenty-Five

THE OATH AND THE RAVEN

February 17, 1855
James

THEY FOLLOWED THE directions Bridewell had provided and found themselves arriving at a grand estate well outside London at dusk. Torches burned at the gate. Armed guards checked invitations with the rigid discipline of soldiers. This was no secret salon—it was a fortress.

James helped Helena down from the carriage, both masked. Hers was simple—black silk with delicate silver tracery. His was equally understated, designed not to draw attention but to blend with the crowd of similarly concealed faces.

Inside, masked guests milled beneath chandeliers and velvet drapes. The air buzzed with wealth and intent. This wasn't curiosity or dabbling. This was commitment.

"Vexley's here," Helena whispered.

James spotted her near the fire. Tall. Green silk beneath a half mask. Not hosting. Commanding.

"She's entrenched," he murmured. "Not merely a member. A power."

Helena's hand tightened on his arm. "Which means we need to be perfect tonight. One misstep and she'll destroy us."

The crowd began to shift, drawn toward a raised platform at the far end of the ballroom. Candles flickered. Conversations died.

A hush fell.

A cloaked man entered—beaked mask, deliberate steps. The Raven.

Power radiated from him like heat from a flame. Every eye turned. Every conversation stopped.

Talon Bridewell broke the silence. He stepped forward, voice clear and fervent.

"We stand at a crossroads," he declared. "For too long, Britain has been ruled by incompetence disguised as tradition. By birthright instead of merit. By cowardice cloaked in ceremony."

Murmurs of agreement rippled through the crowd.

"But we are not here to complain," Bridewell continued. "We are here to act. No half measures. A single blow can cripple the current regime by removing this thorn that has caused us so much trouble."

James felt Helena stiffen beside him. *A single blow. Removing a thorn.* The language was unmistakable and building to a crescendo.

The Raven took over then, his voice low and deliberate.

"We stand on the cusp of reshaping Britain. The diplomatic gala is our opportunity. The Bramble must not leave it alive."

The words hung in the air like smoke.

Assassination.

James forced himself to stay still. Forced his breathing to remain steady. Beside him, Helena's mask hid her expression, but he felt the tension radiating from her.

Bridewell, masked but still identifiable, unfurled a map on the table—the interior of a large building. Patrol routes marked in red. Entry points circled. Timetables noted in precise handwriting.

"This diplomatic gala," the Raven pronounced, "is the perfect stage for chaos. The Bramble plans to give a speech. He'll have few guards. You each know your part."

"His speech alone could rouse half the Commons back to the queen's side," someone muttered.

"Which is why he must not live to deliver it," the Raven answered coolly.

Helena's whisper was barely audible. "They're serious. They mean to kill someone."

James felt revulsion coil in his gut. His hands wanted to reach for the map, tear it to shreds, arrest everyone in this room.

Instead, he stood perfectly still and listened.

Vexley spoke then, her voice cold and precise. "This isn't symbolic. It's a reckoning. The monarchy has cloaked cowardice in medals and ceremony for too long."

The Raven's gaze swept the room. "At the gala, we strike. The Bramble falls. And Britain wakes to a new reality."

Then he raised a gloved hand. "But first—you must swear. Those who stand here tonight must pledge themselves to the Society. To our cause. To our methods."

The group formed a loose circle around the table. James and Helena moved with them, maintaining their place among the conspirators.

"Repeat after me," the Raven commanded. "Our loyalty is to the Society."

"Our loyalty is to the Society," the crowd echoed.

James forced himself to speak the words. Each one tasted like ash.

"Our strength is in our unity."

"Our strength is in our unity."

Helena's voice joined his, steady despite everything. They had no other choice.

The oath rang hollow—but necessary.

When it was done, the Raven nodded once. "You are bound now. To each other. To this cause. There is no turning back."

James felt the weight of those words settle over him like a shroud.

IT WAS LATE when the gathering finally concluded. Guests began to disperse, masks still in place, identities still protected.

As Helena and James headed for the door, Bridewell intercepted them. He clapped James on the shoulder with false camaraderie.

"I knew you two would fit in perfectly. The Society has high hopes for you, given your standing in society. Your passion tonight was most convincing." His smile didn't reach his eyes. "But conviction must be demonstrated. The Society does not embrace new members lightly."

"We won't disappoint you," James said.

Bridewell's gaze shifted to Helena. "See that you don't. Lady Vexley will be watching closely. She has a particular interest in your… development."

The threat was clear.

Outside, the night air was sharp and cold. James helped Helena into the carriage, then climbed in after her.

The moment the door closed, Helena pulled off her mask. Her face was pale.

"That was difficult," she said quietly. "Listening to them spout treason. Assassination."

"The Bramble," James murmured.

"And at a public event. This is beyond anything we imagined."

James clasped her hand. "We'll stop them. But from this point on, we've crossed a line we can't easily uncross."

They rode in silence for a moment. Then Helena said, "We need to be close to the gala. Visible. Useful. Let them believe we'll help them set the stage. If we know the location and the date, we can determine who the Bramble is."

James nodded. "Then we place ourselves among the patrons and patronesses. Make ourselves indispensable."

"And when the time comes, we force the truth into the light."

"And save the Bramble's life."

Their plan had shifted. Now, they weren't just embedded among the Society. They were racing against time to prevent murder.

WHEN THEY ARRIVED at the Foreign Office Annex to report, Sir Frederick was waiting despite the late hour. The fire had burned down to embers. Lady Josephine stood beside him, her expression grave.

James laid the details out quickly—the oath, the assassination plan, the diplomatic gala, the Bramble.

Frederick's face darkened with each word. When James finished, Frederick dropped a file on the table.

"I believe the woman you saw at the Black Cat was Lydia Montague."

James blinked. "Wait. Lydia? Not Clarissa Montague?"

"Clarissa's cousin. Raised together after Lydia's parents died. Nearly identical in height. Similar in bearing. From a distance, in the right mask and cloak—easily mistaken. Lydia's been using that to her advantage."

Helena moved to James's side. "Then the woman we saw at the Black Cat—"

"Wasn't Clarissa," Frederick confirmed. "But someone who's been very careful to let everyone think otherwise."

Josephine added, "Clarissa's tied to Sableport, but she's not part of the Society. Lydia's using her—her name, her clothes, her access. To get to people. To spaces. To trust."

Helena's voice was quiet. "So we chased the wrong woman."

"No," Frederick corrected. "You followed the trail she wanted you to, and it led you here. Now it's time to follow the real one."

He opened the file, revealing photographs and documents.

Lydia Montague stared back at them from a formal portrait—sharp features, calculating eyes. Similar to Clarissa but with something harder beneath.

"Lydia becomes the thread we pull," Helena said.

James added darkly, "We're not just infiltrating the Society anymore. We're dismantling them. And Lydia Montague is where we begin."

Frederick met his gaze. "Then you'd better move quickly. We need to identify which diplomatic gala they're targeting—there are three scheduled in the next month. And we need to determine which speaker is the Bramble. At least four prominent figures are scheduled to address various events."

Josephine added, "The Society was careful. They didn't specify which gala or which speaker. That's by design—knowledge shared only in fragments to limit exposure."

"So we need to find out the specifics," Helena said.

"And quickly," Frederick replied. "If the Bramble dies, Britain loses one of its strongest voices for stability. And the Society wins."

James looked at Helena. Her jaw was set, her eyes determined.

They needed to identify which gala, which speaker, and when. Stop an assassination. Expose Lydia Montague. And bring down the Black Rose Society.

Time was no longer their ally.

Chapter Twenty-Six

A Calculated Performance

February 24, 1855
Helena

THE INVITATION HAD arrived a few days ago, cream colored and edged in gold. Lady Pemberton's Winter Ball. One of the season's most coveted events.

Helena had planned to decline.

Then Bridewell's note had arrived.

Attend. Observe. Report.

Now she stood in her dressing room, watching her maid fasten the clasp of her glittering necklace, and tried not to think about what she'd become.

A spy in silk. A traitor in diamonds.

"You look lovely, my lady," the maid said.

Helena managed a smile. "Thank you, Mary."

Lovely. Yes. That was the armor she'd wear tonight. Charm and grace and her father's name. Tools for coaxing secrets from unsuspecting victims.

Her stomach turned.

THE CARRIAGE RIDE to Lady Pemberton's estate passed in a blur of gaslit streets and cold February darkness. When she arrived, the ballroom blazed with chandeliers and hummed with conversation.

Helena paused at the entrance, scanning the crowd. Diplomats, military officers, society's finest. All glittering and unsuspecting.

She was taking stock of the room when a low voice spoke near her shoulder.

"Lady Helena."

She turned. Sir Talon Bridewell stood beside her, immaculate in evening dress, a glass of champagne in hand.

"Sir Talon." She kept her voice light. "I didn't expect to see you here."

"I'm full of surprises." His smile didn't reach his eyes. "Walk with me."

They moved to a quieter alcove, away from the crush of guests.

"I need your eyes and ears tonight," Bridewell said quietly. "Your father's colleagues—many of them are here. I want to know who still moves in diplomatic circles. Who attends the important events."

Helena nodded slowly. "The upcoming galas?"

"Among other things." He paused. "I also want to know who's vulnerable. Affairs. Debts. Indiscretions. People who might be... persuaded to see things our way."

Her throat tightened. "You want me to listen to gossip. Gather secrets."

"I want you to have conversations," he corrected. "The kind you've been having your entire life. Only this time, you'll remember what you hear."

He handed her a small card with names written in neat script.

"These are the names I want you to attend to. Be subtle. Be charming. And report back to me before the evening ends."

He walked away before she could respond.

Helena stared at the card. Five names. Five people she'd known for years. Five individuals who'd done nothing wrong.

She slipped the card into her reticule and stepped back into the ballroom.

Lord Knox stood near the refreshment table, silver haired and affable. He'd been her father's colleague once. Had visited their home for dinner parties. Had brought her sweets when she was a child.

Now she would use him.

"Lord Knox." She approached with a warm smile. "How wonderful to see you."

His face lit up. "Lady Helena! My dear girl, you look radiant. Your father would be so proud."

The words struck like a blade. Would he? Would her father be proud of what she was doing?

She pushed the thought aside. "You're too kind. Are you enjoying the ball?"

"Immensely. Though I confess, I'm more looking forward to the Royal Society gala next week. The Lancaster House event, you know. Supporting war widows and orphans—a worthy cause."

Helena's pulse quickened. Lancaster House. One of their three suspected targets.

"I hadn't heard the details," she said lightly. "Will it draw a distinguished crowd?"

"Oh, very. Half the diplomatic corps will be there. Prince Albert's considering an appearance. And Sir Reginald Prescott is scheduled to speak."

She filed the information away. "Sir Reginald? How lovely. His speeches are always so moving."

"Indeed. Though between you and me…" Lord Knox leaned closer, voice dropping, "I worry the war talk will depress the ladies. But I suppose it's appropriate, given the cause."

"Quite." Helena smiled. "And the other upcoming events? I've rather lost track of the social calendar."

He listed three more galas, including the Diplomatic Reception and an opera benefit. Each with its own distinguished guest list.

Helena made mental notes of everything.

When she finally excused herself, Lord Knox squeezed her hand warmly. "Your father was one of the finest men I knew. I'm glad to see you carrying on his legacy."

She walked away before the guilt could show on her face.

The next target was easier. Colonel Hartwell's wife, a sharp-tongued woman who loved to gossip.

"Lady Helena, how delightful." Mrs. Hartwell's smile was brittle. "I was just telling Lady Vincent about the unfortunate situation with poor Captain Morrison."

"Oh?" Helena accepted a glass of champagne from a passing footman. "I hadn't heard."

"Gambling debts." Mrs. Hartwell's voice carried a gleeful edge. "Quite substantial, I'm told. His father had to cover them. The shame of it."

Helena filed the name away. Captain Morrison. Vulnerable. Desperate for money.

"How dreadful," she murmured. "And your husband? How is the Colonel?"

Mrs. Hartwell's expression soured. "Bitter as vinegar, if you must know. He blames the generals for Balaclava. Says the whole campaign is mismanaged. I keep telling him it's unpatriotic to say such things, but he won't listen."

Perfect. A disaffected officer with grievances against command.

Helena made sympathetic noises and extracted more details before moving on.

By the time she'd worked through the list, her face ached from smiling. Her chest felt tight with self-loathing.

She was collecting leverage. Building cases against innocent people. And for what? So Bridewell could recruit them or bend them toward treason?

"Lady Helena."

She turned to find Lady Agatha Vexley standing before her, resplendent in dark-emerald silk. Her expression was cold.

"Lady Vexley." Helena kept her voice steady. "Good evening."

"Is it?" Vexley's eyes narrowed. "You seem quite busy tonight. Circulating with remarkable ease."

"I'm renewing old acquaintances."

"How convenient." Vexley stepped closer. "I wonder if you're truly committed to our cause, or merely playing at rebellion."

Helena's pulse spiked. "I've done everything asked of me."

"Have you?" Vexley's smile was sharp. "Bridewell may trust you. I don't. Not yet. You're too polished. Too perfect. It makes me wonder what you're hiding."

Before Helena could respond, another voice cut in.

"Agatha, don't bore the girl with your paranoia."

Lady Eleanor Bennett appeared beside them, elegant and composed.

"Eleanor." Vexley's tone cooled. "I was merely—"

"Testing her loyalty? How tedious." Eleanor's gaze swept to Helena. "You've proven yourself useful, my dear. That's what matters. Ignore Agatha's suspicions. She sees traitors everywhere."

Vexley's jaw tightened. "Caution isn't paranoia."

"No, but this is tiresome." Eleanor turned away dismissively. "Come, Helena. I believe Lady Pemberton is looking for you."

Helena followed, relief flooding through her. But as they walked, Eleanor leaned close.

"A word of advice. Vexley's instincts are usually correct. Don't give her reasons to doubt you."

Then she was gone, disappearing into the crowd.

Helena stood frozen. A warning? Or a threat?

She was composing herself when a familiar face appeared.

"Lady Clarissa." Helena smiled. "I didn't know you'd be here.

It's been ages since I've seen you."

Lydia—posing as her cousin Clarissa—returned the smile warmly. "I almost didn't come. But I'm glad I did." She linked her arm through Helena's. "Walk with me?"

They moved toward the terrace doors, away from the noise.

"I wanted to thank you," Lydia said quietly. "For welcoming me into the fold. It's lonely sometimes, carrying such weight."

Helena's chest tightened. The girl sounded so sincere. So earnest.

"We all carry it," Helena said carefully.

"Yes, but you make it look effortless." Lydia's expression turned wistful. "I have important work coming up. Arrangements to check. I'll be traveling soon."

Helena's instincts sharpened. "Traveling where?"

"Here and there." Lydia smiled. "Making certain everything is in place for... well. You'll know when it's time."

"For which event?"

Lydia's smile turned mysterious. "The right one." She squeezed Helena's arm. "I'm so grateful you're part of this. It means everything to have allies I can trust."

She drifted away, leaving Helena staring after her.

Lydia thought they were friends. Thought Helena was genuine.

The guilt twisted deeper.

She found Bridewell in his study an hour later. The ball continued downstairs, but he'd withdrawn to conduct business.

"Report," he said without preamble.

She pulled out the mental notes she'd catalogued. "Lord Knox mentioned three upcoming galas. Lancaster House, the Diplomatic Reception, and the opera benefit. He said Prince Albert might attend Lancaster House. Sir Reginald Prescott is scheduled to speak there."

Bridewell's expression didn't change, but she caught the flicker of interest in his eyes.

"Go on."

"Colonel Hartwell is bitter about Balaclava. His wife says he blames the generals. He might be sympathetic to our… perspective."

"Good. Who else?"

"Captain Morrison has gambling debts. Substantial ones. His father covered them, but he's vulnerable."

Bridewell made notes. "Excellent. You've done well."

Helena should have felt relief. Instead, she felt sick.

"There's another matter." Bridewell set down his pen. "More delicate."

Her stomach dropped. "Sir?"

"Herr Pruhsfeld, the Prussian diplomat, needs to meet with our inner circle. Quietly. Day after tomorrow."

"I don't understand. How does that involve me?"

"He'll arrive at Lord Cavendish's residence at three o'clock. The meeting will take place upstairs. But we need… a distraction. Something memorable that keeps all eyes elsewhere."

Helena's mind raced. "What kind of distraction?"

"You're a diplomat's daughter." His smile was thin. "You'll think of something."

She stared at him. He wanted her to create a scene. To orchestrate chaos while they conducted their treason upstairs.

"I'll need help," she said quietly.

"Then recruit it. Carefully." He leaned back. "Thirty minutes, Lady Helena. That's all we need. Can you give us that?"

She thought of James. Of Prudence. Of how easily they could stage something convincing.

"Yes," she said. "I can give you that."

"Good." He dismissed her with a wave. "Report back after it's done."

HELENA SENT A message to Sir Frederick requesting an urgent

meeting. The Foreign Office Annex was dark when she arrived past midnight. But Frederick was waiting, along with Lady Josephine and Adrian.

She reported everything. The information she'd gathered. The upcoming galas. Bridewell's request for a distraction.

Frederick took notes, his expression grim. "Lancaster House. Prescott is speaking. That could be it."

"Or it could be the Diplomatic Reception, where Mr. Caldwell is speaking," Josephine said. "Or the opera benefit with Signor Bellini."

"Any of them could be targets," Adrian added.

"Do whatever it takes to stay in Bridewell's good graces," Frederick told Helena. "You need to be part of whatever he has planned."

She sank into a chair, exhaustion pressing down on her. "Bridewell wants the distraction day after tomorrow. Three o'clock at Lord Cavendish's residence."

Frederick nodded slowly. "We'll use it. Engineer a distraction that draws all attention. What do you need?"

"James," she said. "And my aunt Prudence."

Adrian raised an eyebrow. "What are you planning?"

"A scandal," she said grimly. "The kind everyone talks about."

Frederick studied her. "This is taking a toll on you."

"I'm fine."

"No, you're not." His voice was quiet. "But you're managing it. That's what matters."

She wanted to argue. To say she wasn't managing anything. That every conversation with Bridewell left her unsettled. That Vexley's suspicions were grating on her. That she found Lydia's masquerade as Clarissa repugnant and detested pretending to believe her lies. That she barely recognized herself anymore.

But she just nodded. "What choice do we have?"

"None," Frederick said. "Not until we know which event they're targeting. Not until we can stop them."

Helena stood. "Then I'll keep going."

She walked out into the cold London night, pulling her cloak tight against the chill.

Somewhere in the darkness, she was still herself. Still Helena Ashford, daughter of a diplomat, believer in honor and duty.

But that girl felt very far away tonight.

Chapter Twenty-Seven

THE PRICE OF SECRETS

February 26, 1855
James

THE PLAN WAS theatrical. And of course, Prudence had suggested it.

James stood in Lord Cavendish's drawing room, champagne in hand, watching Helena circle Lady Pemberton as she looked for her opportunity. Prudence held court near the window, entertaining three elderly matrons with scandalous gossip about the prince's latest hunting party.

All perfectly innocent. All perfectly positioned.

Upstairs, Bridewell wanted to meet with a Prussian diplomat, Herr Pruhsfeld. Thirty minutes. That's all they needed to keep every eye in this room focused on the spectacle.

James checked his pocket watch. Twenty-seven minutes remaining.

Helena moved closer to Lady Pemberton, who sat resplendent in ivory silk near the fireplace. A footman passed with a tray of wine glasses—deep-red Bordeaux, the kind that stained.

James positioned himself near the door, ready.

Helena reached for a glass just as Lady Pemberton shifted in her seat.

The collision was perfect.

Wine arced through the air in a crimson spray, splashing across Lady Pemberton's ivory gown in shocking streaks.

Gasps erupted around the room.

Lady Pemberton surged to her feet, staring down at the spreading stain. "My gown!"

"Oh!" Helena's hand flew to her mouth. "Lady Pemberton, I'm so terribly—"

Then Prudence's voice cut through the shocked silence like a theatrical blade.

"Blood!"

Every head in the room turned. Conversations died midsentence.

Prudence swayed dramatically, one hand pressed to her forehead. "There's blood everywhere! Helena, you're bleeding!"

"Aunt Prudence, it's wine—"

"*Wine?*" Prudence's voice rose to a pitch that could shatter crystal. "You're telling me you've been stabbed and all you can talk about is WINE?"

James bit the inside of his cheek to keep from smiling.

"Lady Prudence," James said, moving toward her with appropriate concern. "I assure you, no one has been stabbed—"

"Then explain the *carnage!*" Prudence gestured wildly at Lady Pemberton's wine-stained gown. "Look at her! She's drenched in—in—" Her eyes rolled back dramatically. "I can't... the sight... I feel faint..."

She collapsed backward into a convenient chair with all the grace of a tragic opera heroine.

The room erupted.

"Someone fetch smelling salts!"

"Get the physician!"

"Open a window!"

"Should we send for Lord Pemberton?"

Helena dropped to her knees beside the wine-stained Lady Pemberton. "I'm so terribly sorry. I don't know how I was so clumsy. Please, let me help—" She lifted her handkerchief.

"Don't touch it!" A matron shrieked. "You'll make it worse!"

Servants rushed in from all directions. Footmen, maids, the housekeeper—all drawn by the commotion. One brought smelling salts for Prudence, who waved them away weakly while moaning about her "delicate constitution." Another brought cloths to dab at Lady Pemberton's ruined gown.

Perfect chaos.

James glanced at his watch. Twenty-three minutes remaining.

He moved to the window, ostensibly to open it for air, but positioned himself where he could see the second-floor windows in the wing across the courtyard. Through the glass, he caught movement in Lord Cavendish's private study.

Four figures.

One wore a hooded cloak—the Raven, identity concealed. Another wore a distinctive Prussian military uniform. Herr Pruhsfeld. The other two were unmistakable: Bridewell and Eleanor.

James fixed the details in his mind. The Raven's height— perhaps five-foot-ten. Medium build. Moved with controlled grace. Pruhsfeld gesturing emphatically. Papers spread across the desk. Bridewell taking notes.

"Major Westwood, don't just stand there!" Lady Pemberton's shrill voice pulled his attention back. "Help Lady Prudence to the settee!"

James turned to find Prudence being supported by two footmen. She had one hand still pressed to her forehead in distress.

"The shock," she murmured. "I've never been good with… with… violence."

"It's wine, madam," one of the footmen said carefully.

"Wine violence!" Prudence wailed.

James crossed to help, carefully positioning Prudence on the settee where she could continue her performance. She caught his eye for just a fraction of a second—a glint of pure mischief— before her expression collapsed back into theatrical suffering.

"Perhaps I should have some brandy?" she gasped. "For the nerves?"

Helena continued apologizing to Lady Pemberton, who was now surrounded by servants attempting to blot the wine from her gown.

"Ruined," Lady Pemberton moaned. "Absolutely ruined. This was French silk!"

"I'll replace it," Helena said quickly. "I'll commission a new gown from your dressmaker. Two gowns. Whatever you wish."

James checked his watch again. Fifteen minutes.

The drawing room doors opened and Lord Cavendish hurried in, looking harried. "What's happened? I heard shouting—"

"An accident, my lord," Helena said, standing quickly. "I'm afraid I've ruined Lady Pemberton's gown."

"And traumatized Lady Prudence," added one of the matrons helpfully.

Cavendish's gaze swept the room—wine stains, weeping women, servants rushing about with cloths and smelling salts. "Good heavens."

"I'm so terribly sorry to cause such disruption," Helena said. "Please, send me the bill for Lady Pemberton's gown."

"Nonsense," Cavendish said, though he looked like he rather wished all the guests would politely leave. "These things happen. Lady Pemberton, are you quite all right?"

"I will survive," Lady Pemberton said with martyred dignity. "Though my afternoon is destroyed."

Prudence let out another theatrical moan from the settee.

James suppressed a smile and glanced toward the window again. Ten minutes remaining.

The hooded figure moved across the study. The Raven was preparing to leave. James tried to get a better angle, but the mask obscured everything. The figure moved with deliberate grace— too controlled to be casual, too practiced to be amateur.

Could be anyone.

The Raven disappeared from view. Moments later, James

caught a glimpse of a hooded figure slipping out a side door into the courtyard. Gone.

"Major Westwood," Prudence called weakly. "Would you be so kind as to escort me to my carriage? I fear the excitement has quite undone me."

"Of course, Lady Prudence."

He helped her to her feet. She leaned on his arm, still playing the fragile invalid, though he could feel the strength in her grip.

Helena was still apologizing profusely, surrounded by fussing servants and disapproving matrons.

James checked his watch one final time as he helped Prudence toward the door. Five minutes remaining.

By the time they reached the entrance hall, the crisis in the drawing room was beginning to subside. Lady Pemberton had been escorted upstairs to change. The wine-stained cushions had been removed. The servants had dispersed.

Helena emerged, looking genuinely distressed. "I cannot apologize enough—"

"Don't worry yourself, my dear," Lord Cavendish said, though his smile didn't quite reach his eyes. "Accidents happen."

Prudence straightened suddenly, all signs of weakness vanishing. "I believe I'm feeling better now. How strange. It must have been a passing spell."

"How fortunate," Cavendish said dryly.

They made their farewells and climbed into the waiting carriage. The moment the door closed, Prudence's performance dropped entirely.

"Well," she said brightly. "That went rather well."

Helena covered her face with her hands. "Lady Pemberton looked ready to murder me."

"Nonsense. She'll dine out on this story for months." Prudence adjusted her hat. "The time I was nearly assassinated by a wine glass at Lord Cavendish's."

James caught Helena's eye. "Was it enough?"

She nodded. "Thirty minutes of perfect chaos."

"Your aunt deserves an award."

"I'll settle for that brandy I requested," Prudence said. "Purely medicinal, you understand. For my delicate nerves."

Helena managed a laugh, but James could see the strain in her eyes. The weight of what they were doing. The cost of every deception.

James looked out the carriage window at the London streets rolling past.

They'd given Bridewell his meeting. His thirty minutes.

And somewhere in that exchange, another piece of treason had been committed.

THAT EVENING, BRIDEWELL summoned James to a private club on the edge of Mayfair. Discreet, certainly. And shut to anyone without the right name.

James arrived to find Bridewell waiting in a back room. Lord Percival Grey sat in the corner, watching with that calculating smirk. Lady Vexley stood by the fireplace, arms folded.

"Major Westwood." Bridewell gestured to a chair. "Please, sit."

James sat, every nerve on alert.

"This afternoon's distraction was… adequate," Bridewell said. "Though I'm curious how Lady Helena managed to recruit her aunt so quickly."

James kept his expression neutral. "Lady Prudence is devoted to her niece. And she enjoys dramatics."

Grey chuckled. "That much was evident."

Vexley's eyes narrowed. "I still think it was too convenient. Too perfectly timed."

"Wasn't that the precisely what was asked for?" James asked.

"Perhaps Lady Helena is simply competent," Bridewell said. "Which brings me to why you're here, Major. We need something more substantial from you."

James's pulse quickened. "What kind of something?"

"Information." Bridewell leaned forward. "Admiral Whitmore frequents the Admiralty Club. Retired, but still well-connected. He knows troop deployment schedules."

James's blood ran cold. Information about troop movements. Active treason.

"You want me to question him."

"I want you to have a conversation," Bridewell corrected. "You're a former officer. You served in Crimea. He'll trust you. Men like him love to talk to fellow soldiers."

"What specifically do you need to know?"

"When reinforcements ship to Crimea. Which regiments are being rotated home. Any planned withdrawals or strategic shifts." Bridewell's gaze was steady. "This isn't idle curiosity, Major. Lives depend on this information."

"Whose lives?" James asked quietly.

Grey's smirk widened. "The right ones."

Vexley stepped closer. "Are you having second thoughts?"

James met her gaze. "No. I'll do it."

"Good." Bridewell stood. "Tomorrow night. The admiral dines at the club every Thursday. Get close. Earn his trust. Report back immediately."

James nodded. "Understood."

As he turned to leave, Vexley spoke again. "One more thing, Major. Don't ask questions about our plans. You'll know what you need to know when you need to know it."

He looked back at her. "And if I need context to act effective-ly?"

"Your job is to follow orders," she said coldly. "Not to under-stand the larger picture."

James held her gaze for a long moment, then left.

Outside, the London fog had rolled in thick and cold. James walked through it, mind churning.

They didn't trust him. Not fully. He was a tool. Useful, but expendable.

Which meant Helena was too.

THE ADMIRALTY CLUB smelled of cigar smoke and old leather. James found Admiral Whitmore exactly where Bridewell said he'd be—at a corner table, nursing a brandy, looking lonely.

James approached carefully. "Admiral Whitmore? Major James Westwood. I served under Colonel Blackwood in Crimea."

Whitmore looked up, eyes brightening. "Blackwood? Fine officer. Sit, sit. Always glad to meet a fellow soldier."

James sat, signaling for a drink. "I heard you'd retired, sir. Well-earned, I'm sure."

"Retired, yes. Though they still ask my opinion now and then." Whitmore's smile was bitter. "Not that anyone listens."

"The War Office can be… stubborn."

"Stubborn? That's generous." Whitmore took a long drink. "They're sending good men to die for incompetent generals. Balaclava was a massacre. And they want to call it heroism."

James saw his opening. "I heard Sir Reginald Prescott plans to give a speech about it. Honoring the fallen."

Whitmore snorted. "Honoring the waste, more like. Six hundred men charging entrenched artillery because someone misread an order. And now they'll spin it into propaganda to keep the war going."

"You don't think we should continue the campaign?"

"I think we should stop throwing lives away." Whitmore leaned forward, voice dropping. "You want to know the real travesty? Two more regiments shipping out next week. Fresh meat for the grinder. And the Third Regiment finally coming home in March—what's left of them."

James's chest tightened. Exactly the information Bridewell wanted.

He hated himself for asking the next question. "Which regiments are shipping out?"

"The 14th and the 22nd. Poor bastards." Whitmore shook his head. "And the supply situation is a nightmare. Half the equipment doesn't arrive. The other half arrives broken. But do the generals care? No. They just order more charges."

James let him talk. The Admiral was drunk and angry and desperate to be heard. He revealed deployment schedules, provisioning troubles, command disputes. Everything.

And James took note of it all, feeling the weight of each word.

This was treason. Real, tangible treason.

When Whitmore finally wound down, James thanked him and prepared to leave.

"Major Westwood."

James turned back.

"You seem like a good man," Whitmore said quietly. "Don't let them use you. The War Office, the generals—they'll chew you up and spit you out. Protect yourself."

James managed a nod. "Thank you, sir."

He walked out into the cold night, Whitmore's words echoing in his head.

Don't let them use you.

Too late for that.

BRIDEWELL'S STUDY WAS lit by a single lamp when James arrived at midnight. The Raven stood in the corner, hooded and silent. Lady Vexley and Lady Eleanor flanked Bridewell's desk.

James reported everything. The deployment schedules. The supply problems. Whitmore's bitterness.

Bridewell took notes, expression pleased. "Excellent work, Major. This confirms what we suspected."

James kept his voice steady. "May I ask how this information will be used?"

The room went silent.

The Raven's head turned slightly. Though James couldn't see his face, he felt the weight of his gaze.

When the Raven spoke, the voice was distorted—low, deliberately obscured. "You'll know when it's time."

Vexley's tone was sharp. "Your job is to follow orders. Not ask questions."

Eleanor's voice was softer, but no less firm. "Trust that we have a plan, Major. Your role is essential. But you only need to know your piece. The less you know, the safer you are."

"Safer how?" James pressed.

"If you're questioned," Bridewell said calmly, "you can't reveal what you don't know."

James looked at the Raven. The hooded figure stood motionless, watching. Calculating.

"I understand," James said finally.

But he didn't. Not really.

They were using him. Keeping him blind. And when things went wrong—because they always did—he'd be the one left holding the knife.

Bridewell dismissed him with a wave.

James walked out, every instinct screaming that something was wrong. The Raven's presence. The compartmentalization. The refusal to answer questions.

They didn't trust him.

Which meant they were planning something he wouldn't approve of.

Chapter Twenty-Eight

LANCASTER HOUSE

February 26-27, 1855
Helena

HELENA STOOD AT the tall windows of her sitting room, gazing out at the pale winter light slanting through the bare branches. The fire crackled, casting restless shadows across the walls, but its warmth did nothing for the tension coiling in her chest.

The past ten days had been a careful dance of inquiry and distraction. She and James had combed through diplomatic calendars, reviewing every scheduled gala, every announced speaker. Three events had stood out as possibilities. Adrian had helped them pare down the list, but with the Society sharing information only in fragments, they'd been left guessing.

Then, two days ago, Bridewell's summons had arrived: *You are expected at Lancaster House for assistance with preparations for the Royal Society gala. Arrive at noon on the 27th.*

Lancaster House. One of their three candidates.

She went still.

The Black Rose Society had just confirmed their target. Not only that—they'd delivered it directly into her hands, as if rewarding her for playing the game well enough to earn the final move. The gala at Lancaster House wasn't a possibility anymore. It was the answer.

But which speaker was the target? The guest list included half a dozen prominent figures who could fit the Society's vague description of the Bramble—diplomats, military advisors, members of Parliament. Any one of them could be marked for assassination.

Officially, the evening was in support of the Royal Society for the Welfare of War Orphans & Widows, a cause that had drawn the patronage of London's most influential hostesses and the backing of key diplomats. By assisting the patronesses organizing the event, their "volunteer" efforts provided a convenient pretext to stay close to the preparations.

But while their work needed to appear innocent—overseeing the final details, arranging seating charts, ensuring the evening ran smoothly—their true purpose had to remain hidden.

Helena wrapped her arms around herself, staring down at the street below. With their new roles within the Black Rose Society, they were walking on the edge of a precipice, and any misstep could mean disaster. If the wrong people realized they were more than helpful members of the social set, if their presence raised the wrong suspicions…

She inhaled slowly. They would have to be visible, but unobtrusive; engaged, but unnoticed. And, above all, they would have to ensure that the gala ended without catastrophe.

And yet, no amount of planning could account for the unknown. Not when they still didn't know which man the Society intended to kill.

She turned from the window and settled at her writing desk, reaching for a fresh sheet of paper. There was one last thing she needed to do today before tomorrow's gala preparations overtook her.

She dipped her quill into ink, hesitating only briefly before setting it to the page. The letter had to be persuasive but not alarmist.

Lord Thomas,

I find myself troubled by certain matters that have come to my attention and feel it would be best if we spoke. I would be most grateful if you would call upon me at your earliest convenience. Today, if at all possible.

Once sealed, the note was dispatched.

When Thomas arrived later that morning, Helena greeted him with a warm smile, though it did little to mask the tension in her stomach. The butler led him to her sitting room, where a fresh tea service awaited, but Thomas barely glanced at it. His shoulders were tense beneath his finely tailored coat, and when he took his seat across from her, he gripped the armrest as if steadying himself.

"Your note sounded urgent," he said without preamble, his voice taut. His gaze flicked to the door, then back to her. "I imagine this isn't about polite conversation."

Helena folded her hands in her lap, carefully composing her words. "It isn't." She met his gaze evenly. "I've been looking into Sableport Maritime."

His reaction was instant. His fingers curled tighter around the armrest, his jaw clenching as he exhaled sharply through his nose. "Why?"

"Because I was concerned for you," she said simply. "My father's diplomatic connections still open a few doors. I asked the right people." She hesitated just long enough for the weight of her next words to settle. "What I learned worries me greatly."

Thomas swallowed, his Adam's apple bobbing. "Helena..." His voice was quieter now, edged with desperation. He glanced toward the window, as though expecting someone to be watching.

"Sableport is not what it seems," she continued. "Investors who ask too many questions—who try to pull out—are disappearing. Drownings. Falls from high places. Accidents, they say, but those close to them aren't convinced. People whisper about spirits and curses, but I don't believe in ghosts, Thomas. I do, however, believe in men who will go to great lengths to protect their interests."

Thomas shot to his feet so quickly that his chair scraped against the floor. He paced to the fireplace, his hands braced on the mantel as he stared into the flames. When he finally spoke, his voice was tight, almost hoarse. "Another letter came yesterday. No signature—just a warning to remember my 'obligations.'"

Helena's pulse quickened. "And do you intend to?"

He turned to her, his expression grim. "I've already sold over half my shares. I was planning to wait before divesting the rest, but now—" He raked a hand through his hair, disheveling it. "Now I wonder if I'll live long enough to see that happen."

"Thomas, listen to me. If you leave London for a time, it will give you space to make your next move safely. No one would question it—not with everything going on. You could claim stress, a desire for peace at your country estate."

He gave a short, humorless laugh. "They might not question it, but would they allow it?" He cast a glance at the fire. "If I disappear, if I try to run—"

"Not run," she corrected. "Withdraw. Retreat to your country house. It's safer than waiting for them to decide you're a liability."

Thomas was silent for a long moment. The flickering firelight cast sharp angles across his face, deepening the worry etched in his features.

"You never used to be this ruthless," he murmured, searching her face.

She smiled, though there was little warmth in it. "I never used to have reason to be."

A long pause, then finally, he nodded. "Perhaps you're right." His fingers flexed at his sides, his breath unsteady. "Some time away might be best."

Helena stood and reached for his hand, squeezing it briefly. "I think so."

Thomas exhaled, some of the tension in his shoulders easing—but not all of it. His expression was still drawn tight, his movements tense as he released her hand and reached for his hat. "I'll leave within the week."

"Good."

He hesitated, as if about to say something else, but instead he gave a short nod and strode to the door. Helena watched him go, the knot in her chest easing ever so slightly. She should have told him days ago.

He was leaving, though. Which meant he would be safe.

At least, she prayed he would be.

HELENA AND JAMES arrived at Lancaster House the following day promptly at noon. The afternoon sun slanted through the towering windows, casting golden streaks across the parquet floors.

The grand reception room hummed with purposeful activity. London's most influential patronesses had gathered to finalize preparations for tomorrow evening's gala—a charity event in support of the Royal Society for the Welfare of War Orphans & Widows. It was the kind of occasion that drew diplomats, members of Parliament, and foreign dignitaries, which meant security had become a Crown concern.

Sir Frederick Woolsy stood near the windows, reviewing documents with two palace officials. As the Crown's representative overseeing security arrangements, his presence was expected—even welcomed. Lady Josephine stood at his side, lending her considerable social influence to smooth any ruffled feathers among the patronesses.

Lady Agatha Vexley had arrived early. She stood at the far end of the room, stirring tea and observing the assembled women with cool detachment. When her gaze flicked toward Helena and

James, it lingered just long enough to be noticed before moving on, as if dismissing them.

Helena exchanged a glance with James. They moved toward the center of the room, postures easy, expressions neutral, but both keenly aware that Vexley watched them.

Lady Margaret Fairfax presided over the main table like a general marshaling troops. Around her sat the event's key patronesses—women whose influence could make or break a social season. Helena recognized most of them: Lady Ashcombe, sharp-tongued and impatient; Lady Vincent, whose diplomatic connections rivaled Helena's father's; the Dowager Countess of Pembroke, who attended everything and approved of nothing.

Helena took her seat beside James just as Lady Margaret cleared her throat.

"Shall we begin? Sir Frederick has graciously agreed to coordinate security arrangements with the palace. Sir Frederick?"

Frederick inclined his head. "Thank you, Lady Margaret. Given the… prominence of tomorrow's guests, the Crown has requested certain precautions. Nothing conspicuous—we don't want to alarm anyone. But additional footmen at key entrances, staff names checked against the household lists, that sort of thing."

Lady Margaret took a slow sip of tea. "Security is always such a delicate matter, isn't it? One wants guests to believe they're attending an evening of refined entertainment—not arriving at a military encampment."

"Precisely," Frederick agreed. "Subtlety is key."

Helena inclined her head. "The challenge lies in ensuring everything remains secure without it feeling oppressive."

James added, "Too visible a presence might make our foreign guests uncomfortable."

"Quite right," Lady Josephine said smoothly. "We've made some minor adjustments—a few staff changes, additional footmen stationed discreetly. Nothing that will disrupt the evening's flow."

Frederick's eyes flickered past Helena and James—brief, almost imperceptible—but his meaning was clear. They all knew what wasn't being said.

The conversation shifted naturally to seating arrangements and last-minute details. Helena pulled her knife to slice the wax seal from a fresh packet of name cards and began arranging them.

"Too many names, too little time," she murmured.

Lady Prudence materialized at her shoulder. "Am I allowed to comment when your brow starts to crinkle like your father's?"

Helena didn't look up. "Only if I'm allowed to ignore you. I'm attempting to solve a diplomatic disaster involving seating Lord Vincent and the French ambassador."

"Then by all means, save Europe." Prudence set a folded card beside the pile. "But perhaps move Lord Vincent two seats down. Lady Ashcombe has a sharp fan and no patience."

Helena allowed the barest smile. "Noted."

"You're handling this admirably," Prudence added in a lower voice. "I only wish the circumstances didn't require it."

She swept away in a rustle of silk.

Helena glanced up to find Vexley still watching her. Their eyes met across the room. Vexley's expression didn't change, but something cold flickered in her gaze before she looked away.

THE MEETING PROCEEDED efficiently. Lady Margaret assigned final tasks—flowers, musicians, receiving line protocols. Lady Josephine made polite suggestions while Frederick ensured security concerns were quietly addressed. Helena and James spoke sparingly but offered measured agreement where needed, supporting but never leading.

Just as the patronesses began to gather their things, a footman entered and announced Sir Talon Bridewell.

The room's energy shifted subtly. Bridewell was known in

these circles—a wealthy gentleman with parliamentary connections and philanthropic interests. His presence at such a meeting wouldn't raise eyebrows.

Frederick greeted him with a cordial nod. "Sir Talon. A pleasure."

Bridewell returned the nod with a smooth smile. "Sir Frederick. I hope I'm not intruding. Lady Margaret was kind enough to invite me—I've taken an interest in the orphans' cause."

"Not at all," Frederick said. "We were just finishing." He gathered his documents. "Lady Josephine and I have another engagement. Thank you all for your cooperation."

With polite nods to the assembled women, Frederick and Josephine departed.

Bridewell's smile widened as his gaze swept the room. "Ladies, your dedication to tomorrow's success is admirable. I wonder if I might borrow Lady Helena and Major Westwood for a moment? There are a few details regarding tomorrow's arrival protocols that could benefit from their perspective."

Lady Margaret waved a gracious hand. "Of course. We're nearly finished here in any case."

Helena's fingers tightened slightly around her teacup. From the corner of her eye, she saw Vexley shift forward, positioning herself to follow.

Bridewell turned and strode from the room. Helena fell in step beside James, and behind them came the unmistakable click of heeled footsteps.

Lady Agatha Vexley.

Of course.

ONCE IN THE corridor, Bridewell's civility vanished. The air cooled. His smile evaporated. He led them down a side hallway, away from the main reception rooms, before finally stopping and turning to face them.

"You understand what's required," he said, voice low and clipped. "Your position within the Society depends on my associates meeting no resistance tomorrow."

James stiffened. "Security cannot appear compromised. Too few guards and Sir Frederick will raise alarm."

Bridewell's gaze sharpened. "Then strike the balance. Over-correction is how people reveal themselves."

Helena kept her posture relaxed, her expression composed. "We'll adjust the rotations. Discreetly."

A glint of satisfaction flickered in his eyes. "Good. See that it's done."

If only she knew who the Bramble was. The Society shared only what it chose to, even with its supposed loyalists. The identity of their intended target remained maddeningly out of reach.

Bridewell glanced sidelong at Helena. "You've been useful. Tomorrow decides whether that continues."

Helena kept her expression neutral. "We understand what's at stake."

"Good," he said. "Your roles place you at the center of influence. That makes you valuable—and vulnerable."

Behind them, Vexley's voice cut through like a blade. "They've been given much responsibility—for newcomers. Trust is not usually so freely extended."

Helena turned to face her. "Results have a way of clarifying things."

Vexley's expression didn't soften. "Then tomorrow will be revealing."

"Enough," Bridewell said. "We've placed our pieces. Let's see who plays them well."

Vexley crossed her arms, her voice tight. "Loyalty used to be measured in sacrifice. Now a pair of newcomers—fresh-faced and favored—are handed influence? Perhaps if I'd fluttered my lashes at the right man, I'd be standing where they are."

Helena met her gaze steadily. "Results speak for themselves. We'll let ours do the talking tomorrow."

Vexley's nostrils flared, but before she could retort, Bridewell cut in with a cold glare. "That's enough, Agatha."

Lady Vexley's face reddened.

"I selected them deliberately because the major has experience with guards and rotations," Bridewell continued. "That decision is not open to debate."

Without another word, he strode down the hall, boots striking sharply against the floor.

Vexley's eyes narrowed. "Don't embarrass him," she hissed. "I'll be watching you."

She pivoted and disappeared back toward the reception rooms.

Helena stared after her, jaw tight.

THEY MOVED QUICKLY through a side corridor, descending a narrow staircase behind a velvet-draped alcove. The passage was clearly designed for servants—narrow, unadorned, hidden from guests. Moments later, they slipped into a modest study tucked away from the main rooms.

Sir Frederick waited beside a cluttered desk. Papers were spread across the surface—letters, maps, guard placements. Lady Josephine stood near the window, keeping watch.

Frederick looked up sharply. "You weren't followed?"

"No," James said. "Bridewell assigned us to manipulate security coverage. Lady Vexley's suspicious, but she has nothing concrete."

Frederick handed them a folded paper. "The final list of speakers for tomorrow's gala. Each name has significance, but one stands out—Sir Reginald Prescott. We suspect he's the one they call the Bramble."

Helena's pulse hitched as she scanned the list. Prescott—her father's old friend. She remembered him laughing in their drawing room, always smelling faintly of cigars and bay rum. He'd been one of the few who'd visited after her father's fall. One of the few who'd remained loyal.

And now the Society wanted him dead.

She forced her voice steady. "He's respected on both sides of the Channel. If the Society succeeds, they'll devastate Anglo-French relations."

James gently touched her arm. "We won't let that happen."

"We need strong security," Frederick said, voice low. "No detail overlooked. Yet not so airtight that the Society suspects we know their plans."

Helena nodded. "We'll coordinate the lists and have each servant vouched for. Make it seamless."

James inclined his head. "But if the Society sees us doubling the guard, they'll vanish."

A small line appeared between Frederick's brows. "Precisely. Strike a balance, but watch the path they plan to use. We can't lose them now."

Josephine's gaze flicked between Helena and James. "They trust you enough to have you 'help' from the inside?"

Helena's stomach turned. "Yes. Bridewell insisted we manipulate the security plan. He said it would prove our loyalty."

Frederick's mouth set into a grim line. "I hate that you're forced into weakening our defenses. But for the sake of stopping them…" He exhaled. "Be careful. They'll watch your every move."

Helena hesitated. "There's another matter. Thomas Chadwick—he's deeply invested in Sableport Maritime. Hawthorne introduced him, and Thomas has been receiving threats since he started asking questions."

Frederick's expression darkened. "How deeply invested?"

"Enough that divesting quickly would be noticed. I convinced him to leave London for his country estate. He'll be safer there."

"Good," Frederick said. "Getting Thomas out was wise. Sableport's been on our radar since the Duke of Westbridge's death—we suspect they orchestrated it, possibly funded by the same interests behind the Black Rose Society. But the company's extraordinarily well-insulated. Legitimate maritime trade on the surface, a web of silent partners and false names beneath. Every time we've tried to find proof, the trail goes cold."

James frowned. "And the investors? How many are complicit versus duped?"

"That's the question we can't answer. Most appear genuinely ignorant—Thomas among them. But someone's orchestrating it all, and they've been careful." Frederick's jaw tightened. "We can't risk moving on suspicions alone. If we act without proof, the entire network will scatter and go to ground. But once the gala is secure, we'll shift our focus."

Josephine added quietly, "In the meantime, getting Thomas out was the right move. One less innocent caught in the crossfire."

Frederick shifted a map on the desk. "Now, about Prescott's speech. He plans to reaffirm Britain's commitment to the Crimean campaign. Make the case for holding the line against Russian expansion."

Helena's chest tightened. Prescott had always believed in diplomacy backed by strength. Her father had taught her the same. "He'll rally support for the war."

"Precisely what the Society doesn't want," James said. "They've positioned themselves as reformers opposed to foreign entanglements. Prescott's speech undermines their platform."

Frederick's expression darkened. "More than that. Prescott has credibility on both sides of the Channel. If he makes a compelling case and the Society silences him, it won't just be murder—it could unravel Anglo-French diplomacy. Russia would see Britain as weak, divided. The alliance would fracture."

Helena felt the weight settle over her. "So they don't just want him dead. They want chaos."

"Exactly," Frederick said. "Which is why we can't let them succeed."

AN HOUR LATER, Helena moved through the grand corridors of Lancaster House, James at her side, reviewing the final placements of staff and security.

Despite all their careful planning, they were walking a knife's edge.

As they passed the tall double doors of the entrance corridor, Helena spotted Amelia. She stood near the gilded console, posture straight, chin high, reading from a list and practicing a polite curtsy.

Her sister looked composed—elegant even—but Helena caught the way her fingers twisted the ribbon holding her notecards.

James followed her gaze. "Amelia?"

Helena nodded. "Lady Josephine asked her to assist with greeting foreign guests. She'll be stationed near the main entrance."

"Is that wise?"

Helena's voice tightened. "Probably not. But if I try to stop her, she'll ask why I was allowed to help and she wasn't. And I can't tell her the truth—not about the Society, not about the assassination plot. She thinks this is just a charity gala."

James said nothing, but his hand brushed hers lightly.

"She wants to prove she belongs. And if I pull her back now, she'll think I don't trust her. Worse, others might wonder why."

They moved on, but Helena couldn't stop seeing the determined set of her sister's shoulders.

She stopped near a gilded mirror, catching James's reflection as he studied their security notes.

"What if we can't protect them all?" she whispered. "Prescott, the other dignitaries, half of London's elite will be here tomorrow."

James turned to face her fully, his expression resolute. "We will. We've come too far to fail now."

Helena nodded, her resolve solidifying. She would do whatever it took—just enough sabotage to maintain their cover, yet enough oversight to foil any lethal strike.

A wordless vow passed between them: They would walk this razor-thin path side by side. And if they failed… she didn't know if she could live with what followed.

Chapter Twenty-Nine

THE RESCUE

February 27, 1855
James

LATE AFTERNOON HAD given way to early evening by the time James found himself pacing near a tall window in Lancaster House. The security plan—deliberately flawed, riddled with gaps—was set. Tomorrow's gala loomed. But all James could think about was the hypocrisy of what they'd done.

There were two arrangements now: what the Society expected to see and what Sir Frederick's people truly meant to do. It was a trap within a trap. And James had designed both.

Instead of confirming the lists or mapping exits, his thoughts circled the lies they'd planted. One misstep and both plans could collapse. The Society would see the ruse, and the Crown's agents would be too late.

In Crimea, his men had died because someone they trusted had given away vital information. A single betrayal had turned a plan into a death trap. Now he was the one handing over information, ensuring the watch was altered—just enough—to let enemies slip through.

He supported the Crown. He fought for it, bled for it. And yet here he was, pretending allegiance to the Black Rose Society, feeding them just enough to keep their trust while working against them. Was this what Ethan had done? Was this what it had felt like—walking that edge, knowing every deception tightened the noose?

He remembered how Ethan used to linger in doorways, silent and sharp eyed, carrying secrets like they might explode. He'd assumed it had been the stress of war, but now he saw it differently—the exhaustion, the calculation, the constant pretense. Every lie felt like a weight added to the wrong side of the scale.

James inhaled slowly. This was different. He wasn't betraying anyone—not this time. He was trying to prevent a massacre. If that meant playing the traitor again, so be it.

A burst of noise shattered the stillness.

He turned as a disheveled man rushed past the doorway—dust streaked, flushed, eyes wide with panic. Not just a messenger with bad news. This one looked like he was fleeing for his life.

James met Helena's glance and followed the man into Sir Frederick's office.

The stranger was already speaking in a hoarse rush. "Please. I need to speak with you—it's urgent."

Sir Frederick gave James and Helena a nod, then guided the man into a side room. Lady Josephine followed, concern sharpening her features.

James studied the newcomer—fists clenched, breath uneven, desperation bleeding through his calm. A man who had barely made it out.

"Who is he?" James asked quietly.

"Samuel Greene," Sir Frederick said. "One of my informants."

Helena went still beside him.

Samuel drew a shaky breath. "Sir—I've just come from the leather district. Nathaniel Clarke's in danger. He took a coded message from the Society." His voice dropped. "They know. They're going to kill him—but not before they tear every secret out of him."

Helena's fingers curled against her skirts. James felt a protective anger coil in his stomach. Nathaniel might have been self-serving, but he wasn't reckless. If he'd risked taking something from the Society, it wasn't just important—it was invaluable.

"Where is he?" James asked.

Samuel swallowed. "They've got him in an old warehouse near the tanneries. I barely got away to warn you."

As James and Helena turned for the door, Sir Frederick said, "Take our horses."

They rushed from Lancaster House to the stable yard, mounted swiftly, and tore onto the cobbled streets, hooves striking hard against the stones. The city blurred past in streaks of gaslight and dark alleyways.

The moment they turned onto the lane leading into the leather district, a wall of stench hit James—rotting hides, acrid chemicals, the heavy stink of tanneries. It was the kind of place where bodies could disappear.

Dusk bled into the alleyways. Windows above them were shut tight, but James felt unseen eyes tracking them.

Samuel twisted in his saddle. "There," he whispered, jerking his chin toward a squat warehouse with a sagging roof. "He's inside—three, maybe four men holding him."

James pulled his horse to a stop behind a cluster of barrels. The windows were boarded up, the heavy doors barred from the inside. Only the side entrance, slightly ajar, offered a way in.

"All right," James said, swinging down. "We go in fast, take them before they know what's happening."

Helena dismounted beside him, adjusting her coat and lifting her kerchief into place. "We get in, get Nathaniel, and get out."

James nodded, adjusting his own to cover his face. No hesitation.

They slipped through the side entrance, the reek of old leather and chemicals closing in around them. Somewhere inside, a chair scraped against the floor, followed by a thump and a low grunt.

Nathaniel.

James inched forward, knife gripped tight. Helena mirrored him, steps near silent. A flickering oil lamp cast moving shapes on the far wall.

As they crept closer, the room unfolded before them—a crude interrogation den. Nathaniel Clarke sat bound to a chair, his head lolling forward, his wrists rubbed raw. His face was battered, blood drying along his temple.

Four men occupied the room. One crouched near Nathaniel, murmuring something. "You're holding up longer than I expected." Irritated, he straightened and reached for a wooden cudgel.

Two others lounged nearby, nursing bottles of whiskey. The fourth was pawing through a satchel, distracted.

James lunged first, his fist cracking against the speaker's jaw. The man crumpled without a sound.

The second man lurched to his feet, fumbling for something behind his coat. Helena rushed him—not with precision, but with speed and desperation. She didn't duck so much as charge, ramming her shoulder into his ribs. He grunted, stumbled back a step, and she seized the chance to drive her knee into his thigh. When he doubled over, she shoved him hard. He went down in a sprawl.

James turned just in time to block a club aimed for his head. He caught the attacker's wrist, twisted, and slammed the man backward into a stack of crates. Wood splintered under the weight.

A fourth man shouted and charged at Helena. She flinched, eyes darting. Her hand closed around a heavy whiskey bottle still sitting on the table. No time to think. She swung it hard and caught the side of his head. The glass didn't break, but he reeled, stunned. She swung again, lower this time. He dropped, clutching his side.

Samuel darted through the chaos, knife flashing as he slashed Nathaniel's bindings. "We have to move."

Helena spun, breathing hard. Four men down. No movement.

James crouched beside Nathaniel, gripping his arm. "Can you stand?"

Nathaniel coughed, wincing as he flexed his wrists. "'Ardly." His voice was hoarse.

James hauled him up, bracing himself. The man's full weight tested his knee, but it held. "We need to move."

But Nathaniel wasn't looking at James—he was frantically patting down his coat. His bruised fingers trembled before they found what they sought.

Nathaniel pulled a folded scrap of paper from inside his coat. His grip was weak, but his eyes burned with triumph.

"I got it," he rasped. "The message."

Helena barely spared the parchment a glance before gripping his arm. "Then we need to go—now."

James slung Nathaniel's arm over his shoulder, half dragging him toward the exit as Samuel pushed open the side door. The alley beyond yawned dark and narrow.

The warehouse groaned behind them—a shifting of bodies, the rustle of fabric against wood. Then a muffled curse.

Someone was getting up.

Another voice, hoarse with pain. "Bleedin' hell—what in God's name jus' 'it me?"

James tensed. Footsteps scuffed against the floorboards inside. A scrape of metal—a knife unsheathed. Then the thud of boots hitting the ground.

They were coming.

A second man, voice sharp with fury, spat, "Oi! Get up, you daft sods—they're leggin' it!"

Helena reached the waiting horses first, swinging up in one swift motion. Samuel followed. James hauled Nathaniel into the saddle, securing him before mounting up behind him.

A door slammed open somewhere in the warehouse. A burst of voices—angry, disoriented.

"They've gone!" someone bellowed.

Another voice growled, "Ain't far, neither. We find 'em, we gut 'em."

James didn't wait to see if they'd pursue.

"Go!"

Their horses surged forward, hooves hammering against cobblestones. The city blurred past in smears of lamplight and cold streets. The acrid scent of tanneries faded, replaced by damp, smoke-tinged air.

No shouts followed. No pursuit.

But James knew better than to assume they were safe.

They didn't slow until they reached an old stable closer to the river, its doors half hanging open, the wood warped and splintered. One of the places Nathaniel had named as safe. The sour scent of old manure and stale straw filled the dim interior.

The place was quiet—only the restless stamping of their mounts and their own breathing broke the silence.

James dismounted, looping his reins over a rusted hook before turning to assist Nathaniel. The man's legs buckled beneath him, and he sagged heavily against James.

Helena swung down from her horse, raking a hand through her disheveled hair. "That was too close."

James exhaled, his pulse still hammering. "I think we lost them." He flicked his gaze to the crumpled message in Nathaniel's grasp. "Let's hope whatever you stole was worth the beating you took."

Nathaniel let out a ragged breath, his hand tightening around the paper. "Feels like it better be, don' it?"

Helena righted an overturned bench. "Sit," she ordered Nathaniel, steadying him as he collapsed onto it.

As he sagged forward, she reached for the message, her brow furrowing as she scanned the parchment. "It's encoded," she said after a beat, her voice tight. "But not in anything I recognize."

James moved to her side. "Complicated?"

"Deliberately so. We'll need Charlotte to solve it."

Samuel, still panting from the ride, wiped sweat from his brow. "I'll fetch Dr. Ramsey—and Charlotte." He turned his mount and disappeared into the night.

James crouched beside Nathaniel. "What possessed you to steal this message?"

Nathaniel winced, pressing a hand to his bruised ribs. "'Eard 'em talkin' about a way in, didn' I? Thought if I 'ad somethin' valuable, I could sell it to Sir Frederick. Earn some coin... keep meself safe." He let out a pained chuckle, then hissed through his teeth. "Didn't expect 'em to catch me so bleedin' fast."

Helena's gaze lingered on him, guarded but not unkind. "This might give us details about the assassination."

Nathaniel, still cradling his ribs, eyed them both warily. "So, wot's in it for you?"

James frowned. "What do you mean?"

Nathaniel gave a humorless huff. "I mean—you don't storm a warehouse like that fer free. No one does. So wot am I to you? Leverage? A debt to be called in? Or just the message?"

James didn't answer at once. He crouched in front of Nathaniel, resting his forearms on his knees.

"In Crimea," he said evenly, "I lost men because someone sold us out. Arranged our route. Precise timing. Then he vanished before we set out, giving our plans to the enemy." His jaw tightened. "I watched good soldiers die because I trusted the wrong person."

Nathaniel stilled.

"I won't let that happen again," James went on. "Not to anyone under my watch."

Nathaniel swallowed. "Even a bloke like me?"

"Especially someone like you," James said. "You take risks for us. That makes you *ours*. And we don't trade our own lives for convenience."

Silence stretched between them, broken only by the horses shifting in their stalls.

Nathaniel scrubbed a hand over his face, wincing. "Bloody

'ell," he muttered. "Didn't expect that."

Helena stepped closer. "You weren't rescued for charity," she said quietly. "You were rescued because you matter."

Nathaniel gave a weak, crooked smile. "That's a new one, innit?"

James stood. "You'll be paid. Treated. Kept safe as best we can. After the gala, you decide what comes next."

Nathaniel nodded once, the sharp edge in his expression dulled—not gone, but eased.

"All right, then," he said. "Let's see if this bleedin' scrap was worth the trouble."

He glanced down at the folded paper still clenched in his hand.

"For all our sakes."

Chapter Thirty

A PYRRHIC VICTORY

February 27, 1855 – late evening
Helena

HELENA STOOD AT the threshold of the abandoned stable, watching for the doctor's arrival. Full darkness had fallen, winter night settling cold and sharp. A single lantern burned inside, casting restless shadows across rough walls. The sour odor of old hay mingled with the lingering scent of horse sweat.

She rubbed at a sore spot on her arm—a bruise from the fight. Yet her mind stayed fixed on Nathaniel's labored breathing as he slumped against a makeshift bench.

They had rescued him. But had they been too late?

A hiss of wind rattled the stable doors. Then horse hooves—fast and urgent—approached outside. Helena cracked open the door to peer through it. Sir Frederick Woolsy appeared first, dismounting in a swirl of cloak. Lady Josephine and Charlotte Sinclair followed, then Dr. Sebastian Ramsey with his medical satchel. The group spread through the stable, eyes scanning the corners.

She inclined her head. "Thank you for coming so swiftly. Nathaniel needs attention."

Dr. Ramsey crossed to Nathaniel without a word, knelt beside him, and opened his satchel. "Let's have a look."

He checked Nathaniel's pulse, then gently tilted his chin, examining his pupils in the flickering lamplight. Blood matted Nathaniel's hair near a split along his temple. Fresh bruises darkened his jaw. When Dr. Ramsey pressed along his ribs, Nathaniel let out a sharp gasp.

"Cracked ribs, more than likely," Ramsey muttered. "Heavy bruising. He's lost more blood than I'd prefer. No obvious fracture—thank God—but he's had a hard blow." He looked up at Helena. "He's in rough shape, but he'll recover. Warmth, stillness, no exertion. Strong broth. A week of quiet."

Sir Frederick's gaze swept the stable—over James standing watch near the door, then to Helena. "Samuel told us about the rescue. Are you both unhurt?"

"We're unharmed." Helena gestured to where James stood near the lantern, battered paper in hand. "We secured the coded message Nathaniel stole."

Lady Josephine exhaled. "A bold move, but reckless. We can only hope it was worth the risk."

Helena exchanged a look with James. "If they went to the trouble of putting it in cipher, it's because they can't risk it traveling."

Sir Frederick's voice dropped low. "Then let's not waste a moment. Charlotte?"

Charlotte offered a polite smile and stepped forward. "I'll need somewhere to spread it out."

Helena led her to a rickety table near a shuttered window. James set the folded paper on the scarred surface. The stable fell quiet.

Charlotte settled onto a three-legged stool, lantern light flickering over her hands as she carefully flattened the parchment.

"This cipher is complex, but not unfamiliar," she murmured, pulling out a small notebook. "I've seen variations of it in other Society documents."

Ramsey worked in near silence—"Breathe here," "Hold still,"

"This will sting"—his hands steady as he cleaned the worst wounds and bound Nathaniel's ribs.

Helena forced herself to focus on Charlotte's progress, trying not to let her gaze stray to Nathaniel's battered face.

James joined her beside the table, tension radiating from him. Whatever Charlotte uncovered would set the course of tomorrow. Possibly the rest of their lives.

Time stretched. The scratch of Charlotte's quill. The rustling of pages. Nathaniel's occasional hiss of pain.

Finally, Charlotte straightened.

"The southwest gate," she said. "They'll infiltrate during Prescott's speech."

James let out a sharp breath and shot Helena a look.

She understood immediately. "That's what Bridewell ordered us to arrange."

"Nathaniel nearly died stealing a copy of our own plan," James said quietly.

The room fell silent.

Nathaniel, propped against the wall, let out a weak laugh that turned into a cough. "You're sayin'… I stole your own bloody plan?"

"Not ours," Helena said quickly. "Theirs. But we already knew the southwest gate was vulnerable because we're the ones who weakened it."

Nathaniel stared at them. "So I got meself beaten for nothin'."

"Not for nothing," Frederick said firmly. "You confirmed they're committed to that route. They could have changed plans, used a backup. Now we know they won't." He met Nathaniel's eyes. "Confirmation matters. It changes what we dare do tomorrow. It's worth blood."

But Nathaniel didn't look convinced.

Neither did James.

Sebastian Ramsey didn't look up from his work. "I don't relish risking lives—Prescott's or anyone else's. But information that lets us take them before they slip away? That's worth taking chances."

Helena glanced at him. The quiet weight of his words sank deep.

When she finally spoke, her voice was clear. "Then we'll stop them. We'll protect Prescott. No matter what it takes."

James met her gaze.

Charlotte looked down at the parchment again. "I'll go over this once more to check for errors, but the intent is clear." She traced a line with her finger. "They don't just want him dead. They want to make a spectacle of it."

Helena felt something cold and focused settle in her chest. Then they'll fail.

"If you come across more messages like this, bring them to me," Charlotte murmured to Frederick. "I'm beginning to understand their pattern."

The lamplight threw stark shadows across the dusty floor. Nathaniel lay dozing on a blanket now. Ramsey crouched beside him again, checking his pulse.

Unflinching, Helena thought. The kind of man you'd want nearby when things fell apart.

Sir Frederick folded the decoded notes and slid them into a worn satchel. "We have their plans. We'll position our best guards at the southwest gate, the corridors leading from it, anywhere they think is vulnerable. Quietly—no show of force, but enough to take them when the time is right."

Helena forced a small nod, though her chest felt tight. "James and I will keep the Society's trust. We can't reveal we've discovered their plan. We have to pretend everything is proceeding as they arranged."

Lady Josephine squeezed Helena's hand. "I'm sure you'll manage it with grace. Be cautious."

James stood beside Helena, shoulders taut, expression etched with determination. "We know the route they'll use. That gives us an advantage."

Helena swallowed, recalling the moment Bridewell demanded certain corridors remain lightly guarded. We've come too far to fail.

"Then we're set," Frederick said. "Tomorrow, at the gala, we'll protect Prescott. And we'll finish this."

A chill brushed through the stable—a reminder of the winter air outside and the precarious hours ahead. Helena glanced at James, eyes meeting in a shared vow.

It was victory, yes—but one measured in bruises and blood. They were walking a razor's edge—pretending to aid the Society's infiltration while secretly preparing to destroy it. One misstep and everything would collapse.

But they weren't alone.

They had each other.

And that had to be enough.

Chapter Thirty-One

WHISPERS OF DOUBT

February 28, 1855
James

J AMES WOKE TO the sound of rain against the window, his body stiff from a restless night. By the day's end, everything they'd set in motion would either hold—or unravel.

He splashed cold water on his face from the basin, the shock of it doing little to clear his mind. His reflection in the mirror looked haggard—shadows under his eyes, jaw tight with tension.

A tepid cup of tea waited on his desk, forgotten. He'd prepared it nearly an hour ago, but his mind kept circling back to the warehouse rescue. Helena, slipping past the guards with fearless precision. The way she'd fought—swift, efficient, unafraid. She'd been extraordinary.

And she could have died.

The thought settled like a stone in his chest. He'd felt pride watching her fight, yes. But also something sharper—a visceral fear that he might lose her the way he'd lost his men in Crimea. Not because of enemy action. Because of secrets and lies and the razor-thin line between masquerade and true betrayal.

He forced himself to turn from the mirror, to focus on the half-finished letter on his desk—last-minute adjustments to the guard lists, subtle changes meant to dull the Society's advantage without exposing their hand.

Keep moving. Keep planning.

Every detail he'd fed to the Black Rose Society was balanced by quiet sabotage. But the complexity of it twisted his conscience into knots. What if he'd miscalculated? What if the deception necessary to keep them alive was the very thing that would doom them both?

He was reaching for the pen when footsteps pounded the corridor. A frantic knock rattled the door, followed by it swinging open before he could respond.

Samuel Greene burst through, breathless and disheveled, looking as if he'd run half of London.

"What happened?" James exploded from his chair, prepared for the worst. "Has the Society gone after Nathaniel?"

"No, sir" Samuel said between labored breaths, "Sorry to disturb you, sir." He brandished a folded newspaper, the cheap print smudging his fingers. "You need to see this."

James's brow creased. He extended his hand. "What is it?"

"A gossip rag. Printed this morning."

A creeping dread settled at the base of James's spine as he unfolded the pages. His eyes scanned the opening lines—*Rumors swirl around Lady Helena Ashford and her abrupt engagement to Major James Westwood. Sources suggest the lady's heart remains with her previous suitor, Lord Thomas Chadwick...*

Blood roared in his ears. The article speculated that the engagement was an arrangement in name only, arranged out of desperation or cunning. It implied Helena had lied about her feelings, that she'd welcomed Thomas at her home only two days ago.

Two days ago. The day before they'd prepared for the gala.

Nausea churned in his gut. She had seen Thomas? And she'd never said a word?

Helena had said she'd handled Thomas, whatever that had meant. He'd assumed she meant sending a letter, a polite dismissal. Not a private meeting.

"They're claiming our engagement is a sham," he murmured, voice tight.

Samuel shifted on his feet. "Lady Josephine said I should bring it straight to you. She wants you to go to Lady Helena's home as quickly as possible. Word's already spreading. The house is being inundated with callers."

James exhaled slowly, scanning the lines once more. The column questioned Helena's virtue, painted him as some convenient piece in her larger game. Or was it the other way around?

He slammed the paper onto the desk. "Thank you, Samuel. I'll leave at once."

"Shall I accompany you?"

James shook his head. "No. But keep your ears open. If the Society thinks our engagement is a ruse, it could unravel our position entirely." He paused, voice low. "I won't let that happen."

Minutes later, James was out the door, the scandal sheet crumpled under his arm. He caught the first hackney coach he could hail, spitting out Helena's address in clipped tones.

The ride through London's bustling streets felt agonizingly slow. His mind churned with a mix of protectiveness and doubt.

If Helena had seen Thomas, did she still care for him? *Did she merely feign attraction to me for the sake of the mission?*

He mentally scolded himself. *Don't be an idiot. You trust her.*

But the thought crept in anyway, insidious: If he could wear a lie so convincingly, so could she.

He shoved it aside. It lingered anyway.

The coach lurched forward through the rain-slicked streets. He didn't know if he meant to protect Helena, defend her, or demand the truth.

Maybe all three.

Chapter Thirty-Two

COURTING COMPLICATIONS

February 28, 1855
Helena

HELENA HAD BARELY finished pinning up her hair when voices echoed from the entrance hall below—too many voices, too early in the morning.

She descended the stairs to find the drawing room already filling with callers. Lady Ashcombe perched on the settee, fanning herself vigorously. Lady Vincent stood near the fireplace, teacup trembling in her hand. The Dowager Countess of Pembroke occupied the best chair like a judge preparing to pass sentence.

And they were all staring at Helena.

"Good morning," Helena said carefully, stepping into the room. "This is… unexpected."

Lady Ashcombe's fan snapped shut. "Is it true?"

"Is what true?"

Before anyone could answer, the butler announced, "Lady Beatrice Cavendish," and Helena's childhood friend swept through the door, a folded newspaper clutched in her hand like evidence at a trial.

"Helena." Beatrice's voice shook. "Tell me this isn't true."

She thrust the paper forward.

Helena took it with numb fingers. The headline screamed at her: *DOUBTS SURROUND LADY HELENA ASHFORD'S BETROTHAL*

Her eyes skimmed the text. *Sources close to the family suggest Lady Helena's hasty engagement to Major James Westwood was arranged to save face after Lord Thomas Chadwick withdrew his suit. The lady was seen receiving Lord Thomas at her home only two days ago, leading many to question whether her heart truly belongs to her intended…*

The room fell silent.

"Well?" Lady Ashcombe demanded. "Were you entertaining Lord Thomas in your home while engaged to another man?"

Helena's ears burned. "Thomas came to say goodbye before leaving for his country estate. That's all."

"That's all?" The Dowager Countess's eyebrows rose. "A private visit from a former suitor while your fiancé is nowhere to be found?"

"It wasn't a private visit. My aunt and sister were present."

"Were they?" Lady Vincent's tone suggested she doubted it.

Beatrice stepped closer, voice dropping. "Helena, you can tell me the truth. Is the engagement real? Because if you're being forced into this—"

"I'm not being forced into anything."

"Then why didn't you tell me?" Beatrice's hurt was palpable. "We've been friends since we were children. If you'd truly fallen in love, wouldn't you have confided in me?"

Helena opened her mouth, but no answer came. How could she explain? *I'm infiltrating a treasonous organization and pretending to be engaged for my cover* wasn't exactly drawing room conversation.

The silence stretched.

Lady Ashcombe's fan began moving again. "She can't answer. That tells us everything."

"It tells you nothing," Prudence announced, sweeping into the room in a dressing gown of such violent purple it made several ladies flinch. "It's barely nine in the morning, and you've descended on my niece like vultures on a carcass. Have you no shame?"

"We have every right to—"

"You have no rights here whatsoever." Prudence settled into a chair with theatrical grace. "But since you're so desperate for gossip, I'll give it to you. Helena and Major Westwood met at the Duke of Ashton's ball. He was utterly smitten the moment he saw her."

Lady Vincent sniffed. "How convenient."

"Convenient? It was a disaster." Prudence leaned forward conspiratorially. "He approached her without a proper introduction. Helena gave him such a set-down, any other man would have fled the ballroom entirely."

Despite herself, Helena felt a smile tug at her lips. That part, at least, was true.

"But he persisted," Prudence continued. "Quite romantic, really. Like something from a novel."

"Novels aren't real life," the Dowager Countess said drily.

"No, but love matches are." Amelia appeared in the doorway, arms laden with a flower arrangement she placed on the side table. "And theirs is genuine."

"How would you know?" Lady Ashcombe challenged.

"Because I have eyes." Amelia set down the arrangement and moved to stand beside Helena. "I've watched them together. The way he looks at her—like she's the only person in the room. The way she softens when he's near. You can't put that on."

Beatrice's expression wavered. "But the article says—"

"The article is gossip printed by people who weren't there." Amelia's voice turned sharp. "Were any of you present when Thomas called yesterday?"

Silence.

"Then perhaps you should stop believing scandal sheets over your own friends."

The Dowager Countess shifted in her seat. "Nevertheless, the timing is suspicious. A broken courtship, a hasty engagement—"

"Thomas and I were never formally courting," Helena said quietly. All eyes snapped back to her. "We were friends. That's all. When he began hoping for more, I realized I couldn't return his feelings. So I ended it. Kindly, I hope, but firmly."

"And then immediately accepted Major Westwood?" Lady Vincent's skepticism was clear.

"No. Then I spent weeks refusing to even consider another attachment." Helena met her gaze steadily. "James pursued me. I resisted. Eventually..." She paused. "Eventually, I stopped resisting."

Lady Ashcombe's fan had gone still. "Why?"

"Because he saw *me*. Not my father's legacy. Not my social position. Just... me." Helena's voice dropped. "And I realized I *wanted* to be seen."

The drawing room had gone quiet again, but this time the silence felt different. Softer.

Beatrice's eyes were suspiciously bright. "You could have told me."

"I know. I'm sorry." Helena reached for her friend's hand. "Everything happened so quickly, I barely had time to catch my breath."

"I would've helped you."

"You're helping me now."

Before Beatrice could respond, the butler appeared again. "Another caller, my lady. And... several more approaching the steps."

Prudence groaned. "How many people read that wretched article?"

"All of London, apparently," Amelia muttered.

Within twenty minutes, the drawing room was packed. Neighbors Helena barely knew. Acquaintances who'd never called before. All of them with the same barely concealed hunger for scandal in their eyes.

"Is it true about Lord Thomas?"

"Were you really seen embracing him?"

"Does Major Westwood know?"

"Has he called off the engagement?"

Helena stood in the center of the room, feeling like a fox surrounded by hounds. Amelia fielded questions from one group while Prudence entertained another with increasingly outlandish details of Helena's supposed romance. But the crowd kept growing, and the questions kept coming.

"Ladies, please—"

"Did you accept his proposal out of desperation?"

"Is the major aware of your true feelings?"

"Are you in love with him at all?"

"Yes."

The word landed harder than she intended.

Helena hadn't meant to say it. Certainly not like that—loud and sharp and utterly certain. But something inside her had snapped at the insinuation that James was merely convenient, that she'd simply settled.

Every eye in the room fixed on her.

"Yes," she said again, quieter this time. "I love him."

Had she just lied? Or told the truth? She couldn't tell anymore.

Lady Ashcombe's fan had stopped moving entirely.

"He's brave and principled and stubborn as a mule." Helena found herself smiling despite the audience. "He questions everything, including me. He doesn't let me hide behind propriety or expectations. He makes me want to be honest. To be better."

"But the article—"

"The article is wrong." Helena's voice steadied. "Thomas called two days ago to say goodbye before leaving for his estate. He's a friend, and he was kind enough to offer his regards as he departed. That's all."

"Can you prove it?" someone called from the back.

The butler materialized at the drawing room entrance. "A letter has arrived for Lady Helena. From Lord Thomas Chadwick."

The room erupted.

Helena took the envelope with shaking hands. Thomas's familiar script stared back at her. She broke the seal and unfolded the paper.

Dear Helena,

I write to inform you that I have departed London for my estate in Surrey. Recent events have convinced me that a period of country rest would be beneficial for my health and peace of mind, and your wise counsel helped me see that this is the best decision.

I want to be clear: any rumors suggesting impropriety between us are utterly false. You have behaved with nothing but honor and courtesy toward me. Our meeting yesterday was brief and proper—a simple farewell between friends.

Your engagement to Major Westwood is your own affair, and I wish you both every happiness. Please do not let idle gossip trouble you. Those who know you will recognize the truth.

I remain, as always, your friend,
Thomas

Helena's hands trembled as she lowered the letter.

"Well?" Lady Vincent demanded. "What does it say?"

Helena read it aloud, her voice barely wavering. By the time she reached Thomas's closing, several ladies were nodding approvingly.

"There," Prudence said triumphantly. "Satisfied?"

Lady Ashcombe snapped her fan open. "It does seem quite definitive."

"Of course it's definitive," Beatrice said, her earlier doubt replaced by fierce loyalty. "Helena told you the truth. Perhaps next time you'll believe her before invading her drawing room before breakfast."

The Dowager Countess actually looked chagrined. "We may have been… hasty."

"You think?" Amelia muttered.

The tension in the room eased fractionally. Some ladies settled back into their seats, accepting offered tea. Others began making polite noises about taking their leave. But the underlying current of curiosity remained.

Then the butler announced, "Major James Westwood."

Every head turned.

James stood in the doorway, still in his greatcoat, a copy of the scandal sheet visible under his arm. His eyes found Helena immediately.

The room held its breath.

He crossed to her in three strides, handed his coat and the paper to the nearest footman without looking, and took both of Helena's hands in his.

"Are you all right?" His voice was low, meant only for her, but in the silent room everyone heard it.

"I'm fine. I didn't expect—"

"I came as soon as I saw it." His jaw was tight. "Samuel brought me the paper. I should have been here sooner."

"James, you didn't need to—"

"Yes, I did." He glanced at the assembled ladies, then back to Helena. Something shifted in his expression—a decision made. "Everyone in London seems to think I don't care for you. That our engagement is some sort of arrangement."

"James—"

"Let them think what they want." His voice dropped further, but his eyes held hers with an intensity that made her breath catch. "I know the truth."

Helena's heart hammered. They had an audience. They needed to perform. But the way he was looking at her didn't feel like performance.

"What truth?" she whispered.

"That I'm the luckiest man in London." His thumb brushed across her knuckles. "That marrying you isn't convenient—it's a miracle I don't deserve."

Someone in the room made a small sound—delight or surprise, Helena couldn't tell.

"You don't have to say—"

"I'm not saying it for them." His voice was rough. "I'm saying it because it's true. Because you're extraordinary. Because the thought of losing you—" He stopped, jaw working.

Helena couldn't breathe. Couldn't think. Could only stare at him and wonder how much of this was real.

"So let them print their scandals," James said, louder now, addressing the room. "Let them question the timing or invent secret rendezvous. I know what I have. And I'm not letting go."

The drawing room exploded with chatter.

Ladies surged forward with congratulations, doubts forgotten. Prudence looked vindicated. Amelia was beaming. Even Lady Ashcombe's fan was fluttering with approval.

Beatrice pushed through the crowd to squeeze Helena's arm. "I'm sorry I doubted you," she whispered. "That man is *desperately* in love with you."

Helena managed a nod, still reeling.

James released one of her hands but kept the other, his grip steady. "Have they been interrogating you all morning?"

"Something like that."

"Then we're leaving." He raised his voice. "Ladies, if you'll excuse us, my fiancée needs air."

"But we've just arrived—"

"Then enjoy the tea. Lady Prudence will be delighted to entertain you." He was already guiding Helena toward the door.

They made it to the hallway before Helena found her voice. "James, you didn't have to—"

"Be so dramatic?" A hint of humor touched his eyes. "I'm aware. But you looked like you were facing a public execution."

"I was."

"I know." His expression sobered. "Helena, about the meeting. When you saw Thomas—"

"You don't need to explain."

"Yes, I do." He glanced back toward the drawing room, where voices still buzzed. "Not here. Too many ears. But later. We need to talk."

Something in his tone sent a chill through her. "James—"

"Later," he repeated. "After the gala. When everything's… settled."

"You're frightening me."

"I don't mean to." He squeezed her hand. "I just need you to know—whatever happens tonight, whatever we face—"

The drawing room door opened. Lady Josephine swept into the hall, resplendent in emerald silk.

"There you are!" She smiled brilliantly. "Helena, James, what a lovely surprise to find you both here."

Her timing was too perfect to be coincidence.

"Lady Josephine." James inclined his head. "I didn't know you were calling."

"I heard about that dreadful article and came immediately." Her voice carried clearly back into the drawing room. "Such nonsense. Anyone with eyes can see you two are devoted to each other."

"You're very kind," Helena managed.

"Not kind. Honest." Josephine's gaze moved between them. "I do hope you'll arrive at the gala together tonight. It will do wonders to silence the remaining gossips."

"Of course," James said.

"Excellent." Josephine beamed. "Then I'll see you both there. Try not to let the scandal sheets trouble you. By tomorrow, they'll have found some other poor soul to torment."

She glided back into the drawing room, and Helena heard her voice rise in authoritative greeting to the assembled ladies.

James released Helena's hand slowly. "I should go. Let you deal with the rest of them."

"Will you be all right?"

His expression was unreadable. "I'll manage. Tonight, then?"

"Tonight."

He collected his coat from the footman and paused at the door. "Helena?"

"Yes?"

"What you said in there. About loving—" He stopped, jaw tightening. "Did you mean it? Or was it just for them?"

Her breath caught. The honest answer terrified her. The diplomatic one felt like a betrayal.

"James—"

"Never mind." He shook his head, something unreadable crossing his face. "Forget I asked. Tonight's complicated enough without—" He stopped again. "We'll talk after. When we're not performing."

He left before she could answer.

Helena stood in the empty hallway, her heart pounding, as the voices from the drawing room swelled behind her.

Amelia appeared at her elbow. "Well. That was quite a performance."

"Was it?" Helena's voice sounded distant to her own ears.

"I think something else is happening now." Amelia studied her. "The way he looked at you—Helena, I don't think he was acting."

"He has to. We both do."

"Maybe you started that way." Amelia's voice gentled. "But I don't think you're acting now."

Helena couldn't answer. Because her sister was right.

Somewhere along the way, between the lies and the danger and the pretense, something had shifted. The engagement might have started as fiction, but what she felt when James touched her hand—that was achingly real.

And tonight, at the gala, they would either save each other or lose everything.

Helena straightened her shoulders and turned back toward the drawing room. The scandal would fade. The gossips would move on. But the truth—the complicated, terrifying truth— would remain.

She was in love with James Westwood.

And she had no idea if they would survive long enough for it to matter.

Chapter Thirty-Three

THE GALA

February 28, 1855
James

J AMES STEPPED DOWN from the carriage onto Lancaster House's snow-swept drive, Helena's hand resting lightly on his arm. Behind them, Amelia and Prudence descended in a rustle of silk.

Anyone watching would see a confident couple arriving at a charitable gala. But James felt Helena's tension in the way her fingers pressed against his sleeve—a mirror of his own.

Every eye would be on them tonight. The scandal sheet had seen to that.

They climbed the marble steps into the grand foyer. Chandeliers blazed overhead, casting golden light across elegantly dressed guests. The air hummed with conversation and violin strings.

James swept his gaze across the space, mentally cataloguing exits and vantage points. Somewhere in this glittering crowd were assassins. And somewhere, hidden among Sir Frederick's careful arrangements, were the traps they'd laid.

Unguarded corridors that weren't unguarded. Dimly lit stairwells watched from above. Doors left ajar with guards positioned just out of sight.

On paper, the defenses looked compromised. In truth, they were a snare.

At the top of the entrance hall, Duke Sebastian Cavendish greeted each arrival with practiced grace. Tall, distinguished, utterly unaware that beneath the silk and champagne, a war was unfolding on his polished floors.

"Lady Helena, Major Westwood." The duke smiled warmly. "A pleasure to see you both. The cause of the war widows and orphans lies close to all our hearts."

"Your Grace." James inclined his head. "We're honored to be here."

They moved into the crush of guests. Amelia drifted ahead like a diplomatic ghost—elegant, unobtrusive, watching everything. Prudence paused to compliment a matron's jewelry, providing perfect cover.

"Major Westwood. Lady Helena."

Lady Margaret materialized before them, resplendent in shimmering satin. Beside her stood Lady Eleanor Bennett, serene and unreadable.

"How brave of you both to attend," Lady Margaret said, her sympathy perfectly calibrated. "Not everyone would feel comfortable showing their faces after such… inventive speculation in print."

James kept his smile polite. "We can't allow foolish rumors to interfere with such an important evening."

Lady Margaret's gaze lingered, as if searching for cracks in their composure. "Of course not. True devotion always endures the ink of gossip." She paused. "I do hope tonight proceeds smoothly. Such a large gathering requires careful… oversight."

Something in her tone made James's instincts sharpen. Was that a warning? Or merely small talk?

"Indeed," Helena said smoothly. "Fortunately, the organizers have been thorough."

Lady Margaret smiled. "One hopes so."

She glided away, leaving James uncertain whether she'd just

wished them well or delivered a veiled threat.

"She knows something," Helena murmured.

"Or suspects something. The question is which side she's on."

Before Helena could answer, another voice cut through the chatter like a blade wrapped in velvet.

"Lady Helena. Still glowing, I see. I suppose scandal agrees with you."

Lady Vexley stepped closer, a shadow in dark-green silk. Her eyes fixed on Helena with cold assessment, ignoring James entirely.

Helena held her smile. "You're too kind, Lady Vexley. One does try to maintain composure when being dressed down in newsprint."

Vexley's lips curved. "Yes, I imagine that must've been quite a surprise. Those gossip columnists can be so… inventive. Almost as if they had assistance from within."

There it was. Not quite an admission, but close enough.

"Still," Vexley continued, "I suppose it was clever. What better way to cloak questionable meetings than beneath the veil of romance?"

James's voice turned cold. "There was nothing questionable about their meeting."

Vexley glanced at him—dismissive, perfunctory. "So I've been told. Though it's strange, isn't it? Some of us spend years proving our loyalty and are still passed over when matters of real responsibility arise. And yet others"—her gaze returned to Helena—"arrive with fanfare and are handed the run of the house."

Helena's chin lifted. "Perhaps it's because we're willing to act. Not just whisper behind fans."

Vexley's eyes glittered. "Action is admirable. Until it's reckless."

James stepped forward slightly. "As is fomenting discord in public."

Vexley's jaw twitched. "Just see that you don't disappoint

Lord Bridewell. He doesn't enjoy being embarrassed."

She vanished into the crowd.

James exhaled slowly. "She'll be watching us all night."

"Let her watch." Helena scanned the room. "She thinks I've stolen her influence. She's not entirely wrong. But she's forgotten something."

"What's that?"

"I'm better at this than she is."

Helena guided them toward a cluster of familiar faces. Lady Beatrice Cavendish turned toward them, diamonds glittering at her throat, her smile warm but her eyes sharp.

"I was beginning to wonder if I'd spot you," Beatrice said, taking Helena's hands. "You both look positively unbothered—very well done."

Helena gave a small smile. "Appearances are everything."

Beatrice leaned closer, lowering her voice. "Major, you may wish to keep an eye on the Prussian envoy. Pruhsfeld. There's been talk—quiet, troubling talk—that he's a pawn of the Russians. Here to facilitate the movement of funds. Not for diplomacy, but for influence."

She hesitated. "Some say it's meant to drive a wedge between Britain and France. Others whisper about darker intentions. With your background, I thought perhaps you'd know where to pass that along. Discreetly."

James's chest tightened. "That's deeply concerning. Thank you, Lady Beatrice. I'll see it reaches the right ears."

Beatrice inclined her head. "I knew you were the right man to speak to. Do excuse me—duty calls."

She glided away.

Helena's grip tightened on his arm. "If Pruhsfeld is working with the Russians…"

"Then this isn't just treason. It's foreign influence."

They moved through the ballroom, exchanging pleasantries, always watching. James's gaze snagged on a figure near the refreshment table.

Lord Percival Grey.

The man wasn't mingling. He was observing. Cataloguing. That calculating smirk set James's teeth on edge.

"Grey's here," he murmured to Helena.

"I see him."

James adjusted their path, keeping Grey in sight without approaching directly. But as he turned, a voice cut through the surrounding chatter.

Low. Familiar. Roughened by years but unmistakable.

James went rigid.

His gaze snapped toward a cluster of guests near the pillared archway. A man in evening dress, half-turned away, speaking to a footman. Average height, unremarkable features. But the voice—

Ethan Turner.

It couldn't be. Turner was dead. Or disappeared. Or—

The man moved, and James caught a glimpse of his profile. Older. Harder. But the same.

Blood roared in his ears.

Ethan Turner. Here. Alive. At this gala.

The man who'd sold out his unit in Crimea. The man whose betrayal had gotten good soldiers killed. The man James had trusted.

Helena's hand tightened on his arm. "James? What's wrong?"

He forced himself to breathe. To think. "Nothing. I—thought I saw someone."

"Who?"

He couldn't answer. Not here. Not with Turner standing thirty feet away, casual as you please, as if he hadn't traded British lives for Russian gold.

Turner finished speaking to the footman and melted into the crowd.

James's fists clenched.

"James." Helena's voice cut through the haze. "Talk to me."

"Later." His voice was rough. "I need—I'll explain later."

She studied him, concern etched in her features, but nodded.

Across the ballroom, James spotted another familiar face—or rather, an unfamiliar one that moved with familiar ease.

A footman, silver tray in hand, circulating among guests. Perfectly ordinary. Except James recognized the way he moved. The slight cant of his shoulders. The economical grace.

Adrian.

In disguise. Exactly as planned. Whatever face he'd borrowed tonight, it was good enough to fool the room.

Their eyes met briefly across the crowd. Adrian's gaze flicked toward the curtained archway, then back to James. A message: trouble that way.

James gave an almost imperceptible nod.

Then Adrian's attention shifted sharply. His posture changed—subtle, but James caught it. Adrian had seen something. Or someone.

James followed his line of sight.

Ethan Turner, emerging from behind a pillar, accepting a glass of champagne from a passing tray.

Adrian had recognized him too.

For a fraction of a second, Adrian's mask slipped. Not enough for most to notice. But James saw the shock ripple across his features before the footman's bland expression returned.

Adrian turned away deliberately, moving toward the far end of the ballroom. Avoiding Turner.

But the damage was done. Adrian knew Turner was here. And Turner—if he'd been paying attention—might have caught that moment of recognition.

James filed it away. Another complication. Another threat.

He forced himself to focus on the immediate task. Find Bridewell. Confirm Pruhsfeld's presence. Watch for the assassination attempt.

Near a shadowed alcove, James spotted his target.

Lord Talon Bridewell stood in quiet conversation with a tall man draped in black and gold. That had to be the Prussian envoy. Herr Pruhsfeld.

So Beatrice's information was accurate.

Pruhsfeld smiled easily, gesturing with one hand while Bridewell nodded, face drawn with concentration. They weren't discussing the weather. This was business.

Russian gold flowing into British treason.

James's jaw tightened. That money would fund the Society's rot while British soldiers bled in Crimea. And Bridewell stood there like a merchant at market, trading loyalty for leverage.

"That's him," Helena murmured at his side. "Pruhsfeld."

"And he's not here to make friends with the queen. He's here to fund the enemy."

James glanced at her. Fire and clarity wrapped in silk. "We'll expose them."

"You can count on it."

They lingered near the dais, close enough to observe without drawing attention. James's thoughts circled—bombs, assassins, Turner's reappearance, the possibility of Bridewell discovering their ruse.

One misstep, and everything would collapse.

"James?" Helena's voice, gentle. "You're distant."

"I'm fine. Just observing." He nodded toward Bridewell's corner. "He's with Pruhsfeld again."

Her gaze sharpened. "I'll circle around. See if I can get closer, hear what they're saying."

He caught her hand as she turned. "Helena—" Too much unsaid. He settled for a nod. "Be careful."

Her fingers lingered. "Always."

She vanished into the crowd.

James turned toward the stairs, scanning the upper gallery. He needed higher ground. A better vantage point.

Near the musicians' gallery, he spotted Amelia surrounded by foreign guests, her pleasant chatter about Viennese waltzes disguising her keen surveillance of the floor below.

The footmen all looked legitimate. No unfamiliar faces. No signs of infiltration yet.

But James couldn't shake the instinct to find Helena. To make sure she was safe.

He leaned over the railing, searching the ballroom floor.

No copper silk near Bridewell or Pruhsfeld. No sign of her in the surrounding clusters.

His pulse ticked faster.

She'd said she'd circle around to eavesdrop. But there was no trace of her.

Had she found something? Was she already acting?

Or had something gone wrong?

He forced himself to stay calm. Helena was brilliant. Capable. She didn't need him hovering.

But knowing that didn't quiet the dread coiling in his gut.

Movement near the curtained archway caught his eye—one of Bridewell's men, drifting toward the west corridor with studied nonchalance.

The game was in motion.

James descended the stairs, weaving through dancers until he edged close enough to Bridewell and Pruhsfeld to catch fragments of their conversation.

"If Reginald frames Balaclava as heroism," Bridewell said quietly, "the public will rally. Parliament will follow. Support for the war will surge."

Pruhsfeld's thin smile held no warmth. "Which is precisely what the tsar cannot allow. A united Britain is far more dangerous than a disillusioned one."

James's jaw clenched. Confirmation. Russian involvement. Treason funded from abroad.

Around him, the gala glittered—laughter, champagne, oblivious nobility. They had no idea what moved beneath the surface.

Bridewell and Pruhsfeld parted with stiff bows, both wearing the look of men who'd sealed a dark bargain.

James scanned the crowd again.

Still no Helena.

The dread sharpened into something harder. She should have

returned by now.

Near the refreshment table, Lord Percival Grey spoke in low tones to an older gentleman in a sleek frock coat.

James drifted closer, just within earshot.

"And what of Sir Reginald's speech?" the companion asked quietly.

Grey gave a derisive laugh. "Only that it's meant to rouse sentiment. Balaclava. Heroism. Patriotism. All that rot. After the Light Brigade disaster, it'll have the public weeping and Parliament digging deep. We can't have that."

"The Charge was a tragedy," the man said. "It's already won public sympathy."

"Which is precisely why the speech must never be delivered."

James didn't react. Didn't flinch. Just turned smoothly and moved away.

So Grey was complicit in the assassination. Actively working to silence Prescott.

He filed it away. Another piece of the puzzle.

But Helena—

A flash of copper silk near the west corridor.

Relief flooded through him, sharp and immediate.

She emerged from behind a column, her expression composed but urgent. Their eyes met across the ballroom.

She gave a small nod. Found something.

James started toward her, but a hand caught his elbow.

He turned.

Adrian—still in footman's livery—leaned close as if adjusting James's cuff. "Turner's heading for the southwest gallery. He's meeting someone."

"Who?"

"Don't know. But we need to follow." Adrian's voice dropped further. "Watch yourself. He's armed."

James glanced back at Helena. She'd already turned away, moving purposefully toward the west wing. Whatever she'd found, she was acting on it.

His instinct screamed to follow her. To make sure she was safe.

But Turner was here. Armed. Meeting someone. If James didn't track him now, they'd lose him.

"Lead the way," James said quietly.

Adrian melted back into the crowd, and James followed, keeping distance between them. Around them, the gala swirled on—music, laughter, champagne. Oblivious.

James glanced once more toward where Helena had disappeared into the west corridor.

Be safe, he thought.

Then he turned toward the southwest gallery, following Adrian into the shadows.

The trap was set. The players in motion.

And somewhere in this glittering maze, traitors were about to make their move.

Chapter Thirty-Four

A HIDDEN MENACE

February 28, 1855
Helena

HELENA HAD SLIPPED away from James under the pretense of circling the ballroom. Her true intent was one she knew he'd disapprove of: to eavesdrop near Bridewell and Pruhsfeld. She'd nearly reached the back corridor when a familiar voice called out.

"Lady Helena."

Sir Frederick stepped from a narrow servants' passage, face composed but eyes sharp.

"We've received word of a device," he said, voice pitched low. "An explosive. Hidden somewhere inside Lancaster House. We believe Sir Reginald is the target."

Helena's breath caught. "What can I do?"

"I have people searching every inch." He glanced past her toward the ballroom. "Once dinner is called, you'll have access to the east wing and ballroom while guests are occupied. I want you to check the dais and surrounding areas. Quietly. Thoroughly. If we can't locate it, we may be forced to clear the house."

She nodded crisply. No protest. No hesitation.

"Watch for anything that doesn't belong—not just devices.

Assassins as well." He vanished back into the shadows.

The weight of his words settled over her.

Helena returned to the ballroom's edge, finding Prudence with a practiced smile already in place. In a few quiet words, Helena relayed what Frederick had told her.

Prudence didn't blink. "I'll keep watch. Signal if you need assistance."

Helena spotted James briefly across the room, but then he disappeared with Adrian, moving toward the southwest corridor.

Her chest tightened. *Be safe.*

DINNER WOULDN'T BE announced for another ten minutes, so Helena seized the opportunity to search the upper corridors while the guests were still occupied in the ballroom—this was her best opportunity.

She moved quickly through the eastern wing, mentally noting windows, alcoves, doors. Gaslight flickered along gilt-trimmed walls. Fewer footmen here. Fewer eyes. They'd left these halls deliberately unguarded as part of the trap, but now the gaps made her pulse race.

Every shifting shadow might be hiding an assassin.

She passed drapery with a glance, skirts brushing the floor, eyes scanning the seams of walls and baseboards. Nothing yet. But the devices could be anywhere.

From below, Amelia's laughter floated upward—a practiced distraction, a buffer of normalcy.

Helena checked behind wall sconces, beneath decorative tables, inside empty vases. The corridor yielded nothing suspicious, but she'd done what she could. When dinner was called, she'd focus on the most vulnerable areas: the dais, the ambassador's route, anywhere Prescott would be exposed.

As she headed back down the main staircase, the dinner gong

sounded through the ballroom.

Guests began drifting toward the dining hall in clusters, the room slowly emptying as seating arrangements quietly asserted their social order. Helena lingered at the periphery, smiling through compliments and pleasantries, every sense strained to track exits, staff, anyone who lingered too long near closed doors.

Amelia left the spot where she'd been holding court near the musicians' gallery and followed the others into the dining room as well.

From across the thinning crowd, Prudence caught Helena's gaze and lifted a brow—confirmation. Time to search.

She angled toward her aunt. As she passed, Prudence leaned in, voice soft beneath the rustle of skirts. "Sir Frederick has a message. He suspects a traitor among us. Someone who might know we're acting against them."

Helena's smile didn't falter. "Then they'll learn we can fight back."

Prudence moved to stand watch near the ballroom entrance as Helena approached the podium where Prescott would speak.

The parquet wood floor stretched before her, empty now, her footsteps nearly silent.

At the dais she paused, scanning the space.

Then she saw it.

Something glinted at the base of the podium.

Not polish. Not waxed wood.

Metal.

Her pulse spiked. She pressed one hand briefly to her necklace—three fingers brushing the pendant. Their agreed-upon signal.

Down the hall, Prudence's eyes met hers for only a heartbeat, then she turned and vanished behind a side curtain, headed for Frederick.

Helena exhaled once and turned her focus back to the podium.

She was about to kneel when a voice stopped her cold.

"You shouldn't be here."

Helena froze. The voice was soft, clipped, vaguely familiar. A woman stepped from the shadowed alcove beside the podium—blonde curls pinned neatly, suspicion tugging at her lips.

Lady Clarissa.

But no.

Not Lady Clarissa. Her cousin, *Lydia*.

"No one is permitted to be near the device," Lydia said. "Not tonight. The Raven gave explicit instructions."

Helena straightened slowly, keeping her expression neutral. "I didn't know you'd be attending, Lady Clarissa."

A flicker of tension crossed Lydia's face, quickly masked. "I wasn't meant to. I came to ensure everything was proceeding according to plan. When I saw you—well, I assumed you understood the need for caution."

"Of course," Helena said smoothly. "But I thought it wise to check the placement myself. Sir Bridewell asked for assurances."

That seemed to appease her. Lydia stepped closer, lowering her voice. "We should move. If anyone sees us here, it could draw attention and complicate everything."

Helena glanced toward the base of the podium again, feigning concern. "This one is well-placed."

"Yes." Lydia hesitated. "It has the best opportunity. But there are more. One's in the east corridor, along the ambassador's exit route. I told them it was excessive, but Vexley insisted. Said if the first one failed, the panic would drive him straight into the path of the second."

Helena nodded as if in agreement, though her pulse hammered.

Rapidly approaching footsteps echoed down the corridor.

Lydia tensed. "I shouldn't be seen with you." Her eyes flicked to Helena once more. "Stay clear once this begins. You're too valuable to be caught in the chaos."

Two of Sir Frederick's men emerged from the side passage and seized Lydia.

"Wait—what are you—" Lydia began, but one clamped a hand over her mouth.

The other took her firmly by the arm, guiding her silently toward the exit.

Lydia struggled briefly, eyes wide with betrayal as she looked to Helena.

Helena simply watched, expression composed.

They vanished through the doorway.

Helena turned back to the podium and crouched, fingers steady despite her racing heartbeat.

Attached to the base was a wicked little mechanism of brass, copper, and steel.

A bomb.

A compact infernal machine—brass and steel, its inner workings humming with quiet menace. A clockwork heart ticked faintly beneath the casing, wires looping around a small glass vial dark with powder. Machine oil filled her nostrils. A tightly wound spring pressed against the charge, primed to ignite when the mechanism completed its cycle.

Ingenious in its simplicity. Lethal in its intent.

She forced her breath steady.

She'd spent years studying codes, locks, and the delicate workings of clocks under her father's quiet instruction, recording each lesson meticulously in her notebooks. She had a knack for understanding clockwork—the tension in gears, the precision of springs and levers. As a girl, she'd opened household clocks just to see how they ticked, adjusting their mechanisms until they hummed in perfect rhythm.

Adrian had capably trained them in observation and mechanical principles, but the disarming of explosive devices hadn't been part of the curriculum. Still, the principle was familiar: understand the sequence, identify the trigger, interrupt it without setting the whole thing off.

Her fingers curled around the apparatus, feeling the faint vibration of the ticking mechanism. She eased it loose from the panel, hands trembling for only a heartbeat before focus settled in.

This wasn't mere clockwork. This device was designed with lethal intent.

She inhaled slowly, remembering her father's quiet voice explaining how hidden triggers were often disguised as stabilizers.

A soft footfall behind her made her pulse spike.

She spun.

Prudence stood in the doorway, skirts rustling faintly, expression unreadable.

Her gaze dropped to Helena's hands, then narrowed. "Well. You weren't exaggerating."

Helena straightened slightly, the device still cradled in her palms. "It's active. But stable—for now."

Prudence stepped closer, voice low and even. "Do you need help? Or shall I just stand here and look decorative?"

Helena gave a tight laugh. "Decorative is fine. Just stay back."

"I'll do my best." Prudence's gaze swept the room. "I assume this isn't the only party favor?"

Helena nodded once. "At least one more. East corridor. Vexley's idea."

Prudence's mouth thinned. "Of course it was."

A few curious guests lingered near the far end of the corridor, attention drifting toward Helena's position.

Without hesitation, Prudence pivoted and strode toward them, voice rising in theatrical alarm. "Oh, do be careful with that punch bowl!"

Heads turned instantly. Prudence waved her hands with commanding grace, herding them away with effortless charm.

Helena breathed out and turned back to the bomb.

She pulled back the brass casing, exposing an intricate coil of wires and gears. Two primary leads twisted together. A third wire arched between them. A spring-loaded pin perched over the glass vial.

Decoy wire, her father's voice warned from memory. *They'll hide the true trigger in plain sight, but twist a second to confuse the eye.*

Her fingers followed the fuse's path, searching for the resistance point.

There. The stabilizer wire. Not the decoy, but the real one.

With a steady breath, she flicked open her folding knife. One quick slip—*snip*—and the connection broke.

No hiss. No jolt. No explosion.

Another slow cut, and she eased the fuse free from the spring-loaded trigger.

The clockwork clicked softly. Then… silence.

Helena exhaled, chest loosening.

She'd done it.

She placed the disarmed mechanism gently on the floor. Her legs threatened to give out, but she stayed upright.

Footsteps.

Dr. Sebastian Ramsey approached, brow furrowed—until his eyes dropped to the bomb.

"You disarmed it?" His voice was stunned.

"I did."

"Brilliant." He breathed. "I'll secure it."

Prudence returned, smoothing her gloves. "Amelia's charming them with tales of forbidden Viennese dance steps. She can buy us another five minutes, no more." She glanced at the device, then at Helena. "Tell me there aren't others."

Helena straightened. "There's another. East corridor. Lydia confirmed it before she was taken."

"Of course she did." Prudence eyed the bomb with distaste.

Ramsey accepted the apparatus with careful hands and disappeared into the side passage.

Within minutes, he returned with Sir Frederick.

Helena's eyes instinctively sought James. He wasn't there.

A flicker of disappointment pricked beneath her ribs, quickly suppressed. No time for it.

Frederick's expression was grave as she explained what had happened—Lydia's slip, her confession, the device's design.

He listened closely, then gave a sharp nod. "Well done. You may have saved Prescott's life. But we're not finished." His voice lowered. "If we halt proceedings now, we lose our chance to seize the ringleaders and send half of Europe's diplomats fleeing in panic. That kind of chaos—the Society wins."

Ramsey stepped in. "So we keep the gala going. Let them move first, catch them in the act."

"Exactly," Frederick said grimly. "Helena—keep searching. You're our best hope of locating the others. Sebastian, coordinate with me. Prudence, keep the guests from wandering."

Prudence gave a crisp nod. "Subterfuge is my specialty."

They parted with quiet purpose, each step underscored by rising urgency.

Helena caught Ramsey before he disappeared. "Stay close to Frederick. If another bomb is found—or someone tries to act—you'll be needed."

He nodded and vanished.

Helena turned to Prudence. "We need to check the corridor Prescott will use to reach the dais. Lydia mentioned another device was planted along his route."

Prudence offered a bright smile—too bright. "Lead on, dear."

THEY MOVED SWIFTLY through the east corridor, skirts whispering over polished wood, gaslight throwing long shadows against the walls.

This was the route Lydia had mentioned—the one Lord Prescott would take following his speech. If the Society wanted to guarantee his death in the event their first bomb failed, this was the perfect place.

"Anything?" Prudence whispered.

"Not yet." Helena's gaze swept over decorative urns, behind wall sconces, beneath velvet-draped tables.

Then she saw it.

At the base of a tall Corinthian column, partially obscured by a folding screen, a thin wire protruded just slightly from behind the molding.

"There," she said, already crouching.

Prudence moved to stand watch, subtly repositioning a velvet rope to block the far end of the hall.

Helena eased the screen back.

Behind the column's baseboard, a second device nestled in a hollowed-out cavity—slightly different construction but no less lethal. The same brass and steel casing, but different wire arrangement. The spring looked tighter, the vial of black powder smaller but more volatile.

"Stay back," she told Prudence.

This one was designed for devastation. Not only would Prescott be killed, but anyone standing near him.

She examined the wiring. This version was more complicated, but now she knew what to look for.

A false wire looped across the top. The real circuit was wound in the base, concealed beneath a tensioned pin.

You've done this once, she told herself. *Do it again.*

She cut the decoy first—quick and clean—then slipped the blade behind the pressure pin. One sharp breath. One slow motion.

Snip.

The spring snapped upward, harmlessly. The pin released with a soft metallic click.

Silence followed.

Helena's heart pounded as she extracted the device, cradling it in her gloved hands.

Behind her, Prudence let out a breath. "If you keep this up, I'm going to insist you carry smelling salts."

Helena managed a faint smile. "You handled that superbly."

"I once talked a duchess out of serving roast beef because it clashed with her garden party. Diverting the flow of guests is nothing."

Helena wrapped the disarmed bomb in a linen napkin from a nearby sideboard. "We need to get this to Frederick, but I'm afraid it could explode if it's jostled."

Prudence stepped forward, peering at the device. "Hide it here for the moment, and I'll report its location to him. If one of us trips and we both die in a blaze of misplaced heroism, I'll never hear the end of it from your sister."

Helena slipped the device into an empty champagne crate and tucked it behind the curtain near the servants' entrance, then straightened, brushing dust from her gloves. "I should return to the ballroom before anyone notices my absence."

"Agreed. I'll find Frederick and—"

Prudence stopped mid-sentence, her gaze fixed on something past Helena's shoulder.

Helena turned.

At the far end of the corridor, barely visible in the gaslight's flicker, stood Sir Talon Bridewell.

He wasn't moving. Just watching them.

His expression was unreadable from this distance, but the set of his shoulders—rigid, alert—sent ice down Helena's spine.

How long had he been standing there?

What had he seen?

Bridewell's gaze held hers for one long, terrible moment.

Chapter Thirty-Five

SHADOWS IN THE CROWD

February 28, 1855
James

A FLICKER OF motion ahead—Ethan turning down a side hallway.

James and Adrian pushed through the last cluster of guests and into the corridor. Quiet. Dimly lit.

Far ahead—just a whisper of sound. Footsteps. A door easing shut.

They broke into a run, bootsteps muffled by rugs. At the far end, the door to a servants' stairwell stood ajar.

"He's heading away from the public rooms," Adrian said under his breath. "I think he's trying to escape."

"Your cover. Stay out of sight," James muttered. "If he can identify you later—"

Adrian's mouth twitched. "He won't. I age ten years and drop two social classes in this getup."

Movement above them. James glimpsed Ethan rounding a landing one flight up, his silhouette shadowed by flickering gaslight. Not standing to fight—fleeing.

"Ethan!" James's voice rang through the stairwell.

The figure hesitated—just for a heartbeat—then bolted up the next flight.

They chased him through the servants' levels, past linen closets and storage alcoves, each footstep echoing in the confined space. James's lungs burned and his knee protested the steep stairs, but fury kept him moving. He couldn't let Ethan disappear. Not tonight.

They reached a dim corridor on the upper floor. A side door slammed shut ahead. James crashed through after it, catching the blur of Ethan ducking into a room off the corridor.

No lamps lit.

James hesitated only a second before plunging in.

The salon beyond had the heavy hush of a space long undisturbed. Velvet curtains muffled the music and laughter rising from below. Every creak of the floorboard under James's boot felt deafening.

Then—

Flick.

A match hissed to life.

Its sharp scent cut through the stale air. The flame flared, illuminating Ethan's face in strokes of light and shadow. He stood by the hearth, expression unreadable behind the dance of flame.

James froze. Heart hammering.

Ethan gave a slow smile. "Just wanted to make sure it was you."

The flame wobbled, burning lower. "You brought backup? Afraid to face me alone?"

"Just someone to make sure you don't stab me in the back again." James's voice was gravel edged. "You ran. Why?"

Ethan tilted his head. "Because I knew if you saw me, you'd follow. And I couldn't resist seeing how far you'd chase a ghost."

He dropped the match.

The tiny flame hit the floor and extinguished with a soft hiss. Darkness rushed back in.

The only light came from a trace of moonlight slicing through a gap in the curtains and the faint glow from the doorway behind them.

"Yours is the last face I expected to see," James said, tracking Ethan's shape in the half light. "What are you doing here? Why Pruhsfeld?"

Ethan's voice floated toward them. "Still asking all the wrong questions. Good to know some things never change."

James stalked forward. "Answer me."

Silence. Then: "Because he's willing to help. Because he understands the world isn't won with honor and blind loyalty. You always wanted the war to mean something. I just wanted to survive it. Crimea wasn't a beginning—it was the end. The end of believing England cared about its sons."

James's voice was low and cold. "You let our men die."

"I was ordered to make that trade," Ethan shot back. "One platoon to gain information that could save hundreds. You were supposed to die that day too. Your own general was willing to sacrifice you."

The words settled like ash in James's lungs.

Ordered. Your own general was willing to sacrifice you.

He remembered the general seated beside his cot, speaking in that clipped cadence he'd used during briefings. He'd called it a tragedy. A tactical miscalculation. He'd rested a gloved hand on James's arm and said, "You weren't meant to be there, son."

God, he'd believed him. Because the alternative—that the general had known, had sent them to die—was too grotesque to entertain.

But now…

James swallowed hard. For one raw second, the floor seemed to tilt.

Ethan's voice was low, almost kind. "You were never supposed to come back, James. They counted you among the acceptable dead."

The old wounds roared to life—smoke, screams, the thunder of the blast that mangled Andrews, that buried six others in ash and twisted iron. The leg that still ached when it rained.

And yet.

There was something in Ethan's tone. Something gloating. Satisfied.

In that instant, James's understanding shifted.

No tremor in Ethan's voice. No flicker of remorse. Just that same maddening smoothness—a story spun with just enough pain to make it plausible.

It *sounded* like the truth. Which was exactly why it wasn't.

"You almost had me," James whispered. "For a moment, you nearly did it. That's your gift, isn't it? You don't need facts—just a thread of doubt and a man too tired to pull it out far enough to see it goes nowhere."

Ethan's tone sharpened. "Is it so hard to believe generals would trade lives for advantage? You saw the Light Brigade. You know what they do to good men."

James moved closer, stepping into the moonlight. "I stayed. To serve my queen. You ran."

Ethan stepped back.

James pressed on. "The general might've made tactical mistakes. But you *chose* this path. You *chose* the Black Rose. You chose Russia's coin over your country."

"No," Ethan said. "I saw the truth. And I chose the Society."

"You chose wrong," James snapped. "They want to burn it down."

"At least they're honest about it."

They circled, faint outlines caught in shifting silver and black.

"Don't dress treason in disillusionment," James said. "I've buried men who broke. But you didn't break. You betrayed."

Silence. Then Ethan edged toward the door.

James moved to block him. "Not this time."

"You're making a mistake."

"You already did."

Ethan's voice dropped. "Once tonight's chaos begins, you'll be too busy worrying about Helena to stop us. Or did you think the bombs would spare her?"

James's blood ran cold. Bombs?

"If you've touched her—"

"Touch her?" Ethan raised a hand in mock innocence. "You're the one who let her wander off when she's surrounded by enemies."

"Leave her out of this."

"That unguarded corridor? That was your plan. Clever, really. But maybe ask yourself—how far did you fall by pretending to be one of us?"

James lunged.

They crashed against a side table, glass rattling as shadows clashed in violent motion.

"We. Are. Nothing. Alike."

Ethan's grin turned savage. "You're right."

Moonlight caught the blade—just once—before Ethan struck. His hand moved—fast.

Steel flashed.

Pain flared sharply along James's arm.

"James!" Adrian's voice, urgent from a darkened corner. He pounced from the shadows and twisted Ethan's knife arm, forcing him back. "That's enough."

Ethan snarled, struggling in Adrian's grip. "You should be worrying about your fiancée. You're too late. This night's already turned in our favor."

James's vision blurred, but Adrian was there, pulling the blade from Ethan's grip and tossing it aside. Ethan struggled, but Adrian held firm.

"We don't have time for this," Adrian snapped. "If we don't focus on our mission, Prescott dies—and others too."

James forced his mind to focus. The bombs. The speech. Helena.

"Let me find something to tie him," he ground out.

He yanked a length of curtain cord from the wall and sliced it free. Between them, they dragged Ethan into a chair and lashed his wrists and ankles.

Still panting, Ethan chuckled. "The main attack hasn't even begun and you're already broken and bleeding."

James shoved a handkerchief into Ethan's mouth and tied it tight. "Then we'll meet it head-on."

Adrian's voice came low. "Let's move."

James gave Ethan one last look. Bound, gagged, and faintly smug beneath it all. But contained, and no longer in control.

He stepped back into the light of the corridor, the door clicking shut behind them.

Chandeliers sparkled as if nothing had happened. The orchestra played on. Laughter floated from the distant dining room—light, bright, entirely unaware.

But James felt the war humming beneath every note.

He glanced down at his sleeve—wet, sticking to his skin. The pain pulsed sharper now, blood still warm, but it didn't matter yet.

He met Adrian's gaze. "Frederick first. Then Helena."

Adrian nodded once, handing him a fresh handkerchief. "No time to waste."

James bandaged his arm, then adjusted his coat and straightened. The cut could wait. Everything else couldn't.

They slipped back into the crush of velvet and candlelight.

James scanned the dining room—for Helena, for Grey, for Vexley. For any glint of danger hiding in plain sight.

He wouldn't lose her. Not to the Society. Not to ghosts. Not to Ethan.

Different war. Same stakes.

He'd lost his brothers once.

He wouldn't lose her now.

Chapter Thirty-Six

A CONSPIRATOR'S GAMBIT

February 28, 1855
Helena

SIR TALON BRIDEWELL stood at the far end of the corridor, watching them.

Helena's breath caught. *How long had he been standing there? What had he seen?*

When he walked toward them, her heart hammered against her ribs.

Beside her, Prudence smoothed her skirts with practiced ease. "Good evening, Sir Talon," she said brightly. "I was just leaving to find Frederick. He asked me to check on the floral arrangements in the main hall."

Bridewell's expression remained unreadable. "Did he."

"Indeed." Prudence's smile didn't waver. "Though I confess, these drafts are dreadful. I believe I'll find a warmer corridor before I catch my death."

She swept past him without waiting for a reply, footsteps retreating down the hall with deliberate purpose.

Helena stood her ground, pulse racing. *Don't show fear. Don't let him see.*

Bridewell stopped three feet away, studying her. "And you,

Lady Helena? What brings you to this particular corridor?"

"Checking the route Prescott will take to the dais," she said, keeping her voice steady. "You asked me to ensure the security gaps remained in place. I wanted to verify them myself."

When his expression shifted—not suspicion, but approval, relief flooded through her.

"Good," he said. "Timing is essential tonight." He gestured toward a nearby doorway. "Join me. We should discuss the final arrangements."

She followed, mind racing. *Keep him talking. Learn of any changes. Any surprises he might have.*

The room they entered appeared be a private study. A desk flanked by tall, curtained windows faced two chairs.

"And tonight's Prussian guest?" she asked. "Pruhsfeld—he truly speaks for the Russians?"

A smile crept across Bridewell's face. "He delivers funding, influence, pressure—enough to bend men who mistake position for power. This alliance with France will ruin us. The tsar offers something better."

Helena kept her tone neutral, curious. "You truly believe our salvation lies with Russia?"

"The monarchy drags us toward collapse," Bridewell said, voice tight with fervor. "But a realignment—one led by men of vision—will see Britain rise again. The old order must fall."

She nodded as if convinced. "And tonight's display will ensure that?"

"Tonight is our opening move. We correct the balance. Disruption is merely the means." He lowered his voice. "Prescott's speech—if it reaches the public, will cement loyalty to the Crown. One rousing tribute to the Light Brigade, and tragedy becomes a rallying cry. We can't allow it. Tennyson's damned poem has done enough harm as it is."

Her throat went dry. "But why bombs?"

"One is for him. The others are contingency."

He watched her closely, so she didn't let her expression falter.

"But we're not fools. If the explosions fail, we proceed with simpler means. A shot. A blade. My men are already positioned. His words will die in his throat."

Already positioned? They'd slipped past the guards? Helena forced herself to appear calm. "And if security interferes? Tries to stop them?"

Bridewell's smile was cold. "My men are already among the crowd as guests. They'll strike when the moment comes and disappear into the chaos. No one will know who fired the shot until it's far too late."

A shot. A blade. Operatives hidden among the guests. Backups upon backups.

Footsteps approached. Helena tensed as Lady Eleanor Bennett glided into the room, all composed elegance. Lady Margaret followed a step behind, clearly flustered.

"Talon. There you are," Eleanor said to Bridewell. "Margaret was convinced she saw you slip away."

Lady Margaret's gaze darted between the three of them. "I didn't mean to intrude—I only thought—"

"You thought correctly," Eleanor said smoothly. "Talon needed a moment away from the crush. But as you can see, all is well." She turned to Margaret with a dismissive smile. "The duke was asking after you. Something about the whist tables."

Margaret's relief was palpable. "Oh. Yes, I should—" She nodded quickly to the room. "Forgive me."

She hurried out, footsteps fading rapidly down the corridor.

Eleanor waited until silence settled, then turned to Helena. "Margaret means well. Unfortunately, sentiment and resolve rarely coexist."

"Useful, though," Bridewell said. "Her late husband's connections have given us access we'd otherwise lack."

"True." Eleanor moved to the window, gazing out at the glittering carriages below. "Some people are meant to endure change. Others are meant to impose it."

Helena recognized the opening. "And Prescott? Which is he?"

"An impediment." Eleanor's voice was cold. "He'll stand at that podium and tell a room full of grieving families that their sons died for glory. That the disaster at Balaclava was somehow noble."

"It wasn't?" Helena asked carefully.

"It was a massacre." Bridewell's jaw tightened. "Six hundred men sent to charge entrenched artillery because of a miscommunication. And now Prescott wants to spin it into propaganda for continuing this war."

Eleanor turned from the window. "He'll invoke the poem. Quote Tennyson's pretty phrases about honor and sacrifice. By the time he's finished, half the room will be weeping and the other half will be ready to send their own sons to die."

"We can't allow that," Bridewell said quietly.

Helena kept her voice neutral. "So tonight you silence him."

"Tonight we demonstrate that the Crown cannot protect even its own elite." Eleanor's smile was thin. "When a bomb explodes at the heart of London's finest gathering—when a diplomat dies within sight of the prince—faith doesn't waver. It breaks."

A chill ran down Helena's spine. "The musicians' gallery," she said, as if confirming it. "That's brilliant placement. The sound will carry through the entire ballroom."

Bridewell's eyes sharpened. "You've been thinking tactically."

"I've been thinking practically." Helena met his gaze. "Three devices, you said. The podium for Prescott. The east corridor for panic. And the gallery to ensure everyone hears it."

"Precisely." Eleanor looked pleased. "The corridor serves no strategic purpose. Vexley insisted on the symbolism."

"Where *is* Lady Vexley?" Helena asked. "I'm surprised she isn't here."

"Occupied elsewhere," Bridewell said shortly. "She has her role. You have yours."

Helena shifted her weight. "About the gallery—my sister Amelia was near there earlier. I should make certain she's moved to a safer area before—"

"No." Bridewell's voice was flat.

"But—"

"You'll stay here." He stepped closer. "You've proven yourself capable. Loyalty is another matter. You'll remain in this room until it's time to observe Prescott's speech."

Helena's heart sank. "Sir Talon, I only meant—"

"I know what you meant." His expression was unreadable. "But tonight, everyone remains where they're assigned. No exceptions."

Eleanor moved to stand beside him. "Surely you understand. We can't have people wandering the halls at critical moments."

"And Lady Clarissa?" Helena tried a different angle. "Shouldn't someone ensure she's in position?"

Bridewell's jaw tightened fractionally. "Clarissa was given clear instructions."

"She's late," Eleanor observed. "Unusual for her."

"Should we be concerned?" Helena pressed.

Eleanor shrugged, the gesture elegant and unconcerned. "If she's meant to be here, she will be. If not—events will proceed regardless."

Helena stared at her. "That's remarkably fatalistic for someone orchestrating an assassination."

"Is it?" Eleanor's smile didn't reach her eyes. "I prefer not to pretend the world bends for individual lives. We control what we can. The rest takes care of itself."

"Or doesn't," Bridewell added. "Either way, Prescott does not leave this house alive."

"History will barely notice how."

The casual brutality of it struck Helena silent. They weren't just ruthless—they were coldly indifferent to anyone who wasn't immediately useful.

Eleanor studied her. "You seem troubled."

"Not troubled," Helena said quickly. "Merely… calculating risks. My aunt and sister are both in attendance. I'd prefer not to lose them in the chaos."

"Then you'll appreciate our precision." Bridewell gestured to the window. "The devices are timed. The targets are specific. Your family will be safe if they stay away from the podium and the eastern corridor."

"And the gallery?" Helena asked.

"Will be cleared before the charge ignites." His eyes narrowed. "Why are you so interested in the musicians' gallery?"

Helena's pulse quickened. "I'm simply being thorough."

"Good." He moved between her and the door. "Then you'll be thorough here. With us. Until it's time."

The trap closed around her.

Footsteps sounded in the corridor again—different this time. Confident. Approaching.

"Ah," Eleanor said. "Lord Hawthorne. Right on schedule."

Lord Edward Hawthorne stepped into view beside Duke Cavendish. Polite interest flickered on their faces.

Bridewell turned toward them, momentarily distracted.

Helena seized the moment. She stepped back—once, twice—until the statue's shadow swallowed her.

One more step, and she slipped into the adjoining corridor.

Her heart hammered as she moved quickly down the hall, boots whispering over polished stone.

They'll suspect. But it doesn't matter. I know the plan now.

A bomb. A shot. A blade. Prescott wouldn't survive unless she stopped them.

The Black Rose was thorough. Ruthless. They'd trade lives for their vision without hesitation.

I won't let them.

Footsteps echoed faintly behind her. She ducked through a side passage, vision narrowing to a single purpose.

Find Frederick. Warn him. Then the musicians' gallery.

She ran toward the music, the glittering crowd—and the stage where a man's life hung by a thread.

She had a speech to save.

And a future to fight for.

Chapter Thirty-Seven

A RACE AGAINST TIME

February 28, 1855
James

JAMES PRESSED A hand to the bandage beneath his coat. The bleeding had stopped, but the wound throbbed with every movement. Around him, Frederick's men—still disguised as footmen—moved with tense purpose, casting occasional glances but asking no questions.

He turned a corner as Frederick emerged from a curtained side room. Behind him stood Josephine and Prudence, both wearing a brittle composure.

"James." Frederick's voice was low, urgent. "Staff reported movement on the roof. Might be how they're bringing additional men inside." His gaze flicked to James's arm. "You're bleeding."

"Ethan Turner is here. Alive. I confronted him—he's tied up now. But he warned me Helena was in danger."

Frederick's expression hardened. "Then we move fast. I have men searching for the third bomb. Find Helena. You two, stay close to Prescott. He refuses to cancel—says retreat would humiliate the Crown."

A young agent burst through the curtain. "Sir—Bridewell's people are looking for Lady Helena. They've been told to detain her."

James's chest tightened. "I'll find her."

Frederick nodded. "Go. Josephine, Prudence—keep the guests calm, but position yourselves to help if we need to clear the rooms."

James skirted the ballroom's edge, scanning the crowd. The deliberate security gaps now felt like open wounds. One unguarded hallway to his right sent a chill of foreboding down his spine. Perfect access for an assassin.

The crowd parted slightly, and he pressed forward, cutting down the corridor—

And nearly collided with Helena.

She burst around the corner, breathless, eyes wide. When she saw him, her shoulders dropped with relief.

"James." Her voice shook. "They wanted me to stay with them while the bombs went off—but when Hawthorne arrived, I slipped away. I had to. I'm exposed."

He steadied her with his good hand. "Are you hurt?"

"No. But they're planning multiple attacks—if the bomb fails, they have assassins positioned. And there's a third device in the musicians' gallery."

"Frederick's men are searching for it," James said. "But we need to protect Prescott."

"I couldn't stay with Bridewell," she said. "If he catches me again—"

"He won't." His voice was firm. "We stay together from now on. Prescott needs protection, and so do you."

Relief flickered across her face. Then she noticed his arm. "You're injured."

"It's minor. I'll explain more later. Right now we need to head to the west corridor. Frederick's men swept it earlier. Prescott should be in the side chamber."

He slipped his arm around her waist and guided her forward. His wounded arm pulsed with pain, but he ignored it.

They stepped into a broader hall where moonlight streamed

through tall windows.

Frederick spotted them from a doorway and strode forward. "You're both intact. Good. We haven't located the third device."

"It's in the musicians' gallery," Helena said. "But if the bomb fails, they'll use blades or bullets. One way or another, Prescott dies."

Frederick nodded grimly. "I'll have my men search the gallery now. If they don't find it before the speech, I'll pull them. Too dangerous. You two stay with Prescott. Position guards around him—we might prevent a direct attack."

"They've placed men among the guests," Helena warned. "If the bomb doesn't create panic, something else will."

Frederick's jaw tightened. "The prince is still in the north reception room. That changes things."

He signaled sharply to two nearby agents. "Now. Quietly."

Across the hall, James caught a glimpse of movement—Prince Albert Edward being guided away through a side door, his guards closing ranks around him as if nothing out of the ordinary had occurred.

Frederick gave them a look of hard approval. "Now we need to hold the line." He turned and disappeared down another corridor.

James looked at Helena. "To Prescott. We don't leave his side."

She nodded, and they moved forward together.

Ahead, the corridor glowed with firelight. The orchestra played. The crowd waited, unaware.

The last act had begun.

Chapter Thirty-Eight

THE ASSASSINATION UNRAVELED

February 28, 1855
Helena

HELENA AND JAMES wove through the crowd toward the dais. Sir Reginald Prescott stood near it, encircled by Frederick's guards, each man alert, coats weighted with hidden pistols.

Prescott's relief was palpable when he saw them. "Lady Helena. Major Westwood. Thank God. Frederick keeps pressing me to cancel, but I can't." He lowered his voice. "Public confidence is splintering. Half of Parliament would have us retreat; the other half would have us prosecute the war more fiercely. The widows in this room—they need to know their husbands didn't die for a blunder. If I don't speak tonight, those opposed to the war carry the day."

Helena kept her voice steady. "Two bombs have been disarmed. A third remains in the musicians' gallery—Frederick's men are searching for it now."

"And if they don't find it in time?" Prescott asked.

"Then we clear the gallery before you speak," James said. "But there are other threats. Assassins among the guests. Armed. Waiting."

Prescott's jaw tightened. "I know the risks, Major. But if I retreat now, it sends a message: that terror works. That men like Bridewell can silence the Crown with threats." He met James's gaze steadily. "I won't give them that victory."

James studied him for a long moment. "Then we adjust. If we find the third bomb, then you can give your speech. But no one comes within arm's reach. Any movement toward the dais, we stop. If a weapon is drawn, he is to be brought down at once."

"Agreed," Prescott said.

"And if something goes wrong," James continued, voice hard, "you go down. Not heroically. I'm not suggesting you martyr yourself. I mean literally—you drop flat and let the guards cover you. Understood?"

A flicker of humor crossed Prescott's face. "I'll try to resist the urge to perform heroically, Major."

"See that you do." James glanced at the guards. "Keep the circle tight. No one approaches without authorization."

One of the guards—broad shouldered, sharp-eyed—nodded. "We'll hold the line, sir."

Helena stepped closer to Prescott. "This speech—it matters that much?"

"It has to." Prescott's voice dropped. "Half the people in this room believe the war is pointless. The other half think retreat is cowardice. If I can make them see why we're there—not for conquest, but to keep Russia from controlling the Black Sea— then maybe, just maybe, we can unify them long enough to finish this properly." He paused. "Or at least prevent total collapse."

James exchanged a glance with Helena. "Then we make sure you're alive to deliver it."

"We found it," Sir Frederick announced as he approached. "The third device has been removed."

Sir Reginald nodded. "Then we proceed as planned." He began making his way toward the dais with his guards.

"That means the other assassins will be forced to act," James said.

She nodded. "Be careful."

They separated and eased into position.

Before she could settle near the urn where she planned to observe the guests and watch for assassins, a hand gripped her elbow—hard.

Lady Vexley yanked her into the shadow between two columns, green silk rasping, her fury barely leashed.

"Let go," Helena said quietly.

Vexley's grip tightened. "You treacherous little Judas. I warned Talon you were too polished. Too eager. But he was so delighted to have the diplomat's daughter at his elbow." Her smile showed teeth. "You played us all."

Helena wrenched her arm free. "I did my duty."

"Duty." Vexley's laugh was sharp as broken glass "Is that what you call it? Passing yourself off as one of us? Lying to our faces? Pretending to believe while you gathered evidence to hang us?"

"You were planning to murder a diplomat and blame it on Crown incompetence," Helena said, voice cold. "What did you imagine would follow?"

"I imagined we'd win." Vexley stepped closer, voice dropping to a hiss. "I imagined we would finally show them what power looks like when it isn't dressed in velvet and lies."

"By slaughtering widows in a ballroom?"

Vexley's eyes flashed. "*Widows?*" She flicked a glance toward the crowd. "Look at them—draped in black and still applauding the men who sent their sons to die. They'll weep tonight and sign another petition tomorrow. They are not victims, Helena. They are accomplices with clean gloves."

Her gaze fixed on Prescott; she took a step.

Helena caught her wrist. "Don't."

"Or what?" Vexley leaned in, breath hot with rage. "You'll have me dragged out like some kitchen thief? I'm already ruined. You made certain of that." Her voice turned silky—cruel. "But you'll remember me. You'll remember that I saw you for what you are."

Helena's jaw tightened. "I'm stopping fanatics from killing innocent people."

"*Innocent.*" Vexley spat the word. "There's no innocence left in this room—only comfort. And comfort breeds rot." She jerked her wrist free. "Enjoy your little triumph. It will cost you."

She slipped back into the crowd as if she'd never been there.

Helena exhaled, hands shaking. James appeared at her elbow.

"Trouble?" he asked quietly.

"Nothing I couldn't handle."

His gaze followed Vexley's retreating form. "She's not done. Keep watch on her."

Helena nodded. "If she interferes, we arrest her."

Sir Reginald stepped onto the dais. A hush rippled outward. Gilded fans stilled. Champagne flutes lowered. Helena stood near one of the tall urns flanking the dais, spine rigid, senses sharpened. James positioned himself opposite—still, watchful.

Her heart hammered against her ribs.

"Ladies and gentlemen. Noble friends. Honored widows. Families of the fallen." Prescott's voice carried through the chamber. No dramatics. Just that cool, steady voice.

"We gather tonight not in ease or celebration, but in remembrance."

Helena's gaze swept the ballroom. Too many curtains. Too many guests with tight expressions. She catalogued exits, shadows, every flicker of movement.

"In the Crimea, our soldiers endure cold, hunger, and cannon fire. Many will not return. Some of you know that already. Some of you wait in dread to know it still."

Her breath caught—not from sentiment, but from watching someone walk willingly into the crosshairs. The Society wouldn't allow this speech to finish. Not a matter of if. Only when.

Prescott paused. "You've heard the words. Tennyson gave words to what our soldiers could not speak."

Her chest constricted.

"'Theirs not to reason why, Theirs but to do and die.'"

The words landed like a hammer. Someone sniffled. A gloved hand trembled, lowering a fan.

"They charged not for glory, nor for medals, but because they were told to. And they obeyed. Despite confusion. Despite blunder. And still, they rode."

A flicker of movement. Tall man. Narrow build. Threading through the crowd too deliberately.

There. Right side. Moving toward the dais.

James noticed—she saw it in the angle of his head, the shift in his stance.

"Bravery should not have to answer to incompetence."

James moved like a knife through silk—calm, casual, lethal.

The stranger was close now, beneath the lip of the dais. His hand slipped into his coat.

Steel glinted.

James caught the man's wrist. A subtle pivot, a half step. Their shoulders touched—briefly, concealing the quiet struggle. The blade disappeared. Another man—Frederick's—appeared behind the attacker, hand on his elbow. Gone. Folded back into the crowd.

Prescott continued, unshaken. "If we are to honor those lost, let it not be with verses alone. Let it be with change."

Helena's breath slowed. The applause hadn't begun. But she could feel it building.

"Let command be earned on the field, not inherited in drawing rooms."

A ripple of support. Scattered murmurs. A faint clap—cut short.

Then Prescott pivoted. "Some ask why we remain in the Crimea. Why our men fight and freeze for a distant peninsula most could not find on a map. Let me answer plainly."

Helena straightened. Even James shifted.

"We are not in the Crimea for glory. Nor to expand borders. We are there to keep Russia from seizing control of the Black Sea—a gate that opens into the heart of Europe."

He stepped forward. "If we abandon Crimea, Russia gains control of the straits. That power would not stop at the Danube or the Dardanelles. It would shift the balance of Europe itself. The ports of Constantinople would become staging grounds. The trade routes of the East—ours, France's, Austria's—would be strangled."

A low murmur ran through the room.

"We stand against aggression, not to escalate war but to contain it. If Britain yields now, we send a message not only to Russia, but to the world: that tyranny can advance unchecked, so long as its boots don't yet reach *our* shores."

Helena's chest tightened.

"We are there because peace is not preserved by inaction. We are there because our allies depend on us. And because the men who die under our flag deserve to know their sacrifice holds meaning beyond the mud."

A sharp silence. Then—

"So you say," someone muttered bitterly from the back.

She didn't look. That tone reeked of the Black Rose.

Prescott didn't pause. "And we are there to prove that Britain will not be bullied in the councils of the great powers by opportunists who trade diplomacy for bloodshed."

His voice rose. "We must be better—stronger—in how we fight, and in who we place in command. But we must fight."

A flicker of green. *Vexley?* Then it was gone.

Eleanor's companion whispered to someone nearby. Faint sneers passed between them.

The crowd was splintering. The speech was working—dividing. Exposing.

Then the shift came.

She felt it before she saw it. The air thinned. The back of her neck prickled.

A figure emerged near the left curtain behind Prescott. Holding a silver tray. Moving too deliberately.

Not a servant.

A pistol gleamed beneath the tray.

"Left," she whispered—sharp, urgent.

James turned, already moving.

Prescott's voice lifted: "Let our enemies—foreign and domestic—take note—"

The tray clattered to the floor.

Two deafening cracks shattered the air.

Screams erupted as the guards swept forward. Prescott dropped to the floor, protected by one of Sir Frederick's men. The chandelier above groaned—one bullet caught the chain. Crystals rained down. Someone screamed.

Then the third shot rang out.

James stumbled.

Helena's heart lurched. No.

She didn't think—she launched.

The gunman was turning, pistol swinging toward Prescott on the floor for another shot. Helena grabbed the first thing she could reach—a heavy crystal vase from the nearby pedestal—and hurled it at his head.

It struck him in the face. He staggered.

She crashed into him before he could recover, using her momentum to drive him sideways. They hit the floor hard. Her elbow struck marble—sharp pain bloomed. The taste of blood filled her mouth where she'd bitten her tongue.

He was stronger. Heavier. He tried to shove her off, one hand still gripping the pistol.

She couldn't overpower him. But she could make it impossible for him to aim.

She grabbed his gun hand with both of hers, forcing it toward the floor, using her weight to pin his arm. He snarled, thrashing, trying to throw her off. His free hand caught her shoulder—she cried out as his fingers dug into the bruise from earlier.

But she held on.

"Get off—" He bucked violently.

She drove her forehead into his nose. Felt the crunch. Blood sprayed.

He roared, grip loosening just enough.

She wrenched the pistol from his hand and flung it across the floor, out of reach.

Then guards were there—finally—pulling him off her, slamming him facedown into the marble.

James crashed through a toppled chair, back on his feet, eyes blazing. He reached for her.

Relief buckled through her.

Helena scrambled upright, chest heaving. Her right hand burned—scraped raw. Her shoulder throbbed. Blood filled her mouth.

Sir Reginald climbed to his feet and turned back to the crowd. Calm. Shaken, but whole.

For a moment, he just stood there, gripping the podium rail. His hands trembled slightly. Then he straightened.

"Britain may stumble," he said, voice not quite steady at first but gaining strength, "but she does not fall. Not when her people stand together."

Silence. Shattered crystal glittered across the floor.

Then a single clap—uncertain, testing.

Another joined it. Then a few more.

Some guests remained frozen, staring at the blood, the fallen chandelier, the subdued gunman. Others whispered urgently to companions, already edging toward the exits.

But a widow in black stood, tears streaming down her face, and began clapping—slow, deliberate, defiant.

An officer near the gallery lifted his hand to join her. Then another. A clergyman. A titled lady who'd lost her son at Balaclava.

The applause grew—not triumphant, but raw. Shaken. The sound of people who'd just witnessed violence and were choosing, despite their fear, to stand with the man who'd survived it.

Half the room clapped. The other half stood in stunned silence or murmured nervously to each other.

But it was enough.

They hadn't just protected a man. They'd kept the speech from being silenced by terror.

The Society wanted chaos. They'd gotten resistance instead.

Though not everyone joined. And not everyone was convinced.

Near the back, Lady Eleanor stood motionless. Expression tight. Behind her, Lady Margaret—a subtle tilt of her head. Eyes unreadable. Her gaze flicked to Helena and lingered.

James eased in beside Helena, placing one hand at the small of her back.

"Dramatic enough for you?" he muttered.

"Too close."

His breath warmed her ear. "Close is still alive."

Frederick approached, expression taut. "It's over."

Helena's knees nearly buckled. She exhaled slowly. No lives lost. Not tonight.

"The building?" she asked, voice raw.

Frederick nodded. "The house is secured. No one gets out. We've arrested conspirators we haven't yet identified, but the worst has passed." He gave them both a sharp nod. "Good work."

Then Sir Talon Bridewell appeared at the edge of the crowd.

Not flustered. Not panicked.

Walking with careful, deliberate precision toward Frederick.

His face was composed. Almost serene. But his eyes—his eyes burned with something cold and furious.

"Sir Frederick," he said, voice carrying clearly, "I believe congratulations are in order. You have spared us an unpleasant spectacle."

Frederick turned slowly. "Sir Talon. I'm surprised to see you still in attendance."

"Why should I flee?" Bridewell's smile was thin. His gaze swept the scene—guards, shattered crystal, the subdued gunman. "Though I confess, I am… disappointed."

"Disappointed?" Frederick's tone remained careful.

"That even my own side cannot manage competence." Bridewell stepped closer, hands folded behind his back. "One asks for precision and is given clumsy hands and panic."

Helena's breath caught. He was confessing—because he couldn't resist being heard.

"Sir Talon," Frederick said quietly, "we might speak privately. There's no need to agitate the room."

"On the contrary." Bridewell's eyes found Helena and held. "Let them look. Let them understand what has been done here." His voice softened—almost admiring. "Lady Helena—how exquisitely you played it. The grieving daughter. The disillusioned patriot. The earnest reformer." The smile thinned further. "I believed you. That is my error."

James moved between them. "That's enough."

Bridewell lifted his chin, addressing the crowd as if he stood in Parliament. "Is it? I think these ladies and gentlemen deserve to know how the Crown conducts itself when it fears honest dissent. It sends its creatures into drawing rooms—into charities—into our very conversations."

"Honest dissent?" Helena stepped forward, fury held tight. "You planted bombs in a ballroom full of widows. You took Russian gold to fund treason."

"Treason." Bridewell's laugh was sharp, incredulous. "You call it treason to demand that Britain be led by men of judgment? To refuse a war conducted for vanity and alliances?" He turned slightly, sweeping the room. "We are bleeding in the Crimea while boys with titles play at command. And when men insist it must end, the Crown calls them villains."

"You're not a reformer," Helena said coldly. "You're a fanatic willing to murder innocents to make a point."

"Innocents?" Bridewell's composure cracked—just a fissure, showing heat beneath. "There are no innocents in a nation that applauds slaughter as patriotism. Every vote that sent men to the guns. Every drawing-room cheer. Every handkerchief waved as boys marched away." His eyes burned. "Complicity wears silk as easily as it wears uniform."

Sir Frederick waved two guards forward. "Sir Talon Bridewell, you are under arrest for treason, conspiracy, attempted murder, and receiving funds from a foreign power."

Bridewell didn't resist. He spread his hands, almost gracious. "There it is. Arrest. Silence. A tidy little lesson." His gaze fixed on Helena. "You think you have won. You have only postponed what is coming. This order is already dying."

As the manacles closed, he called over his shoulder, voice ringing to the rafters: "Remember this night. Remember that the Crown hides behind masks and calls it justice."

Then he was gone, dragged into the corridor, still preaching to anyone who would listen.

Another stir in the crowd. Lady Eleanor Bennett being arrested. A moment later, she was brought forward by Frederick's agents, hands already bound.

Unlike Bridewell, she wasn't speaking. Wasn't preaching. Just watching with cold, calculating eyes.

She stopped before Helena, guards on either side.

"Well played," Eleanor said softly. Only Helena and James could hear. "I misjudged you."

"You let Bridewell speak," Helena said. "Why?"

Eleanor's mouth curved—barely. "Because Talon cannot bear silence. He'd rather be caught with an audience than escape unseen." Her gaze flicked toward the corridor where he'd vanished. "I told him to go. He chose to perform."

"And you?" James asked.

"I prefer survival to speeches." Eleanor's voice dropped. "I know when the board has turned—tonight."

"For tonight," Helena said, unwilling to grant her anything.

Eleanor's eyes glittered. "You stopped three devices. You saved one man and one speech." She leaned in a fraction, cool as winter glass. "The Society runs deeper than you know. You've cut off a limb, not killed the beast."

"Then we'll cut off the rest," Helena said.

"Will you?" Eleanor's smile didn't warm. "My usefulness is at an end." Her gaze cut briefly across the ballroom—Parliamentary faces, titled men, clergymen. "But not the thing you're fighting.

"How many do you think you've found?" she murmured. "A handful? Two dozen?" The softest shrug. "There are men who sign laws by day and send orders by night. Men who sit in pews and call it virtue. You cannot clap irons on an idea, Lady Helena."

"We'll try," Helena said.

"Do." Eleanor's voice was almost gentle. "And when you grow tired, remember: every arrest makes a story. Stories recruit."

Frederick stepped in, sharp. "Enough. Take her."

As the guards pulled her away, Eleanor raised her voice—not a shout, just a clear statement pitched to carry:

"Lady Helena is in the Crown's service. She came among us under false pretenses. Remember that."

Several guests gasped. Others whispered behind gloved hands.

Eleanor didn't look back. She didn't need to.

Then Lady Margaret's voice, feather light but perfectly timed, floated over the murmurs.

"Lady Eleanor?" Margaret stood near the back, hand pressed delicately to her throat, expression shocked. "My goodness. I had no idea you were involved in all of this. How dreadful."

Eleanor turned her head, scowling. "Margaret—"

"To think I considered you a friend," Margaret continued, voice carrying. "And all this time, you were plotting murder." She shook her head, the picture of aristocratic horror. "Thank heavens Lady Helena was brave enough to stop you."

The murmurs shifted. Several ladies nodded. The narrative was already changing.

Eleanor's expression went cold. "You opportunistic little—"

"Take her," Frederick repeated, voice harder.

Eleanor was dragged away, still glaring at Margaret, who

watched with an unreadable expression.

Helena caught Margaret's eye across the room. Margaret gave the slightest nod—so subtle no one else would notice—before turning away to comfort a scandalized dowager.

There was something unreadable in that exchange. Helena filed it away.

Within moments, both Eleanor and Bridewell were gone, their voices fading into the night.

Helena stood very still, heart finally slowing. Footmen began offering champagne again—mechanical, awkward. Guests drifted into hushed clusters, whispering behind gloved hands.

Sir Reginald leaned heavily on the dais railing, pale but uninjured.

They'd done it.

Chapter Thirty-Nine

UNMASKED

February 28, 1855 – March 1, 1855
James

"OUR POSITIONS WITHIN the Black Rose are useless now," James murmured, fingers brushing Helena's.

She nodded, throat working. "But at least all of London will know we remained loyal to the Crown."

He laced his fingers with hers—public, unmistakable. Around them, guards moved through the crowd, rounding up conspirators. Guests whispered behind gloved hands. Several stared openly at their joined hands.

Let them stare.

"But we succeeded," he said quietly. "We saved Prescott. We caught the leaders. We'll deal with the consequences."

Helena's gaze tracked Bridewell being led past—head low, irons flashing. He didn't look back.

"Come on," James said. "Frederick will want a full report. And we still need to collect Ethan Turner."

Helena's breath caught. "Turner. I'd nearly forgotten."

"I haven't." His jaw tightened. "East corridor. We left him gagged, tied."

They moved swiftly through the dim halls, past shaken guests who still clung to corners in hushed conversation. The door to the side room stood ajar.

Inside—only makeshift ropes on the floor.

Helena knelt beside them, fingers brushing the frayed edge. "He cut himself free. Or someone helped."

James's stomach dropped. Had he missed a concealed knife? Had one of Bridewell's men rescued Turner?

"He'll surface again," Helena said, standing. Her voice was flat. Exhausted.

James nodded, though frustration burned in his chest. Turner had been right there. Bound. Helpless. And now—

"Major Westwood. Lady Helena."

Frederick appeared at the corridor's end, Josephine beside him. Both looked drawn, years added in a single night.

"Sir Frederick," James said.

"Walk with me." Frederick gestured toward a private study. "We need to talk."

The study was small, windowless. A single lamp burned on the desk. Frederick closed the door behind them.

"Sit," he said. Not an order. An invitation.

James remained standing. Helena sank into a chair, shoulders rigid.

Frederick leaned against the desk, arms crossed. "You stopped an assassination on British soil. Prevented a massacre. Exposed two of the Society's highest-ranking members." He paused. "That's a triumph by any measure."

"But?" Helena asked.

"But the cost is significant." Frederick's expression was grave. "Your covers are gone. Bridewell named you both publicly. By morning, every remaining Society member will know you're Crown agents."

James had expected this. Still, hearing it aloud settled like lead in his chest.

"How many did we arrest?" he asked.

"Fifteen tonight," Josephine said. "Including Bridewell and

Lady Eleanor. But we estimate the Society has at least thirty more members we haven't identified."

"And the foreign interests?" Helena asked.

Frederick's jaw tightened. "Herr Pruhsfeld—the Prussian envoy—he's gone. Left before we could question him. Claimed diplomatic immunity, departed in a private coach within the hour."

"So their foreign entanglements remain largely intact," James said.

"Largely, yes." Frederick straightened. "We still need to investigate a scheme they call Eclipse. Bridewell mentioned it, then abruptly stopped talking as if he'd realized he'd said too much. We don't know what it is yet, but its existence suggests the Society's plans extend beyond tonight's attack."

Helena's hands tightened in her lap. "Then this isn't over."

"No," Frederick agreed. "It isn't. We've wounded them badly—severed leadership, disrupted activities, exposed their methods. But they're not destroyed." He looked between them. "And you're both targets now. Bridewell made that clear."

The words hung in the air.

James had known that too. Had accepted it the moment he'd chosen this mission. But knowing Helena was marked—that she'd carry this danger because of what they'd done together—

"We'll be ready," he said.

"Will you?" Josephine's voice was gentle but pointed. "You've been living false identities for weeks. You've infiltrated, maneuvered, lied to people you knew. Convinced them you were engaged. That takes a toll." She looked at Helena. "And now everyone knows. Your friends. Your family. The world at large."

Helena's composure didn't crack. But James saw the flicker of something in her eyes. Pain. Shame.

"I'll need full written reports from both of you," Frederick said. "But that can wait a day or two. For now, go home. Rest. You've earned it."

"What happens next?" James asked.

"We regroup," Frederick said. "Question the prisoners. Track down the remaining members. And decide how best to employ you henceforth—now that your usefulness in that guise has ended." He paused. "But that's a conversation for tomorrow."

"Tomorrow," James agreed.

Frederick studied them both. "You did well tonight. Better than well. You saved lives. Remember that when the doubts come."

James nodded.

Frederick pushed off the desk. "Go home. Both of you. Get some rest. God knows you've earned it."

Josephine touched Frederick's arm lightly. "We'll handle the interrogations tonight. You two have done enough."

"Thank you," Helena said quietly.

Frederick opened the door. The sounds of the building filtered in—boots on marble, low voices, the distant clatter of a carriage departing.

James and Helena stepped into the corridor.

The door closed behind them.

THEY WALKED IN silence through the emptying halls of Lancaster House.

The ballroom doors stood open. Inside, servants swept shattered crystal, righted toppled chairs, scrubbed blood from the floor.

Helena stopped at the threshold.

James stopped beside her.

"I keep seeing it," she said. Her voice was barely above a whisper. "The gunman turning. The pistol. You stumbling."

"I'm all right."

"You were shot."

"Shot at. Not struck. I'm uninjured," he corrected. "There's a difference."

She turned to him, eyes searching his face. "You could have died."

"So could you." His throat tightened. "When you tackled that gunman—Helena, he was twice your size. If the guards hadn't reached you—"

"But they did."

"Barely."

She looked back at the ballroom. "We survived."

"We did."

"And now we're exposed. The engagement was our cover. Without it—" She stopped. Drew a breath. "What are we now?"

The question he'd been dreading.

Because he didn't have an answer. Not one he could voice. Not when exhaustion pulled at every word, when his arm throbbed and her face was pale with fatigue.

"I don't know," he said honestly. "But I know I don't want to lose you."

Her eyes met his. Something flickered there—hope? Fear?

"James—"

"We're both exhausted," he said gently. "We've been running on nothing but stubborn determination for hours. This isn't the time to make decisions."

She nodded slowly. "You're right."

But the distance between them felt vast.

He wanted to pull her close. To tell her everything burning in his chest—that somewhere between the lies and the danger, he'd fallen in love with her. That the engagement might have been false, but what he felt was devastatingly real.

But the words stuck.

They always had.

"You should go home," he said. "Get some rest. Your family will be worried."

"Amelia and Aunt Prudence are here somewhere," Helena said. "Frederick had them taken to a private room."

"Then find them. Make sure they're all right." He paused. "I'll see you here tomorrow."

She studied his face. "Tomorrow."

Neither of them moved.

The moment stretched, fragile and uncertain.

Then Helena stepped back. "Goodnight, James."

"Goodnight."

She turned and walked down the corridor, spine straight, shoulders back. Every inch the lady she'd been raised to be.

But he saw the exhaustion in her gait. The slight hitch in her step.

She disappeared around the corner.

James stood alone in the empty hallway, the echo of her footsteps already gone.

The danger—for tonight—was over.

He looked down at his bandaged arm, the blood from the knife wound seeping through the linen. A sharp reminder of how close they'd come.

Worth it.

Dawn filtered through the tall windows, turning the marble pale gold as London stirred beyond the walls.

Tomorrow, he'd answer to Frederick. To the Crown. To every choice he'd made.

And tomorrow, if he could find the courage, he'd tell Helena the truth.

Chapter Forty

NEW BEGINNINGS

February 28–March 1, 1855
Helena

HELENA STOOD BY the tall window in the Foreign Office Annex, fingers trailing through condensation on the glass. Morning pressed pale and gray against London's rooftops. The city stirred—carts creaked, hooves clipped cobblestones, church bells tolled the hour.

The world moved forward, unaware.

Behind her, Sir Frederick sat at the long mahogany table, unshaven and rumpled. Lady Josephine stood beside him, one hand resting lightly on his shoulder. Across the room, James leaned against a chair, his injured arm bound in fresh linen.

Helena had gone home last night. Tucked Amelia and Aunt Prudence safely in bed. Collapsed into her own still wearing her ruined gown. Woken three hours later to a summons from Frederick: *Come to the Foreign Office. We need to finish this.*

Now, standing in this quiet room, exhaustion pulled at every thought.

"Her Majesty sends her congratulations," Frederick said, breaking the silence. "And her gratitude. I briefed her this morning on everything that transpired."

Helena turned from the window. "We were simply doing our duty."

"You saved Sir Reginald Prescott's life," Josephine said gently. "And prevented a massacre. That's rather more than duty."

James shifted. "What's the tally of the injured?"

"Three guests were injured by falling crystal from the chandelier," Frederick reported. "None seriously. One gentleman suffered apoplexy from the shock and is recovering at home. No deaths."

Helena exhaled slowly. *No deaths.* After everything—the bombs, the gunman, the chaos—no one had died.

"Bridewell and Lady Eleanor are in custody," Frederick continued. "Both singing different songs. Bridewell claims he's a patriot fighting a corrupt monarchy. Eleanor insists she was following Bridewell's lead and had no knowledge of the full plan."

"She's lying," Helena said flatly.

"Obviously." Frederick's expression was grim. "But she's clever about it. Her statements contradict Bridewell's just enough to create doubt."

The door opened.

Evan Harrington, Duke of Westbridge, entered with Violet Heatherington at his side. Both looked tired but composed.

"Good," Frederick said. "We were just reviewing the aftermath. What's the status on Sableport Maritime?"

Evan dropped a folder onto the table. "The shipping invoices link directly to Hawthorne's ledgers. Every crate bound for the wine vaults bore Sableport markings—some official, some altered. All traceable, yes, but nothing that directly implicates Sableport in wrongdoing."

He paused, jaw tight. "The board denies everything. I sit at that table, Frederick. I hear what they choose to say in open session. But the real decisions are being made elsewhere—by men who have learned how to smile at one another while keeping their ledgers locked."

"How are they concealing their involvement?" Adrian asked.

"By using proxy companies and false ledgers to hide behind," Evan said. "Names borrowed from the dead. Offices that disappear between inquiries."

Violet's voice was precise, controlled. "We traced one set of records to a counting house off Bishopsgate. By the time we arrived, it had been emptied. Signage painted over. One director's signature appears on documents dated last week—but his obituary was printed last month."

"They erase their trail faster than we can preserve it," Evan said.

Frederick's expression darkened. "So they're wounded but not destroyed."

"Exactly," Violet confirmed. "They've shuttered records and burned correspondence. Their investors have gone quiet. But they're still functioning. Barely."

James stirred. "Then the threat remains."

"It does," Evan agreed. "But the damage is visible now. The cracks are spreading. We just need time to widen them."

Frederick nodded slowly. "Credit to both of you for getting what you did. Without those invoices, we'd have nothing."

Violet arched a brow. "We still don't have much. Next time, get me a warrant. I'll even tie it with ribbon."

A ghost of a smile touched Frederick's face.

He turned back to Helena and James. "There's more. One of our men found references in Bridewell's correspondence to something called Eclipse. We don't know what it is yet, but it suggests ongoing schemes."

"And Herr Pruhsfeld?" Helena asked.

"Vanished," Josephine said. "Left London before dawn. We tracked him as far as Dover, then lost him. He's likely back in Prussia by now, but I doubt we've seen the last of him."

"So the overseas connections remain intact," James said.

"Yes." Frederick's voice was heavy. "The Society is wounded—leadership arrested, activities disrupted. But they're not dead. And Project Eclipse suggests they have contingencies we haven't uncovered."

Helena's stomach twisted. They'd won the battle. But the war continued.

"There's one more thing," Frederick said. "Clarissa Montague has been located."

Helena straightened. "Where?"

"Bath. With her aunt. She's been there for three weeks." Frederick's expression softened. "She had nothing to do with the Society. Her cousin Lydia used Clarissa's name and likeness to gain sympathy and access. Clarissa knew nothing about it."

Relief flooded through Helena. "She should be told what happened."

"She has been," Josephine said. "And a public clarification will follow. Her reputation will be restored."

One innocent cleared. One small victory.

Evan and Violet exchanged glances.

"We should go," Evan said. "Let you finish your report."

"Thank you," Frederick said. "Both of you."

They slipped out quietly.

The door closed.

Silence settled over the room.

Frederick stood, bracing his hands on the table. "You humiliated the Society's leaders. Exposed their methods. You'll be seen as threats now. Not assets."

"We know," James said.

"Do you?" Josephine's voice was gentle but pointed. "Because it's one thing to know intellectually. It's another to live it. You're marked now. Both of you."

Helena met her gaze. "We'll be ready."

"I don't doubt your courage," Josephine said. "But courage isn't always enough."

Frederick straightened. "The queen wants you both to continue working with the Crown's intelligence efforts. She's prepared to offer you formal appointments—with resources, support, and legal protections."

Helena's breath caught. "Formal appointments?"

"Yes. No more unofficial arrangements. You'd be placed under Crown authority." Frederick paused. "Think about it. You don't need to answer today."

James nodded slowly.

Frederick glanced at Josephine. "We'll leave you two alone. You've earned a moment's peace."

They moved toward the door.

"Sir Frederick," Helena said.

He turned.

"Thank you. For trusting us with this."

His expression softened. "You earned that trust ten times over."

The door closed behind them.

Helena and James stood in the quiet room.

Alone.

For the first time since the ballroom, truly alone.

Helena's heart hammered against her ribs.

"We should talk," James said quietly.

"Yes."

Neither moved.

The silence stretched, heavy with everything unsaid.

"The engagement," Helena said finally. "It served its purpose."

"It did."

"But I—" She stopped. Drew breath. Started again. "I don't want to give it up. Not if there's something real beneath the pretense."

James's composure cracked. Raw vulnerability flooded his face. "There is. There always was."

Her throat tightened. "When? When did it stop being pretend?"

He stepped closer. "I don't know. Somewhere between the first dance and the last gunshot. Somewhere between the lies and the truth." He paused. "But I know what I feel now. And it's not strategy."

"What is it?" she whispered.

"Love."

The word hung between them.

Helena's eyes burned. "You love me?"

"Yes." His voice was rough. "I tried not to. Told myself it was the mission. The cover. But somewhere along the way, you stopped being Lady Helena Ashford, spy, and became just— Helena. The woman I'd follow into hell. The woman I'd die protecting."

"Don't," she said sharply. "Don't talk about dying."

"Then what should I talk about?" He stepped closer still. "Living? Because that's what I want, Helena. A life. With you. Not as agents playing roles. As ourselves."

Tears spilled down her cheeks. "I don't know who I am anymore. Without the mission. Without the lies."

"Yes, you do." He reached up, cupped her face gently. "You're brilliant. Brave. Stubborn as hell. You throw yourself at armed gunmen and somehow come out standing." His thumb brushed away a tear. "You're extraordinary. And I love you. Not Lady Helena. Not the spy. Just you."

She couldn't breathe. Couldn't think.

"The engagement was a lie," she whispered. "But this isn't."

"No. This is real."

She closed the distance between them, hands fisting in his coat. "I love you too. I didn't want to. It terrified me. But I do."

His arms came around her, careful of his injured shoulder. "Then let's stop pretending. No more lies. No more masks."

"What are we, then?"

"Whatever we choose to be."

She looked up at him. "I choose you."

"And I choose you."

He kissed her.

Not the careful, strategic kisses they'd shared for their cover. Not the brief, uncertain brush of lips in public.

This was real. Deep. Desperate.

His hand tangled in her hair. Her fingers gripped his shoulders. They kissed like people who'd survived hell and found each other on the other side.

When they finally parted, Helena rested her forehead against his.

"We're exhausted," she said.

"We are."

"And we still have a war to fight."

"We do." He smiled. "But maybe not right this minute."

She laughed—soft, shaky. "What happens now?"

"We rest. Separately," he added. "Because we both need actual sleep."

"And tomorrow?"

His hand found hers, fingers lacing together. "Tomorrow, we decide if we want Frederick's offer. Tomorrow, we start figuring out what comes next." He paused. "Together."

"Together," she echoed.

He pressed a kiss to her forehead. "Go home, Helena. Get some rest. I'll see you soon."

"How soon?"

He smiled. "Tomorrow. Dinner?"

"Dinner," she agreed. "A real dinner. Not a mission. Not a pretense. Just—us."

"Just us."

She stepped back slowly, reluctantly releasing his hand.

At the door, she turned back.

He stood in the pale morning light, bandaged and exhausted and absolutely perfect.

"James?"

"Yes?"

"Thank you. For seeing me."

His expression softened. "Thank you for letting me."

She slipped out into the corridor.

The Foreign Office was quiet. Early morning light filtered

through tall windows. Somewhere, a clock chimed the hour.

Helena walked toward the exit, each step lighter than the last.

The war wasn't over. The Society lived. Dangers remained.

But for the first time in weeks—maybe in her entire life—she felt it.

Hope.

Not the fragile, desperate hope of survival.

But the solid, certain hope of something worth fighting for.

She pushed through the heavy doors and stepped into the morning.

London spread before her—gray and gold, waking slowly. Smoke rose from chimneys. Vendors called their wares. The city lived, unaware it had been saved.

Helena drew a deep breath.

The war wasn't over. The Society lived. Dangers remained.

But she wasn't afraid.

Not anymore.

Because whatever came next—whatever threats emerged from the shadows—she wouldn't face them alone.

She had James. She had purpose. She had hope.

And that made all the difference.

She smiled and walked into the morning, ready for whatever tomorrow would bring.

Chapter Forty-One

SAFE TOGETHER

March 2, 1855
James

FREDERICK APPEARED IN the doorway of the library where James and Helena were reviewing intelligence reports. The lines around his eyes spoke of a long day, but his expression carried satisfaction beneath the weariness.

"Bridewell and Eleanor are being held in the Tower, but both have stopped answering our questions," he said without preamble. "Apparently they've decided silence is their best ally."

Helena straightened in her chair. "What about the others?"

"We still don't know who the Raven is, so he's still out there somewhere. Lord Percival Grey was questioned and released. Lady Vexley has gone into hiding," Frederick said. "We're attempting to trace her movements, but she's proving elusive. More concerning—we've intercepted correspondence which implies the Raven is... displeased with her recent conduct."

"What conduct?" Helena asked.

"She sent a threatening message to the Ashford residence. Your aunt intercepted it and delivered it to me. She's concerned."

Helena paled.

James felt his protective instincts flare, but he tempered them.

"How serious is the threat?"

Frederick's gaze shifted between them. "Serious enough that I want Helena away from her residence and under guard tonight. Use the safe house in Bloomsbury. Just a precaution until we've located her."

He looked directly at James. "You'll accompany her, Major. For protection."

Helena opened her mouth—likely to protest—but Frederick continued smoothly. "A guard will be posted at your residence to watch over Lady Amelia, but without you there, she should be safe. Lady Prudence has agreed to serve as your chaperone tonight."

Helena blinked. "My aunt agreed to come with me?"

A small smile played at Frederick's lips. "She was surprisingly enthusiastic, actually."

James felt something shift in his chest. One more night. One more opportunity to speak plainly, now that the masquerade had ended.

"We'll be ready within the hour," he said.

Frederick nodded. "I'll bring you news in the morning." He withdrew.

Helena stood, gathering her papers with careful precision. "James—"

"I'll keep you safe," he said quietly.

Her eyes met his, and he saw more there than he'd expected. Not simply worry over Vexley's threat, but a reflection of his own uncertainty. About them. About what their future would hold. The mission was over. But this—whatever this was between them—wasn't.

AN HOUR LATER, they stood in the foyer of the Ashford residence as Prudence descended the stairs with a carpet bag and an expression of grim determination.

"Well," she said, pulling on her gloves with military efficiency. "A safe house. How terribly clandestine."

The carriage ride through London's evening streets should have been uncomfortable. Instead, Prudence filled the silence with her particular brand of directness.

She sat across from them, studying James and Helena with knowing eyes. "You do realize this charade has become quite transparent?"

"What do you mean, Aunt Prudence? I—" Helena began.

"Oh, don't 'Aunt Prudence' me. I may be a widow, but I'm not blind." Prudence's gaze sharpened. "The Foreign Office recognizes you need protection. Very well. But let's not pretend I'm here solely due to Lady Vexley and her threats."

She looked directly at James, and he met her eyes steadily. There was something reassuring about Prudence's bluntness after weeks of deception and performance.

"You're in love with my niece, Major," Prudence said. Not a question. A statement.

James didn't look away. "Yes, ma'am. I am. And I've already told her."

Helena's sharp intake of breath beside him was audible in the close confines of the carriage.

Prudence nodded once. "Good. She deserves someone who'll admit it."

The carriage rolled on through the darkening streets. James saw Helena's fist clench beside his on the seat. He wanted to take it, to offer reassurance, but not yet. Not here. Not with Prudence watching them both so closely.

They arrived at a small, modest townhouse on a quiet Bloomsbury street. Gas lamps flickered to life as they climbed down from the carriage, casting long shadows across the pavement.

Inside, Prudence surveyed the premises with the thoroughness of a general inspecting a garrison. Two bedrooms upstairs, a sitting room below, a small kitchen at the back.

"Perfectly adequate," she declared. She claimed the larger bedroom with a decisive nod. "Clean and serviceable. Lady Helena, you'll take the smaller room."

"I'll take the sofa, ma'am," James said. "If anyone attempts to enter, I'll be able to prevent them from reaching the stairs."

"Perfectly proper," Prudence announced, as if daring anyone to suggest otherwise.

MRS. BANKS—ONE OF Frederick's people, who kept the house in readiness—had left a cold supper laid out of sliced ham, cheese, bread, and fruit. The three of them sat at the small table, conversation careful and polite. James was hyperaware of Helena across from him, the way the lamplight caught in her hair, the small furrow between her brows that appeared when she was thinking.

Halfway through the meal, Prudence touched her temple delicately. "I'm afraid I have the most dreadful headache coming on."

Helena's concern was immediate. "Aunt Prudence, shall I—"

"No, no. I simply need to lie down." Prudence stood, gathering her things with theatrical efficiency. "I'm certain you'll both manage perfectly well without me hovering."

She fixed James with a pointed look. "I trust you're a gentleman, Major."

"Always, ma'am."

"Mm. Well." Her mouth quirked. "Don't be too much of a gentleman."

"Aunt Prudence!" Helena's face flushed.

But Prudence was already at the stairs. She paused, turning back, and her expression gentled.

"Helena. Your mother would be proud of you." Her voice

softened. "And your father… He'd have approved. Eventually."

Then, briskly: "I shall see you both in the morning. Good-night."

She disappeared upstairs, leaving James and Helena alone in the lamplight.

Helena stared after her aunt, then at James. "She deliberately left us alone."

"Yes," he agreed.

Silence stretched between them, weighted with possibility and uncertainty.

Helena cleared the table, a small domestic gesture that felt surprisingly intimate. James rose to help. Their hands brushed as they reached for the same plate, and both froze.

Helena pulled back, crossing to the window. "I should… retire."

But she didn't move. Just stood staring out at the dark street, her reflection ghostly in the glass.

James moved to the fireplace, adding wood, giving her space. "You don't have to."

She turned. "Don't have to what?"

"Retreat. We're past that, aren't we?"

Helena crossed slowly to the fireplace, settling into the chair opposite his. "Are we?"

James leaned forward, elbows on his knees. "I told Prudence the truth. I'm in love with you."

"I heard."

"And?"

Helena's fingers twisted together in her lap. "And I'm terri-fied."

Not what he'd expected. He waited, giving her space to continue.

"The mission gave us a reason," she said quietly. "A structure. We knew what we were supposed to be. What we were supposed to do. But now…"

She trailed off, and James understood.

"Now we have to decide what's real," he finished.

"Yes."

He leaned forward. "Then let's be honest. Completely honest."

Helena met his eyes, searching for certainty, for truth. "No roles? No performances?"

"None."

She nodded slowly. "All right. You first."

James stood, needing to move for this. He paced to the window, then back to the fire.

"I've been afraid to trust what we have," he said.

Helena remained quiet, watching him with those intelligent green eyes.

"Turner was my lieutenant," James continued. "We planned an infiltration together in the Crimea. Dangerous, but necessary. The night before the operation, he claimed illness. Said he couldn't go."

His voice hardened. "He knew what would happen."

Helena's expression didn't change, but he saw understanding dawn.

"We went in without him. Walked straight into a trap." The words tasted like ash. "My men died. All of them. Only I made it back."

He paused, the weight of it settling in his chest as it always did.

"By the time I got out of hospital, Turner was gone. Transferred. The Colonel didn't believe he'd betrayed us. No proof. Just my word against his reputation." James turned to face her fully. "I never got justice for my men."

Helena's breath caught, but she didn't speak. She simply listened, and that—that was everything.

"I've questioned every instinct since then," James admitted. "Second-guessed every choice. And then I met you. And you made me want to trust again."

He crossed to stand before her. "But what if I'm wrong?

What if I can't tell the difference anymore? Between truth and performance. Between what's real and what's convenient."

Helena rose from her chair, closing the distance between them. "Look at me."

He did.

"I'm not Turner," she said firmly. "And you're not that officer who trusted blindly."

Her hand came to rest over his heart. "You question yourself because you learned from your mistakes. That's not weakness, James. That's wisdom."

"You know the difference between truth and lies," she continued. "Because you've lived in both. And you chose truth."

The certainty in her voice unlocked something in his chest.

"I chose you," he said quietly.

"Yes. And I chose you."

They stood close now, close enough that he could feel her warmth, could see the pulse beating at her throat.

"Are you still terrified?" he asked.

"Yes. Are you?"

"Yes."

Her smile was small but genuine. "Good. At least we're honest about it."

Helena didn't step away. Instead, she took a breath and met his eyes.

"My turn for honesty?"

James nodded.

"I've spent these last few years avoiding love," she said. "After my mother died, my father… fell. He said love ruined him." Her voice went soft. "But it wasn't the love that did it. It was his despair."

James remained still, letting her speak.

"I learned that safety meant protecting my heart," Helena continued. "That needing someone was weakness. That partnerships were traps disguised as care." She looked up at him. "My father taught me that.

"And then you asked me to trust you," she said. "Not to need you—to partner with you. You never tried to protect me from the work. You trusted me and just… worked beside me."

James reached up, cupping her face gently. "You proved yourself every day. To me. To everyone."

"Except to myself," Helena whispered.

The admission cost her—he could see it in her eyes.

"You don't need to prove anything to me," James said. "I already know who you are. You're the woman who defused Bridewell's bombs. Who walked into that gala knowing you might die. Who trusted me even when you were afraid."

Helena's eyes shimmered. "I don't know how to do this."

"Do what?"

"Let someone see me. All of me. Not the agent. Not the role." Her voice broke slightly. "Just… me."

James drew her closer. "Then let me start. I see you, Helena. I've always seen you. And I'm not going anywhere."

They stood so close now that he could count her eyelashes, could see the flecks of gold in her green eyes.

"I love you," James said. "Not the spy. Not the mission. You. Helena Ashford. The woman who's brilliant and brave and terrified. The woman who makes me want to be better than I am."

Her breath caught. "I love you too."

Simple. Direct. True.

He drew her closer, his hand still cradling her face. "May I kiss you?"

"You're asking permission?"

"Always."

Her smile bloomed like sunrise. "Yes."

The kiss started tender—testing, tasting, learning. But certainty grew with each heartbeat, and the kiss deepened. Not desperate. Deliberate. Two people choosing each other with full awareness.

Her hands found their way into his hair. His arms circled her waist, drawing her close. This was different than any kiss before. No mission. No cover. No performance.

Just them.

When they finally pulled back, foreheads touching, both breathing hard, Helena whispered, "We should stop."

"We should," he agreed.

Neither moved.

The reality settled over them—Prudence upstairs, even if deliberately absent. Unmarried. Propriety still mattered.

But God, he didn't want to let her go.

Helena seemed to understand. "Stay with me. Just… stay.

"Not…" She blushed.

"I know." He understood completely. "Just stay."

He led her to the sofa, sitting and drawing her down beside him. She settled against his shoulder with a sigh, tucking her feet beneath her.

They talked as the fire burned low and the night deepened. About everything. About nothing. The mission, yes, but also books they'd loved as children, places they wanted to see, small dreams they'd tucked away.

James memorized her—the way she gestured when excited about an idea, how her voice softened when she spoke of her mother, the feel of her laugh vibrating against his chest.

"What will you do now?" Helena asked. "After all this?"

James considered. "Frederick wishes me to assist in training new men."

"And you?"

"I want to build something. Not just tear things down."

Helena shifted to look up at him. "We could work together. Properly. Analysis, strategy, training."

"Partners in our work as well as our lives?" he asked.

"Yes."

He kissed her temple. "I'd like that."

The fire crackled softly. Helena's warmth seeped into him, into places that had been cold since Crimea. No words were needed now. This silence was companionable, certain.

This was enough.

This was everything.

Helena's breathing gradually evened, her weight growing heavier against him. She was falling asleep.

James held her, watching firelight play across her peaceful face. This was right, he realized. This was home. Not a place, but a person.

His eyes grew heavy. He fought it, wanting to stay in this moment, but eventually sleep claimed him too.

The fire burned down to embers. Outside, London settled into its midnight rhythms. Inside, two people who had begun with lies slept in each other's arms, having finally found truth.

Chapter Forty-Two

CHOOSING TRUTH

March 3, 1855
Helena

GRAY LIGHT FILTERED through unfamiliar windows, soft and hesitant. Helena woke slowly, awareness returning in pieces—the faint scent of wood smoke, the warmth against her side, the steady rhythm of breathing that wasn't her own.

She was on the sofa. James's arm was around her. Her head rested on his shoulder.

Memory flooded back. The confessions. The kiss. Falling asleep in his arms while the fire died and the night deepened around them.

She should feel scandalous. Improper. Instead, she felt… safe. As if all the careful armor she'd built over the years had finally found a place to rest.

James stirred, his breathing changing as he woke. There was a moment of confusion as he registered where they were, then suddenly he recalled it all. He looked down at her, and something warm kindled in his hazel eyes.

"Good morning," he murmured, voice rough with sleep.

"We fell asleep," Helena said.

"We did."

"On the sofa. All night."

His mouth curved. "Terribly improper."

Helena felt an answering smile tug at her lips. "Scandalous."

They sat there a moment longer, neither quite willing to break the spell. Then footsteps sounded on the stairs.

They sprang apart like guilty children, Helena smoothing her rumpled dress while James ran a hand through his disheveled hair. The effort was futile—they both looked exactly like two people who had spent the night on a sofa together, fully clothed but thoroughly compromised.

Prudence appeared at the foot of the stairs, perfectly composed, her gray dress crisp and her expression serene. She took in the scene—the dying embers, the rumpled clothes, the obvious all-night conversation—and her eyebrow rose a fraction.

"Good morning," she said. "I trust you both slept well?"

Her tone suggested she knew exactly what had happened. Or hadn't happened.

"Aunt Prudence—" Helena began.

Prudence waved a dismissive hand. "I'll prepare coffee. Sir Frederick should be arriving shortly."

She moved toward the kitchen with deliberate unconcern, leaving Helena and James to exchange glances.

"She's not even pretending to be surprised," Helena whispered.

James's smile was rueful. "I doubt she expected anything else."

Frederick's knock came precisely at nine, brisk and businesslike. Helena went to answer, trying to smooth her dress one more time, knowing it was hopeless.

Frederick stepped inside with his usual efficiency, papers tucked under one arm. He found them arranged in the sitting room—Helena and James on the sofa with careful space between them, Prudence reading by the window with studied disinterest.

"Lady Vexley has been found," Frederick said without preamble.

Helena's pulse jumped. "Where?"

Frederick's expression went grave. "She was pulled from the Thames early this morning."

Silence fell heavily in the room.

Helena shifted uncomfortably. "She's dead?"

Frederick nodded. "The Yard are treating it as murder. But given the circumstances—her falling out with the Raven, her increasingly erratic behavior—I suspect he judged her a liability."

James's hand found hers, squeezing once. She felt a complicated tangle of emotions—relief, yes, but also a pang of sadness. Vexley had been bitter and dangerous, but she'd also been desperate. And the Raven had discarded her like a broken tool.

"The immediate danger has passed," Frederick continued. He studied them both, and Helena saw his sharp eyes register the rumpled clothes, the way they sat close despite the careful space between them, the indefinable something that had shifted.

He didn't comment. But a small smile played at the corner of his mouth.

"I suggest you both go home. Rest. You've earned it."

It was more than dismissal from the safe house, Helena realized. It was a reprieve. The present business was finished.

She and James exchanged glances. What now?

Frederick moved toward the door, then paused. "Lady Helena. Major Westwood."

They turned.

"I'll expect to see you both at the Annex later today. There's work to be done. Different work. But important nonetheless."

"We'll be there," Helena said.

Frederick nodded. "Good." He paused, and that small smile deepened. "Oh, and congratulations."

He left before they could ask what he meant.

Prudence stood, closing her book with a decisive snap. "I'll just… check upstairs. Make certain I haven't forgotten anything."

Her exit was even more obvious than her theatrical headache the night before.

Helena and James were alone again, standing in the morning light. Everything felt different. The night had changed things, had stripped away the last of their carefully maintained distance.

Helena spoke first. "We began with a lie."

James turned to her. "Yes."

"The engagement. The mission. All of it." She stepped closer. "But this is real."

"Yes."

Helena took a breath, steadying herself. "Last night, I told you I was terrified. I still am. But I'm more terrified of not having this." She gestured between them. "Not having you."

James crossed to her in two strides. "What do we do now?"

The question was genuine—he was truly asking, not assuming. That, more than anything, solidified her certainty.

Helena considered. She thought of her mother, who had loved deeply and well. She thought of her father's despair after losing that love, how he'd taught her that safety lay in independence. She thought of last night's confessions, of James's honesty about Turner, of her own admission that she didn't know how to let someone see all of her.

"We plan a real wedding," she said.

James's expression shifted—surprise, hope, joy. "Is that a proposal?"

Helena laughed, the sound lighter than she'd felt in ages. "No. It's my declaration."

He grinned. "Then allow me."

James took her hand properly. Not for show. Not for the mission. For them.

"Helena Ashford." His voice was steady, certain. "I'm not good at speeches. I'm better at action. But you deserve words. True ones."

Helena's heart hammered against her ribs.

"I've spent months in shadows," James continued. "Wearing masks, playing roles. And then I met you. And you made me want to step into the light. You made me want to be the man I was before Turner's betrayal. Before my leg was shattered. Before I learned to doubt everything."

His thumb traced circles on her palm. "I can't promise I'll never be afraid. I can't promise I won't question myself. But I can promise I'll choose you. Every day. Every choice. I can promise I'll trust you, even when it terrifies me."

He drew a breath. "Will you marry me? For real this time. No ruse. No false front. Just you and me. Side by side in all things."

Tears blurred Helena's vision, but her voice was steady. "Yes. For real this time. Yes."

The kiss sealed the promise. Different than last night's kiss—that one had been discovery. This was commitment. This tasted like the future.

"Are we quite finished with the dramatics?" Prudence's voice floated down from upstairs. "I'd like my breakfast!"

Helena and James pulled apart, laughing, foreheads touching.

"She has impeccable timing," James murmured.

"She's had years of practice," Helena said.

She pulled back enough to look at him properly. This was her life now. James. Prudence's dry humor. Real family. Not the isolated existence she'd accepted as inevitable. Something better. Something real.

Something chosen.

James touched her face gently. "Ready?"

For what? Everything.

"Always," Helena said.

They walked toward the kitchen hand in hand, toward Prudence's grumbling, toward breakfast and coffee and the comforts of routine. Toward a future they were building together, piece by careful piece.

In the kitchen, Prudence sat at the table with a cup of coffee, looking supremely unbothered by the fact that she had made it herself.

"Finally," she said, looking up at them. "I was beginning to think I'd have to come fetch you." She studied their joined hands, their matching expressions. "Well? Are we celebrating or mourning?"

"Celebrating," Helena said with a grin.

Prudence nodded once, satisfied. "Good. Then we have a wedding to plan. A real one this time."

She stood briskly. "Three weeks should be sufficient if you have the banns read this Sunday. Though barely. There's so much to do. Guest lists, flowers, the breakfast…"

She was already planning, already organizing, already taking charge with the efficiency that had run the Ashford household for years.

Helena sat, pulling James down beside her. His hand found hers under the table, squeezed. She squeezed back.

They began with a lie. The fake engagement, the mission, the carefully constructed cover. But they were ending with truth. With choice. With partnership freely given and freely accepted.

And that, Helena thought as Prudence enumerated the endless tasks ahead of them, was what mattered.

Not how they began.

But how they chose to continue.

"Helena, are you listening?" Prudence asked.

"Yes, Aunt Prudence."

"The guest list. We'll need to start with family, then Frederick and his people from the Annex."

James's thumb traced small circles on Helena's palm. She glanced at him, found him watching her with an expression that made her heart skip.

Three weeks until they married. A real marriage. No cover. No mission.

Just two people who had found each other in the shadows and chosen to step into the light.

Chapter Forty-Three

THREE WEEKS

March 3–31, 1855
Helena

T HEY ARRIVED AT the Foreign Office Annex midmorning to share the news and return to work. Helena's hand rested in the crook of James's arm as they walked through the familiar corridors, Prudence following with her customary composure.

The meeting room door stood open. Inside, Amelia and Josephine sat with Frederick, clearly waiting.

"Frederick told us you were permitted to return home," Josephine said, rising with a warm smile.

Amelia studied them with knowing eyes. "It took you so long to arrive that I assumed either something terrible had happened… or something inevitable."

Helena tried to subdue her grin as James's hand found hers. "We're engaged," she announced. "Properly. Genuinely. Permanently."

The room went still.

Then Amelia gasped with delight. Josephine's smile deepened. Frederick nodded with satisfaction. And suddenly Helena was swept into embraces, Prudence's arms surprisingly fierce, Amelia laughing.

"When?" Amelia demanded, pulling back to study Helena's face. "How soon?"

"March thirty-first," Prudence said calmly. "I've already arranged for the banns to be read tomorrow."

Amelia's eyes went wide. "Three weeks? THREE WEEKS?" She whirled on Prudence. "You're giving me three weeks to plan a proper wedding breakfast?"

"I'm giving you three weeks to assist with a proper wedding breakfast," Prudence corrected. "I've already begun the arrangements."

"Assist?" Amelia's tone suggested this was the greatest insult she'd ever received. "My dear Prudence, I don't assist. I orchestrate."

"Then orchestrate within reasonable bounds," Prudence said. "The guest list is finalized. Fifty people."

"Fifty?" Amelia looked stricken. "That barely covers—"

"The Foreign Office alone, yes, I've heard your argument," Prudence interrupted. "Nevertheless. Fifty."

Amelia turned to Helena with theatrical desperation. "Tell me I at least have creative freedom with the flowers? The menu? Something?"

Helena, caught between amusement and alarm, ventured: "The flowers?"

"Roses, peonies, lilacs," Amelia said immediately, already mentally arranging. "All white and cream, nothing garish. Perhaps touches of pale pink—"

"It's March," Prudence observed. "Half of those aren't in season."

"Then we'll force them in hothouses." Amelia's chin lifted. "This is Helena's wedding. She deserves proper flowers."

"Expensive flowers," Prudence corrected.

"Proper flowers," Amelia insisted.

Frederick cleared his throat, drawing their attention back. "Perhaps we might discuss the actual wedding before planning the entire breakfast?"

Amelia waved a dismissive hand. "The wedding is simple. Vicar, vows, done. The breakfast is where the real work lies." She turned back to Helena. "Now, about the menu. I'm thinking four courses minimum. Each with wine—"

"We're planning to get her married," Prudence said. "Not drunk."

"One doesn't preclude the other," Amelia replied with a sweet smile.

Josephine, who had been quietly observing, stepped forward. "I'll help coordinate," she said gently. "Between Amelia's vision and Prudence's practicality, I'm certain we can create something lovely."

"Thank you, Josephine," Helena said gratefully.

James, who had been watching this exchange with growing amusement, leaned close to Helena. "Should we be concerned?"

"Probably," Helena whispered back.

Amelia was still enumerating plans. "Kedgeree, obviously. Cold salmon. Roasted fowl. And champagne—the good French champagne, not that English nonsense—"

"Amelia," Prudence said warningly.

"—which I'll personally oversee," Amelia finished, undaunted. She pulled a small notebook from her reticule. "I've been sketching table arrangements for weeks."

"Weeks?" Helena blinked. "But we only just—"

"Oh please." Amelia's grin was unrepentant. "I've been planning your wedding since the day you walked into Lady Beatrice's musicale on James's arm and looked at him like he hung the moon."

Helena felt her face heat. "I did not—"

"You absolutely did," Amelia said. "Even when you were pretending it was all a ruse, anyone with eyes could see." She tapped her notebook. "So yes, I've been planning. And now that it's actually happening, I refuse to let a mere three-week deadline stop me from making it perfect."

Helena took in the room—Amelia's infectious enthusiasm,

Prudence's steadying restraint, Josephine's quiet organization, Frederick's amused tolerance, James's hand still holding hers.

Surrounded by warmth and chaos. This was family. Real and chosen.

She was no longer on the outside looking in.

THE FOLLOWING MORNING, Helena sat in St. George's Church in Hanover Square, Prudence and Amelia on either side of her. James sat a few rows back with Adrian, both men in their Sunday best.

The vicar's voice carried through the sanctuary: "I publish the Banns of Marriage between James Westwood of this parish and Helena Ashford of this parish. If any of you know cause or just impediment why these two persons should not be joined together in Holy Matrimony, ye are to declare it."

Silence answered. Helena's breath caught.

This was real. No mission, no cover. Just her name and his, spoken aloud before God and the congregation. Public commitment.

James's eyes found hers across the pews, and he smiled.

After the service, they walked out into pale March sunlight. Prudence adjusted her gloves with satisfaction.

"Well," she said. "That makes it official."

Amelia linked her arm through Helena's. "One reading down, two to go. And then you'll be properly, irrevocably his."

Helena's heart was too full for words.

TWO DAYS LATER, Frederick summoned them to his office at the Foreign Office Annex.

"Your work in the field has, unfortunately, come to an end," he said without preamble. "But your expertise is invaluable."

He opened a leather portfolio on his desk and drew out a folded piece of paper. "We've been examining correspondence intercepted from remaining Society members. This was found in a coded message between two operatives we're tracking."

He unfolded it carefully and laid it flat.

The message was brief. No signature. Just three lines in rushed, uneven script:

Eclipse rising. The Raven silent. Phase Two begins.

Helena leaned forward. "Phase One was the assassination attempt at the gala. What is Phase Two?"

Frederick's expression was grim. "That's what we need to determine. The assassination failed, but they're proceeding anyway. Which means either they achieved something else that night, or the failure itself served their purpose."

He gestured to the message. "We need to understand their patterns. Their methods. The way they think and plan and change course when plans fall apart. You've both been embedded in the Society's ranks. You know how they speak, how they justify their actions, how they bind loyalty to ideology. That knowledge is too valuable to waste on direct pursuit."

James's jaw tensed. "You're reassigning us."

"I need you analyzing intelligence, not chasing shadows," Frederick said. "Since the Black Rose Society knows you're allied with the Crown, you'll never be permitted at one of their meetings again. I've assigned Adrian to become our next man placed inside their ranks. Miss Sinclair will continue breaking their codes. Lady Arabella is already positioned in their outer circles, gathering what she can."

He paused. "You've done the dangerous work. Now I need you doing the planning and assessment—predicting their movements, finding the patterns, identifying where they're most vulnerable."

Helena straightened. "We'll need complete access to all Society intelligence. Everything you have. If we're to predict their next move, we can't work from partial information."

"Agreed," Frederick said. "I'll have everything brought to a private study. You'll have complete access."

He outlined their specific assignments—Helena would focus on assisting Charlotte with cipher breaking and intelligence assessment. James would train new agents in tradecraft while also analyzing operational patterns.

"Different work," Frederick said. "But no less important. The Society isn't finished. The Raven is still out there, still planning."

The days settled into a new rhythm. Helena and James worked side by side at adjacent desks. She decoded intercepted correspondence while he reviewed operational reports. Their hands would brush when passing papers. Their eyes would meet across the workspace.

Partnership in a new form.

One afternoon, Frederick paused by their desks, observing them working in comfortable synchrony. A small smile played at his lips.

"You work well together," he said. "I expect great things from this partnership."

By Friday, Helena stood in the modiste's shop on Bond Street, ivory silk pooling around her feet.

The gown was simple and elegant—ivory silk with a fitted bodice, long sleeves tapering to points at her wrists, and a full skirt supported by crinolines. Delicate lace trimmed the neckline and cuffs. Nothing ostentatious. Nothing that would draw attention away from the moment itself.

Prudence studied her niece with approval. "Your mother would have loved this."

Helena's throat tightened.

"But what about the veil?" Amelia circled, inspecting. "And

the gloves must be proper length. Belgian lace, I think."

"As long as they don't interfere with the sleeves," Helena said.

The modiste scrambled to keep up with Amelia's additions while Prudence offered measured corrections.

Left alone for a moment before the mirror, Helena studied her reflection. She looked different than the woman who had walked into Bridewell's study weeks ago. Softer somehow, but not weaker.

She had chosen this. Chosen him. Chosen a life beyond the mission.

THE SECOND READING of the banns came and went. After church the following week, Helena and James walked through Hanover Square, his arm offered in easy companionship.

"Regretting this yet?" he asked.

"Not even slightly." She paused. "Though I may regret letting Amelia plan the breakfast."

James laughed. "I heard she's importing orchids."

"From where?"

"I'm afraid to ask."

By the end of the second week, Frederick had delivered on his promise. A private study at the Foreign Office now held stacks of intelligence reports, intercepted correspondence, maps marked with Society safe houses, and lists of known agents.

Helena stood before the largest table, documents spread in a careful arrangement. James worked beside her, cross-referencing names against locations.

"They're fragmenting," Helena said, studying a pattern that had emerged. "Look—after Bridewell's arrest, the inner circle scattered. But they're not operating independently."

James traced a line between three marked locations. "They're communicating. Careful, coded messages. But Charlotte's been breaking them."

"Which means we can track their movements." Helena picked up one of Charlotte's decoded messages. "This one mentions 'the northern cell.' And this one references 'awaiting word from the west.'"

"They've divided into regional operations," James said slowly. "Smaller, harder to infiltrate. But also harder to coordinate."

"Unless they have a central authority still directing them." Helena met his eyes. "The Raven."

"He's gone silent," James said. "According to every intercept, no one's heard from him since Vexley's body was discovered."

"Which means he's either in hiding, or…" Helena trailed off.

"Or he's planning something that requires complete silence." James set down the paper he'd been holding. "Eclipse. Phase Two. Whatever it is, he doesn't want anyone knowing about it until it's already in motion."

Helena moved to the map, studying the marked locations. "They'll need to communicate eventually. To coordinate. That's when we'll find them."

"And when we do, we'll be ready." James came to stand beside her. "Frederick's right. This is strategic work. Finding the pattern before they know we've seen it."

"Does it bother you?" Helena asked quietly. "Not being in the field?"

He considered. "No. Not if it means we're the ones who see what's coming before they do." He looked at the Eclipse message, still pinned to the board. "Whatever Phase Two is, we'll find it."

Helena's hand found his. "Yes. We will."

THE DAY BEFORE the wedding arrived in a flurry of activity. Flowers filled the Ashford residence—arrangements appearing in every room.

Amelia directed their placement with military precision. "No, no, the peonies go on the LEFT."

"They're flowers, Amelia," Prudence said. "Not soldiers."

"Flowers are EXACTLY like soldiers. They must be in formation."

Through the chaos, Josephine moved with quiet efficiency, ensuring everything was actually ready despite appearances.

"Trust me," she told Helena. "Tomorrow will be perfect."

But as evening fell, Helena felt her nerves rising. Not about marrying James—about that, she was certain. But about being the center of attention. About all those people watching.

Prudence found her alone in the drawing room.

"Your parents married in this house, you know," Prudence said quietly. "In this very room. Your mother was terrified too."

Helena turned. "She was?"

"Oh yes. But your father..." Prudence's expression softened. "He made her laugh. Right before they said their vows. And then she wasn't afraid anymore."

"What did he say?"

Prudence smiled. "He whispered: 'At least we'll be terrified together.'"

Helena laughed, tears pricking her eyes. "That sounds like something James would say."

"Then you've chosen well."

HELENA WOKE ON her wedding day to pale dawn light filtering through her bedroom curtains. Butterflies danced in her stomach, but beneath them lay certainty.

This was right. This was real.

Amelia burst through the door, trailing maids with the dress. "You're awake! Good! We have so much to do!"

Prudence followed with jewelry. Josephine brought tea.

The preparation became a ritual—hair dressed and pinned, gown fastened with careful hands, her mother's pearls at her throat, the lace veil settling over her face.

Helena looked at herself in the mirror. The woman looking back was both familiar and new.

Prudence stood behind her, placing gentle hands on her shoulders. "You look beautiful. Like your mother." Her voice went soft. "She'd be so proud."

Helena's throat tightened. She wished her mother could see this. Wished her father had lived to approve. But James was waiting.

And that was enough.

The carriage ride to St. George's passed in a blur. Prudence and Amelia sat across from her—Amelia chattering about the breakfast arrangements, Prudence quiet and composed.

Helena barely heard them.

The carriage stopped. The church doors opened. Guests rose. Music began.

And there, at the end of the aisle, stood James.

Three weeks ago, they were still pretending. Three weeks ago, this had been a lie.

But now—now it was the truest thing Helena had ever done.

She stepped into the church. Sunlight streamed through the windows, casting colored light across the stone floor. James's eyes found hers, and everything else fell away.

This was real.

This was theirs.

This was forever.

Chapter Forty-Four

THE WEDDING BREAKFAST

March 31, 1855
Helena

THE SCENT OF lemon cake and early spring drifted through the drawing room of the Ashford residence. Windows stood open to mild March air, letting pale sunlight spill across parquet floors. Daffodils and primroses filled the vases. Everywhere, laughter floated softly.

Helena stood near the terrace doors, one hand wrapped around a champagne flute, the other resting on James's arm. His warmth grounded her. His smile—half-guarded, half-reverent— never strayed far from hers.

Lady Amelia was already holding court beside the breakfast table, gesturing with a strawberry-topped scone as she regaled two footmen with an embellished tale of their carriage being hijacked by geese in Surrey.

"It could only happen in Surrey," she insisted, before spotting Helena and waving the scone in her direction.

"She's been telling that story to everyone," James murmured.

"I gave her free rein with the planning," Helena replied. "She earned it."

In truth, Helena was grateful. For the noise. For the comfort of it. For the silver ribbons threaded through the garlands and the quiet clink of china. For the illusion, however temporary, of peace.

At the next table, the Duke of Westbridge leaned slightly toward Violet, his tone pitched for her alone but not quite quiet enough to escape Helena's notice.

"Well," Evan murmured, raising his glass, "they've managed to get married. Meanwhile, I'm still waiting for you to say yes."

Violet didn't look up from her plate. "I said yes. Just not yet."

"The Black Rose—"

"—is still out there," she finished quietly. "When it's done, Evan. When we've finished what we started. Then I'll marry you."

He was quiet for a moment. "You know I'd wait forever."

"Let's hope it doesn't take that long." But her hand found his beneath the table.

Prudence joined them near the terrace, her gown in dusky-rose silk that suited the season. "It's a fine thing," she said softly. "Seeing you both standing still for once."

James inclined his head. "We were promised dancing. We've learned to take our promises seriously."

Lady Josephine clinked her glass gently beside the hearth. Conversation stilled. She stepped forward, elegance wrapped in navy silk, and held the floor without needing to raise her voice.

"To Helena and James," she said, her tone firm but affection-ate. "May your marriage remain a source of courage and clarity. And may your shared purpose only deepen the joy between you."

Glasses lifted. Murmurs of agreement rippled through the room.

Prudence moved to stand beside Josephine, her voice steady. "To a niece who was never meant to be ordinary. May your boldness always be tempered by wisdom—and may your husband have the good sense to keep up." Her mouth curved. "Marriage, after all, is its own kind of battlefield."

Laughter followed—real, honest, lingering.

When it faded, Frederick stepped forward, raising his glass with measured precision. "To Helena and James. May your partnership remain sharp enough to meet the challenges ahead—and your love strong enough to outlast them." His gaze met Helena's briefly. "Trust, once earned, is the rarest and most enduring form of strength."

He drank. The room lifted their glasses as one.

Helena felt the weight of it—the love, the faith, the hope. All of it offered freely. All of it earned through fire and the slow, steady work of becoming someone worth trusting.

The string quartet struck up a country waltz. James set down his glass and held out his hand.

Helena let him lead her to the cleared space near the hearth. Their hands fit without adjustment. Their steps fell into rhythm—their first dance as husband and wife.

She rested her cheek lightly against his shoulder. "Did you ever think we'd reach this day?"

"No," he murmured. "But I never stopped hoping."

The music swelled. Other couples joined—Adrian partnering with Josephine, Violet and Evan finally taking the floor together. Even Arabella was swept into the dance by a persistent young lieutenant.

Helena closed her eyes and let herself simply be. No plotting. No calculating. No masks.

Just this. Just James. Just them.

When the waltz ended, they didn't immediately step apart. James's hand lingered at her waist.

"What are you thinking?" he asked quietly.

"That I'm grateful," she said. "For all of it. The danger. The fear. Because it led here. To you."

His throat worked. "Helena—"

"No speeches. Not today." She smiled. "Just stay here. With me. In this moment."

He drew her closer. "Always."

The afternoon stretched on, golden and gentle. Guests lingered over tea and cake. Amelia told three more stories, each more embellished than the last. Frederick remained near the hearth, speaking quietly with Josephine and Prudence—the three forming a triangle of calm authority.

Adrian caught Helena's eye once from across the room and raised his glass in silent salute. She returned the gesture.

They had walked through fire. And somehow, impossibly, they'd come through to the other side.

As twilight edged against the windows, guests began departing. Carriages were called. Coats retrieved. Farewells exchanged with promises to call soon.

Finally, only family remained. Amelia directed the staff. Prudence sat near the dying fire with Josephine, heads bent in quiet conversation. Frederick had disappeared into the study with Adrian, already discussing the work that waited beyond this brief respite.

James drew Helena toward the terrace. The air had cooled with the evening's approach, but it wasn't unpleasant. Stars were beginning to appear.

"Two months ago," James said, "I walked into that ballroom thinking I was attending a routine assignment. Play a role. Gather intelligence. Report back."

"And instead?" Helena prompted.

"And instead I met you." He turned to face her fully. "And everything changed."

She moved closer, until they stood barely a breath apart. "We began with a lie."

"We did."

"The engagement. The charade. None of it was real."

"No," he agreed. "But this is." He took both her hands. "You are. We are."

She rose on her toes and kissed him—soft and sure. When she pulled back, she saw the future in his eyes. Not perfect. Not without danger. But theirs. Chosen. Earned.

"Ready?" she asked.

"For what comes next?" He smiled. "Always."

They turned toward the house together. The windows glowed warm. Inside, family waited. Tomorrow would bring new challenges—Frederick had hinted as much. The Society wasn't finished. The Raven still moved in shadows. Work waited.

But tonight was theirs.

James laced their fingers together as they crossed the threshold, leaving the cool March night behind, stepping into warmth and light and the life they'd chosen.

The door closed softly behind them.

Epilogue

A Future Forged in Fire

April 3, 1855
Helena

T HREE DAYS HAD passed since their wedding. Three days of stolen peace—mornings on the terrace, evenings by the fire, no masks and no pretense. Just Helena and James, learning what it meant to simply be.

The terrace off their bedroom had become their refuge. Three months ago, she'd stood at these doors—locked for three years—and forced the bolt open. A small act of defiance. A promise that she could open herself to love without losing herself the way her father had. She'd told herself that one day she'd sit here as her mother had, with tea and morning light.

She'd been wrong about one thing. It wasn't tea she wanted. It was this—James beside her, bare feet on warm brick, no masks between them. Not teatime contemplation, but shared silence in the aftermath of choosing each other.

The wrought iron table still bore the faint scorch mark from an earlier experiment with Lady Josephine's Turkish coffee blend. The bricks still held yesterday's warmth, reluctant to yield it to the spring air.

Helena sat barefoot, a shawl wrapped around her shoulders.

James was beside her, one leg stretched out, the other bent so his knee brushed hers beneath the table. His hand cradled a porcelain cup, steam curling upward in the morning light.

Her toes pressed against the sun-warmed stones. Three months ago, she'd stood at this threshold but couldn't step through. Now here she sat, unguarded and unafraid.

No performance. No masks. Just them.

The city stretched beyond the terrace walls—loud, restless, still brimming with danger. But for the first time, Helena didn't feel like she was standing at the edge of a battlefield alone.

She studied the rooftops, the chimney smoke rising in lazy spirals, the distant Thames catching the morning light. "I used to think peace meant the absence of danger," she said quietly.

James glanced at her. "And now?"

"Now I think it means having someone beside you when danger comes. Not safety. Partnership."

His fingers found hers beneath the table. "That's a far cry from the woman who believed love was a trap."

"That woman was terrified of needing anyone." She turned to face him, their foreheads nearly touching. "This woman knows the difference between need and choice."

"And which is this?"

"Both," she said simply. "And I'm not afraid of either anymore."

They lapsed into silence, companionable and warm. The kind that came when there was nothing left to prove.

The sound of a man's footsteps on the stairs broke the quiet.

Helena straightened. James's hand went instinctively to where his knife would have been, had he been dressed for work rather than wearing shirtsleeves amid this borrowed quiet.

But it was only Frederick's voice, apologetic, from the doorway. "Forgive the intrusion. Your sister sent me up. I wouldn't interrupt your first days of marriage if it weren't significant."

James rose, extending a hand. "Come in, sir."

Frederick stepped onto the terrace, a leather portfolio under one arm. "I thought you'd want to know—Bridewell has been permitted to leave England under conditions that ensure he will never again hold influence here. His properties have been seized, his titles rendered meaningless in all but name. As for Lady Eleanor, she departed for the Continent. Her withdrawal from English society is widely understood to be permanent. Neither will trouble the Crown again in any public way."

Helena nodded, feeling a weight lift she hadn't known she was carrying. "Good."

"But that's not why I came." Frederick's expression shifted, became more serious. "Something has changed. We've received our first correspondence from within the Society itself—someone calling themselves 'the Shadow.'"

He set the portfolio on the table and drew out a single folded letter. The seal was broken—a dark smudge of wax that might once have been shaped like a crescent moon.

Helena took it, unfolding it carefully.

The handwriting was educated but hurried. Not panicked— deliberate.

Sir Frederick,

I write at considerable risk. I have a place within the Black Rose Society, and recent events have forced me to question what we have become. What began as pursuit of reform has twisted into something I can no longer support in good conscience.

You have disrupted our undertakings, but the threat remains. The Raven has divided us into smaller circles, each blind to the whole. I am uniquely positioned to observe, and I intend to provide intelligence as I am able.

This is the first of what I hope will be many messages. I cannot reveal my identity—not yet. The Raven's reach is long, and his suspicion keen. But I can offer what I see and hear, in hopes it will aid your efforts to dismantle what we have built.

Watch for my messages. They will be coded, sent by such means as I can contrive. Trust will be earned slowly, on both sides.

For now, know this: The Society is not finished. It is re-forming, more carefully than before. Project Eclipse moves forward. New people are being drawn in. The game has not ended—it has merely changed.

I remain hidden, but not silent.

—The Shadow

Helena read it twice, then passed it to James.

Silence stretched as he scanned the contents. Finally, he looked up. "Someone inside is turning."

"Or pretending to," Helena said quietly.

"Precisely my concern," Frederick said. "The Shadow—whoever they are—could be genuine. A disillusioned member seeking redemption. Or they could be the Raven's tool, feeding us misinformation."

James studied the letter again. "The handwriting suggests education. The phrasing is careful—someone used to crafting messages."

"And the seal?" Helena asked.

"Deliberate obscurity," Frederick said. "Nothing that could identify them, but distinctive enough that we'll recognize future letters."

Helena's mind was already working through implications. "If they're genuine, they're taking an enormous risk. The Raven would kill them without hesitation if discovered."

"Which is why we must proceed carefully," Frederick said. "We can't act on this intelligence without verification. We can't ignore it either."

"What do you need from us?" James asked.

"Analysis," Frederick said. "When future messages arrive—and I believe they will—I'll need you to evaluate them. Look for patterns, inconsistencies, anything that suggests deception or confirms authenticity. You know how the Society operates. You've seen their methods firsthand."

Helena nodded slowly. "We'll watch for their patterns. See if the Shadow's intelligence aligns with what we already know."

"And if it does?" James asked.

"Then we may have our first real advantage," Frederick said. "A source within their circles. Someone who can tell us what they're planning before they act."

He gathered the letter back into the portfolio. "I'll leave this with you. Study it. In the coming weeks, I'll forward any additional messages we receive. Build a picture of the Shadow— how near they stand to the inner councils, their trustworthiness, their motivations."

"And in the meantime?" Helena asked.

"In the meantime, Major Blackwood continues his work infiltrating their circles. Miss Sinclair continues breaking their codes. And you two—" He glanced between them. "You help me guide the course we'll follow when the Shadow's intelligence starts flowing."

Frederick moved toward the door, then paused. "Enjoy your peace while you have it. The Society is regrouping, and when they move again, we'll need to be ready."

Then he was gone, footsteps receding down the stairs.

Helena and James sat in silence for a long moment.

"The Shadow," James said finally. "Do you think they're genuine?"

Helena considered. "Someone risked exposure to send that letter. Whether from conscience or calculation, I don't yet know. But they're playing a dangerous game."

"As are we all." James reached for her hand. "Frederick was right about one thing. We've earned this peace. A few weeks to rest, to settle into our new life."

"Before the next storm," Helena said.

"Before the next storm," he agreed. Then, more quietly: "We began with a lie, you know."

She looked at him.

"The engagement," he said. "The charade at that ballroom. I thought it was just another assignment. Another role to play."

"And I didn't trust you," Helena said. "Didn't trust anyone. I thought partnerships were just another kind of trap."

"What changed?"

"You did." She leaned into him. "You let me see past the mask. The man who carried Turner's betrayal like a wound. The man who was terrified of becoming what he'd been taught to hate."

James's jaw tightened. "I never thought I'd feel peace again. Not after Sebastopol. Not after Turner. I kept waiting for the next betrayal."

Helena brushed her temple against his. "But it didn't come. You were seen. And trusted anyway."

"You brought me home," he said, turning toward her.

She kissed him then—slow and sure. No performance. No fear. Just Helena and James, choosing each other again.

When they parted, she rested her hand over his heart. "I suppose this is what it is to give oneself without reserve."

James smiled faintly. "It's quieter than I imagined."

She laughed softly. "We'll remedy that later."

He rose, offering her his hand. "Come. Let's have breakfast. Like ordinary people."

"We're not ordinary people."

"No," he agreed. "But we can pretend. For a few hours more."

She took his hand and let him lead her inside.

Behind them, the city woke to another day. The Society still whispered in shadows. The Raven still watched and planned. The Shadow had emerged, offering intelligence that might be salvation or trap.

Work waited—assessment, preparation, the slow careful effort of dismantling what remained of the Black Rose.

But they had time now. Time to build what they'd begun. Time to strengthen the foundation before the next storm came.

And when it did—when new players entered the game, when the Shadow's messages started flowing, when the final confrontation came—they would be ready.

Not as pieces in someone else's game.

As partners who had chosen each other, again and again, until that choice became unbreakable.

The Society wasn't finished.

Neither were they.

THE END

In the months ahead, new faces would join the struggle against the Black Rose Society. Charlotte Sinclair never intended to step into the field. But when the Crown requires a fresh name to move among the Society's re-formed circles, Sir Frederick chooses hers. Ciphers won't be enough—she'll have to become someone else entirely. And Major Adrian Blackwood—sharp, dangerous, and infuriatingly capable—wasn't part of the plan. But he just might be the key difference between surviving the work and being swallowed by it.

About the Author

Sheridan Jeane writes historical romances that will take you on a romantic, excitement-packed journey. Her Victorian-era novels will transport you to a world of spies, intrigue, and deliciously sensual moments. But don't let the corsets fool you, Sheridan's stories are anything but stuffy!

Sheridan is the daughter of an artist/art-therapist/professor mother and an opera-fanatic/computer engineer/knowledge-guru father. Growing up, she assumed all families routinely converted their garages into well-stocked art studios complete with a potter's wheel, kiln, and every color of acrylic paint under the sun. Didn't most second-graders nail shingles on the roof of the new 2-car garage their dad built? And didn't everyone's parents host the occasional after-opera cast party? No? Who knew? Not Sheridan!

Her parents had grand plans for her from the very beginning. Her mom always said she thought the name "Sheridan" would look great on the cover of a book someday! Talk about fate!